The Regency

LORDS & LADIES
COLLECTION

*Two Glittering Regency
Love Affairs*

A Scandalous Lady
by Francesca Shaw
&
The Gentleman's Demand
by Meg Alexander

The *Regency*
LORDS & LADIES
COLLECTION

The Regency

LORDS & LADIES
COLLECTION

Francesca Shaw &
Meg Alexander

MILLS & BOON®

*First published in Great Britain 2005 by
Harlequin Mills & Boon Limited,
Eton House, 18-24 Paradise Road,Richmond, Surrey TW9 1SR*

THE REGENCY LORDS & LADIES COLLECTION
© Harlequin Books S.A. 2005

The publisher acknowledges the copyright holders of the
individual works as follows:

A Scandalous Lady © Francesca Shaw 2002
The Gentleman's Demand © Meg Alexander 2001

ISBN 0 263 84573 7

138-1005

*Printed and bound in Spain
by Litografia Rosés S.A., Barcelona*

A Scandalous Lady

by

Francesca Shaw

Francesca Shaw is not one, but two authors, working together under the same name. Both are librarians by profession, working in Hertfordshire, but living within distance of each other in Bedfordshire. They first began writing ten years ago under a tree in a Burgundian vineyard, but although they have published other romances, they have only recently come to historical novels. Their shared interests include travel, good food, reading and, of course, writing.

Chapter One

Nicholas Lovell, Earl of Ashby, swung his quizzing glass at the end of its ribbon and listened to the
rising hum of anticipation from the well of the theatre below him. From his vantage-point in the box
he could see virtually the entire sweep of the Theatre
Royal, the swirl of colours from the ladies' silks and
satins, the subdued gleam on the gentlemen's formal
evening wear. As usual the Bath audience had paid
hardly any heed to the curtain-raiser, chattering, gossiping and waving to acquaintances throughout it.
But now the mood had changed to one of heightened
expectation.

Perhaps, he mused, his friends had not exaggerated the charms and talents of the Royal's chief attraction, Mademoiselle Lysette Davide, the sublime
interpreter of Shakespeare. And tonight there was
the added piquancy of knowing that those privileged
enough to procure a ticket would be witness to her
last performance of the season. But, no, despite everything, he could not summon up the enthusiasm
to join in his friends' excitement. He closed his eyes
and leaned back in the gilded chair.

'For pity's sake, Lovell, do wake up and show a bit of interest. The performance is about to start.' George Marlow leaned over and poked him unceremoniously in the ribs with his quizzing glass.

Nicholas raised one dark brow laconically, and resumed his bored scrutiny of Bath society, chattering in the stalls below.

George, persisting in the face of his friend's uncharacteristic ennui, added, 'I tell you, La Belle Davide is well worth the wait.'

'He's right, you know,' Lord Corsham contributed. 'Worth sitting through that tedious ballet for. Have another glass of champagne, old chap. You haven't had enough to drink, that's your trouble.'

The last of the quartet, Sir William Hendricks, whose box it was, peered anxiously at the programme. 'It isn't Shakespeare, is it? Can never understand a word the fellow's on about.'

Nicholas laughed, roused from his indolent mood by the look on his old schoolfriend's face. He well remembered Hendricks's struggle to concentrate on any literary endeavour at Eton, being more enamoured of the sports field and cockpit than his books. 'Don't worry—it's not Shakespeare. Why do you bother with a box, old chap? It can't be worth the expense.'

'Well, one does, you know. After all, one never knows when one might want to come along—and I can tell you, ever since we discovered Mademoiselle Davide we've been here virtually every night she's performed.' He sighed gustily. 'If I could just kiss her hand.'

'And the rest of her,' George Marlow remarked, with a meaningful grin.

Nicholas was surprised by his companions' calf-struck demeanours. After all, George had kept a string of actresses for the past few years, yet all the men were behaving like schoolboys whenever this particular woman's name was mentioned.

'So what's stopping you?' he enquired, irritated. 'She's only an actress, and we all know what that means. Enough money and you can kiss her from head to toe, never mind her hand.' It had taken a lot to persuade him to come out this evening. He had only arrived in Bath that afternoon—reluctantly obeying a summons from his elder sister Georgiana—and had had no intention of doing anything but having a good dinner and several glasses of brandy with his brother-in-law Henry.

'*Only an actress!*' Indignation mottled Sir William's cheeks. 'She is pure, unsullied, a goddess—the Unobtainable!' His companions, equally earnest, nodded solemnly.

They had all of Nicholas's attention now. He swung round away from the stage and regarded the three young men with amused disbelief on his lean features. 'There is no such thing as an unobtainable actress. You three are either getting old or you have all lost your touch!'

'Damn it, Nick,' Lord Corsham growled indignantly. 'No one succeeds with her. It isn't just us. Not even you could storm those unsullied ramparts—I bet you!'

'I can't be bothered to storm anything,' Nicholas rejoined with a quirk of his firm lips. 'Look, the curtain's going up.'

He turned away as Frederick Corsham grabbed his sleeve. 'Not even if I wager Thunderer?'

He had all the Earl's attention now. 'Are you serious, Freddie? I thought you'd never sell that animal, never mind wager him.'

'It's a safe bet,' his friend replied breezily, sitting back as the limelights were turned up and the curtain rose on the first scene of *The Castle Spectre*. 'Even you couldn't do it.' The other two nodded solemnly. They all knew few women could resist Nick's dark charms if he chose to exert them, but they also knew of Miss Davide's formidable reputation for virtue.

'Done—and I haven't even set eyes on the lady.'

At that moment Lysette Davide was standing in the wings having a furious, whispered argument with Mr Porter, the manager of the Theatre Royal. 'I never thought you meant it!' he said. 'I'll raise your fees to…to…12 pounds a week,' he added wildly. 'Damn it! That's as much as Mrs Jordan was getting in her heyday.'

'Not now, Mr Porter! I am retiring after this performance and that is final. Now, *please* leave me!'

Lysette checked her dark wig again, smoothed down her white diaphanous skirts and took a deep, not entirely steady breath. In the three years she had been on the professional stage she had never lost her pre-performance nerves, and tonight, the very night that she was going to declare her retirement, she felt as nervous as a kitten. And the hissed interchange with Mr Porter had only served to make things worse.

Her cue came and she swept on to the centre of the stage, tall, almost regal. The theatre erupted into a storm of applause from all levels and footstamping from the common folk up in the topmost tier.

* * *

From the vantage-point of Sir William's box, overhanging the stage, Nicholas had a perfect view of the Unobtainable Miss Davide. And for the first time that evening he was paying attention. It was not just that she was a very beautiful young woman, tall, shapely, elegant, but that she had great presence. While she was on the stage, even when she was not speaking, she held the eyes of all the theatregoers, and when she did speak for the first time there was a collective intake of breath from the stalls. Her voice was strong, carrying, yet mellifluous, with a slight hint of a French accent.

The play was a farrago of nonsense, of course, a typical fashionable Gothic melodrama, yet she made it sound like Shakespearean verse. For the first time in weeks Nicholas felt his boredom disappear. He had begun to worry about his lack of interest in all his old pursuits. Gambling had lost its excitement, the pursuit of the fair sex had lost its lure, and he had taken to leaving parties early, and more or less sober.

His circle had begun to comment, and the only person pleased with this apparent reform of a notorious rake was his land agent, who found all his correspondence answered promptly and with interest.

The truth was that, at the age of twenty seven, the Earl of Ashby was growing restless with the pursuit of pleasure for pleasure's sake. His sister, the redoubtable Georgiana, had told him he needed to marry and settle down, to ensure the future of the earldom by producing an heir. But, unsettled and restless as he was, Nicholas was damned if he was going to marry one of the eligible ninnies that his sister found for him on a regular basis. And, much as his ancestral estates in Buckinghamshire were beginning to tug at his conscience, the thought of sobriety and conformity with a 'suitable' wife who had neither wit nor conversation filled him with dismay.

His eyes did not leave the tall dark figure as the play progressed. The drama involved ludicrous plots, abandoned orphans and a wicked villain who emerged, cloaked and masked, to seize the heroine, but Nicholas took in none of that. One part of his mind enjoyed the spectacle of Miss Davide's beauty, the other reflected that, if he had to spend a week in Bath at his sister's beck and call, then the pursuit and conquest of such a woman would be more than compensation.

The curtain fell for the first interval and a waiter came in with a tray of champagne and canapés. After the man had departed, all three of his friends turned to Nicholas and demanded with one voice, 'Well?'

Nicholas grinned, stretched out his long legs and raised his glass in a toast. 'To the Divine Miss Davide, and to the three of you for giving me something to do for the next week.'

'You are very confident,' Lord Corsham remarked.

'He's got cause,' George Marlow replied ungrudgingly. 'When has he ever failed with a lady? I don't know how you do it, Nick, but you've got the devil's own luck.'

'Probably signed his soul away to Old Nick.'

'No such thing,' Nicholas protested. 'All one

needs is a certain charm, flair…all the things you three are so sadly lacking.'

'I shall ignore that slur,' Sir William said amiably. 'And at least you've cheered up. You'd become so damnably sober we were thinking of sending for your physician. We had better set a time limit on this wager—shall we say the end of next month?'

The interval ended and the play resumed. Miss Davide, not on stage again until the next scene, sat in her dressing-room as her dresser powdered her shoulders and arranged her fichu. She leaned forward, carefully checking her hairline to make sure no betraying blonde curl was escaping, and touched a cloth to her darkened brows.

'First half went well, ma'am,' her dresser, Florence, remarked. She looked at her mistress's reflection in the mirror, automatically checking the heavy stage make-up which covered the naturally pale skin. She always thought it a pity that Miss Davide covered that lovely mass of blonde hair: soft, it was, like spun gold. And the dark eyebrows made her green eyes look hazel. But the perfection of her features was all hers and owed nothing to the artistry of the stage.

'Thank you, Florence. It did go well, did it not? Still, I will confess I am very nervous about my announcement—and Mr Porter is deeply unhappy with my decision. Now, you are sure that you will be content to work for Mrs Scott next season?'

'Oh, it's an honour, ma'am, with her being so well known. But I shall miss you; you've been so kind to me.' Her mistress's slender hand with its long tapering fingers came up and briefly touched her own.

'You will have me crying, Florence. Do not say anything else.' At that very moment there was a knock on the door. 'I must be on stage now. Please bring my hand-glass and powder.'

Despite it being the middle of a scene, there was another storm of applause when Miss Davide resumed the stage. The second half went by as if in a dream: the villain was vanquished, the orphan reunited with his sister and all ended well.

Lysette took four curtain calls, but then held out her hands to still the applause. 'Dear friends, I have an announcement to make. What I have to say is difficult, for I have valued your loyal support these past three years, but the time has come for me to leave the stage.'

There was a gasp, then a cry of 'No! Shame!' but she held up her hand again.

'I know that what I have said will disappoint you, but my mind is made up. Goodnight, thank you and goodbye to you all.'

She swept a final deep curtsey and left the stage, her cheeks hot, tears pricking the back of her eyes, leaving uproar behind her. For many reasons she did not regret her decision, but that was not to say it was not hard to leave behind the thrill of a life so different from that she had been brought up to. Mr Porter rushed up, red-faced, his arms waving in agitation.

'I never thought you would go through with it— now hear what you have done! They are rioting out there!' He had to raise his voice above the sound of rhythmically stamping feet.

'Get a grip, Mr Porter,' the young lady who until a few moments ago had been Lysette Davide commanded briskly. 'They will have another favourite by next season. Your profits will be assured,' she added wryly. Three years' acquaintance with the theatre manager had taught her precisely where his priorities lay.

Her hand was on her dressing-room door when the stage doorman Stebbings came panting round the corner. 'Are you coming along to the Green Room, miss? There's a dozen or so nobs all wanting to see you, and I won't answer for the consequences if you don't make an appearance,' he said anxiously.

Lysette sighed, very tempted to plead a headache, to get the doorman to give her apologies, but then a sense of duty got the better of her. After all, it was for the last time. 'Very well, Stebbings. But only the most faithful gentlemen who always call—you know the ones.'

She hastily checked her appearance in the mirror, whisked a trace of powder over her high cheekbones and rubbed a smudge of lamp-black from under her lower lashes, then hurried along the dingy corridors, parsimoniously lit by the occasional oil-lamp. Mr Porter was not going to spend money on frills and furbelows behind the scenes, but he had invested in the Green Room, where his actors met favoured members of the audience.

The scene which greeted Miss Davide's eyes as she pushed open the door was a familiar one. A dozen gentlemen clad in evening dress, glasses in hand, were discussing the evening's performance and her astounding announcement, while one or two of the more callow youths glowered at each other in jealous silence from the corners of the room.

As she walked in the room fell silent, then she was surrounded, bouquets and ribboned boxes pressed upon her, and from every side expressions of dismay at her decision and pleas to reconsider rained down. Smiling, nodding, responding with the grace that so marked her, Lysette gave no indication that this was yet another performance.

'Red roses, my lord, they are enchanting!' she was saying encouragingly to the tongue-tied seventeen-year-old heir to one of the nation's greatest families, when the door half opened again and she heard Stebbings expostulating on the other side.

'I'm sorry, gentlemen, but Miss Davide isn't seeing anyone else now.'

'She will see me,' a lazy voice declared coolly, and a tall, dark man strolled in, closing the door firmly behind him.

'Lovell!' Lord Franklin exclaimed. 'Didn't know you were in Bath, old man. Now look here, this won't do, you know—this is in the nature of a private farewell by Miss Davide's most faithful admirers. And quite frankly,' he added, low-voiced as he stepped forward to shake hands with the newcomer, 'we could do without any competition from you!'

Nicholas clapped his old acquaintance from White's Club on the back and grinned unrepentantly. 'I have been a silent admirer of Miss Davide for some time, and I am sure you are going to introduce us.'

Lord Franklin made the best of it, 'Miss Davide, may I make known to you Nicholas Lovell, Earl of Ashby? Lovell, Miss Davide.'

Nicholas bowed low over her proffered hand. 'Madam, your most devoted servant.'

Lysette inclined her head in response. 'My lord,' she responded calmly, not inclined to like this sardonic, self-assured man in his immaculate evening clothes. He was attractive enough, she admitted grudgingly, elegant certainly, without being in any way a dandy, but his self-possession made her want to oppose him on principle.

Despite her long practice in managing attentive gentlemen she found herself swiftly isolated from the rest of the group. His lordship's broad shoulders effectively blocked the others and the way he filled her champagne glass felt almost possessive.

Lysette's irritation grew, but she let none of it show on her face.

Nicholas, however, was close enough to see the sudden flare of annoyance that turned her hazel eyes green, and the infinitesimal tightening of her perfectly painted lips. He was intrigued. In his not inconsiderable experience actresses were piqued when eligible gentlemen ignored them, not when a new admirer came their way. This was going to prove one of the most satisfying wagers he had ever accepted; suddenly the prospect of winning Thunderer at the end of it was insignificant compared to the delight of conquering Miss Davide.

His facial control was as good as hers, but something of the hunter in his thoughts reached her and she felt herself strangely excited and unsettled by this man. Why this should be when she handled every other importunate gentleman with grace and firmness was a mystery.

Startled by this discovery, she looked up sharply to meet his dark blue eyes. Nicholas looked down and locked his gaze with hers, quite deliberately holding the moment like a caress, his mouth curving in an unspoken invitation. He was not surprised to see the flush that touched the creamy skin over the high cheekbones, but he was taken aback as she haughtily raised her dark brows and remarked coldly, 'I am neglecting my other guests, Lord Lovell. You must excuse me.'

So, she did not like to seem too obvious, Nicholas mused. Well, it would make the chase all the more piquant, and he had, after all, the entire week before he had planned to leave Bath. He was carrying in his breast pocket a small gift he had bought for his sister: an antique cameo he had found in an obscure little jeweller's in the City. It was not particularly valuable, but it was unusual and, even to a masculine eye, pretty. Georgiana, irritating though she might be, was still his favourite sister, and he had purchased it on a whim for her. However, the Bath jewellers would furnish another gift for his sister.

Lysette took a step forward, expecting him to move aside and allow her to rejoin the main group. To her annoyance he did no such thing, remaining still while she now found herself in dangerous proximity to him. She opened her mouth to ask him to move when he forestalled her by producing a small, flat jeweller's case.

'Miss Davide, will you honour me by accepting this small token of my admiration?'

Lysette took the box in her long fingers and regarded him levelly. 'Why, thank you, my lord. Perhaps I should make it clear that acceptance confers no promise of anything else whatsoever. I only ever accept gifts in appreciation of my performance *on the stage*.' There could be no mistaking the implication of her words, and normally such a very frank hint meant that she had no further trouble with the gentleman concerned.

But this gentleman…this one was different, and obviously prepared to be quite as frank as she. 'That is making the situation very clear, ma'am.' His lips quirked in amusement as he moved aside slightly. 'Are you always as blunt?'

Despite the fact that he had given her the space to pass by, Lysette surprised herself by not moving. 'I rarely find it necessary, my lord, to be any more explicit, but I have discovered that many gentlemen have…how shall I put it?…a misconception that all actresses also follow another profession.' Again she felt the flush mounting her cheek. What was it about this man? Why could she not simply ignore him, sweep past him and join the other…safer… gentlemen?

She felt as though she was fixed to the spot, but then he moved again, bowing as he said, 'But I am monopolising you, Miss Davide, especially as this is your last appearance. Perhaps I could call upon you tomorrow. May I have your direction?'

'I never receive at home, sir,' she said repressively as she passed him, but he noted with interest that her previously still hands touched nervously at the dark curls that fringed her neck, and her manner as she began to speak to the other gentlemen was slightly less assured.

Florence appeared in the doorway and began the familiar task of gathering up bouquets and posies.

Nicholas watched from his vantage-point, sipping his champagne, as Lysette worked her way round the room, making her farewells and allowing her hand to be kissed by those she knew best.

At last she paused in the doorway, her head held high on the slender column of her neck. He admired the almost classical elegance of her form, the fine gauze shawl draped over her bare arms highlighting the translucence of her skin. The diaphanous stage gown moulded her slender form, emphasising the narrowness of her waist and the grace of her carriage.

What was her background? he wondered. She was a very fine actress—her protestations of virtue just now had been almost convincing—but surely she had to be simulating that air of good breeding, of being one of the Quality? And then she was gone.

Back in her dressing-room Lysette allowed Florence to help her out of her gown and into the simple walking-dress she had arrived in. She was fastening the bonnet strings as Stebbings tapped on the door.

'I'm a bit worried, miss. There is such a crush out front—and at the stage door too. I'm not sure how long it's going to take me to get you a carriage, or even a chair, miss. I think you had better wait a while: they'll go home after an hour or two—I can fetch you some supper in.'

Suddenly Lysette wanted to be out of the theatre and home more than anything. It was over, all the pretence, all the fairytale glitter and unreality, and she had her real life to return to. The thought of being trapped here for even another hour was insupportable.

'No, Nathaniel, I shall go home on foot.'

'But you'll be recognised, miss,' Florence protested, her face screwed up in worry.

'Give me the cloak I used in Act One, Florence, the one with the big hood. If I take off my bonnet and pull up the hood I should pass unrecognised. Is that basket you brought in last week still here? I can put my reticule in it and I will seem to be one of the dressers going home.'

'Yes, miss, here it is. Look, your bonnet will go in too, and if I tuck this cloth over no one will know.' The dresser pulled up the cloak, twitching the ends together in front to cover the modestly dark walking-dress. 'Oh, do take care, ma'am, I shall miss you!' She gave Lysette a convulsive hug, the tears running down her cheeks, then burst into real sobs as Lysette pressed a package into her hands, dropped a kiss on her cheek and slipped out.

Stebbings had been right; the crowd was thick around the stage door. Lysette drew up the hood close around her face, hunched her shoulders under the heavy folds of the cloak to disguise her height, and slipped, almost unheeded, through the throng.

But one pair of eyes marked her progress, one pair of eyes saw through the disguise. The Earl of Ashby, seated comfortably in the vantage-point of his carriage, watched the huddled figure reach the corner of Beaufort Square, glance back and straighten up to her full height before melting away into the darkness.

Little fool! What the devil was she doing, walking alone at this time of night? He had intended following her carriage or chair in his own conveyance, but now he opened the door and jumped down. 'Go home, William, I will walk.'

Lysette, too, was beginning to regret her decision to walk. Despite the lanterns and flambeaux outside each house, the streets were haunted by pools of shadow and frequent alleyways loomed like black pits. More than once she shrank back as groups of men, some of them the worse for drink, passed her noisily, but most worrying was the feeling that she was being followed. Once or twice she stopped and drew into the side of the path, but she could see no one behind her.

She told herself not to be such a ninny, but it was with relief that she reached Walcot Street. She still had to negotiate the area in front of the penitentiary for fallen women, which often attracted attention from undesirables, but once clear of that the street became increasingly respectable in a modest way.

Again she stopped, the hairs on the back of her neck prickling, but this time there was no mistaking the fact that she was being followed, and very closely. Two hulking figures in frieze coats quickened their pace and before she could cry out or run she found herself bundled roughly into a side alley.

Frightened though she was, Lysette was not going to give in easily. One man had a callused hand over her mouth and she bit down hard, causing him to yelp and cuff her over the ear. Half stunned, she staggered, but still swung the heavy basket at the other man, catching him on the corner of the head and knocking off his hat. The smell of sweat and drink was nauseating and Lysette's stomach heaved as she struggled with the second man, trying to catch her breath enough to scream.

Increasingly terrified, she reacted instinctively to his groping hands, raising her knee sharply into the man's groin and being rewarded by his croak of pain. He staggered back, swearing viciously and clutching himself. 'Get the bitch, Clem,' he snarled.

'I think not,' a cultured voice said with soft menace, and the entrance to the alleyway was suddenly blocked by a tall figure silhouetted against the lamplight. Seconds later, after a brisk flurry of blows from a cane, both men were reeling off down Walcot Street.

A wave of nausea hit Lysette and her knees buckled. Before she could sink on to the muddy cobbles, strong arms encircled her and she was lifted and held against a broad chest. A familiar voice said firmly, 'Now, you are not going to faint until you tell me where you live.'

'My lord...' she gasped out, relief flooding through her weak limbs. 'Oh, thank you.'

'Do not thank me,' he replied almost roughly. 'You were a damn fool to be out here alone at this time of night. Now, tell me where to take you.'

'Para...I mean, number eight. Just up the road, here on the left.'

Nicholas Lovell did not appear to notice her hesitation, but put her on her feet, took her arm, picked up the basket, and set off slowly in the direction she indicated.

Lysette clutched gratefully at his strong arm, then staggered as the shock of what had so nearly happened hit her. Nausea hit her and she doubled up, drily retching. The Earl shifted his grip, lifted her firmly in his arms and carried her up the street.

'Here we are, safe and sound,' he said soothingly,

his breath grazing her forehead. 'Number eight...but there is no light. Surely your maid is waiting up for you?'

Her thoughts were almost too hazy to deal with this situation, but after a moment's panic she found that at least part of the truth would serve. 'My companion had to go to her sister's bedside; her husband is very ill.'

'But where is your maid?' He set her carefully on her feet while keeping a firm arm on her elbow. His eyes were shadowed under the brim of his hat, but Lysette was very conscious of his sharp regard.

'I...er I sent her with Margaret, to carry things...er, calvesfoot jelly...and so on,' she added rather wildly.

'Hmm. Give me your key.' Nicholas unlocked the panelled door, holding it open as she slipped past him into a front room which was dimly lit by a well-banked fire.

Lysette stooped to light a taper from the coals and touched it to a branch of candles on the mantelpiece where it reflected in the mirror, filling the little parlour with muted light. She turned, schooling her face into polite gratitude. 'Thank you my lord—' she broke off as she realised that he was not only in the room, but that the front door was firmly closed.

Before she could protest he had walked past her, through into the kitchen behind, and was trying the back door, satisfying himself that it was secure. He rejoined her and, seeing her pale face, sat her firmly in the fireside chair and stated, 'Tea, I think.'

Weak-kneed as she still was, Lysette struggled out of the chair, only to find herself pressed back into it again. 'My lord, I am grateful to you, but this is

entirely unnecessary—and you should not be here!'
In her alarm it came out sounding ungracious.

'If you had slightly more regular domestic arrangements, ma'am, I would not need to be!' he
rejoined tartly, and without as much as a by-your-
leave he disappeared into the kitchen.

Lysette could hear the fire being riddled and the
clang of the kettle being held under the pump, and
suppressed a half-hysterical giggle at the thought of
his elegant lordship involved in domestic chores.
She supposed he must know how to make a cup of
tea, although it seemed unlikely that he ever penetrated to the kitchen regions in his own elegant
home. Goodness knows what he was making of the
cottage, which was doubtless far from what he expected of a leading actress's abode.

He emerged from the back room carrying two
bone china cups and placed one of them on the table
beside her. Lysette took a grateful sip from hers,
watching the Earl cautiously over the rim. He stood
by the fireside, one foot on the fender, looking as
incongruous in the cottage as a big cat in a dog
kennel. He drank his tea with a grimace and she
pulled herself together with an effort and a passable
imitation of her Green Room manner.

'I thank you, my lord, for saving me this evening
and for your kind attention. But I must not keep
you—I am sure you would far rather be drinking
brandy with your friends than sipping Bohea with
me!'

'Not at all, ma'am—a refreshing change. And my
sister would doubtless tell me it is better for me.
Now, how many bedrooms have you?'

'Two…I mean, how dare you, my lord! That is a most unseemly question!'

'Is it?' he asked maddeningly. 'It seems entirely practical to me. I can hardly leave you alone, and I am sure your companion would not wish me to invade her bedchamber. However, doubtless I can make myself comfortable on that couch.'

Lysette jumped to her feet, deeply discommoded. 'Sir, what you suggest is outrageous! My reputation will be in tatters!'

One dark brow rose mockingly. 'My dear Miss Davide, forgive me for stating what may be a truism, but you are—or were—an actress.'

'Oh!' Lysette stamped her foot in sheer frustrated fury. Nothing seemed to dent his assurance and he said the most outrageous things, in such a way as to make them sound common sense. 'I have already told you this evening, I am not *that* sort of actress!'

Nicholas sketched her a bow. 'Oh, yes, you did hint at that earlier. Well, in that case I will be quite safe on the couch, will I not?'

'You…you…you are totally impossible!'

'So I have been told. By the way, Miss Davide, did you realise that when you are angry that slight French nuance in your speech quite disappears?' The dark head bent over the teacup and he appeared quite impervious to her simmering fury.

Lysette glowered at the rangy figure, so very much at home on the hearthrug, the elegant cut of the dark blue superfine cloth moulding athletic shoulders, the long legs more than capable of standing the fashion for a tight cut. 'As I am not French, it is not surprising that the accent is not permanent,' she snapped. 'Now, my lord, grateful as I am—will

you please go?' Although what exactly she was going to do if he chose not to was hard to say.

'My dear Miss Davide—or whatever your real
name is—has it not occurred to you that those ruffians may well be hanging around out there, waiting
for me to leave? It is highly likely they followed us
here: that type tends to be fairly persistent, in my
experience, and I have no intention of leaving you
to their tender mercies.'

The irony was that this was not her home, and if
only Lord Lovell would leave she could make her
escape with safety. But she was in a total dilemma:
she could not tell him that this cottage belonged to
Margaret, her old nurse, who was indeed away with
her sister, but if she did not, he would stay. But at
least, thank goodness, Mama would not be fretting.
Over the last three years she had grown used to her
elder daughter's unpredictably late hours and would
have long since retired to bed.

Nicholas Lovell watched the play of emotions
suddenly transform the previously well-controlled
face of the beautiful young woman before him. He
was puzzled, not a state he often found himself in.

She was not French, that much had quickly been
established. Nor was Lysette Davide her name, but
again, that was normal practice for the stage. Nor,
he very strongly suspected, seeing her complexion
close up, was she a brunette. But she was a genuine
actress of talent, and something more… He stroked
his chin, contemplating the enigma as she took an
impatient few steps around the room. She genuinely
wanted him gone, despite her fear of the footpads—
and that was a real mystery if she was what she

purported to be. And Nicholas Lovell did not like a mystery he could not solve.

Lysette stopped pacing and stood before him, looking up at him with greenish hazel eyes that were becoming shadowed with tiredness and reaction. 'My lord, please…' It was irresistible, even if it was not what he had intended—yet. Her face was tipped up to his, her lips soft and full, her eyes imploring. The subtle scent she wore, like honeysuckle on a warm summer night, had fretted at his senses since he had first come close to her in the Green Room. Now, so near, it filled his nostrils.

Before he could stop himself Nicholas reached out and stroked one finger gently along the fine line of her jaw. She started, her lips parting unconsciously in an invitation he could not resist. He bent and kissed her, catching her in his arms and drawing her into his warmth, his strength. For a moment the slender, supple figure was pliant in his arms, the lips returned the pressure of his, hesitatingly, with a naïveté that was the last thing he expected. Then she jerked back, abruptly freeing herself, anger turning her eyes a pure, hard green. Instinctively her hand came up to strike him and Nicholas parried the blow with the palm of his hand. The sound of the slap rang through the small room, then she was gone, in a flurry of skirts.

Nicholas listened to her footsteps as she ran upstairs, the slam of a door, the unmistakable click of a key turning in a lock. He stood absently rubbing his tingling palm, a look of rueful surprise on his face. Of all the things he had expected to discover this evening it was not that Miss Davide was not only Untouchable, but, quite literally, untouched.

Chapter Two

Camilla Knight who, until a few moments ago, had called herself Mademoiselle Lysette Davide, leant against the panels of the bedroom door until her convulsive breathing stilled slightly. The sentimental wool-work picture hanging over the narrow bed swam in and out of focus in the firelight and she wondered if she was going to faint. Gradually the image of a child clutching two kittens became clear again and the possibility receded.

'How could he…?' she whispered into the silence of the shadowed room. Then, 'No, I will *not* think about it!' The touch of Nicholas Lovell's mouth still seemed to burn on her lips, but she forced herself to ignore it. It was far more important to think about how she was going to escape and get home with Lord Lovell occupying the front room. Three years of living a double life had left Miss Knight with a skill for ingenuity and subterfuge unknown amongst other unmarried ladies of her class, and one amorous and over-gallant peer was not going to trip her up now, just when she had renounced it all and was about to return to safe respectability. But any amount of ingenuity was not going to make this very real man disappear.

Camilla bent and touched a taper to the smouldering coals in the grate then lit the two candles on the mantelshelf. The simple room that she used nightly to transform a society lady into an actress and back again now seemed unreal in the flickering light. It was stark: there was little in there except a bed, a dressing-table with ewer and jug, soap and clean towels. No clothes, no personal belongings, nothing to hint at the real person who inhabited it for a short while. In contrast the rest of the little house was redolent with the personality of Miss Margaret March, the family's old nurse, retired since Camilla's younger sister left the nursery, but still very much a personality in the household. Once Miss March had been drawn into the subterfuge she had kept her mistress's secret faithfully night after night, despite her somewhat confused disapproval of these 'goings-on'.

But tonight Miss March was at her desperately sick brother-in-law's bedside and this absence threatened to break the secret wide open. Camilla opened the curtains and looked out. The cottages on Walcot Street all had small yards and gardens sloping steeply up to meet the far larger ones of the elegant houses of the Paragon, which arched along the crest of the hill above. The lights in the salon of her mother's house shone out directly above, so much higher that in the darkness it seemed to be on a clifftop. Safety was so near and yet so far away. It could be on the other side of Bath for all the help it was as a refuge to her now.

Normally she would have long since taken off her

wig and maquillage, having a short conversation with her old nursemaid as she did so. Then she would have slipped up through the concealed gate in the wall between the gardens, climbing the steep steps through the shrubbery to the back door, left on the latch for her. Now Camilla gazed longingly at her escape route, resting her hot forehead against the glass. It was going to be a long night.

The old clock on the landing produced one wheezy chime, but Camilla could still hear Nicholas moving about downstairs. There was the rattle of the poker in the grate, the sound of the pump in the kitchen, his footsteps on the boards. It seemed he was having trouble settling down to sleep.

Camilla shivered, despite the fire in the grate. She wrapped the quilted counterpane around her shoulders and settled back on the bed, tucking her feet up under her. She was aching for sleep, but determined not to drop off. She had to escape before morning: if his lordship were to see her in daylight her careful disguise would be swiftly penetrated. Stage make-up was never designed to be seen in the harsh light of day.

Now her double life was all over she could hardly believe she had got away with it undiscovered for so long. Three years! But then most people saw only what they expected to see, and that was not Miss Knight, the elder daughter of one of Bath's respectable widows, disporting herself on the professional stage!

Just over three years ago the newly bereaved Mrs Knight had arrived to take up residence in the city with her daughters. Camilla had been eighteen, Ophelia fourteen, and Mrs Knight had been planning her elder daughter's come-out when her unfortunate husband had succumbed to the seizure that carried him off. It had been no surprise to the family that the estate in Cambridgeshire was entailed on a distant cousin, but Mr Knight's sudden demise, and the subsequent discovery that their means were reduced from very comfortable to merely modest, had been a shock.

Mrs Knight had heard that one could live genteely in Bath on the income they had at their disposal and they soon found a respectable house in the Paragon. But the widow had no head for finance, and Camilla had rapidly found herself assuming the responsibility for the family funds. They were fortunate indeed that the elder son of the family solicitor from Cambridge had set up his own practice in Bath, and Mr Arthur Brooke had soon been established in their confidence as both friend and trusted adviser.

The true state of affairs revealed by Camilla and Mr Brooke's study of the account book had been depressing in the extreme. The Knights had been faced with the prospect of moving to dowdy apartments, discharging all but one of the servants and devoting all of their income to day-to-day living. There would be no money for either daughter's come-out, nor funds for dowries.

It was pure chance that had led Camilla to the shocking solution to their problems. After a particularly gloomy session discussing investments, Mr Brooke had offered to take her to the theatre and Camilla had readily accepted, desperate for a little diversion. Besides, private theatricals had long been a passion of hers, and their circle in Cambridgeshire had been unusually rich in other enthusiasts. Visits and house parties in the neighbourhood had invariably included charades, playlets and poetry readings, at which she excelled, and she had missed it very much since their move to Bath.

In the carriage driving back from the play she had been silent, the germ of an idea growing deep within her.

'A penny for your thoughts,' Arthur Brooke had prompted gently in his rather dry manner. Although only thirty, he was already adopting many of the mannerisms of his elderly father. 'Are you thinking about tonight's performance? I thought it very good.'

'I could do that,' Camilla blurted out impulsively.

'I beg your pardon, my dear Miss Knight, do what?'

'Act, go on the stage!'

'But why would you want to do anything so...so improper?' The shock in his voice hardly gave her pause, for the outrageous scheme was growing in her mind even as she answered him.

'Why, to make money, of course! Have we not agreed only this morning that my family's circumstances are straitened indeed? And what other talents have I?'

'But, Miss Knight, only consider what you are suggesting! A respectable match is surely not out of the question? You are educated, well-bred and very, er...' she could almost feel him blushing in the dark '...er, personable, if I may make so bold.'

'And with no dowry and no influential friends to promote my come-out, no amount of education, or even looks, are going to assist me, Mr Brooke. I cannot delude myself. Who,' she finished rhetorically, 'is going to offer for me now?'

There was a short silence, then he said, with shy diffidence, 'I will! Miss Knight, may I have the honour...?'

Camilla rushed in before he said the words. 'No. I thank you, sir, but I cannot accept an offer made out of kindness.'

He managed to keep the relief out of his voice very well, she thought, as they had continued back to the Paragon amicably enough. It had never been mentioned again.

But the idea of making an income from the stage was fixed in Camilla's mind. The very next morning, dressed modestly and heavily veiled, she ventured down to the Theatre Royal and sought an interview with Mr Gordon Porter, its actor-manager. One rendition of a scene from *As You Like It* and Mr Porter was more than interested in this prospect—especially when the anonymous young lady lifted her veil to reveal a lovely, expressive face to match the grace and elegance of a well-turned figure.

The manager was less enthusiastic about the hard-bargained terms she exacted from him, along with a promise never to enquire about the true identity of 'Lysette Davide'. But Mr Porter was no fool, and he soon realised his investment had been a good risk. Miss Davide rapidly became wildly popular, particularly with the gentlemen in the audience, and her salary rose accordingly, season by season.

A heavily disapproving but intrigued Mr Brooke threw himself into the investment of this scandalous income, and by diligence and some strokes of great good fortune they saw the nest-egg grow far beyond

Camilla's original modest dream. Now the Knights' comfortable home was secured, Ophelia's future well funded, and Mrs and Miss Knight could look forward to a respectable future.

These comfortable recollections ceased abruptly as Camilla thought about Nicholas Lovell ensconced downstairs, blocking her escape and threatening her with exposure. The clock struck two. Camilla climbed carefully off the bed, knelt down and applied one ear to the floorboards. All was silent—she would have to risk it now.

She crept down the steep stairs, hugging the inside of the treads to minimise the creaking of the old wooden boards, and peeped through the half-open door into the parlour. He was not on the couch! Her hand flew to her mouth as she scanned the room, then her eyes fell on the long shape stretched before the guttering fire.

Nicholas was lying full-length on the hearthrug, a sofa cushion behind his head. He had taken off his jacket and loosened his neckcloth and his body was totally relaxed in sleep. Camilla stood transfixed on the threshold. He looked younger, gentler, his lean features softened by the depth of his slumber. His lashes lay black on the high cheekbones, and in the flickering firelight his mouth seemed to flex into a smile.

Camilla fought down a totally irrational impulse to cross to him and brush back the lock of dark hair that had fallen on to his forehead. She should be out of the back door and away, not standing here remembering that outrageous kiss and wishing he would wake up and do it again!

With a shiver Camilla pulled her pelisse closer

across her shoulders, lifted her skirts and tiptoed into the kitchen. The big back-door key was in its usual place behind the flour-bin. She pulled it out with infinite care, stopping every few moments to listen, the sound of her heart thudding loudly in her ears. She slipped the key into the lock, then with painful slowness turned it.

The lock gave a harsh click which rang out like a pistol shot in the silent cottage and from the room beyond she heard Nicholas Lovell sigh and turn over, but he did not wake. Seconds later she was out in the chill April air, securing the door behind her and running up the steep path to the shrubbery which masked the door in the wall. With trembling fingers she lifted the latch and was through, pausing only to arrange the screen of falling ivy again before she closed it and climbed up between the clipped box hedges to the kitchen door.

Four hours later Nicholas Lovell woke stiff and cold before a fire reduced to a pile of smoking ash. For a moment he lay, eyes closed, trying to remember where he was and how he came to be there. The memory came back with a jolt of pleasurable anticipation and his mouth twisted in sensual recollection. He sat up, stretched, got to his feet and padded through to the kitchen, wincing as his stockinged feet met the chill of the flagstoned floor.

A few seconds with his head under the pump was enough to bring him fully awake and he stood for a moment listening. All was still in the little cottage. It would be fascinating to see what Miss Davide was like in the daylight and discover how she would react to him when they met again… Nicholas hefted the heavy kettle off the range and filled it. He riddled the fire, threw on some more coal, making no effort to do it quietly, and listened again. Surely that would have woken her?

He made the tea absently, his mind on his strategy for the morning. The capture of the intriguing Miss Lysette Davide—or whatever she was really called—was going to be too piquant to be rushed. Besides, he had five days to fill before going back to Town, and the thought of filling them with the chase was pleasurable.

There was still no movement from the room above. Nicholas climbed the stairs, glanced into the front room, the door of which stood open, found it empty and went to tap on the second chamber door. There was no response, so he tried again, calling out, 'Miss Davide? Good morning! I have made some tea…'

Still silence. Could she really be so heavily asleep? Then he remembered the fatigue in those hazel-green eyes the night before. He should really leave her to sleep, but he could not leave without speaking to her, and he must leave soon or risk being seen by the neighbours. She might be an actress, but she would guard her reputation, and he doubted she flaunted her gentlemen callers in such a way.

Nicholas knocked again, then gently eased down the handle and looked round the door. Not only was the chamber empty but the curtains were drawn and the bed obviously unslept in. He stepped inside and for a moment of disbelief blinked at the empty room, not trusting his own eyes. There was no wardrobe, no cupboard or trunk to hide in. The floor under the bed was visible and empty. He strode to the window, but the casement was stiff and had obviously not been opened for some time. He scanned the little yard below, sloping upwards to the high wall of the Paragon gardens above. But even if she had opened the window there was no way to climb down.

The front bedroom was equally unsatisfactory: it was exactly what it appeared—an elderly spinster's chamber, devoid of hiding places. Nicholas went back to the landing, closing the doors behind him. For a long moment he stared down into the little hallway below, his hands on his hips, his brow furrowed in thought. Unconsciously he pushed back the lock of hair Camilla had been so drawn to the night before.

Well, she must have gone out through the back door; there was no other explanation. But the door was locked and there was no key to be found. The front door was also locked, but the key was on the inside, exactly as it had been left when they had entered the night before. Nicholas went back into the kitchen and peered through the window, but all he could see was the high stone wall all around the yard, and the tangle of ivy and bushes screening the even higher wall at the foot of the gardens of the Paragon buildings.

'How the hell did you get out of here, Miss Davide?' he asked into the silence. 'And why?' It was her house, he was the interloper. But then the memory of that curiously innocent kiss came back to him. Either she was the most accomplished actress he had ever come across or she was indeed as pure as she had wanted him to believe. And if that were the case, then finding herself alone with a man might well have prompted her to take flight. But to where?

Ten minutes later he was locking the front door and slipping the key back under it. He would go home, have a wash and shave and a good breakfast—and send one of the grooms to keep a discreet eye on the little cottage in Walcot Street.

Mrs Knight was already pouring her second cup of chocolate when her elder daughter wandered, heavy-eyed, into the sunny breakfast parlour.

'Good morning, Mama, good morning, Ophelia.'

'Ah, there you are, my dear!' Mrs Knight raised her rather short-sighted blue gaze from the pages of the *Bath Intelligencer* and regarded Camilla anxiously. 'So unlike you to sleep in on such a lovely sunny morning. I was about to send Blisset up to see whether you were awake yet.'

'Oh, Mama!' Ophelia broke in, 'No wonder poor Camilla is so fatigued. How could you forget? It was her final performance last night!' At almost eighteen, Ophelia had much of the blonde prettiness that had made her mother so admired in her time, but she had too something of her father's sharp intelligence and spirit.

Mrs Knight blinked vaguely at her daughters. 'Oh, yes, I had quite forgot. Do forgive me, my dear. Did it go well?' The widow had managed to cope with her daughter's outrageous career by dint of largely ignoring it, persuading herself that Camilla's performances at the Theatre Royal were no different from those enacted at a private house party. Her understanding of financial matters was not strong, and she had been so sheltered by her late husband that the restoration of their fortunes appeared more as a happy accident than due to the actions of her daughter.

And besides, Camilla acknowledged, it was easier all round if Mama did not think too much about her scandalous behaviour. It was enough to give any respectable matron a fit of the vapours. Well, from this morning onwards the entire Knight family would be precisely what they appeared—respectable, modestly well-off ladies: ornaments of Bath society.

This comforting train of thought was punctuated by a shriek from Ophelia, who had purloined the inside pages of the newspaper from her mama and was conning them whilst demolishing her third slice of bread and butter with healthy appetite. 'Camilla! Look—do look! You are all over the paper!'

Her sister nearly dropped her cup before she realised that Ophelia was reading the theatre reviews. For one wild, mad moment she had imagined that the encounter between herself and Nicholas Lovell had somehow reached the gossip columns. She pressed one hand to her breast as if to still her wildly beating heart, before saying, as calmly as she could manage, 'Do read it Ophelia.'

'"*Finest performance of a dazzling three-year career…Mr Bradley also giving a strong reading…*" oh, never mind him! "*…crowned it all with a shocking announcement to theatregoers…riot in the pit…*" Were they really rioting? How exciting!' Ophelia's eyes sparkled with excitement. 'Oh, how I would have loved to be there! "*…resolute in the face of the pleas of her loyal audience…a sad loss* *to the Dramatic Art...noisy scenes outside the Theatre lasting into the small hours...'''*

'A complete exaggeration,' Camilla remarked calmly as she buttered a slice of bread with an almost steady hand. 'There was some disappointment at my announcement, which I confess was very gratifying, but it is a storm in a teacup and will all be forgotten in a week.'

Ophelia was scarcely listening. She was wrestling to fold up the broadsheet pages to show an engraving which purported to be that of Mademoiselle Lysette Davide. 'What a terrible likeness,' she declared, wrinkling her nose.

'So I should hope. Just think what would befall us all if anyone recognised your sister,' retorted her mama faintly, then rallied as a happy thought struck her. 'My dears, I have just thought. We can all go to the theatre again now!'

'Not for a week or so, please, Mama,' Camilla protested. The way she was feeling this morning, she did not care if she never saw the inside of a theatre again!

For his part Lord Lovell spent a restless day, largely engaged in avoiding his sister Georgiana. The Countess of Forres was eager to question her brother as to why he had not returned home until the morning, fearing that he was, once more, reverting to his old rakish ways, instead of conserving his energies for the pursuit of a wife. This had been her intention in inviting him to stay with her, and she expected—nay, demanded—that he dance attendance on her through an elaborate series of social events.

Aided and abetted by his brother-in-law Henry, Nicholas had managed on his arrival to elude her hints, invitations and downright orders to accompany her to dances, soirées and afternoon tea parties, at which he knew full well a succession of eligible young ladies would be paraded before him.

His valet was just smoothing the set of his evening-coat across his broad shoulders when the under-footman appeared at his bedroom door. 'Martins is returned, my lord, and said you had asked to see him at once.'

'Send him to Lord Forres's study. I will be down shortly.' Released finally by his valet, his appearance having passed muster to the standards of that demanding critic, Nicholas ran lightly down the staircase of Georgiana's house in the Crescent. Martins had spent all day watching the little house in Walcot Street, and surely by now he would have gleaned enough intelligence for Nicholas to track down the elusive Lysette Davide. She could hardly stay away from home all day.

The groom was waiting in the panelled masculine sobriety of Lord Forres's retreat. A taciturn, self-confident man, he touched his forelock as his master entered.

'Well, Martins, what news do you have for me?'

'None, my lord, I'm afraid.'

'None?' Nicholas's dark brows rose. 'You have been there since eight this morning, man, somebody or something must have occurred.'

'No, my lord. The place has been deserted. No one in, no one out. I took young Ben with me—he's a reliable lad, my lord—and I set him off to find a back way in—but there is none. I left him on watch and tried both the alehouses in the street. Thought someone there would know something.'

Nicholas stood frowning into the darkened garden. 'Good man. And what did you discover?'

'Not a lot, my lord. The house is occupied by an elderly lady—governess type by the sound of it. No one else lives there, no one else visits. She goes out a lot, but keeps herself to herself. Name of Miss March. Shops locally, pays her bills on time, very quiet. Not so much as a pet parrot.'

Nicholas grinned at this unusual touch of whimsy from the groom. 'You are sure about the parrot?'

'Dead sure, my lord. Do you want me to go back and watch the house again overnight?'

'No, you have done enough for one day. Send Wilkins; we will give it one more shot. Now go and get yourself a good dinner.' He tossed Martins a coin.

As the door closed behind the man Nicholas dropped into one of Henry's wing-chairs and stretched out his feet towards the fire. He steepled his fingers and looked through them at the dancing flames, his mind pondering on the enigma that was Miss Davide. To all intents and purposes she had walked into that cottage as though she owned it; she'd moved about the little rooms with an ease that spoke of long familiarity.

She knew that house well; he was sure of it. Then a thought came to him. Could she be disguising herself as the old lady? After all, she was an actress, and a fine one at that. But then he remembered the bedroom, so obviously and typically that of an elderly lady. Whatever Miss Davide might disguise herself as outside, there would be no need to continue the pretence in the privacy of her own home. And why should she disguise herself in any case?

Nicholas was still pondering pleasurably on aspects of the previous evening when the door flew open and a voice declared triumphantly, 'There you are, Nicholas! Really, what are you about, skulking in here? Benson announced dinner quite fifteen minutes ago!'

'Good evening, Georgiana.' Nicholas got reluctantly to his feet. 'I am afraid I quite lost track of the time. That is a particularly handsome turban. Is it new?'

The Countess inclined her head graciously at the compliment. Never beautiful, she was none the less a striking woman who dressed to advantage to show off her Junoesque figure and height. Strongly coloured silks and taffetas showed off the family jewels and the new pieces which an indulgent husband showered upon her every time she produced for him another child. As the family now consisted of four boys and a girl, her lord had every reason for thus rewarding her.

'Do not seek to divert me, Nicholas; what is going on? Why are you having surreptitious meetings with your grooms in the study?' Her deep blue eyes, so like his, fixed on his face.

'I do not believe Henry objects to me using his study,' Nicholas remarked mildly. 'I can hardly stand around in the mews at this time of night giving my men their orders. May I take you into dinner?' He offered his sister his arm and she gave him a frosty stare as she laid her fingers upon the dark blue superfine of his sleeve and turned with him towards the hall.

'Mmm. Do not think to bamboozle me, Nicholas! You know perfectly well I have no objection to you using the house as you wish, but you are up to something. Something disgraceful in the way of a wager, I will be bound!'

'How well you know me. I can hide nothing from you, sister dear. It revolves around a particularly fine horse and a wager I have entered into with George Marlow and his friends.'

Lady Forres snorted. 'I should have known it. Now, what are you doing tomorrow afternoon?'

'Er...nothing in particular.' Thinking of Mademoiselle Davide, he realised too late that he had fallen straight into his sister's trap.

'Good. Then you are coming with me to Lady Richardson's. She has just had a sculpture gallery added to her house and has invited a select party to view it. The cultural environment will do you good and I need an escort.' She ignored her brother's upcast eyes and persisted. 'Horses and wagers indeed! Besides, there is someone I am particularly anxious for you to meet.'

'Oh, good,' replied Nicholas in a voice of deep gloom as they entered the dining-room.

Lord Forres was already seated, but he got to his feet as his wife and brother-in-law entered and grinned at the expression on Nicholas's face. 'For goodness' sake, Georgiana, leave the man alone,' he admonished lovingly. 'And let us get on with our dinner.'

Despite the fact that there were only the three of them dining that evening, Lady Forres maintained the standard of food and presentation for which she was justly famed. Course followed course, each accompanied by a fine wine from Lord Forres's extensive cellar.

Georgiana showed every sign of wishing to probe further the question of his bet with George Marlow, and at the mention of a horse Henry's ears pricked and he too joined in the interrogation. Nicholas had no desire to discuss the terms of the bet and seized on the only other subject he knew Georgiana could reliably be diverted upon.

'So who is this person you are so desirous of my meeting tomorrow?' he asked innocently. 'A sculptor? Lady Richardson's architect? A visiting Italian artist, perhaps?'

Henry immediately lost interest and reverted to studying the cheeses before him. Georgiana, however, took the bait and dropped the subject of the wager. 'Do not be disingenuous, Nicholas, it does not suit you—you are too old to act the *naïf*. Mind you,' she added darkly, 'you always were!'

Nicholas tried, and failed, to look hurt. His elder sister had always done her best to order his life, but despite their constant sparring there was a deep affection between them. And, provided Georgiana was not nagging him, he always enjoyed coming to the household with its boisterous children, Henry's affable hospitality and Georgiana's lavish table.

His sister set down her empty glass with decision and looked hard at her handsome brother. Really, the boy was far too good-looking for his own good; and those looks combined with his intelligence, wit, social standing and undeniable wealth made him such a catch she could not believe he had wriggled free for so long. Well, not for much longer, if she had anything to do with it! He was twenty-seven years old; high time he was married and setting up his nursery. If Lady Forres had anything to do with it, Nicholas Lovell would not be leaving Bath unengaged to a highly eligible *partie.*

Recalling herself swiftly, she announced, 'The young person I wish you to meet is Lady Richardson's niece, Miss Emilia Laxton. Such a well-bred, well-connected young woman.'

'And how old is this paragon?' Nicholas asked warily. This was all too familiar. Georgiana appeared to think that the younger the débutante the more suitable she would be for reforming her rake of a brother.

'Er...I believe she is, er...seventeen.'

'A schoolroom chit, in other words! Save me, dear sister, from yet another vapid giggling miss without an idea in her head—or indeed anything else.'

'No, indeed, you are being most unfair, Nicholas, to dismiss Miss Laxton out of hand. She is extremely well-connected. The granddaughter of the Earl of Olney and, I understand, the heiress of her uncle, Sir George Laxton. I only want to see you settled and happy, my dear, and she would make you a very conformable bride.'

Nicholas grimaced. He too felt an increasing desire to be settled and happy—but not with some child selected by his sister on the basis of her place in *Debrett's* or the size of her fortune. He wanted a companion, someone with character and intelligence—and looks and spirit, of course. Someone like...He remembered the touch of Lysette Davide's lips on his last night, the flash of anger and intelligence in her eyes, the piquant mystery of her. Of course an actress, of whatever quality, was totally ineligible, but if he could find a respectable young lady with some of those qualities he would be only too happy to marry her.

Yes, he would go to Lady Richardson's and endure it with every appearance of pleasure, and no expectation of meeting anyone of any interest. Meanwhile there was still a wager to win and the delectable Miss Davide to find and conquer.

Chapter Three

No one observing Lord Lovell's urbane expression as he bowed gracefully over his hostess's hand the next day would have guessed that he was at the reception under duress. Certainly Lady Richardson, intensely gratified by the presence of one of the most good-looking and eligible bachelors of the Ton, read nothing but polite interest in his handsome features as he enquired about her new sculpture gallery.

'Well, my lord, we did feel it was time we found more fitting accommodation for the treasures Lord Richardson brought back from the Grand Tour. For so long they have been in very cramped surroundings in our London residence—they could not be properly appreciated there. But here we have not only space for our own sculptures, but also those my late father-in-law had installed in the Berkshire house.'

Nicholas smiled warmly at his hostess, who responded by turning a hue almost as rosy as her afternoon gown. 'A most striking arrangement, ma'am, and, if I may be so bold to venture an opinion, so very indicative of your own taste.'

Lady Forres shot her brother a warning look over the shoulder of their hostess. Lady Richardson might be fooled into thinking she had just received a compliment, but Georgiana, herself inwardly shuddering at the over-ornate, gilded décor, knew better.

'Well, for myself I cannot wait to look around; it looks quite fascinating,' she interjected hastily. 'Give me your arm, Lovell, and let Lady Richardson attend to her other guests. We must not monopolise her.'

The ladies bowed to each other and Nicholas guided Georgiana off towards the far end of the new sculpture gallery. A footman approached with a tray of glasses and Nicholas secured a glass of Madeira for them both. 'Nicholas,' Lady Forres warned, *sotto voce*, while smiling and nodding to an acquaintance. 'None of your tricks now. Do behave, please!'

One dark brow rose quizzically. 'Sister, dear, what can you mean? I am being perfectly polite about this ghastly room.'

'I know you are, you wretch, so why do I feel as though I am sitting on a keg of gunpowder every time you open your mouth?' Her blue eyes regarded him shrewdly; she was not displeased by what she saw. Even a sister's critical eye could detect no flaw in the cut of his coat or the perfection of his neck-cloth or gleaming Hessian boots. And the fashion for tight trousers, while fatal to those of short limbs or a portly disposition, enhanced the rangy elegance of Lord Lovell's frame. As for his looks—well, he took after his father, said by many to have been the best-looking man of his generation.

As brother and sister strolled slowly down the length of gallery, it seemed that an inordinate number of ladies turned to regard them. But Lady Forres, who did not delude herself into thinking it was her new gown that was causing the interest, could see no sign of Miss Laxton, her quarry for the afternoon.

Ah, there she was! Lady Forres spied the young lady sitting demurely on a chaise-longue, partly hidden by an orange tree in a pot. The girl rose politely to her feet when she saw the older woman bearing down on her, but her eyes dropped when she saw Nicholas. 'Miss Laxton, how do you do? You are not acquainted with my brother, the Earl of Ashby, I believe? Lovell, Miss Laxton.'

Miss Laxton dropped a curtsey without raising her gaze to Nicholas. 'Miss Laxton,' he murmured, wishing she would look up. His sister had been right; she really was the most beautiful child: dark brown curls clustered round a small, perfectly shaped head and cascaded on to her slender white neck. Her features were regular, her face heart-shaped and her complexion one of true roses and cream. After a long moment she shyly met his gaze, revealing a pair of pansy-brown eyes and an expression of apprehension.

Lady Forres saw her friend Lady Richardson advancing on them and permitted a small smile to play around her lips, answered by an almost imperceptible nod from the betoqued head of the older woman. The two of them had put their heads together over this meeting, and both had agreed that the match was highly desirable, for many reasons.

'Emilia, my dear,' Lady Richardson cooed, 'why do you not show his lordship the fountain at the far end of the gallery? I am sure he will enjoy the view afforded of the orangery from there.'

'That sounds delightful,' Nicholas responded, offering Miss Laxton his arm. Her fingers, as they settled lightly on his sleeve, trembled slightly. As they moved away from the two matrons he said lightly, 'Come, Miss Laxton, I am not so much of an ogre as to make you tremble, am I?'

'Oh, no, my lord!' she protested, her startled eyes flying to meet his amused gaze. 'It is just that my aunt said that you were such a connoisseur, and I know nothing about classical art. In fact,' she added, all in a rush, 'I think these statues rather ghastly.' She looked so conscience-stricken at this admission that Nicholas laughed out loud.

'In what way?' he asked encouragingly.

'So cold and white. And there are bits missing— see, that one has no arms! Why could they not be mended before being placed in the gallery? And then there are all those huge men wrestling with sea monsters—it really is not the sort of restful thing one would like to live with, is it?'

Nicholas obligingly viewed the fountain to which she was referring. It had been set into the end wall of the gallery and indeed, over-muscled marine gods appeared to be locked in mortal combat with improbable sea creatures. 'I have to agree with you, Miss Laxton, not restful at all. I suspect the architect has seen the Prince Regent's latest additions to Carlton House and has been inspired by them.'

This interchange appeared to have exhausted Miss Laxton's source of conversation for the moment and they stood side by side in silence in front of the tumbling water, Nicholas wondering just how soon he could politely make his escape. Miss Laxton was undoubtedly a delightfully pretty débutante, but five minutes in her company was more than sufficient.

Outside in Laura Place a hired chaise drew up and three ladies descended on to the flagged pavement before Lady Richardson's house. Mrs Knight ran a critical eye over her daughters' gowns and, more than satisfied, ushered them into the hallway. 'One good thing, my dear,' she remarked to Camilla as they climbed the stairs to the reception room. 'Now you are no longer going to the th...I mean, going out in the evenings, you will be able to accept so many more invitations for parties and dances.'

'Indeed, Mama,' Camilla responded, as a maid conducted them into a side room to remove their pelisses and tidy their hair. 'But I shall have to account for the sudden improvement in my health which now, after three years, allows me to go about in the evenings.'

'Oh, that is easily done: the Bath air, the waters, a new physician—there are any number of reasons one can give.' Mrs Knight flapped her hands vaguely and led her small party out to meet their hostess.

Camilla stepped confidently into the salon behind her mother. She knew she was looking her best, in a new afternoon gown of pale moss-green with a simple flounce. Her tall, slender figure needed no distracting frills or ornamentation to detract from any faults, and in keeping with her unmarried status she wore only a simple pearl necklace and matching earstuds. Although her clandestine life had forced her to make excuses for rarely attending evening events, Camilla had nonetheless a wide social circle, many of whom would be present at this reception.

Passing through the salon, she was soon caught up in conversation with a cheerful group of young ladies of her acquaintance. She accepted a glass of orgeat and eyed the over-ornate gallery warily. Lady Richardson was an excellent hostess, but unfortunately her money and connections did not confer good taste in interior design. Camilla maintained a lively debate on the quite dreadfully unflattering hat brims which had just come into fashion, while mentally stripping the room of its ornament and substituting a few well-placed statues and potted palms.

Ophelia, wandering wide-eyed at her mother's heels amidst the crowd of classical sculptures, was inclined to giggle at her elders' flowery enthusiasm for the display. After a few moments she glimpsed Miss Laxton at the far end, made her excuses and hurried towards her best friend.

On reaching her side she was pulled up short by the sight of Miss Laxton's companion, a devastatingly handsome man. Emilia was directing an anxious, silent signal for help to her, and Ophelia was only too happy to oblige. What was Emilia doing with this man when Ophelia knew she had contracted an attachment to Edward Ormond, the younger son of Sir James Ormond, the City banker?

Well, if her dear friend needed help with this particular gentleman, Ophelia was only too ready to oblige! 'Miss Laxton, good afternoon. What a charming party!'

'Good afternoon! My lord, may I introduce Miss Ophelia Knight? Miss Knight and I attended Miss Atherton's seminary together. Miss Knight, may I make known to you the Earl of Ashby?'

Ophelia dropped a curtsey, and raised bright eyes to his lordship. 'My lord, are you resident in Bath?'

'Visiting my sister Lady Forres, Miss Knight. I am rarely in Bath, but I realise now what I have been missing, and will visit more frequently in future.' This child was enchanting, and with none of Miss Laxton's shyness.

Ophelia twinkled back responsively. Unlike her friend, she had not the slightest objection to flirting with a handsome man such as his lordship. 'Oh, so you are attracted by classical sculpture then, my lord? Is there none to be seen in London? Surely the British Museum is full of that sort of thing.'

'I was referring rather to the charming company one encounters in this city, Miss Knight,' Nicholas responded gallantly. Miss Knight intrigued him: she was very young, as young as the gauche and silent Miss Laxton, but there was something about her...

'Have we met before, Miss Knight?' he enquired as the three of them turned and began to stroll back up the gallery.

'I think not, my lord. I have not been to London since I was quite a child, and I do not come out until this Season.'

'Forgive me my error,' Nicholas responded lightly. But that strong sense of having met either Miss Knight or someone very like her persisted.

'There is your sister, dear Ophelia,' Miss Laxton cried, still anxious to widen the circle and remove herself from the uncomfortable presence of Lord Lovell.

Nicholas turned at her words and saw Camilla framed against an empty niche. She was laughing at a story one of her group was telling, her head tilted back slightly, her blonde curls falling from a high knot. Her profile was almost Grecian in its purity and cool perfection of line, and Nicholas thought he had never seen a more beautiful woman.

He glanced automatically at her left hand, but she wore no wedding band. He guessed her age to be perhaps twenty or twenty-one, slightly older than the other débutantes. Perhaps that accounted for her poise and air of quiet self-assurance. And if her younger sister's features had stirred something within his memory, then that feeling was much stronger now.

'Will you not introduce us, Miss Ophelia?' He had met her before—but where? Surely he could not have forgotten such looks and presence?

Ophelia, with an inward sigh, for she was well aware that in the presence of her sister no attractive rake was going to be sparing any attention for her, led the way over.

Camilla had perhaps two heartbeats' notice of the arrival of the man she had spent half the previous night with. For a moment she thought she was going to faint, the shock of seeing him was so great. Then, with an almost superhuman effort, she called up every vestige of acting skill she had ever possessed and stood with nothing but an expression of polite interest on her face.

'Camilla, may I introduce the Earl of Ashby, who is anxious to be made known to you? My lord, my sister Miss Knight.' Ophelia wondered why her sister had gone so pale and why she was suddenly so still, so rigid. Why, Ophelia thought with a sudden flight of fancy, one might almost think she had stepped out of the empty niche behind her, a statue come to life.

'Miss Knight, good afternoon. You will forgive me, but have we not met before? In London perhaps?'

'Good afternoon, my lord.' Camilla murmured. 'I am afraid I do not recall our having been introduced. Perhaps you are mistaken.' It was not the truth, of course, but it was not quite a lie either: after all, he had been introduced to Lysette Davide, not to Miss Knight. He had not recognised her, she was sure of that, but something about her had piqued his interest, that was certain. There was a look in those quizzical blue eyes that worried her. It was obvious that her cool words had not satisfied him and he would not give up until he had placed her in his memory. The impression of him as a hunter that had come to her in the Green Room was back.

She caught a glimpse of her own reflection in one of the long glasses which lined the room between the niches and was reassured. No, surely he would not recognise in this blonde, pale, composed and calm English débutante the brunette actress with her husky French accent and bold stage make-up. And the chaste simplicity of her gown spoke of nothing but the débutante.

'Are you in Bath long, my lord?' she enquired politely. 'Will you be subscribing to the Assembly Rooms and concerts?' With any luck he would say he was just passing through, hated Bath and would never set foot in the place again!

'I am staying with my sister, Lady Forres, and I had intended a short visit only on this occasion. Normally I do not find much to keep me in Bath.

However, I feel I have greatly misjudged the city and I may well extend my stay.' How he managed, without any change of expression or tone, to imply that this was entirely due to her presence, Camilla was at a loss to know. The man was an accomplished and dangerous flirt, if not an out-and-out rake.

In one part of her mind she was amused to have the unique opportunity to observe his technique with women from—as he thought—two very different worlds. But, intriguing as that might be, she could not but be aware that she was in very grave danger, and a tension far greater than any stage fright she had ever suffered was gripping her nerves. One word from Lord Lovell and she would be ruined, irretrievably and for ever. And Ophelia would be tarred with the same brush.

His lordship was signalling for a waiter, and when the man arrived he took two glasses from the tray and offered one to Camilla. As she accepted it her hand shook slightly, and observing it Lord Lovell was taken aback. Why was this cool, poised creature trembling? He was used to displays of nerves from very young débutantes, but in this woman it seemed at odds with her outward assurance.

Camilla glanced round for her sister, anxious to turn this dialogue into a three-way conversation, but, thoroughly bored and somewhat resigned to his lordship's lack of interest in anyone but her older sister, Ophelia had rejoined her schoolfriend at the end of the gallery. Now they sat, heads close together, giggling behind their hands at the carefully placed fig-leaf on a statue of a very minor Greek god.

'I am sure Lady Forres must be delighted that you

are extending your stay, especially if you do not normally find Bath congenial,' Camilla observed, wondering if she sounded as banal as she thought she did.

Nicholas grimaced. 'I had intended staying five days. But now I have made a wager with some of my friends. To win it I must stay in Bath for a while. So...' he smiled at her, transforming his lean and somewhat saturnine features, '...my plans for next week are overset and I think I will have to console myself by experiencing all of Bath's attractions.'

He was rewarded by a slight blush on Miss Knight's pale cheeks. She might look as though flirtation was beneath her, but she could respond to it like the next woman.

Camilla had indeed been in no doubt as to which attractions he had been referring to. Try as she might, the memory of his mouth, warm, experienced and demanding, came flooding into her mind and the blush deepened. Her fingers crept to the curls clustering against her throat, and she smoothed them unconsciously. Nicholas frowned, his memory piqued again by that gesture.

Collecting herself with a huge effort, she smiled back at him. 'Somehow, my lord, I do not think you will find taking the waters to be an attraction, but if you have not spent much time here before you may not be aware of how delightful the countryside is around the city.'

'That does indeed sound more attractive than sipping sulphurous waters—not that I had intended to try, I must admit! Do you know of any rides in particular that you could recommend?'

Camilla, not seeing the trap, fell right into it.

'Yes, indeed, my lord. My sister and I often ride out: there are many routes through the woods or across the hills which I can recommend.'

'Capital!' Nicholas smiled warmly into her green eyes. 'Then might I hope you will act as my guide? Perhaps, if this fine weather persists, you and Miss Ophelia might like to ride with me tomorrow afternoon?'

'Why, thank you my lord. What a kind thought. However, we have a previous…'

'Riding!' Ophelia appeared beside them as if by magic, her arm linked through that of Arthur Brooke, whom she had obviously just waylaid. 'How lovely! With spring so much in the air, I am longing to gallop along the downs. Thank you, my lord.'

'Unfortunately Miss Knight was just telling me you had a prior engagement,' Nicholas said with a wicked glint in his eye, looking from one sister's eager face to the other's warning frown.

Ophelia turned a puzzled face to her sister. 'No, no, Camilla. What can you be thinking of? Why, it was only this morning we were agreeing how dull this week was set to be!'

'Yes, well, we can discuss that later, Ophelia. Mr Brooke must think our manners have gone wandering! Good afternoon, Mr Brooke, how pleasant to find you here admiring the new gallery.' In her relief at seeing him, Camilla was rather warmer in her manner than normal in greeting her old friend and man of law, a fact reflected in the smile that appeared on his normally serious face.

'Indeed, yes, I am. And a most pleasant surprise to find you all here, Miss Knight. An interesting

interpretation of the Graeco-Roman style, but I think
the architect has succeeded in carrying it off.'

'I must confess to finding it somewhat chilly,'
Camilla replied with a smile. 'But I am forgetting
my manners. Lord Lovell, may I make known to
you Mr Brooke? Mr Brooke, the Earl of Ashby, who
is staying in Bath with his sister Lady Forres. Mr
Brooke has a legal practice in the City, my lord, and
is an old and good friend of ours.' She laid a hand
on Arthur's sleeve as she spoke, acting on an instinctive desire for support, and saw his lordship's
brows draw together slightly at the intimacy.

'My lord.' Mr Brooke bowed somewhat stiffly,
disliking the sight of a man of fashion standing quite
so close to Miss Knight. He had never met his lordship, but he knew of the other man's reputation as
a rake and was well aware that he was attracting
many feminine glances as he stood there in his
London clothes.

Ophelia had been waiting with poorly concealed
impatience for the introductions to be over.
'Camilla, you must be mistaken about our engage-
ments tomorrow, for I am certain we have none.
Surely you recall discussing it?'

With a rather stiff smile Camilla capitulated,
knowing from long experience that Ophelia would
be blind and deaf to looks and hints. 'How foolish
of me to have confused the days! It seems, my lord,
that we are able to take up your kind invitation after
all. I wonder if we would be able to make up a small
party…Mr Brooke, would you be able to accompany us?'

Arthur, aware of an almost infinitesimal pressure
on his arm, replied with deep regret, 'I am very sorry

indeed to have to refuse such a treat, but tomorrow I am engaged with one of my clients—a very elderly lady who is in the very frailest health—and I cannot see my way to changing the appointment.'

Nicholas, aware that there was an undercurrent present, glanced from Arthur Brooke's face to Camilla's and wondered if, despite the solicitor's sombre appearance, he would find himself with a rival to cut out. 'What a pity you cannot join us. However, may I call at two o'clock tomorrow? And if I might enquire of your direction?'

'We live in the Paragon, my lord.' She opened her reticule and handed him a card. As she looked up she saw a reminiscent smile playing around his lips.

'Lord Lovell? I have said something to amuse you?'

'I beg your pardon, Miss Knight. I know little of Bath and yet it seems that on this visit I am drawn to that particular district. Why, only last night I had a most singular encounter in Walcot Street.'

'Indeed, my lord?' Camilla said repressively. 'I understand that parts of that street have an unfortunate reputation. It is not an area my sister or I would frequent.'

'Well, my experience did begin with a rather unpleasant encounter with footpads, but ended rather more…pleasurably.' A reminiscent smile curved his firm lips, earning him a severe look from Arthur Brooke, who suspected that expression had something to do with the location of the house for fallen women in Walcot Street.

Camilla's heart was beating in her chest like thunder. He knew! He must know! He had recognised her. Then as her shock subsided she realised he was not teasing her, nor looking to entrap her. No, what she had glimpsed had been a genuinely private recollection of pleasure. The thought that he recalled her like that set her heart fluttering, and once again her own memory of that kiss returned to heat her blood.

'I see my mother is waiting for us. Goodbye, Mr Brooke, I do hope you find your client in better health. Until tomorrow then, my lord, but please do not trouble if the weather turns bad; we will not look for you in that case. Goodbye.' Camilla extended her gloved hand and Nicholas took it, returning the pressure slightly in a formal handshake. But the movement brought her close to him, the hem of her skirts fluttering against his legs as she turned from him towards the door and a slight waft of the warm honeysuckle scent she wore touched his nostrils.

He swung round to watch her as she walked through the door into the salon, her mother and sister at her side. That nagging memory was back again. Where on earth...?

'Lovell!' Georgiana was at his side, looking disapproving and most effectively breaking across his train of thought. 'What have you been about, monopolising Miss Knight for so long? People will talk. And you have neglected Miss Laxton disgracefully, I quite despair of your manners!' Seeing his eyes following the departing Knights, she added, 'Very good family, but no money—that matters not to you, of course—but I tell you frankly, Nicholas, she would not have you. No young lady who has been in society as Miss Knight has will tolerate your wayward behaviour and raking about. You need a nice little innocent who will adore you for what she thinks you are,' she added tartly.

His sister's complaints rolled off Nicholas's broad shoulders, preoccupied as he was with the mystery of Miss Camilla Knight. Frowning, he turned to his sister. 'I beg your pardon, Georgiana. Were you saying something?'

'Oh, you are quite impossible, Nicholas!'

The Knights' carriage was making its way with painful slowness over Pulteney Bridge, which was choked with carrying chairs, pedestrians and several riders making their way towards Sydney Place. 'Oh dear,' Mrs Knight lamented vaguely as she looked out of the carriage window. 'I had meant to walk up from Laura Place and call in at Miss Little's for that bonnet she was trimming for me. Oh, well, never mind. We can walk down tomorrow…'

'We cannot accompany you, Mama, unless you choose to go before luncheon,' Ophelia said with excitement, patting her curls. 'Camilla and I have been engaged to ride out with Lord Lovell.'

'Lovell,' her mama echoed, as if searching her mind to place the name. 'Oh yes, indeed, Lady Forres's brother the Earl of Ashby.' She looked sharply at her daughters. 'He should have presented himself to me before engaging to take you anywhere. And where did you meet him, my dears?' Her mind, although normally vague, was sharp enough when it came to the subject of eligible men and her lovely daughters.

'Why, in the sculpture gallery, Mama,' Ophelia prattled happily, not noticing how unusually silent

her elder sister was. 'You did not venture in, I believe.'

Mrs Knight gave a delicate shudder. 'No, indeed.
I stayed in the salon. All that chilly white marble,
and those unclothed figures… Hardly the place I
would have thought suitable to entertain young
ladies. But you were saying about Lord Lovell?'

'He is rather old, of course,' Ophelia opined solemnly. 'Why, he must be all of thirty.'

'More like seven and twenty,' Camilla interjected
suddenly, then returned to gazing out of the window.

'Well, that is old anyway. And everyone says he
is a terrible rake, but he does not look like one to
me…'

'I sincerely hope you have no idea of such
things!' Mrs Knight protested. 'When I was your
age I would not have heard the word, let alone
thought to use it in the presence of my mama! And
if he is,' she added firmly, 'then you are certainly
not riding out with him tomorrow or indeed any
day.'

Up to that moment Camilla would have been delighted to hear her mother deny Lord Lovell the
house. Now, perversely, she felt a stab of alarm and
a strong inclination to soothe her parent's fears. 'No,
indeed, Mama, I believe Lord Lovell has suffered
the fate of many eligible bachelors. Because he
has—doubtless unintentionally—raised the expectations of many a matchmaking mama, he has been
labelled a rake. He seemed most truly a gentleman,
and of course, we will take Higgins.'

The image of their dour and deeply respectable
groom rose in Mrs Knight's mind in a truly reassuring manner. No, there would be no inappropriate

behaviour with Higgins to hand! 'Very well, my dear. Indeed, if one can be assured he is not, er…what Ophelia said…it has to be admitted he is a most eligible man.'

Aware she was being regarded beadily by her mama Camilla flushed, but said steadily, 'Now, Mama, you know we have agreed that the circumstances of my…' she hesitated '…former occupation dictate that I may never marry. I am now, as we have agreed, quite ineligible.'

'Oh dear, I know you say so, Camilla, but surely, after perhaps a year, there will be not the slightest danger that anyone will ever find out? You cannot condemn yourself to spinsterhood, though I appreciate your offer to remain at my side as a support and companion in my old age.'

'Mama, you know it would be quite dishonourable of me to marry a man knowing there is a risk this might come out—imagine the scandal if it did! And no man would marry me if he knew. But it is not something we should be discussing now. And as to Ophelia, she is far too young for Lord Lovell.'

'*Well*,' Ophelia declared, 'you may say so, but I know that Emilia's aunt Lady Richardson, and Lord Lovell's sister Lady Forres, are plotting to marry Emilia off to the Earl! And she is the same age as I am! So there!' She leaned back with a triumphant smile upon her pretty young face.

'That would be an excellent match indeed!' Mrs Knight exclaimed. 'I must congratulate Lady Richardson, for if this is true she is a most notable matchmaker. Little Emilia Laxton and an earl—why, it gives me hope for your prospects, Ophelia dear!'

'Well, I cannot dispute that I would like to be a countess,' Ophelia agreed. 'And Lord Lovell is very handsome,' she added, with a sideways look at her elder sister. 'But he is also very old... What exactly does a rake do?'

'Did I not hear that Miss Laxton had formed an attachment?' Camilla enquired hastily, hoping to turn the conversation somewhat from the subject of his lordship. She was inclined to agree with Ophelia's first statement, and heartily disagree with the second. It was not Lord Lovell's age that troubled her...

'Oh...er...no, not really,' Ophelia said hastily, with a glance at her mother. But she only managed to look the picture of guilt and Mrs Knight caught her up immediately.

'If you are helping Miss Laxton conceal a clandestine flirtation, Ophelia...' she began warningly, her pale brows furrowed.

'No indeed, Mama,' her youngest daughter hastened to assure her. 'It is no secret. She makes no secret of her attachment to Mr Ormond, but despite his papa's great wealth, her mama will not countenance the match.'

'A City banker! Well, I am not surprised. And he is a younger son, is he not?'

'Yes...but he is going to have a wonderful career as a university professor and make his name, you know. He is ever so learned and already something frightfully important at Oxford...or is it Cambridge?' She broke off, her nose wrinkled with the effort of remembering.

'Emilia Laxton married to a scholar?' Camilla exclaimed. 'What an inappropriate match! She is a sweet girl but she does not—and I suspect never will—have a serious thought in her head!'

'She knows she is not bookish, but she says that is not what Edmund needs. She says he needs a good wife, someone who will look after him when he becomes too immersed in his studies to eat, and she will be that. Emilia says she will nurture his genius!'

'Goodness!' said Mrs Knight weakly. 'How forward young people are these days. Well, the sooner she is married off to the Earl of Ashby the better, is all I can say.'

'Indeed,' her elder daughter agreed with somewhat less conviction. Why should the thought of Miss Laxton's marrying Nicholas cause her heart to jolt so? She scarcely knew him, and she had acknowledged that she would—could—never marry. But almost unbidden her gloved fingers came up to caress her lips, as if re-tasting the sensation of being kissed by him. Suddenly very anxious that the subject should be closed, Camilla turned her gaze once more to the honey-stone terraces of Bath, and the thronged streets through which the coachman was making his careful way back to the Paragon.

The Earl in question was also seated in a carriage and gazing out of the window, doing his best to ignore his sister's steady flow of observation, criticism and general commentary on his character, prospects and lack of stability. 'Settle down and raise a family,' she was saying firmly. 'It is about time you had an heir. You are not getting any younger...'

'Doubtless you are right, Georgiana.'

'I am always right! Do you not wish to be settled?

Can you not imagine the benefits of marriage to Miss Laxton?'

'I am not averse to marrying and settling down, my dear, but, beyond the undoubted charms of Miss Laxton's countenance and youth, I can think of few worse things than to be leg-shackled to a pretty little chit with nothing between her ears than the latest Paris fashions or the newest novel!'

'Nonsense, Nicholas! I agree she is young, and by no means a bluestocking, but then you are not noted for intellectual or cultural pursuits,' Georgiana added, tartly, before continuing, 'but she is malleable. You can mould her to suit you...'

'I do not wish to marry a lump of clay. I want to marry a woman of character and intelligence,' Nicholas protested, then turned a wicked look on his indignant sister. 'Not, of course, that I am averse to a pretty face, a well-rounded figure, a pair of warm lips...' As he expected, she shot him a furious glare and subsided into silence. The conversation was becoming scandalously inappropriate.

A pair of warm lips...soft and inviting...now that did stir memories. He resumed his unseeing scrutiny of the street and turned his mind back to that moment when Miss Davide had quivered responsively in his arms, her face upturned to his, her full lips trusting yet eager against his own, the scent of her filling his nostrils, warm and seductive.

The scent of her! Why, of course, that was it—that subtle, lingering sweetness of honeysuckle, warm against a summer wall, but here warmed by her skin, *that* was what had been in the back of his mind, and that was what he had smelt again that afternoon as Miss Knight had turned to leave!

It couldn't be…the idea was too preposterous to entertain…Camilla Knight was so fair, so unadorned with paint or patches, so undoubtedly respectable. But he knew that women could transform themselves with the application of maquillage, and to cover that pale glory with a wig, a brown hairpiece, would be simplicity itself, especially to one who had all the skills of the theatre at her disposal. He remembered again how the younger sister had piqued his memory when he had first seen her.

But if it were true why should someone like Miss Knight, undoubtedly of the Quality if not of the very first ranks of the Ton, take to the stage? The whole world was aware of how society regarded any young lady who had an association with the boards. After all, the term 'actress' was often no more than a euphemism for a whore, the fiction of being on the stage a cover for being kept by a gentleman as a complaisant friend, always willing, always available…

'Lovell!' Georgiana repeated sharply, her previous words lost on her oblivious brother. 'I begin to wonder if you are quite well. Perhaps you need to take a physick!'

'Sorry, my dear, I was admiring Mr Nash's artistry. You were saying?'

'I will ask you again. Are you dining in this evening?'

Nicholas pulled himself together. 'I think not. I agreed to meet George Marlow and Sir William Hendricks this evening. I shall be out till late, so please do not concern yourself on my part.'

And over dinner and a hand of cards he would make a few discreet enquiries of his theatre-loving friends about the history of the mysterious Mademoiselle Lysette Davide. Before the evening was out he intended to discover if she and the graceful Miss Camilla Knight were one and the same woman.

Chapter Four

'Lovell! Are you going to bid or sit there gazing at the wallpaper all evening?' George Marlow asked plaintively. He had an excellent hand which was getting no support from a partner who appeared to have his mind on something else entirely.

'Um? Oh, yes, right…three hearts.'

George sighed inwardly and cast his eyes up to the ceiling moulding, a careless gesture which did not go unnoticed by the other pair, who hastily changed their tactics.

'Not got your mind on this, have you, Lovell, old man?' Lord Corsham enquired slyly. 'Now, what can you be thinking of, I wonder?'

The three friends were agog to discover what had transpired between the Earl and Miss Davide the previous night. In the scrimmage outside the Theatre Royal they had entirely lost sight of him and were now waiting to hear how the bet was going. On the other hand, none of them was going to broach the subject directly, and Nicholas Lovell was being quite infuriatingly discreet.

Sir William Hendricks played a card and winked

across the table at his partner. 'Been out on Thunderer today, Freddie? Making the most of him while you've still got him?'

'Judging by our comrade's silence, I believe I have little to fear,' Lord Corsham replied languidly, taking a sip of his brandy. 'I haven't noticed any message asking me to hand him over...'

Nicholas lowered the fan of cards in his hand and grinned with a sudden flash of white teeth at his friends. 'There is no need to fish, gentlemen. The answer to the question you are all studiously avoiding asking is "not yet". Now, can we finish this hand?'

'Not if you aren't going to concentrate,' George said bitterly, poking a plump finger at the diminishing pile of coins in front of him. 'I can't afford to play *against* you at any time, but I'm damned if I'm going to play *with* you if you can't keep your mind on the cards!'

The ice having been broken, the other two were not going to give up. Freddie Corsham raked in his winnings and picked up the scattered cards. 'Turned you down flat, then, did she?' He shuffled the cards and began to deal. 'An unusual experience for you, Nick.'

'I wouldn't call escorting a lady home being turned down, exactly,' Lovell replied calmly, picking up his cards and eyeing them impassively.

'She let you take her home!' Hendricks choked on his brandy. 'You lucky dog! Where does she live?'

It was the opening Nicholas was looking for. 'Oh, don't any of you know?' They all shook their heads mutely. Damn! He let none of the disappointment show on his face and kept his eyes on his hand. 'Two diamonds.' The bidding went round twice before he continued. 'I would have thought you faithful admirers would know everything there is to know about the Divine Miss Davide. Surely you are on her doorstep daily with bouquets of flowers?'

George looked particularly downcast. 'Her love of privacy is notorious, old man. Even that old rogue of a theatre manager doesn't know where she lives: we've all tried to bribe the information out of him.'

'And Mr Gordon Porter would sell his own mother for ten guineas,' Hendricks added darkly. 'So if he won't sell the information it means he doesn't have it.'

Nicholas won a trick and scooped the cards towards him, thought for a moment and led with trumps. So, Miss Davide was secretive to a quite extraordinary degree. That tended to support his theory that she and Miss Knight could be one and the same woman. But even as he thought it he wondered again: it was such an incredible suspicion to have. It was possible to believe that a rather fast young widow might hazard her reputation on the stage, but a well-bred, single girl of great beauty...why she would be risking everything! Any hope of a marriage of even the most modest respectability would be lost if the knowledge of such a double existence came out.

Nicholas and George won the next two hands, which cheered up the impecunious Mr Marlow to such an extent that he pulled the bell and, when his butler arrived, ordered the best brandy to be brought up. Nicholas ignored the light badinage between the three men that filled the interval, his thoughts again turned to Camilla Knight.

If they were one and the same, then it seemed inconceivable that the débutante he had encountered today would permit any behaviour of the sort that would win him the wager—and in any case, there was no circumstance in which he was going to start seducing virgins!

Unless of course Miss Knight was such a good actress that playing the innocent was just another role and she truly was leading a double life, with or without the knowledge of her mother and sister. And that would be such an incredibly dangerous thing to do—why, if it came out the entire family would be ruined, including young Ophelia. But could even the most accomplished actress have feigned the innocence in that kiss last night? He could have sworn she had never been kissed by a man in her life before.

On the other hand he could be completely mistaken, taken in by a look, a gesture, the scent of honeysuckle. It was hardly conclusive. The other three were still watching him, obviously hoping for further revelations about their goddess. He had no intention of telling them any more about his evening—and even less about the night. On the other hand he had his pride, and leaving them with the impression that he was on the verge of success when it seemed highly likely that however this turned out he was not going to win the wager, was not a good move.

'However, despite my limited success last night, I have to tell you, gentlemen, that I am not making room in my stables for Thunderer yet.' He won his trick and took his time over his next card, letting the other three hang on his words. 'Miss Davide appears to have left town.'

'Ah, standard female tactics!' Freddie advised wisely. 'Playing hard to get: you remember that little filly I was keeping in that apartment off Drury Lane last year? Took me weeks to win her over, but it was worth it...'

There were howls of outrage from Marlow and Hendricks. 'Come off it, Freddie! Hardly the same class of girl at all! She was just hanging out for more money. How can you compare Miss Davide to an opera dancer!' George spluttered.

'What are you going to do?' William asked, intrigued.

Nicholas pushed his chair out from the card table and stretched his long legs out. 'Go home and go to bed, I think.' He ducked as George lobbed a guinea at his head and grinned. 'I've left a groom keeping watch on the house—and no, Freddie, I am not going to give you her direction. I have no intention of being cut out by you, you rake! But it's a long chance of finding her, I suspect.'

'So, giving up and running back to Town, are you, old boy?' Hendricks asked.

'No such luck! Georgiana has me pinned down for a full week of endless soirées and parties. Have you seen Lady Richardson's new sculpture gallery yet? No? Well, take my advice and steer well clear of any invitation to do so. I was dragged along there today for an interminable afternoon in the company of cold marble and silly débutantes. Mind you,' he added casually as he got to his feet, 'I did meet a Miss Knight who seemed something out of the com-

monplace. Haven't come across the family before—
anyone know anything about them?'

He kept his face indifferent, but was surprised at
the frisson of excitement that he felt at mentioning
her name. Obviously the excitement of the chase, he
told himself.

George and Freddie shook their heads, but
William Hendricks replied, 'Oh, yes, quite a good
Cambridgeshire family, I think. My mother knows
Mrs Knight, and there's a younger sister too, who's
quite a lively girl, but the older sister doesn't go
about much. A bit of an invalid, I think—Mama
used to invite them all to evening parties, but only
the mother used to come. Young Miss Ophelia isn't
out yet.'

So, Miss Knight did not go abroad in the evenings
because she was delicate! He had rarely seen a
healthier-looking young woman—so unless she had
made a recent miraculous recovery she had other
things keeping her busy in the evenings.

Bidding farewell to his friends and refusing the
butler's offer to call a chair, Nicholas strolled along
Charles Street from George's lodgings, around
Queens Square and turned uphill into Gay Street.

The clock of St Mary's Chapel was striking two
as he passed it and the town was quiet, although
candlelight in many windows and the scurry of the
occasional sedan chair bearing its occupants home
showed that not everyone was abed.

Nicholas stopped in the Circus and looked up.
The sky was clear, which explained the nip in the
air, and the stars twinkled icily. Despite the brandy
his head was as clear as the sky above and his blood
raced in his veins. If he had been at home on his

country estates he would have taken a horse out and galloped away this restless excitement; as it was, he carried on walking, striding up Brook Street briskly despite the slope.

Tomorrow he would see Miss Knight again, and then, with the knowledge he had gained this evening, he should be able to solve this puzzle. But it would be a pity if they proved to be one and the same woman...he was not quite sure why, but, yes, it would be a pity.

While the Earl was losing sleep puzzling over her identity, Miss Knight was experiencing just as much trouble sleeping herself. When she woke from a fitful doze, the sunlight was slanting across the polished boards of her bedroom floor from the window looking eastwards over Walcot Street and the river.

For a moment, as she rubbed the slumber from her eyes, she wondered why the sight should make her heart beat faster, then she remembered she was engaged to ride out with Lord Lovell that afternoon. If the unpredictable spring weather turned showery then the excursion would be cancelled, which was, of course, the best possible outcome under the circumstances.

She pulled the bellrope for her morning chocolate and wriggled to sit up against the pillows. Smoothing down the counterpane, she studied her long fingers, unadorned by rings and likely to remain so. The realities of her new life as Miss Camilla Knight, respectable spinster of Bath, were beginning to dawn on her. It had been all very well not having much of a social life when she could go to the theatre every night, experience the thrill of danger as she stepped out onto the stage, the fizzing of excitement through her veins as night after night she overcame stagefright, honed her skills in a particular part, curtseyed again and again to tumultuous applause.

And who would miss the insipid company of débutantes and chaperons when one could have the adoration of gentlemen admirers, safe in the confines of the Green Room? Shy young men at parties proffering compliments and nosegays were as nothing compared to outrageous adoration, the offer of diamonds and pearls, sumptuous bouquets of heavy-scented hothouse blooms…

She had spoken with genuine conviction of the impossibility of her ever marrying and of her intention to support her mama and see her sister well married. But the emptiness of it all suddenly yawned before her on this beautiful spring morning. Even spinsters past their first flush of youth—as she soon would be, she told herself bitterly—could hope for late happiness and a suitor. But the risk of discovery of her scandalous past would never leave her. If she was discovered they would all be ruined, and in any case, she could never enter into marriage dishonestly deceiving her husband.

It meant she couldn't even flirt, Camilla thought dismally as she sipped her cooling chocolate. And Lord Lovell was most certainly a man with whom it would be a pleasure to flirt! Camilla could not recall ever feeling this way about any man she had met before: attracted, excited, and not a little afraid, both of herself and of his reputation as a man who was never short of female company, a man who would never have to try too hard.

Her fingers strayed to her lips as if to retrace the impression of his mouth on hers. It must be because he had kissed her, that was all. She recalled with a shiver the sensation of his lips, then pulled together her unruly thoughts. After all, one would remember one's first kiss; it did not mean that one was seriously attracted simply because the memory was so vivid, so real…

Her thoughts were rudely interrupted by the eruption of Ophelia into her chamber. The younger Miss Knight was wearing her new riding-habit, a garment of deep sky-blue and of a rather more fashionable cut than her mama really approved of.

'There you are! Why are you still in bed? Look what a gorgeous morning it is!'

Ophelia tugged back the curtains to their fullest extent and gazed out over the city.

'I am thinking,' her sister responded coolly. 'And why on earth have you changed so soon? We are not going out until two, and not at all if it rains.'

Ophelia pouted prettily and Camilla felt a little frisson of alarm at the sight of her little sister aping a grown-up so charmingly. The thought of Ophelia catching Lord Lovell's eye was curiously unsettling, despite the fact that she had just convinced herself that he, along with every other eligible man, was not for her.

'It is quite the nicest thing I have,' Ophelia was explaining, fidgeting around with the things on her sister's dressing-table. 'Maria Frogmorton is coming around this morning and it is *miles* nicer than the riding-habit she has just had tailored. Hers is positively *dowdy*.'

'So it is not for Lord Lovell's benefit, then?'

Camilla teased, feeling somewhat reassured. The response was even more consoling, and very typical of Ophelia.

'Oh, no! After all, he is *so* old… But on the other hand, it would be wonderful if my friends were to see me with him; he has *such* a reputation. And I think he is handsome, do you not?' She did not wait for Camilla's answer, but twirled round from the dressing-table, a string of rose quartz beads in her fingers. 'You never wear these, Camilla. May I borrow them to go with my new afternoon dress? You know, the deep pink one.' Ophelia lifted them to her throat without waiting for a reply.

Camilla knew perfectly well what 'borrow' meant in Ophelia's vocabulary. 'Yes, you may have them.' After all, rose quartz beads were not the sort of thing that dutiful spinsters wore with their sensible twill dresses in anything but deep pink… Yes, it really would be best if the weather were to change and it poured with rain this afternoon.

As she thought it a black cloud moved in front of the sun and she jumped out of bed with an exclamation of alarm. 'Oh, no! Look at that cloud!'

'It is all right,' Ophelia reassured her, 'it is just the one—look, it is passing over now. I am starving. I will see you in a minute in the breakfast parlour.' She bounced out, leaving a sudden silence behind her. Camilla sighed, pushed back the coverlet, and padded barefoot to the washstand.

The morning passed with agonising slowness. More than once Camilla crossed the morning-room to the mantelshelf and tapped the clock, as if in doing so she could hasten the minutes. Fortunately her mama and Ophelia were occupied about domestic concerns, and were not witness to her restlessness.

After a cold collation, Camilla went to her chamber to change from her simple morning-gown into her riding-habit. Unlike Ophelia's, it was not newly tailored, and not quite in the highest kick of fashion, but the soft green suited her colouring and moulded itself to her slender, high-bosomed figure. Her maid was just positioning the light veiling on her hat when Camilla heard the front door open, and the sound of voices in the hall below as the footman admitted their visitor.

Her heart turned a giddy somersault in her chest, and she spread her fingers across the front of her jacket, as if to calm its hectic beating. She counted slowly to one hundred, an old trick to counter stage-fright, and pushed in her hatpins with a firm hand. Breathing deeply to quell the sudden spark of panic at the thought of confronting Nicholas again, she descended the staircase, then, summoning all her ability to act the part of the proper young woman engaged in a pleasant afternoon's activity, Camilla pushed open the door and entered the drawing-room.

Nicholas Lovell got to his feet with an easy grace that belied his height. He was dressed for riding in a coat of deep blue that echoed the colour of the warm gaze he now turned upon her. In two strides of his gleaming boots he was across the Turkey rug, bowing over her hand, but not before she had glimpsed the gleam of sensual appreciation in his eyes. Her cheeks felt warm and she felt her fingers curl into his.

'Miss Knight, good afternoon. As you can see,

the weather has favoured us: it is quite clement for our excursion this afternoon.'

Camilla released her hand and replied coolly, 'Indeed sir, although it seemed less than favourable earlier on.'

She crossed and seated herself primly on the sofa next to her mama, who looked pink-cheeked, animated and almost pretty. Lord Lovell had obviously charmed her in a very short time, and Camilla doubted that her mother's strictures against rakes, uttered only yesterday evening, prevailed this afternoon!

Ophelia had not yet made her entrance, and for a brief moment Camilla wondered if she had deliberately delayed her entrance so as to make a bigger impact. This unworthy thought, and the twist of jealousy accompanying it, she swiftly suppressed.

'I must apologise for Ophelia's time-keeping, my lord,' Mrs Knight gushed. 'It is a failing quite frequently found in the young, I regret to say. I am happy to add that my elder daughter is always punctilious in such matters, are you not, my love?'

Camilla knew her mother was complimenting her for Lord Lovell's benefit. Mama was always so transparent in such things, and appeared to have acquired no more skill or subtlety as she grew older. She would be praising her harp-playing, which was non-existent, or her embroidery—which was indifferent—before long.

Nicholas's smile was almost a grin. 'Indeed, ma'am. I am sure Miss Knight aims to act to the highest standards in whatever she undertakes.'

Camilla was half-way to raising a glass of ratafia to her lips, and only the keenest eye could have detected the momentary pause this comment gave her. Had she imagined the emphasis his lordship had placed upon the word 'act'? She swiftly chided herself against over-reaction to such a slight comment, and sipped her refreshment.

Any further chit-chat was forestalled by Ophelia finally making her entrance. She looked young, fresh and absurdly pretty in the blue habit, but to her relief Camilla noticed that his lordship scarcely reacted, bowing over the débutante's hand with polite correctness, before resuming his seat and picking up his glass of Canary once more.

A short silence ensued, then the three ladies verbally collided as each spoke at once.

'Well, I hope the outing is enjoyable...' Mrs Knight began.

'If Maria Frogmorton calls, tell her I am out riding with his lordship, will you, Mama?' Ophelia supplied eagerly.

'Perhaps we should go, while the weather holds...' Camilla suggested.

Lord Lovell got to his feet, bowing to Mrs Knight. 'Do not concern yourself, ma'am. I shall ensure that the ladies are returned secure to you by four o'clock.'

Mrs Knight's hand crept up to her lace cap as if to correct its angle, and she smiled at the Earl. Really, the gossip surrounding him must be sadly amiss if this encounter were anything to go by. Lord Lovell was not only dashing and handsome in his superbly cut riding clothes, but his manners were of the highest order of correctness and charm, a combination one seldom encountered, the widow reflected wistfully.

Could she dare to hope for an alliance of one of her daughters with such an eligible man? Of the two, Camilla was closer to his lordship in age and interests, and unless she was very much mistaken the true source of his lordship's attentiveness. But Camilla had declared that her sacrifice was absolute: she could never marry, for fear of scandal. And yet... For the remainder of the early afternoon Mrs Knight fell to pleasant musings on how such an outcome might be achieved. Her daughter a countess...

Camilla noticed with an inward touch of satisfaction the way Lord Lovell's eyebrows rose at the sight of the two mounts which Higgins led round to the front door. Miss Knight, who normally kept a prudent eye on the family expenditure despite their now comfortable circumstances, had no trouble at all in opening her purse strings for either carriage horses or her own and Ophelia's hacks.

It gave Mrs Knight, as she confessed to her daughters, a 'warm glow' to drive around Bath behind a pair of outstanding dapple greys which quite outshone those of her less fortunate friends in both manners and appearance, but it was the Knights' riding horses which were the envy of every other young lady with aspirations to cut a dash in local society.

The late Mr Knight had been a keen rider to hounds and had enjoyed nothing more than to spend the day in the saddle, whether going about his business on the estate or indulging in some sporting exercise or another. In consequence he had had a knowledgeable eye for a horse and had been happy to see both his daughters well mounted—provided they'd met his exacting standards of horsemanship.

Camilla had inherited his excellent seat, and had
also learned well from his example when it came to
choosing her horses. Ophelia, equally confident on
horseback, made up in somewhat reckless enthusiasm for her less elegant style and was more than
happy with the rather showy, although sweet-
tempered black mare her sister had found for her.

However, it was not Blackbird, whiffling hopefully into her young mistress's gloved hand for a
piece of apple, who caught his lordship's eye, but
the chestnut gelding who was attempting to drag the
leading rein from the groom's hand as he took violent exception to a piece of paper blowing past.

'Stand still, drat you, you stupid bru…animal,'
Higgins growled, turning his own mount to keep
from getting entangled in both sets of leading reins.
'Now then, Miss Ophelia, don't you stand there like
a ninny, girl! You take Blackbird's reins while I sort
out this… Stand, will you!'

Ophelia ran to the head of her mare, not at all put
out by the groom's plain speaking. Having freed one
hand, Higgins took a firmer grip on the chestnut, but
found the Earl already at its head, one hand on the
bridle just above the bit.

'Yes, yes, I know…it could have been a wild pan-
ther in disguise. You were quite right to be alarmed,'
he was saying soothingly. The gelding rolled one
eye at him, obviously unconvinced, but prepared to
stand there all day if his ears were scratched in the
precise way Nick was doing.

'That there animal doesn't have the brains it were
born with,' Higgins said forthrightly, his Norfolk accent strong. 'And I don't care how much you say
about his looks and his gait and his staying power,

Miss Camilla!' He swung down out of the saddle and, looping his rein over his arm, went to toss Ophelia up on to Blackbird.

'Well, I agree he is hardly the most intelligent horse in the world,' Camilla agreed, smiling her thanks to Nicholas as he offered his clasped hands to give her a leg up. 'But he is a wonderful ride if one just does the thinking for him.' She settled in the saddle and arranged the folds of her riding-habit one-handed, holding the reins firmly in the other. 'Thank you, my lord, Kestrel is quite calm now. He really is quite provoking, because he will stand like a rock in the face of real danger, like a fierce dog or a bull, but he imagines all sorts of monsters in shadows or paper.'

Nicholas took the reins of his own horse from his groom and mounted, saying, 'That will be all, Little, thank you. I will not be needing you for the rest of the day.' He swung round to ride alongside Camilla, his eyes on Ophelia, who was riding ahead of them, engaged in an earnest argument with Higgins about whether her new riding-boots were suitable.

'Frippery things,' he was grumbling. 'You take a toss and have to walk home five miles in those and you'll be sorry.'

'Nonsense,' Ophelia retorted. 'I would ride Robin and you would walk in your nice sensible boots!'

'An unconventional groom,' Nicholas observed drily to Camilla.

'He is indeed,' she laughed. 'He taught us to ride, you know, and found us a terrible trial. And, what was worse, our old nurse Margaret used to tell him off for using strong language! There he would be, poor man, with one or other of us at the end of the leading rein, shouting, ''Keep those bl…heels down Miss!'' and going red for want of all the words he would like to be using. But he was a good teacher, and the most reliable and sensible man you could hope to find. Papa placed the greatest confidence in him, and Mama does the same. She even listens to him when he says she cannot take the carriage to visit some friend or other who lives up a particularly steep hill, in case it is too much for the horses, so she takes a chair instead, although she says it makes her seasick.'

'I can see he was a good teacher,' Nicholas commented.

'Yes, she does ride well, does she not?' Camilla watched her young sister confidently handling the black mare as they negotiated the busy junction of Broad Street, the Paragon and Lansdown Road.

He did not answer until they too had turned into Lansdown Road, for Camilla was waving at the occupants of a passing carriage and was then occupied in convincing Kestrel that Bath chairs—which he saw every day of his life—did not conceal tigers, and that he could quite safely trot on up the hill.

'Miss Ophelia has a very confident manner on a horse,' he said at length, 'but it is not on her riding that I formed my opinion of Higgins's expertise as a teacher.'

To his surprise Camilla neither blushed at the compliment, nor disclaimed modestly. 'You think I ride well?' she enquired, smiling at him. When he nodded she added disarmingly, 'Well, I can take no credit for it: after all, Papa had us well taught, gave us good horses and every encouragement, and I expect I inherited his talent for it, so I can hardly congratulate myself.'

'Despite what you say, you are a better horsewoman than your sister, who one supposes has had the same advantages, so I think you may claim it as an accomplishment.'

Camilla laughed. Out in the fresh air with the natural roses blooming in her cheeks, not a trace of artifice about her and with her well-bred and charming frankness, Nicholas once again found himself convinced that he was mistaken in thinking that in Miss Knight he had found the elusive Mademoiselle Davide.

The riders slowed to a walk as the long hill stretched in front of them. Camilla told herself firmly that the Earl doubtless made agreeable conversation, well sprinkled with compliments, to any young lady he found himself in company with. Further, she thought, with even more resolution, allowing herself to be charmed was a thoroughly dangerous weakness with any man, but especially this one.

It was very pleasant to be made to feel that you were the centre of his world and that he found you endlessly fascinating and highly attractive. But the sensible thing to do would be to turn the conversation away from personal matters and to put him firmly in his place by discussing the weather, the view and the latest programme of concerts at the Lower Assembly Rooms.

She was therefore somewhat surprised to find herself, as though under some inner compulsion, smiling at Nicholas and saying lightly, 'I must thank you for telling me I have an accomplishment. I have very few, you see—only two, as I thought—so it is a great relief to be told I have a third!'

'And what are the other two?' he asked quizzically. An unusual young woman indeed! He was going to be disappointed if she admitted to excellence in playing the harp and doing watercolour sketches.

'They are a secret, my lord.' Her eyes twinkled at him and he smiled back wickedly, making her heart miss a beat. Hastily she added, 'At last we are nearly at the top! It is one of the disadvantages of Bath that everywhere one goes there are hills. The views, of course, are superb, and one can hardly complain about a lack of exercise.'

The Earl was not to be diverted. 'It is really too bad of you, Miss Knight, to tease me with secrets! Surely you cannot be ashamed of your accomplishments?' Unless, he thought, one of them was a talent for acting...

'Hmm...perhaps I will tell you one then, provided you promise not to tell anyone else, for my attorney says it is a most unfeminine talent.'

Ophelia trotted up, interrupting their *tête à tête*. 'Which way shall we go? Straight on towards Lansdown is the best for a gallop.' Blackbird sidled and curvetted, impatient at being kept sedately by the other horses.

'Are you wishful to gallop, my lord,' Camilla enquired, 'or would you prefer to hack around the top of the hill and admire the views?'

'Let us gallop and shake the fidgets out of our horses' feet. We can admire the views later at our leisure.'

That was enough for Ophelia, who touched her

heels to Blackbird's sides and was off at a brisk canter, Higgins swinging in behind her at a distance, but still keeping a sharp eye on the flying figure.

Camilla would have followed her example if Nicholas had not leaned over and put a hand on her rein. 'Not so fast, Miss Knight! You promised to tell me a secret and I really cannot let you go until you do so.'

Chapter Five

There was a heartbeat's silence as Camilla, the previous conversation blown from her mind by the wind on the hill, met Nicholas's steady, unsettling, gaze and felt her conscience give a guilty lurch. Had she mentioned a secret? Then she remembered—her so-called 'accomplishments'. Really, she must keep a tighter guard on her tongue around the Earl. He was far too perceptive!

'Oh, very well.' She laughed across at him. 'Do you promise not to tell? Well, I am an accomplished investor, even Mr Brooke our attorney says so, although he does not approve. I am prudent, of course, for we cannot afford to take risks, but even with allowing many tempting gambles to go by I flatter myself that I do very well.' For a moment she thought a look of disappointment crossed his face at this revelation, but it had to have been a trick of the light. 'Are you shocked by my secret, my lord?'

'By no means! We will have to compare notes, for I too enjoy speculating. But I am sorry to hear that you are not more of a gambler, Miss Knight: do you never take risks?'

The long look Camilla gave him revealed nothing of her thoughts, then she smiled and said frankly, 'I cannot afford to take risks, my lord: neither with my money nor with my reputation. What a man—what the Earl of Ashby—may do with impunity, Miss Knight must approach with great caution. But we are being left behind by Ophelia, do let us gallop!'

Nicholas reined back his horse to enjoy the picture of Camilla, perfectly balanced on the chestnut, her veil whipping back with the speed of its pace. It was tempting to ask the Knight family to stay at Ashby during the hunting season. On second thoughts, perhaps that would be raising expectations in Mrs Knight's breast. Her daughter was an unconventional young woman, he mused. Unconventional enough to lead a double life? But surely not. That speech about not taking risks had rung true. With a slight shrug he touched his own mount with his heels and gave it its head.

Two sets of hooves pounded over the short clipped turf, and Nicholas was just thinking that the nibbled grass was a sure indicator of rabbits, and therefore of holes, when Camilla swung to the left, calling back, 'Mind the warren!' over her shoulder. Yes, she would look magnificent on the hunting field, tireless and fearless.

His more powerful animal came up neck and neck with hers and for a moment they let the horses race before reining back as they approached Ophelia and Higgins. They had come to a halt at the edge of the hill where the gorse grew thickly and the groom had withdrawn to a respectful distance while Ophelia, who appeared to have spotted something in the scrub, urged the reluctant mare forward.

'What on earth is that?' she asked the groom, her voice just reaching the other two as they trotted up.

She was leaning down, prodding something with her riding crop, when Higgins suddenly shouted, 'Leave that alone, Miss Ophelia!' and spurred forwards.

It was too late—with a furious buzzing a cloud of wasps rose in the air around the black mare and her rider. Ophelia was flapping at them with one hand, struggling to control the panicking mare with the other, then there was a shrill whinny from the horse and it bolted clear out of the mass of furious insects and past them.

'Oh, no, Blackbird has been stung! Higgins...' Camilla had no need to finish the sentence, for the groom was already spurring his horse after the retreating mare.

Nicholas stood in the stirrups, watching the two riders as they vanished over the slope. 'He is catching her up.'

'I thought he would,' Camilla said calmly, although she looked a little pale as she stroked a soothing hand down Kestrel's neck. 'There is no cause for concern. Ophelia has a very good seat, and I have rarely known her take a tumble. Blackbird will calm down once she is clear of those wretched insects. Honestly! It is just like Ophelia to stir up a wasps' nest!'

'Shall we follow them, Miss Knight?'

'No, not immediately, if you do not mind, my lord. She will be mortified that you have seen her lose control of her mount, and it will be worse if she has an audience for Higgins telling her off and lecturing her all the way home on the correct way to treat wasp stings in horses! We will ride round the crest for a short way, if you like, and admire the view, then we can return without making too much of a to-do about the entire incident. That would only alarm Mama.'

'Certainly; I would be sorry to cut short our ride, so long as you are sure there is nothing I can do. Will you lead on? I am sure you know the best—' Nicholas broke off as her mount suddenly bucked violently, snatching frantically at the bit and shaking his head wildly.

'Oh, no! Kestrel has been stung too!' Camilla concentrated on keeping her seat and tried to head the frantic horse away from further danger, for the stragglers from the wasps' nest were still buzzing ominously.

Camilla was conscious of Nicholas keeping his mount close to hers, but not crowding her, and she was grateful that he did not make matters worse by rushing to take her reins, for that would only panic Kestrel more. Then she was suddenly stabbed by a burning pain in her right wrist, just as Kestrel gave another wild plunge. She dropped the reins and found herself clinging to the pommel as the chestnut took the bit between his teeth and careered off towards Lansdown. Faintly behind her she could hear the sound of pursuing hooves, then all her attention was focused on trying to hang on despite the pain as the furious wasp, trapped in the cuff of her glove, stung her again.

She tried to drag her right glove off with her teeth while reaching for the reins with her left hand, but Kestrel, panicked by pain, was plunging through the gorse so erratically that she had to keep grabbing the pommel just to keep her seat. And in front of her the steep scarp edge was coming closer and closer. It was perfectly possible to walk a horse down the slope, but a frightened animal at the gallop would inevitably fall, taking her with him.

Camilla had just reached the conclusion that she must kick her foot free of the stirrup and jump clear when she was aware of Nicholas's bay pulling up on her right side. He turned its head, attempting to force Kestrel away from the edge and on to the flat plateau, but the chestnut, further excited by the other galloping horse, would not be turned. Just when Camilla was convinced they would all go over the edge together Nicholas leaned over, seized Kestrel's bridle and dragged his head round.

Both horses plunged to a halt in a mêlée of hooves and tossing manes, and Camilla fell off with a thump that knocked every vestige of breath from her body.

She was sitting there whooping with the effort of dragging some air back into her lungs when she realised that Nicholas was kneeling beside her tugging urgently at her glove. 'Aargh!' was all she could manage to gasp out as the pain of the kid cutting into her swollen wrist lanced up her arm.

'Keep still,' he commanded roughly, pulling a pocket knife out and slitting the fine kid until he could peel it back over her hand. 'There. How many times did it sting you?' he asked, shaking out a thoroughly squashed wasp and stuffing the glove in his pocket.

Camilla was still gasping and wordless. Her wrist hurt abominably, her whole hand was on fire and her head was spinning. The part of her mind that was treacherously female was also telling her that she looked frightful and undignified and that Nicholas was being quite revoltingly unsympathetic and practical.

'At least twice by the look of it,' Nicholas remarked, his head bent over her wrist as she lay back on a tussock, too shaky to sit up. Why could he not just make it better and stop touching it? she thought irrationally. Then her nose was full of the smell of spirits and something cold splashed on to her skin. For a moment it burned appallingly, then amazingly the pain began to ebb into something that was almost tolerable.

Her breath came back with a rush and she sat up, pushing off her hat and veil which were hanging by two pins from her disordered hair. It brought her breast to breast with Nicholas, who was kneeling beside her, her hand still in his.

The realisation hit her that she was sprawled on the ground, her habit almost to her knees, her hair round her shoulders and so close to Nicholas that she could see that his eyes were not pure blue but had flecks of black in them. Her wrist felt as though it were on fire, but that was suddenly nothing beside the fact that she had fallen off her horse in a most undignified manner in front of this man, after as good as boasting about her skills as a rider.

There seemed to be only two options: she could burst into tears, which was very tempting, or lose her temper, which she proceeded to do. 'Well, help me up!' she demanded sharply. 'I cannot sit here all day while you splash brandy about!'

'You termagant!' he said indignantly, and

promptly leant over and kissed her full on the mouth.

With a gasp of surprise Camilla fell back and found herself trapped under Nicholas's body, his mouth still fastened on hers, his hands exploring the weight of her tumbling hair.

It might be only the second time she had ever been kissed, but there had scarcely been a waking hour when Camilla had not thought about that moment in the cottage when he had taken her in his arms. This time, despite being dizzy, half-stunned and thoroughly unprepared, she responded to him instinctively. Her lips opened softly to his demand and Nicholas responded immediately, his tongue entering to seek out her own. Almost of its own volition, her tongue-tip met his, tasting, inciting him to deepen the kiss. She felt his fingers tighten in her hair as he shifted his body weight above her, and her hands came up to cup his head. It was as though another Camilla altogether was in his arms, answering him kiss for kiss, meeting his ardour with her own untutored desire.

Nicholas groaned, deep in his throat, an exciting, primal sound that stirred her very bones. Then his lips left hers, trailing warm kisses across her cheek to her ear, nuzzling until his teeth found and teased the soft lobe and the sweet honeysuckle scent of her hair.

Camilla gasped, her body arching instinctively towards his. For one electrifying moment it felt as though every inch of their bodies were touching, then he pulled away, supporting himself on his elbows as he looked down into her face with an unreadable expression.

The hot blush swept up from her toe-tips to the roots of her hair as the enormity of what she was doing hit Camilla. 'My...lord,' she managed to stammer out. But she could not tear her eyes from his, however much she wanted to close them, blot out the reflection of herself in those dark blue depths.

Suddenly he smiled down at her, then his fingers gently smoothed the tangled curls off her hot forehead. 'We really should not be doing this, you know,' he drawled.

'Of course I know we should not!' she retorted angrily, the hot blush being replaced with a cold realisation of just how outrageous her behaviour was.

Nicholas shifted his weight slightly, sending a wave of aching desire through her prone body. 'Stop that!' she snapped, pushing at his chest, then breaking off with a cry of pain as her stung wrist rasped against the cloth of his jacket.

Nicholas got to his knees, gently supporting her into a sitting position. 'Your poor wrist. I know I ought to apologise, but you are *such* a temptation, Miss Knight,' he said ruefully, pushing his hair back off his face. The look of mingled indignation and shame on her face prompted him to add, 'I took advantage of you, I know it. Berate me as you will, you cannot reproach me as much as I reproach myself. I must take you home. Your poor mama will be frantic with worry.'

Camilla still found herself unable to speak. With eyes downcast she let herself be lifted gently to her feet. For the second time in three days she was supported shakily in Nicholas's arms, but this time her entire body was crying out at the shaking the fall had given her. As the excitement of his passionate kisses ebbed from her, the pain of her wrist and the protest of her bruised muscles flooded in.

'Ouch!' She winced as she took her weight on both legs, looking around for the horses. Nicholas bent to retrieve her hat, then used his long fingers to untangle her hair. Transfixed, she stood almost meekly as he pulled the pins from the curls, then gathered the heavy mass in his hands and twisted and pinned it back into a semblance of order.

Camilla put up her hands and was surprised at the competence with which he had restored her coiffure. Shakily she put on her hat, straightening the veil. 'Thank you, my lord,' she said formally. Then, trying to lighten the atmosphere, added, 'You make a very good ladies' maid.'

His eyes crinkled as he grinned wickedly. 'Thank you, ma'am, it is all down to practice.'

Camilla blushed hotly again and began to limp towards Kestrel, who was standing meekly beside Nicholas's bay, cropping the grass and looking as though nothing on earth would disturb his calm manner. She took a trailing rein and began to check him over for stings, taking refuge from the necessity to look at or speak to Nicholas. 'You silly boy, did those nasty wasps hurt you, then?' she crooned to the gelding, stroking the soft muzzle.

Nicholas's voice close behind made her jump. 'Can you ride, or do you want to sit up in front of me?'

The very thought made her gasp. 'No…no…I will be fine, thank you, my lord!' She forced herself to turn and face him. 'Please, if you will just give me a leg up.'

Nicholas bent to do as she asked, looking up with concern at the involuntary murmur of pain she made as her bruised behind made contact with the saddle. 'I am all right, my lord, I will merely be somewhat bruised tomorrow.'

'I do wish you would call me Nicholas,' he said softly as he checked Kestrel's girth. 'After all, I think we know each other well enough by now.'

The blush stained Camilla's cheeks again as she dug her heel into Kestrel's side. 'There is no need, *my lord*, to taunt me with my forward behaviour. I would be very grateful if you could manage to forget everything which has passed between us this afternoon: my wits must have been disarrayed by the fall.'

As Nicholas swung up into the saddle and followed her back towards the Bath road he murmured to himself, 'And you, Miss Knight, have disarrayed rather more than my wits.'

The sheer discomfort of her bruises forced Camilla to rein Kestrel into a walk, although she was in a fever to get home and bid goodbye to the Earl. His behaviour was still causing her deep confusion as she rode, gaze fixed between Kestrel's alertly pricked ears, cheeks still flushed red with embarrassment and mortification.

If he was a rake, then why had he not ravished her as Mama always warned most men would do, given the slightest encouragement? In fact, the whole of polite society appeared to be organised to protect innocent young women from the inevitable ruin that would result from finding themselves alone with a gentleman for more than ten minutes!

Nicholas had certainly taken advantage of her quite dreadfully forward behaviour—but only up to a point. It was he who had drawn back, not she who had resisted him. Even in her innocence she was aware that her response to him would have goaded most men beyond restraint.

Camilla risked a sideways glance at the Earl as he rode level with her, but a full ten feet away. He was looking at the road ahead, sitting relaxed in the saddle, the reins in his right hand, the left one resting on his thigh. As though he felt her eyes on him, he looked across and asked, 'Are you sure you can hold the reins? I will lead Kestrel if your wrist is paining you.'

She managed a mumbled refusal and a shake of her head, then her eyes shot back to him as he remarked, almost conversationally, 'You should not feel ashamed of acting naturally, you know.'

'Naturally!' The word came out as a cross between a gasp and a squeak. Camilla got control of her voice and said, as repressively as she could, 'I am well aware that gentlemen regard that sort of thing in quite a different light, but I can assure you, sir, that kissing gentlemen in any way at all, let alone…' Words failed her.

'Passionately?' he supplied helpfully.

'P…well, yes, passionately…I mean, that is not something which is natural to a lady.'

Nicholas snorted with amusement. 'Not to all ladies, I must admit, but in my experience the vast majority…'

'We are discussing *ladies*, are we not?' Camilla

demanded, not at all wishing to hear about his previous experiences.

'Indeed we are, as well as their weaker sisters. Really, Camilla, what *do* you think happens once people are married?'

She looked so scandalised that he laughed out loud. 'No, I do not mean the er…practical details, I mean in people's heads. Do you imagine that all young ladies, once married, go through life shrinking from their husbands or calmly putting up with the incomprehensible desires of men?'

Camilla's brow wrinkled as she thought about it. Mama, in her few guarded references to the subject, had intimated that the marriage bed was something that a well-bred lady endured in order to present her lord and master with an heir and that she would achieve her own happiness in the production and upbringing of children. Loose women, Mama implied, either pandered to men's base nature for material gain, or in a few quite frightful instances because their own unnatural passions led them astray. 'Lady Caroline Lamb!' she would whisper in appalled accents as the worst example she could think of. The scandalous wife of the long-suffering William Lamb was a byword for outrageous abandonment to sensuality and excess.

But the sensations Nicholas aroused when he kissed her felt anything but unnatural, and it was very hard, even after the event, to think of them as wicked. Embarrassing, yes, thoroughly shocking, certainly…but oh, so very natural!

He had been watching the play of emotion on her face and said gently, 'You know, you are a very beautiful, very intelligent, very talented young woman, Camilla. It is no good looking suitably modest, because you are not a fool. You know your own worth. You have just discovered that you are also a very warm, very passionate woman and one day a very lucky man is going to discover that too. Then you will discover the pleasure such passion brings between a man and a woman.'

His words filled her with such emotion that her eyes swam with tears and she had to bite hard on her lower lip before replying calmly, 'This is a most improper conversation, my lord, but before we terminate it and while we are being so frank I should tell you that I have no intention of marrying— ever—so the entire subject is quite irrelevant.'

'Not going to marry! Of all the damn fool…I beg your pardon…incomprehensible decisions! Why on earth not?' He made no attempt to conceal his incredulity.

'I intend being a support to Mama in her widowhood,' Camilla said repressively. 'Oh, look! Is that not Higgins coming towards us?'

Nicholas stood in his stirrups and shaded his eyes with one hand. 'Indeed it is—your knight in shining armour coming to save you from the dragon.'

The thought of the irascible Higgins in the role of St George was so diverting that Camilla was smiling as the groom cantered up. Once he had dealt with Miss Ophelia his thoughts had immediately turned to his other charge, left all alone with A Man, and he had hurried back. He could see little to concern him in her expression but the state of her hair and her habit were another matter.

'Miss Camilla, what have you been doing?' he demanded with his usual lack of respect. 'You look as though you've been pulled through a hedge back-wards!'

'Kestrel was stung and so was I and I fell off. But other than bruises and a very painful wrist I am quite all right,' Camilla replied soothingly, ignoring his disapproving sniff, for she understood the depths of his concern for her. 'His lordship has been looking after me,' she added, not able to resist seeing how Nicholas would react.

The Earl shot her a very old-fashioned look before informing Higgins that as far as he could see Kestrel had come to no harm either. 'And how is Miss Ophelia?'

The groom turned his horse's head and fell in beside them. 'Fell off,' he said curtly.

'What! Oh, no! Is she hurt?' Camilla demanded.

'Only her pride and her...er...seat. But your mama has put her to bed and called in Dr Willoughby.'

'Goodness! I hope she does not ask him to see me as well. I hate being physicked. Please do not say anything when we get back, Higgins.'

'She'll take one look at you and see what you've been up to,' Higgins said dourly, fortunately unable to see Camilla's hectic blush from his position alongside Nicholas. 'Falling off! And you call your-self a rider!' He dropped back a few paces, but could be heard muttering to himself as they began to de-scend towards the city.

Nicholas caught Camilla's eye and raised his left eyebrow quizzically, throwing her into even more confusion. 'Falling off indeed, Miss Knight...'

'I will turn down Guinea Lane. There is less chance of being seen by anyone I know than if we go straight down to the junction with Broad Street. I am very much obliged for your escort, my lord, but there is no need for you to continue further than that point,' she added coolly. To be seen with a man and in such a state of disarray, even accompanied by her groom, would cause eyebrows to be raised and tongues to wag for the rest of the week.

Nicholas fortunately grasped the situation without having to have it spelt out and parted from them with a polite bow. 'Thank you for a most delightful excursion, Miss Knight. I enjoyed it immensely and I feel I have experienced more of the true beauties of Bath than less fortunate visitors may hope to. Please present my compliments to Mrs Knight, and my best wishes to Miss Ophelia for a rapid recovery.'

Camilla was so cross with him that she could do no more than incline her head in response. Beauties of Bath indeed!

Fortunately she and Higgins managed to reach the front door without encountering any acquaintances, and Camilla's luck continued to hold, for her mama was so taken up with her younger daughter that Camilla was able to slip into her room without being seen.

Tugging the bellpull for her dresser, Camilla cast off her hat and veil and began to pull a brush through her hair, wincing at the pain in her wrist. Mary bustled in, all ready for a good gossip about the afternoon's ride, only to be confronted by the sight of her mistress, hair full of tangles, riding-habit stained with grass and with a swollen and reddened wrist.

'Oh, Miss Camilla, what have you done? Not fallen off as well, have you?'

'Yes, Mary, I have indeed. Now, can you get hot water sent up? Because if I do not sit in a bath straight away I am going to be so stiff tomorrow I shall not be able to walk. And can you get something for my wrist? I have been stung by a wasp.'

Mary immediately set to, organising a footman to bring up the wide saucer bath and set it before the fire she insisted on lighting, bullying the maids into staggering up and down stairs with cans of hot water in double quick time and hurrying in and out herself with towels and soap.

The resulting bustle was sufficiently distracting to keep Camilla's mind off her troubles for a few minutes, but once her dresser had helped her out of her habit and into the bath, arranged the screen modestly around her and left her to soak, there was nothing to keep Nicholas Lovell out of her thoughts. She tried to focus her mind on soaping herself while keeping her right wrist, bandaged with some herbal poultice that Cook swore by for stings, out of the bath, but for some reason the silky warmth of the water, the scented glide of the soap over her skin, only made the remembered sensations more acute.

She let her thoughts play over those moments in his arms, recalling the warm, demanding pressure of his mouth on hers, the arousing weight of his body, the springing life of his hair under her palms. If he ever kissed her again, she would have learned... He must be right that she was naturally passionate—but could she believe him when he implied it was something to be admired and welcomed? Or was it just the ploy of a seducer?

But if he had wanted to seduce her, why had he not done so there and then? Camilla's sense of the ridiculous gave her the answer: seducing virgins was probably more comfortable and convenient in a bed than on hard, scratchy ground in plain view of any passing rider, and one was certainly at less risk of being stung by wasps!

Or if he was not intent on seduction, then was he simply amusing himself with an extreme form of flirtation? Unless he was heartlessly setting out to ensnare her feelings there was only one other explanation—he was seriously intending to pay court to her. And that, Camilla told herself firmly as she reached forward to wash between her toes, was ridiculous. The highly eligible Earl of Ashby would not be looking to modestly circumstanced daughters of deceased county gentlemen for a bride! Every scheming mama in society would have the Earl of Ashby at the very top of their list of marriageable men, as he would know very well. He was rich, well-bred, well-connected—and undeniably charming and good-looking.

Her breath caught on a little sob and she lay back against the high back of the bath. Of course he did not have marriage in mind! And if he did…if he did, then it would be even more painful, perhaps the most painful thing she could imagine, for she could never marry him. And what could be worse than having to refuse the man you loved? she thought drearily, trailing her fingers through the cooling water.

Then her rational mind caught up with her wandering thoughts and she froze. She loved Nicholas!

No surely not, surely one could not fall in love on the basis of four—no, five—encounters?

Painfully, for her bruises were stiffening, Camilla climbed out of the bath and reached for a large towel. Swathing herself in the folds of fine linen, she curled up in a chair by the fire and thought back. Nicholas in the Green Room: arrogant, assured, devastatingly handsome, a big cat on the prowl. Nicholas in the alleyway fighting off the footpads: courageous, strong, physical. Nicholas in the cottage: immovable in his insistence on protecting her, disturbing with his kiss, vulnerable as he slept. Nicholas in the gallery: urbane, an aristocrat with his society mask in place, yet with a dangerous current of provocation running deep in everything he said. And finally the Nicholas of that afternoon: a pleasant companion, a fine horseman, a man who was prepared to have a frank conversation with her, an arousing lover…

Oh, yes, Camilla thought miserably, she *was* falling in love with Nicholas Lovell, Earl of Ashby. There was no doubt of that. She loved everything about him, from the way his eyes crinkled when he laughed to his arrogant self-confidence. She would never be free of the yearning for his kisses, for his caresses, for the sound of his voice and the touch of his mind. And he, whatever his intentions, had awoken her with a kiss like the Prince with the Sleeping Beauty—only there would be no happy ending to this particular fairytale.

Chapter Six

Nicholas stifled a yawn behind his napkin, resisting the temptation to consult his pocket watch for the third time in as many minutes. He had returned from his excursion with Camilla to find Georgiana waving a gold-edged invitation and upbraiding him for forgetting that they were engaged—yet again—to go out to dinner. This time his indefatigable sister had manoeuvred a meeting with Lady Cynthia Fitch, the sister of the fifth Earl of Langford. The lady in question was seated beside him, prattling endlessly about whatever crossed her mind. She appeared to be able to do this without engaging her brains in any way, he thought, savagely rehearsing exactly what he was going to say to his sister when they returned to the Crescent that evening.

Lady Cynthia was undoubtedly well-bred, extremely well-dowered and even, if your taste ran to china dolls, pretty. She was blonde, with a mass of natural curls. Her dimples were constantly on display as she simpered and her long black lashes swept down frequently to veil her somewhat protuberant blue eyes every time his lordship addressed her.

God! Nicholas thought, passing her the salt, three hours married to this peahen and he would either have committed murder or have gone insane. What a contrast to his companion of that afternoon! Camilla was another blonde, to be sure, but her eyes reflected her thoughts, the working of a lively intelligent mind. Companion was the right word for her—it was a pleasure to be in her company. But more than that, when he kissed her... Nicholas firmly repressed the thought, which was undoubtedly an arousing one and highly unsuitable for the dining-room.

He looked across the candlelit table and saw Georgiana watching him beadily from the other side of the ornate epergne. As far as he could see, for the intervening heaps of hothouse fruit and flickering candles, she was glaring at him. Obviously he was not making the required effort with Lady Cynthia. Ruefully he raised his eyebrows at her and received in return exactly the look with which she had greeted his return from illicit outings with the gamekeeper when he had been a boy.

'And a more charming pair you could never hope to see,' Lady Cynthia twittered beside him. Nicholas, who had no idea what she was talking about, found himself instinctively glancing at her plump cleavage, then catching the eye of his brother-in-law, who was sitting on her other side. Henry turned a snort of amusement into a polite cough and looked away, dabbing his eyes with the corner of his napkin.

'Pair?' Nicholas asked, firmly swallowing a feeling of incipient hysteria.

'Why, yes, did I not say? My dear brother has bought me a *pair* of lovebirds. One has to keep them together, my lord, or they pine away.' She lifted her eyes coyly to meet his. 'They are so sweet, the way they bill and coo.' Despite what her mama had said, she had been finding the Earl somewhat hard going, but now she had his attention she was not going to let the opportunity slip away. Emboldened, she added, 'You must come and see them my lord. Tomorrow, perhaps?'

Appalled, Nicholas sought for an excuse. 'Why, thank you, Lady Cynthia, that sounds er... enchanting. However, as tomorrow is Sunday I was going to church...'

'You will be attending Matins in the Abbey? Why, so do we. Perhaps you would care to return afterwards for luncheon? Mama would be delighted to meet you.'

Nicholas was conscious that Lord Henry was watching him with scarcely veiled amusement at his predicament. 'Er...actually I was intending to attend the church in Walcot Street. The sermons, I understand, are particularly uplifting. And long,' he added desperately, 'very long. I do find a long sermon particularly satisfying, and this particular clergyman draws heavily on comparisons between the Old Testament and classical scholarship.'

His brother-in-law was now red in the face and choking. Georgiana, unable for reasons of decorum to speak across the table, sent her incorrigible husband a look which promised later retribution.

Nicholas's guess that the threat of a long intellectual sermon would effectively quash Lady Cynthia's enthusiasm for mutual church-going proved correct. She seemed momentarily daunted, then, remembering her Mama's instructions, rallied. 'But you could join us for luncheon afterwards, my lord? And tell us the more interesting portions of the discourse? I am sure that if *you* explained it to me I would be able to understand it.'

'Delightful as that sounds, Lady Cynthia, I regret that I am engaged for the remainder of the day.'

'Oh, dear.' Deflated, Lady Cynthia turned to converse with Lord Forres and Nicholas breathed again.

His sister, having overheard most of his shameful prevarication, was not amused. 'I sincerely trust the sermon at St Swithin's will be every bit as lengthy and scholarly as you say, Lovell,' she said later that evening as they travelled back in the carriage through the night streets of Bath. 'I am delighted, of course, that you have turned to the church, even if it is somewhat belated. But why on earth St Swithin's?'

'Oh...I spotted it when I was riding by this afternoon and thought it looked interesting.'

'The day you take an interest in church architecture, Lovell,' Georgiana remarked grimly, 'I shall eat my bonnet! You are up to something.'

Nicholas, who had had no idea until he said it that he had even noticed the church which stood at the fork of Walcot Street and the Paragon, realised that it was undoubtedly the church attended by the Knights. Camilla must be on his mind even more than he was consciously aware of. Well, he would confound his sister by attending Matins tomorrow.

The next morning dawned sunny and bright and

Nicholas strolled along the Paragon in good spirits. Exposure to Lady Cynthia the night before had had quite the opposite effect to that intended by Lady Forres. Far from being captivated, he had come firmly to the decision that all the débutantes he had met in the last year were either vapid, boring or too conventional in their obedience to society's rules for young ladies. The only woman he had met whom he could imagine spending his time with was Miss Knight. One would never be bored with Miss Knight—provoked, stimulated, irritated, perhaps— but never bored.

Startled, he found himself seriously considering her as a wife. It would not be a brilliant match, but not an ineligible one either. As Earl of Ashby he had no need to marry for either money or connections—provided he chose a well-bred woman, he could do as he pleased. And Miss Knight pleased him very much...

But what if his faint suspicion that she was Miss Davide were true? An actress was quite another matter. And yet...and yet Camilla was patently innocent, however passionate she was in his arms. Her responses to him were instinctive, not learned: he had enough experience to recognise artifice when he encountered it. Opera dancers and actresses were skilled in being whatever their protector of the moment wanted them to be, and both of you played the game of make-believe. Yet she seemed to have that damned sobersides of an attorney in her pocket: surely a man like that would not represent such an abandoned creature as an actress. Unless of course he was courting her himself...

Nicholas pulled himself together as he found himself in front of the Knights' door. It was opened by the footman, who expressed himself deeply regretful that the ladies were not at home. 'They have gone to church, my lord.'

'Rather early, surely?' Nicholas queried, wondering if after all they had not walked down to the more fashionable Abbey.

'Services at St Swithin's do commence rather early, my lord. Would you care to come in and wait?' Samuel had heard all about the interesting Lord Lovell from Camilla's maid and, in common with the rest of the servants' hall, thought he sounded just the ticket for Miss Camilla.

'Thank you, no. I will meet the ladies out of church.'

A short walk further along the Paragon brought his lordship to the small forecourt in front of St Swithin's. The verger at the door opened it for him, but one swift glance inside revealed the Vicar in full flow in the pulpit. A soft snore from the elderly gentleman in the back pew was hardly a vote of confidence in the engrossing nature of his discourse, so with a polite nod to the verger Nicholas retreated to the sanctuary of the churchyard. It was a pleasantly sunny morning, it would be no hardship to lean against a tombstone and await the emergence of the congregation.

Inside it was cool and dark. Camilla wrenched her attention back to the Ephesians for the fourth time with a guilty start. She had welcomed the necessity to attend church this morning: not only would the need to concentrate on the service banish all thoughts of Nicholas, but it would also give her the opportunity to reflect in tranquillity on her forward behaviour of the day before.

Her eyes rested on her prayerbook, clasped between her gloved hands. Unfortunately the exercise of penitential thoughts about her behaviour simply raised the most vivid recollection of the nature of her transgression—and her partner in it. Camilla shut her eyes as a little frisson of remembrance shot up her spine. His hands, his lips, the turf yielding beneath their bodies...her near compliance.

'No!' Camilla realised she must have whispered it aloud, for Ophelia turned her head and gave her a puzzled look. Camilla stared back repressively, noting that Mama was dozing, very discreetly, her head hardly nodding. That was a relief; she was unlikely to notice her elder daughter's shocking lack of attention to the service.

She felt as heavy-eyed as though she had not slept, although quite the opposite had been true. She had fallen into a deep, dreamless sleep, almost as though she had been drugged, then woken with a sense of excitement. Camilla had swung her legs out of bed, then winced with the shock of stiff limbs and aching bruises. At once the memory of the fall and all that had followed it had filled her mind and she had not been able to banish it since.

Mrs Knight had been too preoccupied with worrying whether Ophelia was well enough to attend church to notice that her elder daughter was also moving with less than her usual grace and was uncharacteristically silent.

The Vicar droned on, and in an effort to focus her mind Camilla fixed her eyes on the altar rail. This did not answer the purpose at all—quite the contrary, for the image of herself walking slowly towards it rose unbidden in her mind. She saw Nicholas waiting expectantly for her to join him, the pews full of her friends and relatives, the church heavy with the scent of orange blossom and lilies; she heard the swish of silken skirts as she trod the stone flags on her uncle's arm. The scene in her mind was softened by the fine gauze of her wedding veil…

This fantasy was enough to see her through the last hymn and the dismissal, and even their departure from the church, with the organist playing softly in the background, did not dispel it until they reached the door, where the Reverend Mr Wise was paying close attention to the Quality in his flock, shaking hands and effusively replying to his patron's comments on his sermon.

'Indeed, yes, my lord,' he was saying, 'a most interesting interpretation of the text, I always think. Good day, my lord! Ah, Mrs Knight, Miss Knight, Miss Ophelia: I trust I find you all in good health on this beautiful spring morn!'

Leaving her mama to make polite conversation, Camilla wandered a little way away to look at the view. St Swithin's stood at the point where Walcot Street climbed steeply up to meet the end of the Paragon. The church, built of golden stone, jutted out on a raised platform to allow for the difference in level of the two streets which met on the far side of it. There was a fine view across the valley of the River Avon from the west end, but from this side, where the small churchyard sloped in two directions, the view was of the rear of the Paragon buildings,

their gardens sloping steeply down, and of the
Walcot Street cottages and their own rear yards.

And standing there, both hands resting on the iron
railing surrounding the burial plot, was Nicholas
Lovell. Camilla could see nothing of his face, and
all his attention seemed riveted on the view. Her
heart leapt with joy at the unexpected sight of him
before the inevitable apprehension filled her.
Camilla felt the colour rise in her cheeks and was
thankful for the fact that she had seen him first and
could compose herself before facing him again.

What was Nicholas doing here? Camilla walked
slowly down the slope towards him, taking in the
sight of his broad shoulders in the admirably cut
blue superfine jacket, the length of his muscular legs
moulded by the tightly strapped trousers, the curl of
his hair just visible at the back under his hat. Then
she saw he was looking at the back of their house
and her heart leapt again: he must be thinking about
her!

Nicholas was thinking about Camilla, certainly,
but not in a way which would have given her cause
for anything but deep anxiety. Twenty minutes spent
leaning on the fence in the sunlight, imagining
Camilla Knight once more in his arms, had been
curtailed abruptly. Some unconscious part of his
mind had been regarding the landscape spread before his unseeing eyes, and now his gaze sharpened.
Nicholas slowly looked up at the towering buildings
of the Paragon stretching along the crest to his right,
then he studied the way their gardens tumbled down
to the wall of the yards belonging to the cottages
facing on to Walcot Street.

Eyes narrowed against the sunlight, Nicholas

counted along until he could identify the Knights' residence, then repeated the process for Miss Davide's little house. The garden of one met the yard of the other, wall to wall. So that was how it had been done! Nicholas realised he was gripping the iron railing so hard it hurt, even through the leather of his gloves. 'Mademoiselle Davide' had had a key, had let herself out of the kitchen door as he'd slept and must have slipped through an unseen gate in the dividing wall. Once the other side she had become, once again, the highly respectable Miss Knight.

'Damn!' He said it out loud. 'Hell and damnation!' Just when he thought he had found an eligible bride, a woman he could not only tolerate being tied to but one with whom it would be a positive pleasure to spend the rest of his life, she turned out to be an actress!

Nicholas dropped his head and stared at his clenched hands on the railing. And yet...her reputation as the Unobtainable was no lie, no fabrication for the billboards. Mademoiselle Davide—Camilla Knight—was the virgin that her background and breeding would lead one to expect. An outspoken and passionate virgin, but a virgin none the less. He remembered her behaviour in the Green Room, the skillful way she had handled importunate gentlemen, the way she had made her terms for accepting gifts quite plain.

And yet...she was still quite ineligible. Whatever her reasons for taking this quixotic path—and he assumed they were financial—she had placed herself beyond the boundaries of polite society. If anyone were to discover just who Mademoiselle Davide really was, the Knight family's only recourse would be an immediate retirement to a life of seclusion in the country. Thank goodness he had found out before he had made her a declaration! What would she have said? Her vehement statement that she would never marry made sense now: but the cynical part of his mind, the part that remembered the constant scheming of society mamas, made him wonder if her resolution to do the right thing would have remained firm in the face of a declaration by the Earl of Ashby. It was a good thing he had not gone into the church: he could leave Bath now, not see her again. No harm had been done...

The muffled sound of footsteps on the turf made him turn round slowly. Walking down between the gravestones was Camilla, a graceful figure in a deep amber walking-dress and pelisse, a velvet bonnet in the same shade with a curling brown feather on her head. She smiled at him, a smile of such pleasure and warmth that his breath caught and every sensible resolution flew out of his head.

'Lord Lovell! I did not look to see you here!' She held out her gloved hand and shook his, apparently unaware that Nicholas was uncharacteristically lost for words. 'Will you not join us for luncheon? I know Mama would be delighted.'

Camilla was pleased with the calm air of social poise she had conjured up. Inside her heart was beating frantically and she had a wild urge to throw herself into his arms, but she told herself firmly that this was just another part to play and continued to smile.

'I...I am afraid I am leaving Bath this afternoon, Miss Knight. I called to say goodbye and to enquire about your health and Miss Ophelia's after your falls yesterday. Your footman told me you were here.'

'Oh!' All Camilla's disappointment showed on her face and her lip quivered very slightly before she gained control of herself. 'Oh, your friends will be sorry to lose your company, my lord. Must you go?'

Nicholas knew he should say he had urgent affairs to attend to on his estate, in Town—anywhere but here. He had never before had the slightest trouble ridding himself courteously and generously of any romantic entanglement; now he found himself incapable of simply saying goodbye and walking away.

'Well…I… Perhaps there is no great urgency for a day or two,' he capitulated. God, he was a fool, but the look of sparkling pleasure on her face was reward enough.

'Then you will have lunch with us,' Camilla pressed, trying to achieve a more ladylike control of her emotions, which had been turned upside down by the sight of Nicholas. Her common sense, her sense of what was right and honourable to do, was telling her that she must be true to her resolution never to marry. Her fantasies and hopes were quite different: she wanted to be in his arms again, she wanted his lips on hers, she wanted him to fall in love with her.

They turned and walked up the slope to join Mrs Knight and Ophelia, who were unfurling their parasols and looking round for Camilla. 'My lord! Good morning!' Mrs Knight beamed with approval at the sight of her elder daughter on the Earl's arm.

What a handsome couple they made! 'Were you in church too? I did not see you.'

'Good morning, ma'am.' Nicholas doffed his hat and bowed to the ladies. 'I am afraid I arrived too late for the service.' He caught Ophelia's eye: she was giving him the quizzical look of a young lady who knew perfectly well he had had no intention of attending divine service. 'I called at the house to enquire about Miss Ophelia's health after her fall yesterday.' He felt Camilla's hand clench on his arm. So! She had not told her mama that she too had had a fall. He closed his arm up to his side, squeezing Camilla's hand for a fleeting moment.

Reassured by the unspoken message, her heart pounding at the momentary contact with his body, Camilla managed to say brightly, 'I have invited Lord Lovell to luncheon, Mama.'

Mrs Knight's thoughts flew to the menu for luncheon, desperately recalling what she had agreed with Cook for today's meal. She had planned only a light cold collation for luncheon, but there was the lobster for this evening: that would do if Cook prepared a hollandaise sauce and some syllabubs for dessert…gentlemen did so enjoy sweet things. None of this frantic thought showed on her face as she made polite conversation with Nicholas while they walked down the Paragon.

'Such an interesting sermon you missed, my lord,' she said, without a blush for the fact that she had slept through a good part of Mr Wise's discourse. 'Such a stimulating speaker…oh, good morning, Mrs Frobisher!' She broke off to bow to a passing acquaintance. Hah! so much for her snide implications that her Daphne would find an eligible husband long before either of Mrs Knight's two girls. 'That was Mrs Frobisher—the Dorset Frobishers, you know,' she confided. 'She has three daughters, quite charming. They rise above the handicap of the family features by sheer force of personality.' Having thus reassured herself that if Lord Lovell came across the three Misses Frobishers he would be already prejudiced against them, she carried on happily along the Paragon, bowing and nodding to other members of the Quality, who like the Knights, were returning home from church.

Once inside the door she shed her bonnet and pelisse and turned to her daughters. 'Do take his lordship through to the Green Salon, girls, I will join you shortly.' As the door closed behind them she bustled downstairs. 'Mrs Powes! Mrs Powes! Here is Lord Lovell come for luncheon, now what can we do with that lobster?'

'Lord Lovell? Oooh, ma'am! What a good thing Miss Camilla's home. Mary, get that lobster out of the scullery and the pan on the boil. Now, don't you worry, ma'am, we'll get you a luncheon up fit for His Majesty, poor man, let alone Lord Lovell.'

Upstairs in the Green Salon, Camilla sat on the sofa watching her sister flirting outrageously with Nicholas Lovell, who was teasing her back in much the same way as he would a favoured niece. 'Did you really come round to ask about me, Lord Lovell?' she was asking, opening her hazel eyes wide at him.

'But of course, Miss Ophelia. I was hardly able to sleep a wink last night for thinking about yesterday.'

His voice held the slightest hint of wickedness,

and although he was not looking towards her Camilla knew perfectly well what he was referring to. She took a large sip from her glass of ratafia and almost choked. She had no fear that Nicholas would tell anyone about what had happened between them yesterday, but equally she had no illusions that he would not refer to it again, however obliquely, to tease her. And if he was telling the truth, the thought that he had lain awake thinking about her made her feel quite hot and confused.

Ophelia, who knew just how well the dark green brocade of the curtains set off her colouring, had perched decoratively in the window-seat and was half turned to look down the garden. Despite her preoccupations Camilla smiled slightly, knowing how long her sister had been practising in front of the mirror to achieve just the right turn of the head to show off her enchanting profile to perfection.

'Do come and look at this view my lord,' Ophelia was saying. 'It is one of the reasons we took this house. See—' she patted the seat beside her encouragingly '—if you sit here you can see right across the Avon.'

Nicholas strolled over, but did not sit. He stood, one hand on the window-frame, looking down. Camilla, suddenly irrationally jealous of her little sister, got to her feet and joined the two of them.

With his eyes fixed outside the room she risked a long look at his averted face. Then she saw that he was not focused on the charming view across to the wooded slopes behind, but was looking down into their garden. Camilla followed his gaze and realised he was staring at the gate in the wall between their garden and the back yard of Miss March's cottage in Walcot Street. Hidden by hanging ivy on the far side, on this face of the wall the gardener kept it trimmed and clear and the route which took her from being Mademoiselle Davide to being Miss Knight was plain to see.

Her eyes flew to his face and saw his eyes narrow speculatively. Camilla gave a little gasp and immediately his attention was all on her. Surely he must have guessed! At any moment the accusation would come and her double life would be exposed. But Nicholas's face revealed nothing but polite interest in the view. 'Yes, it is a fine view, and what a charming garden you have.'

His blandly expressed words concealed his feelings. What he could see from the window confirmed what he had suspected in the churchyard. He had had time to get over that shock, but Camilla's face had betrayed, fleetingly, her guilty secret. She swiftly had her face under control again, but her eyes were still wide with shock and fear, startlingly green. The sensible, the kind thing, to do would be to contrive to send Ophelia out of the room and to reassure Camilla that her secret was safe. And, after lunch, pursue his plans to return to London, putting the whole thing behind him as a pleasant but disappointing interlude.

Camilla wondered vaguely if she was going to faint. It seemed very probable. Her body stood there, apparently calm, while her stomach seemed to have disappeared and her brain whirled. Ophelia's chatter seemed to come from a long way away. What was he going to do? Leave in disgust at her deception? Tell polite society that she was beyond the pale? Expect her to behave as an actress was supposed to behave—the way she had so very nearly behaved yesterday?

He did none of these. Instead he was all concern, taking her lightly by the elbow and steering her back to her seat on the sofa. 'You are pale, Miss Knight. Are you sure you are fully recovered from your fall yesterday?'

For once Ophelia proved a welcome distraction. 'A fall? Camilla, you did not tell me? Does Mama know you fell off too?'

'No, she does not,' Camilla replied sharply. 'And I beg you, Ophelia, do not tell her. She will only worry—and do you want her to forbid us to ride out?'

Ophelia jumped to her feet. 'Heavens, no! Do you think Mama would?'

At that most awkward moment Mrs Knight swept in, full of confidence that her luncheon table would not shame the most exacting society matron. 'Would do what, my dears?'

Ophelia and Camilla looked blankly at each other, momentarily lost for words. They need not have feared, for Nicholas interjected smoothly, 'I had just asked Miss Knight and Miss Ophelia whether you would all be my guests tomorrow night at the first fireworks and musical evening of the Season in the Sydney Gardens. The weather appears to be holding well, and of course I will reserve a box.'

'Please say yes, Mama,' Ophelia pleaded. She had never been allowed to attend such a grown-up entertainment before. Camilla simply sat back against the sofa cushions and felt a wave of relief sweep over her. He had not guessed! He could not have done and still have invited them all out. She had been mistaken, had panicked unduly. For the first time she truly realised what a very dangerous game she was playing, yet like a gambler in the grip of his addiction she could not stop, could not do what she knew she ought and let Nicholas slip out of her life for ever.

Mrs Knight had not the slightest intention of saying no to such a flattering invitation and one which, she hoped, would bring her girls to the notice of society matrons who might include them in further expeditions. To go to the Sydney Gardens in the company of the Earl of Ashby had a cachet indeed! It was true that Camilla was insistent on her ridiculous refusal to consider marriage, and Ophelia was a little young for him, but Mrs Knight still had hopes of Camilla relenting, and at the very least he could only lend them all consequence.

It was a splendid luncheon, and Ophelia for once demonstrated tact and did not comment on the unusual lavishness of the spread. Mrs Knight was feeling ten years younger with the presence of such a handsome young man in the room, and charmed by his lordship's thoughtfulness and attention to her wishes. 'Is there perhaps another gentleman of your acquaintance who you would like to join us tomorrow evening, Mrs Knight? There is no shortage of space in the box and it would balance the party and—should you permit dancing—would provide another partner acceptable to you.'

'How thoughtful of you, my lord.' Mrs Knight beamed, hiding her racing thoughts. Who could she invite who would not distract Camilla in any way from his lordship? Ah, yes, the very man! 'Shall we invite Mr Brooke, my dears?'

Ophelia, who would not have cared if her mama had invited the Archbishop of Canterbury just so long as she could be seen in Nicholas Lovell's company, agreed instantly. Camilla, saying nothing, recognised the danger to her daydreams in the invitation. Arthur Brooke, eminently sensible, aware of every detail of her scandalous other life, and knowing her as well as he did, would immediately tell her to sever a connection which could only lead to exposure. The fact that he would be perfectly right was no consolation whatsoever!

'Then that is settled,' Mrs Knight said happily. 'I will send Samuel down with a note this afternoon. It was so fortunate that your invitation is for tomorrow night, my lord, for we would have been unable to accept otherwise.'

'Why is that, Mama?' Camilla enquired calmly, trying to pull herself together. The entire meal felt like the sort of nightmare she used to have when she dreamt she was acting in a ten-act play without knowing any of the words.

'I had quite forgot to tell you, my love, today has been so busy, but I have received a letter from Lady Ellwood—our close friends and neighbours from when we lived in Cambridgeshire, my lord—and she has confirmed the invitation to the house party she spoke of in her last letter. We must leave on Wednesday, for I am sure she will want my assistance in preparing for so many guests.'

Ophelia squeaked with pleasure. 'Mama! How wonderful!' She turned to his lordship and began to prattle happily. 'Lady Ellwood always has the most wonderful house parties—so many people, and you would never think they would all get on together, but she is such a wonderful hostess and everyone enjoys themselves. Even the Archdeacon joined in the theatricals last time...'

'Theatricals?' Nicholas asked lazily, passing the sugar to Mrs Knight.

Ophelia caught Camilla's horrified expression and blushed scarlet to the roots of her hair. She might be scatterbrained but she was not stupid and she understood, far more clearly than her Mama, the necessity to keep her elder sister's scandalous secret.

'Oh...merely charades, a little verse-reading, you know. After all, the Archdeacon would hardly participate in anything else...' Her voice trailed away and she looked down into her empty syllabub glass.

'Cambridgeshire?' Nicholas enquired, apparently unaware of Ophelia's confusion and the silence of the other two ladies. 'Is that the Lord Ellwood who has such a fine string of racehorses? I believe my father knew him.'

The relief around the table was almost palpable. So the entire family knew what Miss Camilla had been up to. He supposed, now he thought about it, that it could hardly be otherwise, given the practicalities of running a double life.

Mrs Knight was earnestly remarking on Lord Ellwood's success in the Derby, but Nicholas's mind was elsewhere. The Ellwoods lived on the Cambridge–Suffolk border, handy for Newmarket. Later that week Freddie Corsham was returning home to his country estate not ten miles from Newmarket. And Nicholas had a standing invitation to Freddie's house...

As he walked away back to Georgiana's house Nicholas acknowledged that after tomorrow night the best thing to do would be never to see Camilla Knight again. But some devil was not going to let him do that just yet. He would take up Freddie's invitation—his friend was bound to know the Ellwoods—and then...and then he would just have to see what happened.

Chapter Seven

'Will you not walk a little along the central promenade and view the lights, Miss Knight?' Mr Brooke enquired earnestly and with a meaning look. He had already risen from his seat in Lord Lovell's box and was offering his arm to Camilla.

Good manners suggested that she should immediately accept but Camilla hesitated, puzzled and somewhat nettled by the solicitor's proprietary air. Arthur Brooke was acting as though he were her elder brother, chaperoning her in company of which he did not quite approve. His manner was correct, but to someone who knew him as well as she did, it was clear he was obviously out of countenance.

'Thank you, Mr Brooke, but I am so much enjoying watching the world go by from here—and drinking this delicious punch—that I would prefer to remain where I am for a while.' She smiled sweetly at him before turning back to watch the throngs that filled the evening's fête in the Sydney Gardens. Rumour had it that two to three thousand people could be accommodated in the pleasure grounds, but this evening, so early in the year, it was quieter, although none the less interesting for that.

At this hour the orchestra was only playing light airs and the dancing had not yet begun on the portable floor which had been laid before the pavilions and boxes. Couples strolled back and forth, admiring the myriad fairy lights and lanterns strung from trees and leading back into the darker grottoes and intriguing labyrinths.

Mr Brooke flicked up the tails of his very correct evening-coat before sitting down again with some emphasis. Camilla wondered why he had positioned himself quite so firmly between Lord Lovell and herself. She would have liked to be able to speak to her host, at least! As it was she could hardly see him, never mind exchange words with him with Mr Brooke's disapproving bulk in the way.

For her part her younger sister, sitting next to his lordship, was in seventh heaven. He was too old, of course, but undeniably handsome and *so* well dressed in his dark evening clothes which fitted like a glove, impeccable white stockings and exquisitely tied cravat. For once Ophelia had no need to compete with her sister, for she could see that Arthur Brooke was keeping Camilla entertained, leaving Ophelia free to bask in the jealous glances of her friends and acquaintances.

It was wonderful—they all seemed to be here tonight, but *they* were all promenading demurely with their parents, and none were seated in such an exclusive box as she was! Maria Frogmorton almost tripped over her own feet, so agog was she by being greeted by Ophelia, who waved languidly from her seat next to the Earl of Ashby. Her chagrin was not helped by her mama, never a subtle woman, speculating audibly on how those Knight girls had acquired such an eligible escort.

All three Frobisher girls, each cursed with their father's large nose, were Ophelia's next triumph. To their mother's irritation they rushed over to speak to their friend, forcing their reluctant mama to follow them and engage Mrs Knight in conversation from between clenched teeth.

Mrs Knight, keeping her triumph off her face with some difficulty, was ecstatic. She had been patronised once too often by Mrs Frobisher, who was the third cousin to an earl and never let anyone forget it. Now she had seen the Knights in company with the Earl of Ashby twice in two days! She would soon be spreading that around all her friends and the invitations to Ophelia and Camilla would flood in.

Nicholas, very much at his ease, knew exactly what was going on and was, surprisingly, enjoying himself. He found Ophelia's puppy-love amusing and rather endearing: he had no fears that she would break her heart over him. He was a convenient foil for her flirtations and a trophy to parade before her equally young friends, that was all.

No, it was her elder sister he was interested in. Not that his plans for the evening in that regard were going very well, thanks to the disapproving presence of Arthur Brooke. Quite what the lawyer had found so unacceptable in Nicholas he could not imagine, but take against him he most certainly had. There was nothing to criticise in his dry, proper manner, but the man was acting like a dog in the manger— it felt almost as though he would growl at any moment.

Nicholas leaned forward and offered to fill Camilla's glass. She smiled and accepted, allowing him another opportunity to admire her elegant evening gown with its pale yellow net overskirt, showing off the amber satin slip beneath. Camilla's white shoulders and the gentle swell of her breasts rose enticingly from the silvery lace of the low-cut neckline which, to her surprise, her mama had approved. Mama had even lent her the best amber set of drop earrings and necklace which Great-aunt Augusta had left her.

It was the first time Nicholas had seen Camilla in evening dress and the effect was yet another nail in the coffin of his good resolutions to break the connection. Last night he had almost talked himself out of his scheme to stay in Newmarket with Freddie Corsham. Camilla Knight was ineligible, totally ineligible. He was certain now she was Mademoiselle Davide, and the sensible thing to do was to obey his head and walk away. But something else was conflicting with the voice of reason. It could not be love: that was not what he was seeking after all. He needed a suitable wife. Outside marriage all that was required was an intelligent and attractive mistress— one who would keep him satisfied in all respects.

Camilla Knight was too virtuous to become any man's mistress, and her past would not allow her to be any man's wife. So why was he so drawn to her? Camilla stood up to exchange a few words with an acquaintance and he was once more struck by her grace and charm. His eyes lingered on the smooth length of her neck, the soft curls of blonde hair gleaming gold in the bright candlelight of the box. Unbidden, the memory of the sensation of her skin, satin against his lips, of the scent of her in his nostrils, the way she had responded when he kissed her, filled his mind.

His thoughts must have been visible in his eyes, for he realised with a start that Mr Brooke was regarding him with overt disapproval. Damn it! The man must be in love with her himself: if he was not very careful Nicholas would find himself called out!

The two men were still eyeing each other warily when the band struck up a dance tune and the first couples took to the floor to form sets for a quadrille. Nicholas got to his feet and asked, 'Will you do me the honour, Miss Knight?' He scarcely waited for her reply before he took her hand and swept her out of the box and on to the dance floor.

Camilla took her place in the set, her eyes glowing, her gloved hand tingling as though he had touched her naked skin. The measures of the dance separated them, brought them together, separated them again, but their eyes kept meeting. Every time it was she who broke the glance first, feeling as though an electric shock had jolted her heart, frightened that her feelings for him were showing all too plainly.

How she got through the intricate dance without a mistake she never knew, but finally the last chords were struck and she was curtseying to her partner, and joining the other dancers in clapping the band. Automatically she turned to return to the box, but Nicholas was beside her, his hand under her elbow.

'What a crush! I do not think you would wish to be jostled by the crowd, Miss Knight. Let us walk a little.'

Almost before she knew it, Camilla found herself

strolling along one of the lantern-lit pathways which edged the bowling green. It was away from the dance floor and the pavilions and on the other side from the famous labyrinth and grottoes, so that even on such a festive night it was relatively quiet.

They walked a short distance in silence, although Camilla was convinced the urgent beating of her heart must sound as loud to him as it did to her. However, when Nicholas spoke his words came as a surprise. 'Is Mr Brooke related to you?'

'Why, no!' Camilla replied, puzzled. 'His father was our family solicitor for years, and now Mr Brooke manages our affairs here in Bath. Why do you ask?'

'He is so very protective of you, that is all. I half expected him to demand to know my intentions. If he is not a relative then I can only assume he is in love with you. He is within an inch of finding cause for a quarrel so he can call me out.' Nicholas sounded quite matter-of-fact.

Camilla stopped in her tracks, completely taken aback by the idea. '*Arthur Brooke* in love with me! Ridiculous!'

Nicholas looked down into her indignant face. 'You are very severe on the poor man. I agree he is not the most brilliant match, but he seems well-bred and is doubtless a good-looking enough fellow if he ever stops scowling.' He added drily, 'And I have never known a poor solicitor yet.'

'You misjudge me, sir, if you think I would look down on Mr Brooke for his profession. He is a good, kind and respectable man, and will make some young lady an admirable husband. But not me—and in any case, he is not in love with me!'

'Are you sure?' Nicholas enquired slyly. 'Why else should he be so antagonistic to me? Miss Knight? I do believe you are blushing.'

'I am not!' Camilla said indignantly, but she was seized by a sudden pang of conscience. She had always taken Arthur's solicitude for granted, never given his friendship a second thought, beyond a strong feeling of gratitude for his help. She had been so sure that Arthur Brooke's declaration that day in the carriage had been purely a kind gesture—but what if he had meant it from his heart? She had treated it so lightly at the time...

'I am certain you are blushing,' Nicholas teased, taking her chin in his hand and turning her face to the light. 'There, I told you so—your cheeks are quite charmingly rosy.' He bent suddenly and brushed cool lips across her burning skin. If Camilla had not been blushing before, she was now. With a gasp she turned on her heel and ran along the gravel path and down a turning towards the sound of tinkling water. She found herself quite alone in the charming little grove, not much larger than an arbor, lit only by a few lanterns and with a cascade of water falling into a pool of artificial rock at the back.

Camilla unbuttoned one glove, pulling it back from the wrist so she could scoop her hand into the falling water. She gasped out loud at its chilly touch, then dabbed it on to her hecticly coloured cheeks. When she straightened she heard Nicholas's footsteps behind her.

He put his hands on her bare shoulders, the fingertips stroking down the satin slopes, gently, insidiously. 'Camilla...' His voice was husky, the note, even to her inexperienced ears, one of sensual longing.

'My lord, this is most improper...' But even as her back stiffened a shudder ran through her frame. She wanted to lean back into the strength of him, to have him encircle her with his arms, his warmth. She wanted to feel his lips on her skin again—and she knew that this was all wrong, that she was behaving like a loose woman, that she must send him away...

A breeze struck the grove and the sharp gust caught the cascade of water, showering her in cold droplets. Camilla cried out at the shock of it and twisted under Nicholas's hands. The movement brought them breast to breast.

Nicholas needed no further prompting. His arms encircled her, holding her tight against him, and his mouth found hers in a long, unhurried, deeply sensual kiss. Camilla melted against him, her hands reaching up to encircle his neck, her fingers first exploring, then tangling, in the springing curls at the nape. Her fingertips discovered the surprising softness of the skin there and she stroked it, innocently unaware of the effect it was having on Nicholas.

Her lips opened under his, inviting the invasion of his tongue-tip. She had been shocked at her own response when he had kissed her on the Downs, but now she was learning her own power to arouse him. Nicholas groaned deep in his throat and his hand moved down from the slope of her shoulder to the soft swell of her breast. Camilla gasped, both at the intimate touch and at the immediate response of her own flesh under his insidious fingers.

The rising tide of her feelings for him pushed

back and then overwhelmed the small voice inside her that said, *No, this is wrong!* But then another voice, almost an instinct, replied, *How can it be wrong when I love him?*

His mouth left hers and she gave a small murmur of protest which turned into a soft gasp of pleasure as he began to nuzzle the exposed curve of her breast above the line of lace. Her fingers closed in his hair and she bent her own head to kiss the dark head, inhale the scent of Russian Leather from his cologne.

Nicholas was aflame, his senses intoxicated by the scent of honeysuckle, by the satiny smooth sensation of Camilla's skin under his questing lips and by the innocent, trusting passion this young woman showed at his very touch. He had known many sensual, practised women, some of the finest practitioners of the arts of love, but none had been as erotic, as arousing as Camilla in her artlessness. And that was why he had to stop this *now...*

He was already lifting his head when two strident female voices broke the silence of the little grove. Feet crunching on the gravel presaged the approach of the speakers. There was only one way out, the way they had come in: the moment he thought it two long shadows fell across the exit. Swiftly Nicholas stepped back behind the only cover, a statue of Venus standing in a large seashell, pulling Camilla with him. She found herself held tight against him, his hand pressed warningly against her lips. She started to protest, then fell silent, shrinking against Nicholas in the shadows as she too heard the voices.

'Shall we rest awhile, Mrs Frobisher? See, there is a bench here.'

'Indeed, Mrs Frogmorton, it looks most pleasant, and I confess I am quite fatigued by the crush of the crowd surrounding the dancing. Chaperonage is so fatiguing.'

The two matrons picked their way across the grove, straight towards the curved bench which stood at the foot of the statue of the goddess of love.

'Oh, good, it is quite dry. I would not wish to stain this new satin overdress,' Mrs Frobisher declared before settling herself.

'A London *modiste*?' her companion enquired sweetly. 'You are so fortunate in being able to wear that difficult shade. On so many people it would make the complexion quite sallow.'

'If one is to speak of shades,' Mrs Frobisher rejoined tartly, 'did you not observe that dress Ophelia Knight is wearing? Periwinkle-blue, and she is not even out! One would have expected white, or cream, perhaps. Although what Mrs Knight is thinking of to allow such a child to attend an evening event of this nature I cannot imagine.'

Nicholas felt Camilla stiffen in his arms and tightened his grip warningly. The two ladies were so close it seemed impossible they would not hear their breathing or the rustle of Camilla's gown against the encroaching box hedging.

'You speak of Miss Ophelia—I am more concerned with Miss Knight herself!' The two shadows nodded in unison: they had finally reached the issue which had been burning in both bosoms all evening. It was quite impossible to give the matter the full attention it required with the eager ears of their daughters so close, but a private stroll gave ample opportunity to thoroughly air the scandalous affair. 'What can Mrs Knight be about?'

'You need to ask that, my dear?' Mrs Frobisher enquired archly. 'I would have thought it was obvious. She might bring that dull lawyer and that chit of a girl along for propriety, but it is the merest window-dressing. Her motive is obvious: she intends to ensnare the Earl of Ashby for her eldest daughter!'

It was Nicholas's turn to stiffen, but worse was to follow. '*Intending* to ensnare him? I would have thought she had already succeeded, such a significant degree of interest he is showing in the girl. Hardly a day passes when they are not seen together, I have heard. He is even escorting the family to church.'

Mrs Frobisher laughed patronisingly. 'Oh, no, he is not yet in her toils. When one moves in such circles, one recognises the situation instantly. My cousin the Earl suffered in just such a way. Encroaching mamas, pressing attentions upon him under every conceivable circumstance. And occasionally…' she paused and lowered her voice '…a gentleman can find himself unwittingly in a delicate situation where quite unreasonable expectations have been aroused by the merest politeness on his part. Naturally, those of the Ton, those with a sophisticated understanding, would not expect anything to come of it, but others have their ambitions fuelled by what is the merest politeness and condescension.

'The Earl of Ashby is too refined to make a sudden, humiliating break from the Knights, but mark my words he will be gone within the next few days and that will be the end of Mrs Knight's little plan. A moment of glory for Miss Knight, but fleeting, fleeting, my dear.'

Mrs Frogmorton, smarting at the implication that she was less well-connected and sophisticated than her friend, swallowed her chagrin and lowered her voice in turn. 'That is as maybe, but things may have gone too far for an honourable withdrawal on the Earl's part.'

There was a sharp intake of breath from Mrs Frobisher. Camilla thought they must discover her at any moment, her heart was beating so hard it sounded like a drumbeat in her chest. 'What *can* you mean, my dear Mrs Frogmorton?'

'Mrs Knight—although the family is well-bred enough—can have no real hope of securing such a brilliant match for her daughter, as you so rightly point out. The Knights are obscure, rural—except of course that very odd uncle one hears about. They do say he has been shut up now, with paid attendants, but that is by the by... Is it not possible that in her eagerness to promote the affair Mrs Knight has been, shall we say, lax in her chaperonage?'

To Camilla, standing in Nicholas's arms, her skin still tingling from his caresses, these words were coals of fire. Her mama had indeed been lax, but how could she ever have imagined her daughter could behave with such shocking impropriety? She wanted to bury her face in his shirtfront, but all she could do was to stand as still as the statue which shielded her, the hot tears of humiliation trickling down her cheeks.

'Surely not!' Mrs Frobisher gasped, half-horrified,

half-thrilled at the revelation. 'Surely a man as worldly wise as Ashby would not allow himself to be entrapped by a scheming mama and those rather obvious good looks. Obviously, there is his reputation…'

'Indeed! And one has to admit he has always previously confined his attentions to married ladies with complacent husbands. There has never been a whiff of scandal.'

'You say so, but what about the youngest Turner child? I saw her out with her nursemaid the other week, and I cannot recall any others in that family with such dark hair…'

'My dear! You do not suggest…?' Mrs Frogmorton's voice was full of appalled eagerness.

'I will say no more, but the dates are significant.' There was short silence following this scandalous *on dit*. 'Do you not think a quiet word with Mrs Knight would be a kindness?'

'Oh, no, dear! She would not take it in the kindly spirit in which it was meant. And besides, however much Mrs Knight may scheme, and Miss Camilla throw her cap over the windmill, Ashby is too canny to let himself be trapped by such provincial manoeuvrings.'

Having thoroughly picked over and criticised the manners, morals and motives of both the Earl of Ashby and the entire Knight family, the two ladies fell silent at last. At length Mrs Frobisher rose to her feet. 'I do declare I am feeling quite peckish. Shall we stroll back to our box? I do not like to leave girls too long with only their governess. One cannot be too careful.'

With a self-important rustle of silks the two ladies

swept out of the grove, blissfully unaware of the devastation they had left behind them.

For a long moment Camilla stood frozen in Nicholas's arms, then with a jerk she freed herself and stumbled into the middle of the clearing. Her skin burned still, not with his kisses but with scalding humiliation. That her name should be bandied around was bad enough, but that Nicholas should hear it was almost beyond endurance.

'Camilla…those old tabbies…' Nicholas began, taking a step towards her. He was stopped by her upflung hand.

She stood, her face averted from him, calling on every vestige of her hard-learned stage control to help her through the difficult speech which lay in front of her.

'No, my lord, let me speak. I must apologise for the vulgarity of my acquaintances and for the embarrassment that I have exposed you to.' He began to protest, but she stilled him again with a gesture. 'No, please let me finish. My mama, as any careful mother would, wishes Ophelia and me to make good, suitable matches.' She paused, drawing a difficult breath before continuing. 'We are an old family, a good, well-respected family, but we have never aspired above our station. And as I have told you, I have no intention of marrying—*ever*.' Her voice shook betrayingly and she paused for a moment to regain control.

'That said, I cannot deny that I have behaved…indecorously when you have…when we have—' She broke off again, defeated by the impropriety of what she was trying to describe. 'But I have *never* sought to entrap you in *any* way. I have been very weak, but…even if you were to offer for me, which I realise is quite out of the question and never your intention, I would refuse you.' As she said the words they seemed to echo in her head with a dreadful finality, and Camilla realised just how much she had secretly hoped he would make just such a declaration. It had been madness, of course, a complete fantasy, but denying it was the hardest thing she had ever had to do.

Camilla's voice became entirely suspended in tears and she broke off, gesturing with both hands to keep Nicholas away. Somehow she controlled herself and turned to face him, her head high. Suddenly salvaging her pride and her family's honour seemed the most important thing. 'As I say, my lord, I have no intention of marrying, certainly not for considerations of the rank or fortune which I readily agree you would bring me. Nor—' she swallowed painfully '—will I allow my judgement to be swayed by strong physical attraction.'

Nicholas, who had only been waiting for her to stop talking to take her in his arms and kiss away the tears, stopped abruptly. He was well used to the cut-throat gentility of the chaperons' corner, where soft words and appearances of concern were simply a front for ambitious mamas, each aiming to place her own daughter higher in the social tree than her neighbour's child. He had been furious to find himself the subject of such malicious tittle-tattle, having been the subject of it many times before. He knew perfectly well how to value it and would not have thought for a moment to blame Camilla or her mother for the rumours.

But her words struck at the core of pride in the

family name and in his lineage, the pride which had nagged him to go away from Bath, not allow himself to become entangled by a young woman who had risked compromise and scandal in such a way. So, Camilla Knight would not allow considerations of his rank and fortune to influence her, would she? He knew perfectly well that he was considered by society—and by the standards of his own family—far above her in rank, fortune and breeding. But it was up to him to decide whom he might favour with an offer of marriage, not for some young woman— however beautiful—to kindly inform him that she valued neither his rank nor his kisses before he had even hinted at an offer!

Nicholas's conscience was pricking in a way which was painfully unfamiliar, but injured pride overrode its promptings. Conveniently forgetting that he had sought out Camilla's company in a very marked manner which would inevitably lead to gossip, he now found himself furious that such gossip had in fact occurred. Dammit, the old biddies were right. Camilla should be extremely grateful to receive a proposal of marriage from him, not coolly telling him that he need not trouble himself to make one!

His face was rigid with suppressed emotion but his voice was cool as he replied, 'Rest assured, Miss Knight, that I perfectly remember your words on the subject and that I had absolutely no intention of putting you to the distress of refusing an unwelcome declaration. It might be felt that I could be forgiven for misinterpreting the warmth of your responses, but let me also assure you that I had no intention of making you any other kind of offer either...'

'Sir! How dare you?' His outrageous words were like a blow: Camilla's eyes blazed and her back stiffened. The fact that he was entirely right and she had behaved outrageously enough to provoke the offer of a *carte blanche* only served to fuel her anger. The only alternative was to blurt out that she loved him, and that was quite, quite impossible.

Now equally furious with both himself and her, Nicholas strode across the short distance which separated them and took her by the wrist. 'Come, come, Miss Knight! Why so proper all of a sudden? You showed none of this delicacy when my lips were on your breast just now. If those two old witches had arrived a little later, would they have found that bench otherwise occupied?'

Camilla brought her left hand up and slapped Nicholas's face so hard the sound rebounded off the rocks of the waterfall. He released her wrist and stepped back sharply, his eyes narrow slits of fury. Camilla swept out of the grove on to the gravel path, intent only on getting back to the box. What must she look like? She dabbed frantically at her eyes with her handkerchief as she went rapidly through the winding dells. Just before she reached the path encircling the dance floor she found Nicholas at her side. He took her arm.

'What do you want? Go away!'

'Be quiet and think,' he snapped. 'Do you really want to give the old biddies something more to talk about? Compose yourself and dry your eyes. We will stroll back to the box as if nothing untoward has happened and you will then doubtless develop a convenient headache and have to return home. And one last thing before we part...'

'*Yes?*' she snapped in her turn.

'I have never had a relationship of any kind with Lady Turner, and the parentage of her youngest daughter is nothing to do with me.'

Camilla turned and looked at him with icy eyes. 'How very sensible of Lady Turner. One can only admire her judgement.' She found herself at the door of their box and opened the door with the air of an actress making a stage entrance. She moved to Arthur's side, 'Oh, Mr Brooke, please would you drive us home? I have *such* a headache. It must have been the punch.'

Chapter Eight

It was the hardest letter Camilla had ever had to write, but after spending Monday night in a state of sleepless, humiliated misery she was determined to put an end to the whole sorry affair with some shreds of her dignity intact.

If she really had been setting out to ensnare the Earl then she would be seeking to retrieve the situation of the night before. The only way to convince him that this was not the case was to end their connection immediately, however painful that was. Camilla screwed up yet another sheet of expensive hot-pressed notepaper and, pushing back her chair, crossed to gaze unseeing out of the window.

'Oh, Nicholas,' she sighed, resting her hot forehead against the cool window pane. 'I love you…' It was the first time she had ever said it out loud, and although it was hopeless it gave her some pleasure to speak the words she would never say to him.

Outside the weather had turned showery and a cold gust sent a spiteful rattle of rain against the window and buffeted the newly emerged blossom on the shrubs in the garden below.

Camilla returned to her writing-desk and dipped her quill in the standish again.

Miss Knight wishes to convey to the Earl of Ashby her deep regret that he should have overheard the unwarranted speculations of some of her acquaintances last evening. Miss Knight begs his lordship to ignore this incident, attributing it to no more than spiteful tittle-tattle.

However, painful though this is, Miss Knight would wish to take this opportunity to assure his lordship that her intentions, and those of her family, have never been other than those of sincere friendship. A gentleman of his lordship's experience will be able, after careful consideration, to place the correct interpretation upon some of Miss Knight's actions which, however foolish, arose only from an inexperienced and passing affection.

Camilla broke off, nibbling the end of her quill. Well, that was the most difficult part over, and she was not displeased with the tone. She had portrayed herself as, at worst, naïve. It was humiliating, but at least it disguised the true depth of her regard for him. Her fingers drifted unconsciously to the edge of her fichu as she recalled the touch of his lips on the skin beneath. He must never know how much she loved him. Resolutely she dipped the nib again.

Under the circumstances of Miss Knight's imminent departure for Cambridgeshire this letter may also serve as a farewell and an ex-

*pression of Miss Knight's grateful awareness
of his lordship's kind attentions to her family.*

The letter seemed to end a little abruptly, but
Camilla could think of nothing further to add which
would not fatally betray her true emotions or the
truth which lay behind its painful composition.

She reached out and tugged at the bellpull, dust-
ing the page with sand while she waited for Samuel
to appear.

'You rang, Miss Knight?'

'Please fetch me a candle and some wax and then
take this letter to the Countess of Forres's residence
immediately.'

Camilla pressed her seal firmly into the melted
wax and handed the letter to the footman before she
could lose her nerve and snatch it back. She heard
the front door shut behind Samuel with mixed emotions. What did she want to happen now? The rational part of her wanted to receive back a polite
note begging her to give the matter not a second
thought and assuring her that the Earl entirely disregarded anything which had passed the night before. She could almost see the page open before her,
the letter ending with polite expressions of his best
wishes for the future and a clear, and final, farewell.

Yet the irrational side of her wanted him to send
back a missive telling her of his regard for her, and
of his intentions to call round to see her as soon as
possible.

But even as Camilla was penning his direction on
the folded letter Nicholas was bidding farewell to
his sister.

'Why are you rushing off like this, Lovell? I thought you were staying at least another week.'

'No, I only said I might.' Nicholas edged towards the door of Georgiana's bedchamber. 'That is a prodigiously fetching nightcap, my dear.'

Lady Forres patted the lace confection complacently. 'Mechlin lace, the finest. But do not seek to divert me, Nicholas. What are you about? Is this anything to do with Miss Knight?' Her clear blue eyes, so like his own, appraised him from amongst the pile of pillows heaped against her immensely fashionable Egyptian headboard. 'A nice girl, as far as I can tell.'

Nicholas gritted his teeth, but produced a convincing air of uninterest. 'Nice enough, I grant you, but the family is hardly what one would call the best match for a Lovell.'

Georgiana put down her chocolate cup upon the nightstand with some emphasis. 'I have never heard such specious nonsense! Since when have you cared for rank? There is breeding there, and sense. You have no need to marry for money or land, let alone connections! Miss Knight is as charming as she is beautiful.' Infuriated by her brother's silent resistance, she warmed to her argument. 'You complain when I introduce you to débutantes, saying that they are shallow and vapid. Just what are you looking for in a woman, Nicholas?'

Nicholas tightened his lips and regarded his sister through narrowed lids. 'I know precisely what I want in a wife, Georgiana, and I will know it when I see her.' As in fact he had already done, not that he had any intention of confiding *that* error of judgement! 'You seem to forget, sister, that I am not twelve years old. I will thank you not to meddle and to leave me to arrange my own affairs.' Lady Forres said nothing, but from the speculative gleam in her eyes Nicholas knew he had done nothing but arouse her interest. 'Now, I must be on my way. I have to call upon Freddie Corsham before I leave Bath. I will write to you from Town.'

Half an hour later Nicholas found Freddie just risen from his bed, sitting at the breakfast table and eyeing the roast beef with a queasy eye. 'Morning Lovell. Sit down—quietly, damn you!—and help yourself to coffee. Evans, a cup for his lordship.'

'Hung over, Freddie?' Nicholas enquired unsympathetically. He had had a fractured night himself, but at least he had not got over-indulgence in brandy to add to his troubles. He helped himself lavishly to bread and beef and fell to with sudden appetite.

Freddie watched him liverishly. 'What are you doing here anyway? Thought you were going up to Town before coming on to Abbotsford.'

Nicholas waved away the proffered coffee and accepted a tankard of ale from Freddie's man. 'That's why I'm here. I'm not coming to Suffolk, I'm afraid. Pressing business.'

'What?' Freddie exclaimed, then winced. 'But I promised my mama that you'd be there! Can't let me down now, old boy.'

'I have no choice. I have to return to Town.'

Corsham held a hand to his aching head and groaned again. 'My aunt Cecilia is coming with her bevy of daughters. Mama was delighted that you'd be around—helps balance the numbers and spreads the burden of entertaining them. We haven't got enough men, even with you there. Please come. I am a desperate man.'

Nicholas, seeing his old schoolfriend look so green, almost relented, then hardened his heart. The last thing he needed was to be among more young women; after the last few days he was determined to confine himself to strictly male company for a while.

He noticed a knowing look suddenly cross his friend's face. Despite the hangover, and his never very alert wits, Freddie was putting two and two together. 'Aha! You don't fool me Nick—you've tracked Mademoiselle Davide down, you cunning dog! You devil!' he added admiringly, seeing Nicholas's mouth tighten. 'I thought you'd given up, but I should have known better. Mind, you've only got until the end of the month to, er, conquer her. I still think Thunderer's safe—and if you come to Suffolk you can ride him and see what you've lost.'

Rejuvenated by his unusual perceptiveness, Freddie seized the knife and carved himself a slab of beef.

'Stop fishing, Freddie, and pass the mustard.'

The two men ate in silence for a while. Freddie's hangover was still severe enough to keep him quiet, while Nicholas had his own thoughts to contend with. Why not go to Suffolk? He did not particularly want to be in Town, that had merely been an excuse for Georgiana, and the thought of going back to his estates in Buckinghamshire did not appeal. It was those very estates which were tugging at him, making him restless for a new life, a wife, a family. He would undoubtedly dwell on what might have been with Camilla Knight, and that was pointless. That incident, that connection, however pleasurable, was at an end.

'You win, I'll come, Freddie. You've worn me down. But I warn you, if your aunt thinks she's going to marry me off to one of your cousins I'll be on my horse and out of there before you know it.'

Freddie paused, a forkful of meat half-way to his lips, a look of appalled sympathy on his face. 'Good God, man! What do you take me for? I wouldn't wish them on any man, let alone a good friend! No need for alarm, though, I'll hold 'em off!' And for the first time that morning he grinned, wondering why his friend looked so serious.

By Thursday afternoon Camilla had come to the conclusion that two days in a closed carriage had given her far too much time to dwell on the events of the last week. Again her mind ran on the footman's return with the same painful effect as probing a sore tooth with the tongue tip.

'Did you find Lady Forres's house easily, Samuel?' she had asked.

'Oh, yes, Miss Knight. His lordship had gone up to Town, ma'am, but the butler said he would forward your letter.'

'Oh…' was all she had said.

Goodness knows when he would receive the note, but that, now, was of secondary importance. Nicholas had left Bath without so much as a word of farewell, not even the chilliest and most formal note.

The words of Mrs Frobisher echoed in her mind. She had remarked that the Earl was too well bred to make a sudden, humiliating break with the Knights.

But that was precisely what he had done, driven by circumstances unknown to Mrs Frobisher, the catalyst.

Mrs Knight was snoozing gently in the corner, the occasional mild snore escaping her. Ophelia had taken the opportunity to remove a novel from her reticule, given to her as a surreptitious parting gift by her friend Miss Laxton, but certain to be unacceptable to her mama.

Camilla leaned back against the squabs and wished she too could sleep. Last night, spent at a friend's in Oxford, had been convivial, but despite her fatigue she had found it hard to sleep in an unfamiliar bed. She just wished that the journey would end and she could submerge her thoughts in the bustle of arrival at Fulbrook Hall and the warm reception she knew they would receive there.

The rolling outline of the Gog Magog hills was increasingly familiar, as was the rest of the quiet Cambridgeshire countryside through which the carriage was passing. Not far away lay their own old home, now occupied by Cousin Stephen Knight, upon whom it had been entailed on the death of their father. Stephen was a second cousin once removed, a pleasant young man, deeply sensible of the distress his arrival at Nevile's Place must have caused his relatives. Camilla remembered with gratitude the care he had taken to make everything as painless as possible and she looked forward to meeting him again. It had helped, of course, that they had known him for years, and the late Mr Knight, accepting the inevitable with good grace, had done much to introduce Stephen to the estate and its workings. In the event, Mr Knight's premature death had surprised everyone, but the effects of his good sense had meant that the transition had been a smooth one.

She was sure Lady Ellwood would invite her cousin to join the house party, for he too shared the interest in amateur dramatics which their hostess enjoyed so much.

Ophelia slipped her novel back into her reticule and touched her mother on the hand. 'Mama! We are just turning into the avenue.'

'Waah?' Mrs Knight, caught out in her doze, woke with a start, her bonnet over one eyebrow. 'I was not asleep my dear, merely resting my eyes. Oh dear, what has become of this bonnet!'

The carriage wheels were crunching on the gravel as the coachman reined back the team by the front porch. The panelled door swung open and, with her usual lack of formality, Lady Ellwood swept out, almost flattening the butler, who was standing deferentially to one side. She was followed by her husband, both her sons, her daughters-in-law and what, to the Knights, seemed a veritable sea of small dogs and young children.

'Louisa! My dear!' Lady Ellwood waited impatiently for the footman to let down the steps, then enfolded her old friend of more than twenty years in a warm embrace. 'You look so well, dearest! How the Bath air has suited you—I swear you do not look a day older than when I saw you last!'

'Emma, how wonderful to see you...' Overcome by emotion, Mrs Knight broke off, fumbling in her reticule for her handkerchief to wipe away her tears. 'It is such a joy...but to be back in Cambridgeshire, where I spent so many happy years...'

'There, there, dear, come inside and have a nice

cup of tea,' Lady Ellwood soothed. 'You are tired
from the journey. Camilla, Ophelia—my dears, how
lovely you have grown!' She linked her arm through
her old friend's and made vague shepherding movements with the other hand towards the door. 'Come
along, all of you, inside.'

By the next day it seemed to Camilla and Ophelia
as if the last three years in Bath had been a dream
and they had never been away from the county of
their birth. When they had lived at Nevile's Place
the two households had been frequent visitors each
to the other, and on the most informal terms. Both
Lord Ellwood and Mr Knight had been supporters
of the Whigs and had spent many an hour in earnest
political discussion over their port. Their wives,
knowing each other since they were young brides,
had against all expectations become firm friends.
Louisa Knight, always prone to an excess of sensibility, had found her confidence boosted by her
friend's no-nonsense manner and energy. It had
never occurred to Emma Ellwood, the daughter of
the largest landowner in the area, that there might
be any restriction on her doing exactly as she
pleased. Aided and abetted by an indulgent older
husband, she had soon become mistress of all she
surveyed and famous locally for her unconventional
house parties.

The present party found itself the next afternoon
seated on rugs spread on the hillside overlooking the
grounds, recovering from a picnic luncheon of some
magnificence.

Lady Ellwood adjusted her parasol and sighed
contentedly. 'Just look at this weather! And yet I
declare this time last week it was positively cold. I

am delighted, for I am quite determined to present our latest dramatic offering in the garden.'

'The garden, Mama?' Her elder son handed his latest offspring to its grandmama and regarded her quizzically.

'Yes, Charles, in your grandfather's grass amphitheatre.' She turned to the Knights to explain. 'You know, my father-in-law was very fond of chamber music and liked to entertain outside to the sound of a small orchestra in the summer? The lawn he created, sheltered by yews and with a raised turf platform at one end, it became quite overgrown—for my husband, as you know, cares little for music. But I have had it restored and I think it will answer perfectly.' Lord Ellwood, who had been sleeping gently under the shade of his hat, opened one eye and regarded his wife indulgently.

There was an immediate buzz of excitement, but Camilla's trained voice cut through it. 'It sounds wonderful, Lady Ellwood. Which piece do you have in mind?'

'Scenes from *The Tempest*, I thought. There are several which are quite unexceptional,' she added hastily, seeing the look of concern on her youngest daughter-in-law's face. 'And so suitable for an outdoor setting.'

Before she went to Bath Camilla would have been the foremost in planning the production, eagerly sharing ideas for casting and production. But now she sat back, leaving the discussion to her hostess, Charles, his wife and Ophelia. It had come as a shock how much she missed the stage, the frisson of excitement and nerves, the applause and approbation of the crowd. She longed to join in immediately with the discussion, but she was wary of exposing her professionalism and deep knowledge. Lady Ellwood knew her too well not to recognise the change in Camilla from the days when she had acted in one of the many charades and playlets that always took place at Fulbrook Hall.

Now she would have to put all her skill into acting the part of an amateur actress! Turning her shoulder on an animated discussion on casting, she smiled at Mrs Francis Ellwood, the somewhat staid wife of the younger Ellwood son. 'Have you taken part in one of Lady Ellwood's entertainments before?' she asked the dark-haired young woman.

'Indeed not,' she replied earnestly. 'Although I am very much looking forward to doing so. Thomas!' She broke off to call to a young child of about two who had escaped from his nursemaid and was toddling determinedly towards the fence separating them from a field of cows. The nurse ran after him and Mrs Ellwood, ignoring her son's wails of protest, turned back to Camilla. 'At first I was concerned about the propriety of play-acting, but, after all, if dear Lady Ellwood is happy to espouse it, there can be no objection. Do you attend the theatre often in Bath, Miss Knight? I believe there is a theatre of some renown in the city, is there not?'

Camilla found herself unexpectedly flustered. 'Er...no, I have not been in the audience often.' That was true enough.

Mrs Ellwood nodded seriously. 'Perhaps you devote more of your time to good works,' she suggested. 'Do you perhaps know my friend Miss Murgatroyd? She is very active in Bath charities, especially in that founded by Lady Isabella King some years ago. Perhaps you have heard of it?'

'I think not,' Camilla replied faintly. 'What is it called?'

'The Society for the Suppression of Common Vagrants and Impostors and the Relief of Occasional Distress and the Encouragement of the Industrious Poor,' Mrs Ellwood recited with justifiable pride.

Camilla firmly suppressed the desire to giggle, and equally the desire to tell Nicholas. How he would laugh! And then she remembered. She had severed all connections; she would never speak to Nicholas again.

'How very comprehensive,' she managed to say, before she was distracted by Charles Ellwood getting to his feet and waving his hat to attract a rider on the track below.

'Oh, look!' Mrs Knight exclaimed with pleasure, shading her eyes with her hand. 'It is Cousin Stephen! How well he looks,' she added, as the young man turned and cantered up the slope towards them. To her disappointment the Earl of Ashby had left Bath somewhat suddenly, dashing her hopes that perhaps there was something between him and her elder daughter. But, although not to be compared to an Earl, Stephen Knight would be a most eligible match for either of his cousins.

Mr Knight sprang down boyishly from his mount, tossing the reins to a footman who hurried forward. He bowed to Lady Ellwood, then, sweeping off his hat, saluted Mrs Knight on the cheek before shaking hands with his cousins and the others present.

Tall, blond and looking younger than his twenty-five years, Mr Knight was blessed with an open and pleasing personality, a conscientious approach towards his estate and tenants and a love of sport. He would never claim to be an intellectual, but his charming manners and willingness to join in and be pleased by whatever his hostess suggested made him a welcome visitor in all the surrounding houses. Those same hostesses—at least, those with unmarried daughters—agreed that it was about time that Mr Knight found himself a wife and settled to domesticity.

He took his place on the rugs surrounding Lady Ellwood, accepted a cold drink and was about to enquire after the Knights' journey when Charles Ellwood exclaimed, 'A fortuitous arrival, old chap, you are just in time to be cast in Mama's latest dramatic enterprise.'

Stephen sat up with enthusiasm. 'Another play, Lady Ellwood? Then count me in!'

Camilla had not realised that her cousin would be interested. 'Do you act, Cousin Stephen? I had no idea.'

'Oh, rather! Over the last couple of years Lady Ellwood has included me in all manner of entertainments.'

'And very good you are too, Mr Knight,' Mrs Charles Ellwood remarked, lifting the baby from her mother-in-law's arms and dabbing its chin with a napkin.

'Thank you, ma'am.' Stephen gave her a charming smile. 'I must confess I enjoy it so much that if the estates ever become mortgaged I will take to the stage as a professional!'

Mrs Knight looked down at her hands somewhat abruptly, Ophelia coughed as though a crumb had caught in her throat and Camilla waved her napkin in front of her face to disguise her mounting colour. 'So warm, is it not?'

'Indeed, somewhat too warm for the children now, I think.' Lady Ellwood got to her feet and brushed her skirts. 'Who will come in the carriages with me and who will walk down?'

Lord Ellwood swung up into the saddle of his cover hack and rode off with his sons to view a barn that needed reroofing. Lady Ellwood, the Mrs Ellwoods and Mrs Knight took the children in the two open carriages, leaving Stephen, Camilla and Ophelia to stroll down the hill back to Fulbrook Hall. Behind them the servants began to fold rugs and pack the hampers into the pony cart taking their time about it in the warm afternoon sun.

Mr Knight offered an arm to each lady, leaving his horse on a loose rein to follow slowly behind. 'You all look extraordinarily well; the climate in Bath must be congenial,' he commented, but it was on Camilla's face that his warm gaze rested. 'I hope you intend to come over to Nevile's Place: I intend a few changes of which I hope your mother will approve. I would welcome your view first, however, for I would not wish to distress her by altering your old home.'

Camilla smiled affectionately at her cousin. 'You are too kind, Cousin; your sensibility and care for our feelings is much appreciated by all of us. I am sure Mama will be happy with any change that you make, for she will know you have only the best of intentions.'

Ophelia seemed very quiet. Camilla was puzzled, for her sister normally sparkled and flirted in the company of attractive young gentlemen. Surely she did not dislike Cousin Stephen now she saw him for the first time in almost three years? Camilla glanced across at her sister and saw that she was walking quietly, eyes downcast, one hand resting demurely in the crook of her cousin's arm. Perhaps she had a headache? It was unseasonably warm that afternoon.

'We are to perform scenes from *The Tempest*,' Camilla remarked as Stephen conducted them carefully over the stile and down on to the hard-packed earth of the carriage drive. 'I expect Lord Ellwood will covet the part of Prospero.'

'Well, he is the only really *old* person in our party,' Ophelia said earnestly.

'Ophelia! Really!' Camilla chided. 'Cousin, I despair of my sister, she thinks anyone over the age of four-and-twenty is quite decrepit.'

Stephen turned his charming smile on his younger cousin. 'Then I must confess to being in my dotage, for I have just passed my twenty-fifth birthday.'

Ophelia raised wide blue eyes to his face and protested, 'Oh no, Cousin, I think that is a perfect age for a gentleman!'

Camilla cast her eyes upwards but managed to keep the smile off her face. So that was what was wrong with Ophelia! Well, this should be quite entertaining and would do Ophelia no harm, for Stephen was far too kind to either snub or take advantage of her. And, who knows, he might find he too was attracted...

Cousin Stephen was undoubtedly an attractive and eligible young man, and under other circumstances she too might have harboured a *tendre* for him. But it was Nicholas who filled her thoughts, and at night when she fell asleep it was Nicholas's lips she felt on hers.

Abruptly Camilla asked, 'And what part would you like to play, Cousin? Ferdinand would be very appropriate, of course.'

'An attractive part indeed, if neither Charles nor Francis cared for it,' Mr Knight replied enthusiastically. 'Who would play Miranda? Yourself?'

A season ago at the Theatre Royal in Bath Camilla had played Miranda to great acclaim from both the press and the audience. But that was Mademoiselle Davide, not Camilla Knight, and she doubted whether she would be able to conceal her experience in the part from her close friends.

'Oh, no, I am too old. Ophelia is nearer the right age, or Mrs Francis Ellwood.'

They had reached the house as Stephen remarked, 'That is as may be, but I am sure Lady Ellwood has already decided on her casting and we will have little to say to it!'

Her cousin proved correct, for after dinner, to which Stephen was invited, Lady Ellwood waved aside the gentlemen's attempts to sit over their port and summoned the entire house party into the salon.

'Now then, we must cast our play,' she began briskly, once they had clustered round her as she sat in her wing-chair, the tea-tray disregarded at her side. 'Charles, pass me my tablets.'

Her elder son found the notebook and passed it to his mother. Lady Ellwood flipped over the pages and cleared her throat. 'Prospero: Lord Ellwood. Ferdinand: Mr Knight. Ophelia, you will be perfect as Ariel. Mary and Clara, you will be the Spirits: there should be more than two of you, perhaps the

Williams girls will join us if their mama approves.
Charles and Francis—you choose between Alonso
and Sebastian.'

'And Miranda?' asked Stephen.

'Why, Camilla, of course.'

'Surely I am too old,' Camilla protested. 'Ophelia
is nearer to the age of the character than I...'

'I do not think it would be *quite* appropriate,
dear,' Lady Ellwood said carefully. 'You and I can
look at the text and make one or two...amendments.
For propriety's sake,' she added looking across at
Mrs Knight. 'And of course, my dear, the part of
Ariel must be carefully...er...amended to make it
suitable for Ophelia.'

Mrs Knight nodded. 'And the costume too must
be most carefully considered! I will not permit
Ophelia to flit about the stage in flimsy gauzes, and
that is that!'

At the same time as Lady Ellwood was taking a
blue pencil to the Bard of Avon's text—much to the
relief of her old friend—Nicholas was stretching his
legs in front of a blazing fire in Freddie's study.
Lord Corsham had arrived home with his usual in-
souciant lack of concern for domestic detail and
without sending ahead to warn his mama, the
Dowager, of his expected date of arrival.

Finnan, the butler, had opened the door on his
master without betraying the slightest sign of being
discommoded by the arrival of not only his lordship
but the Earl of Ashby to swell an already large house
party.

'My lord.' He bowed to Freddie. 'My lord.' An
equally dignified inclination of the head to Nicholas.

'My lady will be distressed to be from home, my lord, but not expecting you this evening has taken her guests to dine at Lady Robertson's.' He took hats and coats and summoned two footmen with a lift of one eyebrow. 'James, put a match to the fire in his lordship's study. William, ensure their lordships' valets have all the assistance they require. My lord, I will set dinner in the Blue Salon if that is acceptable to you.'

Freddie, never one to stand on ceremony, clapped the butler on the shoulder, causing him to wince more with anguish at the impropriety than at the impact of the blow. 'Just the job, Finnan, no need to rattle around in the dining-room. Mother well, is she?'

'Her ladyship enjoys her normal good health, my lord. I regret that Lady Cecilia has taken to her bed with a severe head cold and that two of your cousins have sore throats.'

'Confined to their beds as well, are they?' Freddie asked hopefully, waving Nicholas ahead of him into the study.

'No, my lord, they have bravely put their discomfort to one side in order to accompany your mother.'

'Oh, yes,' said Freddie vaguely, reaching for the decanter. 'Lady Robertson has three sons; I can see why they have forced themselves to go.'

Finnan, who had ambitions to serve in the most correct and formal household, stiffened his back and swept out.

'Poor old Finnan, I'm a great disappointment to him. He loved working for my father—a great stickler, everything done according to the book, and hell to pay if it wasn't. Brandy?'

Nicholas took the proffered glass and dropped

into one of the fireside wing-chairs. He half raised it in a mock salute to his host, but then fell into a brown study, gazing into the flames which were just catching hold of the coals. However well he had suppressed the thought of Camilla on the long journey from Bath, it was at moments of relaxation like this that she filled his mind again.

He put his glass down on the table at his side, knocking his hand against the bowl of pot-pourri as he did so. A faint flower scent rose in the warming air, slightly dusty, but still redolent of the scent of honeysuckle and roses. Damn it! Why could he not forget her? Because she was different, he answered himself. She was beautiful, but then he had known plenty of beautiful women. She was well-bred and elegant, but then there were dozens of more eligible girls on the marriage mart. No, she had *quality*…that was the only word for it. And, whatever she thought of him there was that spark of thrilling sensual excitement that coursed between them every time they touched.

But he owed something to his name…Georgiana might favour the girl, but she did not know that Camilla had made him the butt of every middle-class matron's gossip in Bath. Let alone Camilla's other secret…

'Nick. Nick! Wake up, for heaven's sake, man!' Freddie had obviously been trying to attract his attention for some time, for he raised one booted foot and kicked his friend none too gently on the ankle.

'Ow! What the devil are you doing, Freddie?'

'Just trying to ask you if you want to go up and wash and change before dinner. Wish I had something to think about that produced the same smile on my face…'

'Shut up, Freddie. I was just thinking about my dinner.'

The combination of the best efforts of Freddie's French cook, his brandy and a day spent on the road combined to send Nicholas into a deep sleep, despite his gloomy conviction that he would spend all night thinking about Camilla Knight. His host gave strict instructions he was not to be disturbed, so it was ten o'clock before Nicholas found his way down to the breakfast-room. Freddie, always inclined to think that ten was the crack of dawn, had only just poured himself a cup of coffee, but the Dowager was leaving the room as Nicholas entered.

She paused as he opened the door for her. 'Dear Nicholas,' she patted him on the cheek. 'The Bath air has obviously suited you. And how is your sister?'

'Georgiana is very well, and sends you her best wishes, ma'am.'

'I am sorry to have missed you last night. If my son—' she sent Freddie a withering glance '—ever communicated with his poor mama, then all would have been ready for you and we would all have been at home.' She looked Nicholas up and down with the arrogant rudeness of her class and generation. 'You're as good-looking a dog as your father was— why aren't you married and setting up your nursery?'

Nicholas, normally more than capable of dealing with formidable gentlewomen, flushed slightly. 'I cannot find anyone willing to take me, ma'am,' he said with a slight smile.

'Nonsense. You cannot be trying hard enough. Never mind, I have a houseful of eligible young women here...'

'Most of them with putrid sore throats,' Freddie muttered through a mouthful of beef. 'And those that haven't have squints.'

'Frederick!' snapped his irritated parent. 'Only Arabella has a squint, and her mama has every hope she will grow out of it.' She smiled again at Nicholas. 'Now, for goodness' sake, both of you, get out in the fresh air—I will see you at dinner.'

Nicholas pulled out a chair and raised an eyebrow at Freddie. 'How nice to see her ladyship in such good spirits.'

Freddie shot him a dark look. 'That's what you call it is it? She's already criticised my haircut, my neckcloth, my complexion—too many late nights, too much brandy, unspecified loose living—and the fact that she thinks my trousers are cut too tight. Oh, yes, and why aren't I married yet.'

Nicholas reached for the rolls and butter and the two men ate in companionable silence for five minutes. Freddie finished first, pushing his chair back and looking out at the bright sky with high white clouds chasing across the sun and casting shadows on the newly scythed grass. 'Looks as though the weather will hold: I've got to see a man about a horse—might as well do it today. Coming?'

Nicholas was only too happy to ride out with his friend, and was too preoccupied with his own thoughts to ask where they were going. It was enough to be out in the fresh air, the horse moving easily under him, the low, rolling countryside green and fertile around them.

Freddie, who was a good landlord, despite his air of caring for nothing but enjoying himself, stopped occasionally and spoke to small groups of estate workers they encountered. Nicholas, looking around as he waited for Freddie to finish talking to a man who was clearing a ditch, saw in what good heart the land was and felt a pang of homesickness for his own estates at Ashby in Buckinghamshire.

They gave the horses their heads after that stop and, watching the sun, Nicholas realised they were heading south-west of Newmarket. Eventually Freddie pulled up as they came over the top of a rise.

A substantial grey stone house lay comfortably in a swell of the hillside, terraced gardens running down to the stream below. 'Fulbrook Hall,' Freddie remarked. 'My godmama's place.' He pressed his horse into a canter again, jumped neatly over the gate into the parkland and led the way through an old Tudor gatehouse towards a sprawling stable block.

The head groom came out as they clattered through the arch into the yard. 'My lord! Good morning, gentlemen. Have you come to see the bay gelding, my lord? Lord Ellwood's gone over to the hunt kennels to see the new puppies, but he should be back in ten minutes or so. Would you care to go over to the house and I'll send a boy to tell him you're here?'

'No, it's all right, Griggs, we'll wait.'

'Did you say Ellwood?' Nicholas demanded abruptly, once the man had turned away, calling to the stable boy.

'Yes.' Freddie looked surprised at his friend's tone. 'Do you know them?'

'No,' said Nicholas slowly. 'No…I just thought I might know someone who is part of their house party this week.' Hell and damnation! Of all the houses, it had to be the one where the Knights were staying. He had known they were not far from Freddie's place—why the devil had he not had the sense to ask Freddie where they were going?

Ellwood was bound to ask them back to the house once he and Freddie had finished discussing the horse—how the blazes could he refuse to join them? Meeting Camilla seemed inevitable. If that were the case then he needed to clear his head and prepare for the encounter.

Freddie was heading with single-minded interest towards the horse-boxes. Nicholas put a hand on his arm. 'Look, old chap, those terraced gardens are just the sort of thing I was thinking of having done at Ashby. You wait for his lordship, I'll stroll over and have a look at them for half an hour.'

Freddie turned, a look of astonishment on his amiable face. '*Gardens?* Damn it, Nick…' But his friend was already striding through the archway. Lord Corsham pushed his hat back and scratched his head in puzzlement. 'Nick's behaving damned oddly. Must be in love…'

Chapter Nine

'This stage is quite superb,' Stephen said enthusiastically, taking Camilla's arm as they strolled out through the yew arch on to a gently sloping lawn, enclosed by high hedges and ending in a low turf platform.

'It is lovely,' Camilla agreed, looking round at the fresh greenery of the sprouting yew against the close shaved turf. 'But do you think the audience will be able to hear well?' She looked up at him, a little frown of concern between her arched brows.

Stephen Knight looked down into his cousin's beautiful face and came to the conclusion that he must indeed be a man in love. Camilla glanced away, unaware of his thoughts, measuring distances with practised, narrowed eyes.

'Cousin Stephen, could you go down the lawn half-way, perhaps—I do not think the audience would extend back from the stage any more than that, do you?' She smiled at him, and he reflected that her air of decision, which in another woman might seem merely bossy, was charming.

He walked away, turned and saw she had climbed

the three steps on to the turf platform. She raised a hand to shade her eyes and called, 'A little further back…there, that is perfect.' And she smiled, a smile of pure pleasure, and Stephen looked at the tall slender figure in the pale green muslin gown, jonquil ribbons fluttering from her blonde hair, knotted high for the morning.

Yes, he thought, it must be love. If he could look at all that loveliness and still want Ophelia, not her sister, then he could be sure of his own heart. Ophelia was not as perfect, not as intelligent, not as poised…yet it was Ophelia who made his heart beat faster, who could make his normally fluent tongue stumble over the most commonplace words. But she was very young, and her elder sister not yet betrothed—under such circumstances would Mrs Knight consent to an engagement?

Camilla lifted the pages of script in her hand and took a moment to choose her piece. She felt almost happy this morning. The sun was shining, she was acting again, among friends. Almost she could forget Nicholas. She took a steadying breath and launched into Miranda's words on first seeing Ferdinand. *'I might call him a thing divine, for nothing natural I ever saw so noble.'*

'That was perfect,' Stephen called, strolling back towards the stage. 'I could hear every word. The only problem will be if we cannot all achieve the same projection of our voices as you can.'

'I am sure everyone will manage perfectly well with a little practice. Shall we try a scene now we are here?' Camilla asked as he joined her on the platform.

'I fear you will show me up dreadfully, dear

Camilla. Everyone spoke of your talent, but I had
no idea how beautiful your voice was. Why, if it
were not such a shocking thing to say, one would
think you almost a professional.'

It was indeed a shocking thing to say, and it explained why Camilla coloured and turned hastily
away. 'Oh, I have had lots of practice. After all, we
have been play-acting together for years,' she said
modestly. 'Shall we try this scene?'

Stephen took his part and conned the pages.
'Here?' He cleared his throat and read, his voice
strong and clear in the morning air.

> *'Wherefore weep you?'*
> *'At mine unworthiness, that dare not offer*
> *what I desire to give; and much less take*
> *what I shall die to want...'*

The words came back to her with perfect clarity.
The pages of the script fell unheeded from her fingers and she was back on the stage at Bath playing
Miranda, the heroine. Stephen, swept along with her
reading of the verse, found himself gazing not into
Camilla's eyes, but into Miranda's. The garden
around him became Prospero's island and he
stepped towards her, his face rapt with the magic of
Shakespeare's love poetry as Miranda declared her
love for the young prince Ferdinand of Naples.

'I am your wife if you will marry me.' She took
his hands, her gaze intent upon his face.

> *'If not I'll die your maid. To be your fellow*
> *You may deny me, but I'll be your servant*
> *Whether you will or no.'*

Stephen, in thrall to the part, gathered her into his arms and a silence fell as she finished speaking.

Then the tranquillity was broken by the sound of one pair of hands slowly applauding. Stephen, expecting no one but another member of the house party, hardly moved, but in his arms Camilla froze. Her expression of shock slowly turned to dismay, and at that he did turn, to see a tall stranger standing regarding them sardonically from the nearest archway. No wonder Cousin Camilla was embarrassed— to anyone not aware of the house party's theatrical plans it would appear a most compromising and improper scene.

The man was wearing riding dress which Stephen, a man always careful of his own appearance, recognised as coming from the hands of a master tailor. 'Weston!' he exclaimed, his voice carrying clearly in the clear morning air.

'Schultz, actually,' Nicholas corrected drily, strolling towards them, hat and whip in hand.

Camilla stood staring at the two men, her head in a whirl. Why were they talking about *tailors*? And, more to the point, what was Nicholas doing here? Her heart jolted painfully as she watched him move confidently across the short cut lawn: the length of his stride emphasised by the leg-hugging riding-breeches, the polish on his high-topped boots, the sunshine glancing off his dark, burnished head. She fought down the impulse to throw herself into his arms, cover him with kisses, tell him how much he was filling her thoughts day and night.

His next words drove all thoughts of love out of her head. 'I do not think I have heard such feeling and projection since the last time I was in the Theatre Royal in Bath.'

Camilla felt the blood draining out of her cheeks. She stared at him, the realisation of what had just happened sinking home. He had seen her act as Mademoiselle Davide. In Bath she had chosen to ignore the slight references he had made, the hints he had dropped that he might have guessed at her secret. But now he had seen her—Camilla Knight—acting, as well as she had ever acted. And he was letting her know that he knew she was Mademoiselle Davide.

Ruin was staring her in the face, yet there he was, shaking hands with Stephen, introducing himself as though they had met at White's, acting as if this were a normal social occasion. Would he betray her? Surely he was too much of a gentleman to do so deliberately, but then a slip of the tongue, a little too much wine over the gaming tables, a word in the wrong ear and the world of the Knight family would come crashing down. All hopes for Ophelia's come-out would be dashed, all hopes of the affection that she was sure was budding between Ophelia and her cousin Stephen would be at an end.

Nicholas looked up from where he was standing with Stephen and made a bow. 'Miss Knight.'

She bowed stiffly in return. 'My lord.'

Stephen, a sociable man, was delighted at the discovery that the two were acquainted. 'You know each other, then? But of course, from your reference to the theatre may I assume that you too have just come from Bath? A fine city with many diversions.'

Nicholas smiled thinly. 'Indeed, I found it most…diverting. The theatre, the Sydney Gardens, the rides…'

The colour had returned to Camilla's face with a rush. She knew she was blushing. To cover her confusion she turned away and strolled to the turf steps down to the lawn. But it only gave Nicholas the opportunity to walk towards her and offer his hand to assist her descent.

She forced herself to meet his gaze and was startled by the chill of his blue eyes and the hard set of his mouth. It seemed that he was still angry with her, as angry as he had been as they parted company in the Sydney Gardens.

Low-voiced she asked, 'Have you received my letter?'

'I have received nothing from you,' he replied in clipped tones.

Mr Knight, seemingly oblivious to the atmosphere, enquired if his lordship would join them in the drawing-room for a glass of Canary. 'Not that this is my establishment,' he added hastily, 'but Lord Ellwood is out and about his estate and I am sure he would wish me to offer your lordship his hospitality.'

'Thank you, Mr Knight, but I am here with a friend. A small matter of a horse he wishes to discuss with Lord Ellwood—he is down at the stables now, awaiting his lordship's return.' His tone with Stephen was pleasant but guarded and his eyes on the young man were assessing. If it were not for the fact that he had made it all too clear that everything between them was over, she might almost have thought him jealous. But that could not be; it appeared that Nicholas Lovell did not forgive and was prepared to extend his dislike to her friends, Camilla reflected bitterly.

To her relief the scene was interrupted by the arrival of Freddie and Lord Ellwood, a gun-dog at their heels.

'There you are, Nick!' Freddie called. He turned to Lord Ellwood to make the introductions, then waited, smiling genially, as Lord Ellwood, in his turn, introduced his house guests.

Freddie bowed to Camilla, his eyes sparkling at the sight of such a beautiful young woman. 'Miss Knight, how do you do? And Mr Knight. Your brother, I presume?'

Camilla was probably the only one who heard Nicholas murmur, 'Hardly brotherly behaviour!' She ignored his reference to the scene he had interrupted and, obviously, misinterpreted. Her heart gave a little jump. Could he be jealous?

'Mr Knight is my cousin, Lord Corsham. Do you make a long stay in the country? The weather is so very pleasant, and the countryside so green: we are finding it such a refreshment after residing in Bath.'

Freddie fell in beside her as the entire group strolled back towards the house. He was not the most perceptive young man in the world, but there was something about Miss Knight that piqued him, piqued his memory. Surely he would have remembered such a gem if he had met her before, yet there was something about the timbre of her voice, her gracious carriage, the turn of her head on that long neck...

He pulled himself together and replied to her questions. 'Not sure how long I'm staying, Miss

Knight, but my mother felt I'd been away from the estates too long so it's goodbye to the attractions of Bath and Town for a while. Still, Lovell's keeping me company, and Mama always enjoys Nick's company. Feels it's a challenge to get him married off, don't you know. Mind you, she says he's impossible to please. Still, she won't give up.'

Camilla, only too aware of Nicholas's rigid back ahead of them, could not resist dropping a barb to test whether Nicholas was listening. 'Oh hush, Lord Corsham,' she said lightly with a little laugh, 'Lord Lovell will overhear you, and I am sure he would not wish to be the subject of tittle-tattle.'

Nicholas's neck, between the line of his freshly trimmed hair and the collar of his coat, reddened. So he was listening, as aware of her as she was of him.

Lady Ellwood was very pleased to find her drawing-room full of unexpected guests, especially her godson, of whom she was inordinately fond. Freddie dropped a kiss on her cheek and, settling in a chair beside her with a glass of Canary, brought her up to date with all the news from his mama.

Lord Ellwood, Stephen and Nicholas seemed deep in conversation on the subject of gun-dogs, but Camilla was constantly aware of his cool gaze flicking over her from time to time. She felt very exposed: Mama and Ophelia had joined the two Mrs Ellwoods in a carriage drive, and never had she wanted their presence so much.

The morning was so warm that the long floor-to-ceiling windows had been opened fully. Camilla stood by one of them, grateful for the cooling breeze on her cheek, and tried to order her emotions.

Standing across the room from her, watching her coldly, was the man she loved, the man in whose hands not only her reputation but that of her entire family rested. She wanted to throw herself into his arms and kiss him, yet she wanted to hit him for being so cold, so seemingly hostile. She was so afraid of what he might do with the knowledge of her secret, yet through the fear anger too was rising. He knew, he must have known almost from the beginning about her double life—just how did he intend to use that knowledge?

Abruptly she ducked under the raised sash and stepped down on to the flagged terrace. No one called after her, so she ran lightly down the steps and into the sunken rose garden where she could sit, hidden from the house. With a soft moan she put her head in her hands, cupping her hot cheeks in her palms. How could she desire Nicholas so much yet be so angry with him? How could she love him so, yet be so fearful of his motives? Surely being in love with someone shouldn't be this painful, this confusing?

'You cannot keep running away from me, Camilla.' He had followed her and was standing a few feet away, his arms crossed, his face as hard as his voice.

Camilla sprang to her feet. 'I am not running away,' she denied hotly. 'I just do not choose to be in your company.'

'Indeed? I would have thought you would be seeking me out, imploring me to keep your secret.' His eyes were blue chips of ice and she felt her own anger rising to meet his. At last he was being plain with her, at last he was admitting he knew she was Lysette Davide.

'I would have thought that unnecessary. I believed that your *honour* as a gentleman would have assured your silence. I have obviously misjudged you.' It was taking all her composure and her training to stop her voice from shaking with the anger that suffused her frame.

Nicholas smiled without warmth, without humour. 'Madam, I would do everything in my power, upon my *honour*, to protect the reputation of a *lady*.'

Camilla gasped as though he had thrown cold water over her. 'You…you…' She took two angry steps towards him, raising her hand, fingers curled.

'No, you don't, you hellcat.' He grasped her wrists, his fingers curling tightly around the thin bones and holding fast. 'If you had let me finish I would have added that your sister and your mother are both ladies whose reputations I would do much to protect.'

'And I, I suppose, can go to the Devil?' she asked wildly, her breath tight in her breast.

'Well, madam, you seem hell-bent on getting there without help from me. I hardly expected you to mope when we were apart, but I had not realised the speed with which you would be looking for the next likely mark. Mr Stephen Knight inherited the family estates, did he not? He has no title, of course, but I am sure that sort of financial security is attractive.'

Camilla stopped struggling; it hurt her wrists too much. Fighting for composure, she said icily, 'My friends are not of your business, but I believe I told you when we first met that I am not the sort of actress that could be bought.'

'Gifts of money—or anything else, come to that—hardly seem necessary in your case.' He stood looking down into her furious eyes. 'Every time you have been in my arms it seems all I need to do is this.' And he released one wrist, running the back of his fingers down her cheekbone, down to the swell of her breast.

Camilla reacted, but fractionally, fatally, betrayingly too late. His touch mesmerised her, set the blood in her veins alight. But it was not that which held her still for that fatal second: it was his face, softened suddenly as those hatefully cold eyes dropped from hers and his lips parted slightly as his fingers touched her skin.

Her freed hand came up, but unlike in Sydney Gardens he was ready for her. 'Oh, no, Camilla, you do not get a second chance.' Her wrist was back in that hard, imprisoning grasp and she was jerked against his chest, held tight as he found her mouth and kissed her.

He had kissed her before and each time it had been a kiss which had lived in her memory, coloured her dreams, sent her pulses racing. But this was a kiss meant to punish, to show his anger, to assert himself as master and not a man enslaved by a woman's charms.

Camilla tightened her lips into a thin line, fought with every muscle in her neck and back to resist him and kicked futilely with her thin slippers against his leather-booted shins. He responded by holding her even closer, crushing her breasts against his coat-front, seemingly seeking to draw every breath from her body.

Just when she felt sure she would swoon, he let go of her and she staggered back, grasping the arm of the bench to stay upright. Nicholas's eyes raked her coldly, taking in the crushed muslin and the disarrayed curls. 'You have my word I will say or do nothing which would harm your sister and mother. But you, madam, had better look to your behaviour. If you persist in throwing yourself at every man who crosses your path you will have no need of my assistance in betraying yourself. Or is your unfortunate cousin your insurance, your key to a *respectable* future?'

Nicholas spun on his heel and stalked back towards the house. There was the sound of voices on the terrace and then she heard Nicholas, his voice assured, calm, as though he had spent the last ten minutes discussing the weather, joining the conversation.

Camilla ran across the rose garden away from the voices, in through the open breakfast-room windows and up the stairs to the sanctuary of her room. Mercifully no one saw her.

She slammed the door behind her, turned the key in the lock and threw herself across the bed, pummelling a wild tattoo on the pillows with her clenched fists. 'I hate you, I hate you, I hate you!' she cried, her voice muffled against the bedding. Finally, out of breath, she rolled over on to her back and lay, gazing upwards, unseeing, the beautifully moulded plaster ceiling a mere blur.

Time passed, marked only by the chime of the little clock above the fireplace. Finally, as it struck the hour, she sat up, some semblance of calm restored. So this was real life, this was the reality she had been ignoring for so long, over-confident in the belief that her scandalous double life would never be discovered.

She had taken to the stage with all the courage of ignorance, a blind belief that she would always remain undetected. And as time had passed the belief had grown to the point where the nagging fear had dwindled into nothing and she had felt invincible in her deception.

Well, it had taken one man to shatter that illusion. One man to teach her that not only could she not keep her secret but she could not flirt with love. And now she had paid the price on both counts. The man she loved thought she was an immoral, deceitful hussy. The gossips of Bath were shredding her reputation and she had shocked herself to the core by the discovery of her own deeply sensual nature. Even now, hating Nicholas as she did, she knew that if he walked in, smiled at her, kissed her, caressed her, she would melt into his arms again.

For an independent, spirited, intelligent woman this was a humiliating discovery to make.

'There, that is the last of the invitations,' Lady Ellwood said with satisfaction, passing it to the younger Mrs Ellwood, who added it to a neat stack of gilt-edged cards.

Camilla laid aside the volume of Scott's *Waverley* without much regret and asked, 'How many is that?' The stack by her hostess's hand looked somewhat larger than she had imagined it would be.

'Forty, all told, but I doubt whether we will get

more than thirty acceptances. The Hodgkinsons are
away with his mother in Harrogate and I have invited the Canon, but he rarely accepts social invitations. Lady Browne may or may not…it will all
depend on her bad leg.'

Camilla paused to steady her breathing and then
enquired in a tone of studied nonchalance, 'Have
you invited the Corshams?'

Lady Ellwood rose from her escritoire and
crossed the drawing-room to tug the bell-pull. 'Tea,
I think, my dears.' She settled in a rustling of puce
draperies next to Camilla, picking up the novel as
she did so. 'Ah! Sir Walter Scott. How are you finding this one? I have just finished *Guy Mannering*,
which I found somewhat slow in places.'

'I agree. To be honest, Lady Ellwood, I do not
know why I persist with Scott; I am always disappointed. I will put this one aside and re-read *Emma*.
But you were saying about the Corshams?' She
wanted to add 'and their guests' but dared not.

'Indeed, so I was. Ah, there you are, Wilkins. Tea,
if you please, and a plate of macaroons if Cook has
any to hand.'

'Yes, my lady.' The footman bowed himself out
and Camilla fought down the desire to scream.

'The Corshams?' she prompted again, wondering
if it were her imagination or if Mrs Francis Ellwood
was regarding her with interest.

No, she was not mistaken. 'Why, Miss Knight,'
said Mrs Francis in a rallying tone. 'I declare you
are very anxious to hear about the Corshams' party.
Can it be that a certain young gentleman has the
fortune to have attracted your sympathies?'

Camilla felt the blush spreading to her very hairline. 'Oh, indeed not! Why…why it is simply that it is such a very large house party from all accounts, and I know so few of them…' Oh, what a mull she was making of this! If the other ladies had not been suspicious of Nicholas and herself before, they certainly were now, thanks to her embarrassed reaction.

Lady Ellwood regarded her with approving interest. 'Well, so that is how the land lies! Of course, I am very biased, but he is a wonderful catch: how he has remained single for so long defeats me.'

If the earth had opened up to swallow her Camilla would have been thankful. All she could do, while wondering wildly how Lady Ellwood came to know so much about Nicholas, was murmur, 'He is?'

'Of course!' Lady Ellwood looked surprised. 'The Corshams are a very old family, very distinguished. And of course the estates have always been so well managed. Added to that there is all the property in London too.'

'Oh!' Camilla felt quite dizzy with relief. 'Oh, you mistake me! I hardly know Lord Corsham—the merest acquaintance—although obviously the most amiable gentleman—there is not the slightest attachment between us, not on either side…'

I am protesting too much, she thought wildly. But fortunately further conversation was forestalled by the arrival of tea, and the necessity of giving Wilkins detailed instructions on the delivery of the invitations.

The weather continued warm and dry for the rest of the week, much to Lady Ellwood's relief. If it had been inclement they would have had to repair to the ballroom, but in its classical perfection it was hardly reminiscent of a scented isle, complete with spirits and shipwrecked sailors.

On the night of the performance the ladies were gathered to don their costumes and *maquillage* upstairs in Lady Ellwood's large dressing-room. The Misses Williams had enthusiastically agreed to make up the number of Spirits required, and their mama had been placated by the utter respectability of their garb. Camilla had reflected privately that no Spirit could have moved through the air in that quantity of fabric, but they made a pretty enough ensemble.

Mrs Knight was still clucking about Ophelia's costume, although after much work with the blue pencil the role of Ariel had been rendered suitably anodyne. 'Oh, the skirts of your tunic...' she wailed. 'Whatever you do, do not spin round and show your ankles!' She tweaked at her younger daughter's hems and enquired anxiously, 'Are you wearing both petticoats?'

'Yes, Mama,' Ophelia replied dutifully, edging her bare feet well out of sight under the chair. Her eyes were sparking and her colour high. Her mama put it down to excitement and stage nerves: what her feelings would have been if she had realised that Ophelia had every intention of luring her cousin Stephen into the conservatory that evening in the hope of provoking a declaration, heaven only knows.

Mrs Francis Ellwood, who was possessed of both a sharp eye and an equally sharp tongue, was watching Camilla. She was untwisting her hair from the rags in which she had knotted it all day, and arranging it carefully into the disarrayed locks suitable to a young woman stranded on a desert island.

'You are very quiet, Miss Knight,' Mrs Ellwood observed. 'Are you suffering from stage fright?'

'Oh, yes, indeed,' Camilla replied glibly. In fact she had no fear of either the audience or of the quality of this excellent amateur performance. No, it was the knowledge that Nicholas would be there, watching her. He would be able to compare her acting tonight with what he had seen in Bath. Then the thought struck her: there was another danger. Nicholas, after all, already knew the worst; this evening's performance would not change his opinion of her one whit. But Lord Corsham had also seen her act in Bath—what if he, seeing her tonight, put two and two together?

Then Lady Ellwood's betoqued head appeared around the door. 'Hurry, my dears, all is ready for us to begin!'

Swept along with the discipline of long practice, Camilla's mind cleared of all other thoughts and fears. Treading carefully in her bare feet, ignoring her mother's shriek as she realised that both her daughters were scandalously unshod and stockingless, she made her way downstairs and across the lawn.

The applause that greeted the final act was tumultuous. As she took her bows between Lord Ellwood, robed and bearded as Prospero, and Stephen, flushed with triumph as Ferdinand, she felt once again the familiar rush of excitement and achievement.

The principals stepped back to let the more minor players take their bows, followed by a bashful group

of footmen and bootboys who had been pressed into
service as shipwrecked mariners.

Lord Ellwood was almost incoherent with admiration. 'My dear, you were magnificent. Equal, if not
above, anything I have seen in Drury Lane. Why,
one would have believed you were indeed in love
with Ferdinand—all, of course, in the most refined
taste, as one would expect of you.'

The applause swelled again and the three of them
moved into the centre of the stage to receive the
approbation of the invited guests. Camilla curtseyed
low, and on either side the men raised her hands to
their lips in gallant salutation.

Defiantly she raised her head and stared out over
the improvised footlights into the blurred faces beyond. Virtually everyone had accepted the invitations, over forty people had attended, but it was
Nicholas she sought, and Nicholas she found.

Their eyes met and locked, his dark and stony,
hers bright with excitement and challenge. Suddenly
seized by the desire to shock Nicholas out of his
coldness, Camilla turned to Stephen, who was at her
side, and threw her arms around him. Automatically
her cousin picked up the cue, and they stood locked
in the theatrical embrace which had marked their
final kiss in the performance.

As Stephen released her Camilla sought
Nicholas's eyes again defiantly, but he was no
longer looking at her. His head was bent as he
brushed a speck from the sleeve of his impeccable
evening-coat. By contrast, beside him Freddie
Corsham was clapping with gusto, his ingenuous
face beaming, his voice ringing out, 'Bravo! Bravo!'

Dear Freddie, far too conventional, far too stolid

ever to imagine that a woman like Miss Knight could have led a double life. No, there was nothing to fear from Lord Corsham.

Finally the applause died down and everyone trooped back to the Red Saloon for refreshments. Mrs Knight, scolding furiously, hurried her daughters upstairs and insisted on them putting on stockings and shoes before they could join the rest. 'What can you have been thinking about? Ophelia, as soon as you have tied your garters put on this fichu. Camilla, where is your shawl? You will catch your death…'

The Knights descended the staircase, modestly shod, silk shawls draped over their elbows, and found themselves instantly the centre of attention. All the men clustered round and Ophelia, more than a little piqued, realised that all their attention was on her sister. Even Stephen, she observed with acute annoyance, had taken Camilla's hand and showed no sign of wanting to let it go.

Nicholas had not been the only one to observe that final embrace on stage with anger. Ophelia found herself quite cross with her elder sister: surely she could not be casting out lures for Stephen? She told herself that it was simply the thrill of the performance: still, it would not do to take risks with the man she was now convinced she loved. Unaware that Lord Lovell was observing the play of emotions on her pretty face, she let her brow furrow in thought.

Lady Ellwood had sent round the champagne and Camilla accepted a glass from Freddie, releasing her hand as she did so with a smiling glance at Stephen. Behind him she saw Nicholas, his face unfriendly as his glance took in both the clasped hands and the shared smile.

Stephen stepped back and was lost to her sight in the crowd which immediately surrounded him. Feeling suddenly vulnerable, she turned to Freddie. 'Did you enjoy the performance, Lord Corsham?'

'I'll say I did! Dashed fine, and you, Miss Knight, were magnificent!'

'You are fond of the theatre, my lord?'

'Indeed, yes! Don't understand many of the plays, unless they're comedies, of course—too much philosophising. But I enjoy the acting and the atmosphere. And I have to say, Miss Knight, that you were equal to anything I have seen on the professional stage. Why, I would have to say you are as good in your talent as Mademoiselle Davide of the Theatre Royal in Bath.'

A very dry voice remarked, 'Really Freddie, what a very shocking thing to say to Miss Knight.'

Freddie blushed furiously and shot his friend a hunted look. 'I say, Miss Knight, I do apologise. Lovell, damn good thing you stopped me there. Oh damn…I mean, I apologise for my language, Miss Knight. Don't know what came over me! Not that I meant that you and she were in any way the same…I mean you are a lady…er…'

'Stop digging, Freddie,' Nicholas remarked, not unkindly. 'I think the hole is quite large enough already.'

'There is Godmama waving at me,' Freddie burbled frantically. 'Please excuse me, Miss Knight…'

There was a long silence. It was finally broken when Camilla said frostily, 'Poor Lord Corsham.

You did not have to put him to the blush in that way. It was not kind.'

Nicholas shrugged. 'I thought it for the best. You should thank me: he is unlikely to speculate again on any similarities between yourself and Mademoiselle Davide.'

Camilla, knowing he was right, but in no mood to forgive him, watched silently as he turned to take two more glasses of champagne from a passing footman. Erect and immaculate in the formal evening wear, Nicholas was by far the most striking man in the room, but in contrast to the laughing faces all around, his was set and cold, his eyes glittering.

She glanced round, hoping no one had noticed the tense exchange between them, and realised she had lost sight of her sister. Instinctively she cast round for their cousin. Nicholas, observing her scrutiny enquired, 'Who are you looking for?'

Startled by his abrupt question, Camilla replied without thinking, 'Stephen.'

Still conning the room, she did not notice Nicholas's lips tighten. Then she saw the backs of Stephen and Ophelia disappearing into the conservatory. Ah, good. If their cousin did not declare himself tonight, he was not the man she thought he was. A small smile touched her lips as Nicholas turned back and handed her a glass.

'Something amuses you.' It was a statement, not a question.

'Why should it not?' she replied coolly. 'Everyone is enjoying themselves—except, apparently, you, my lord.'

'Indeed, you seem to have had quite a little triumph.'

'And you grudge me that? How ungracious you are, my lord.' The glass she raised to her lips was not quite steady.

'You are very unconciliatory for someone so much in my power,' Nicholas remarked tightly.

'In your power?' Camilla's brows arched haughtily. 'Why, indeed, I might be, but I have no fear that you would say anything to cause Mama and Ophelia distress. If you betray me, you betray them.'

'You are pleased to be confident in me, Miss Knight.'

'I have every confidence that you would do nothing to diminish your own good opinion of yourself, my lord,' she fired back. 'Excuse me, there are other people I wish to speak to. Friends of mine.'

Weaving her way through the crowd, exchanging nods and pleasantries and receiving compliments as she went, Camilla finally found herself alone on the terrace. She held up her hot face to the cool rays of the moon. An owl hooted from across the park but otherwise she was alone, and the noise from the room behind was cut off abruptly as the heavy curtain swung back across the window.

So that was that then. There could be no going back from that chilly parting. Not wanting to be disturbed, Camilla trod slowly down the mossy steps and into the shadows of the topiary which dotted the lawns. As she did so the noise from the reception room swelled again and instinctively she turned, drawing back against a yew peacock.

A shaft of moonlight suddenly pierced the light, high cloud and illuminated the man standing on the terrace as surely as a theatre limelight. Nicholas, a champagne flute in his hand, stood for a long moment scanning the garden. Then he said out loud suddenly, viciously, 'Oh, to hell with it. To hell with it all,' and threw the glass into the darkness.

There was a sharp tinkle as it hit the slender trunk of a young tree and then he was gone.

Chapter Ten

At ten o'clock the next morning Camilla sat at the breakfast table tearing pieces off a bread roll and sipping at her now cold tea. Her preoccupation was fortunately going unnoticed amongst her companions, who were variously suffering the effects of too much excitement, too much champagne and too little sleep.

Only Ophelia was bright and breezy, her voice loud and animated, causing her mama to say repressively, 'Do try for a little moderation in your volume, my dear, we are all feeling rather fatigued this morning.'

No one but Camilla appeared to notice how Ophelia's eyes sparkled and what an uncommonly pretty gown she had put on that morning. Camilla could hazard a shrewd guess as to why her sister had threaded pink ribbons through her hair to match the rose quartz necklace encircling her neck and why she was almost bubbling with expectation and excitement.

Her suspicions were confirmed when there was

the sound of hoofbeats on the drive, followed shortly by the bang of the knocker on the front door.

Lord Ellwood clutched his aching forehead and grumbled, 'Who on earth is calling at this hour?'

His elder daughter-in-law got to her feet and peered carefully around the draperies at the long window. 'I do believe it is Mr Stephen Knight's horse—that handsome new bay he was riding the other day.'

No sooner had she spoken than the sound of Stephen Knight's voice was heard in the hall and the butler appeared. 'Mr Knight has called requesting the favour of a word with Mrs Knight, my lady. I have shown him into the Blue Salon, madam, while I enquire if Mrs Knight is at home to visitors.'

A look of puzzlement crossed Mrs Knight's face. 'Mr Knight? For me? I cannot conceive what that might be about. Perhaps a problem with one of our old servants... Would you excuse me for a moment, Emma dear?'

Camilla shot Ophelia a very hard stare, but her sister looked back at her with wide, innocent blue eyes. 'More tea, Camilla?'

Aware that Mrs Francis Ellwood was watching the by-play with her usual beady regard, Camellia merely said, 'Thank you, Ophelia,' and passed her cup.

A silence fell, during which no one was so ill-bred as to speculate on the reasons for Mr Knight's early visit. After ten minutes or so the door to the breakfast room opened again on the butler. 'Miss Ophelia, Mrs Knight requests your presence in the Blue Salon.'

Ophelia laid her napkin down with great care,

stood up, smoothing the skirts of her pretty muslin gown, and followed the black-clad figure with a demure smile of apology to her hostess.

This time Mrs Francis Ellwood could hardly contain herself until the door shut once more. 'Well!' she exclaimed, putting down her chocolate cup with emphasis. 'We can all guess what that is about!'

'Can we?' Camilla asked, calmly and repressively.

Mrs Francis was not to be snubbed. 'Oh, you think your mama might not agree to Mr Knight's proposing to your sister as you yourself are not betrothed? After all it is unusual for the younger sister to be turned off first.' Her black eyes were snapping with excitement and a not unpleasurable sense of the elder Miss Knight's discomfiture. After all, as she would observe later to her sister-in-law, Mrs Charles, 'A charming and talented enough young woman, but she does put herself forward for an unmarried girl. Her sister's success will perhaps put her nose out of joint.'

Lady Ellwood, sensitive to the undercurrents around her breakfast table, chided her daughter-in-law gently. 'Yes, we really should not speculate on such a delicate matter. Lord Ellwood, will you be dining at home this evening? I must tell Cook how many covers are required.'

At that point Mrs Knight almost burst into the breakfast-room, her face glowing with excitement, her hands clasped tightly to her bosom. 'Camilla dearest, Emma, dear friends...such joy! Dear Mr Knight—Stephen—has asked for little Ophelia's hand! Such a surprise, such a happiness!'

Lord Ellwood, ever practical, remarked, 'An excellent match, and brings the estate back into the family to boot! You are to be congratulated, madam.'

Mrs Knight, much struck by this thought, sank down in her chair, her handkerchief clasped in her hand. 'Oh, yes, how happy her poor dear lamented papa would have been to see this day!' And promptly burst into tears.

What with mopping up her mama's tears, receiving congratulations from the assembled guests and then, somewhat belatedly, repairing to the Blue Salon to chaperon the newly engaged couple, Camilla did not have much leisure at first to continue brooding on her own troubles.

Her sister and cousin, although receiving her good wishes politely, made no secret of their desire to be alone. Mindful of her mama's wishes, Camilla could not allow that, but she did retire behind a large potted palm and gave them what privacy propriety would allow.

The lovers withdrew to the bay window and, heads close together, exchanged murmured conversation. Camilla sat back and tried to discipline her mind to making lists of items for her sister's trousseau. Then she realised the others had fallen silent, and in parting the fronds saw that Stephen had bent his head to kiss Ophelia gently on the lips.

It was such a chaste, touching and innocent caress that Camilla felt a lump rising to her throat. She had not the heart to intervene and drew back into her corner. But all hope of occupying her mind with wedding lists had been shattered by the sight of that salute. Unknowingly her fingers strayed to her lips, as though feeling again that last angry, punishing kiss that Nicholas had pressed on them in the rose garden.

He would never kiss her now with that gentle adoration that Stephen was showing her sister. Perhaps once there had been a glimmer of hope for them, but now all that was left was the anger and mistrust and that undeniable sensual attraction that sparked between them whenever they touched.

Finally her mama reappeared and Stephen reluctantly took his leave, agreeing plans for the ladies to spend the next day at Nevile's Place, where Mrs Knight could indulge in an orgy of list-making and Ophelia could reacquaint herself with what would be her new home.

Amid the excited bustle of the house, Camilla slipped away into a corner and tried to concentrate on being happy for her sister and not on thinking about a pair of hard blue eyes finding hers across the garden as the play came to an end.

The owner of those same blue eyes was at that moment standing beside Lord Corsham on the banks of his trout lake, which his friend regarded with deep displeasure. 'Damn me if it's not those poachers,' Freddie was saying. 'I keep giving orders for it to be restocked, but every time I go fishing I never catch a darned thing.'

Nicholas stooped to pick up a stick and stirred the mud at the lake edge with it. Freddie, glowering moodily at the water, skimmed a stone across the glittering surface as if hoping to provoke a rise of fish. They stood together silently, Freddie's mind entirely on fishing, Nicholas's on something quite different.

He stirred the muddy water unseeingly, his mind's eye full of Camilla: her slender form caught up in Stephen Knight's embrace on stage, her passion as she declared the lines of the play, the defiance as she deliberately sought his eyes across that crowded garden.

God! He wanted her: wanted to kiss her, undress her, make love to her... He should never have kissed her like that in the rose garden. It was not her he had been angry with, it was himself—and he had taken that anger out on her. Why had he let himself get involved with a woman like that? A woman in her position? She was everything he had hoped of finding in a wife—and she was totally ineligible. Gripping the stick, he hurled it with all his strength at the opposite reed bed, sending a heron flapping upwards in panic and showering Freddie with muddy water.

'I say! Dammit, this is a new shooting jacket, Nick!' He glanced up as more droplets fell. 'Oh, hell, now it's raining! And if we go back to the house we'll be driven out of every room by giggling girls. What was my mother thinking about asking them all to stay?'

'Let's run away, Freddie,' Nick suggested abruptly, hunching his shoulders against the sudden shower. 'Now—today.'

Freddie drew him under a sheltering willow. 'Good idea, but where? London's dead, too early for Brighton, no hunting, too early for shooting anything decent...'

Nicholas frowned. Where indeed? Anywhere without memories of Camilla Knight would do. At that moment, like a messenger from the gods in answer to their question, a rather damp footman rounded the coppice.

'Letter for you, my lord,' he called as he drew near, adding rather darkly, 'Mr Finnan said I was to bring it out, said you wouldn't be far from the house.' He glanced down at his mud-spattered stockings and pulled his jacket tighter around his shoulders.

'Thank you, Jenkins. Cut along back now. No point in you getting any wetter. Come on, Nick, we're half-way between the house and the village—let's go down to the Corsham Arms and have a brandy by the fire.'

Ten minutes later the two of them were sitting comfortably, legs thrust out towards a crackling fire, the soles of their boots steaming gently and bumpers of the landlord's best brandy at their elbows.

'And not a woman in sight,' said Freddie gratefully, slitting the seal on his letter. 'Oh! It's from George—says Bath's pretty dull now that Mademoiselle Davide's no longer there and we've gone. Says he hasn't forgotten that wager and time's running out...' He conned the rest of the page and added, 'Here we are, the answer to our prayer! George says, had we heard about a big mill near Buckingham in three days' time?'

'A prize-fight?' Nicholas raised an interested eyebrow. 'Who's involved?'

'Alfred Dyson, the Slough Bull, and the challenger is some character called Patrick Shaughnessy. Never heard of him, but George writes that he's trained with Thomas Cribb and the smart money's going on him.'

'Capital! Write back to George and invite him and

Hendricks to meet us at the Black Horse in Buckingham. The mill won't be far out of town—probably at Rickett's Farm—that's where they usually hold them. Then we can all go on to Ashby afterwards and I'll promise you a week without any giggling girls! We can play cards and drink claret if nothing else.'

'Damn good idea,' Freddie agreed. 'Tell you what, I'll get my groom to hack Thunderer over along with my curricle and team and you can try him out—see what you've missed, not winning that bet over Mademoiselle Davide.' He shot Nicholas a mischievous glance. 'Don't glare at me, Nick, I've noticed you studiously ignoring my invitations to try him out while you've been here. Not like you to be a bad loser.'

'I've not lost yet; I've got until the end of the month.' Nicholas retorted, draining his glass and getting to his feet. 'Come on, it's stopped raining. Perhaps I'll throw a leg over him this afternoon.'

'Well, I suppose it is asking for a lot, expecting you to seduce a woman when you don't know where she is,' Freddie said fairly to his friend's retreating back, then wondered why the back of Nick's neck suddenly flushed red.

It was past luncheon, and still raining heavily, when the same postboy who had delivered George's letter reached the Ellwoods' estate. The butler, tutting under his breath at the damp state of the letters, brought them to his lordship on a silver salver.

'Bills, bills, one for you my dear—what handwriting your nephew has to be sure!—one for you,

Charles, another bill and a letter for you, Mrs Knight. Somewhat rain-spattered, I regret to say.'

Mrs Knight slit the seal, unfolded the single sheet within and squinted at the heavily crossed and re-crossed lines. 'Camilla dear, can you read it? It is from Miss March—our old nanny, you know,' she explained to Lady Ellwood. 'I cannot make out a word. She *will* write too close together—a habit I was always fearful she would pass on to you girls.'

Camilla rose and took the letter, smoothing down the page and scanning it in the light from the window. 'If only we could persuade her to use a second sheet, but her habits of economy die hard and she will always cross the page to save the postage. Oh dear, someone has died…ah, her brother-in-law.'

'That was hardly unexpected, my dear,' Mrs Knight intervened.

'Yes, but her sister collapsed and was quite ill, and then poor Margaret had to nurse her and the strain in turn made her…oh I cannot read this; it must be *ill*. And now there is trouble with the will and the property and can you ask Mr Brooke to look at it because of course she won't—surely that cannot be ''consume''?—oh no, it is *presume* to approach him herself.'

'What a moment to get involved with this!' Mrs Knight exclaimed in exasperation. 'Of course she cannot be expected to know of Ophelia's happiness, but even so, why she does not simply send a note to Mr Brooke herself I cannot imagine. She knows him well enough.'

'Now, Mama, do not be harsh. You know what trouble poor Marchy has always had with her sister and her nerves. And of course they are in Cheltenham, so she cannot speak to him in person.'

Mrs Knight flapped her hands irritably. 'Well, can you write to Mr Brooke, my dear, and explain? I am sure he will sort it all out in a moment. Such a capable young man,' she added to Lady Ellwood. 'Just like his dear father.'

'Very well, Mama, and I will write to Marchy as well and tell her not to worry. She sounds quite worn down, poor woman.'

Writing to Mr Brooke proved more difficult than Camilla had anticipated. She felt she needed to explain the background to Miss March's current dilemmas, but at the same time she did not feel authorised to go into too much detail about the affairs of her old nurse's sister. Two drafts of Lady Ellwood's expensive hot-pressed paper were consigned to the waste-paper basket. One version had been too wordy, the other too abrupt. Really, it would be so much easier simply to speak to Mr Brooke direct.

Camilla put down her quill and wandered over to the window. The glass was streaked with rain and a wet peacock wandered by, his soaked tail trailing on the gravel. He looked as miserable as she felt.

Oh dear, this would get her nowhere! She felt drained by the anticlimax at the end of the play, drained by trying to be happy for Ophelia when her own heart was in pieces. The house felt like a prison. All people spoke about was weddings and lists and trousseaux; and not being able to share fully in her sister's happiness made her feel so grudging, so guilty...

Then as she sat at the desk and dipped her quill once more in the standish the idea struck Camilla.

It was so simple! She would go to Cheltenham, collect Miss March, reassure her sister that they would consult with Mr Brooke and then return home to Bath! By doing so she could leave Mama and Ophelia happily engaged in wedding plans. She would leave Nicholas far behind and in looking after Miss March and helping her with her affairs she would have something to occupy her unruly thoughts.

Dropping the pen back on its stand, Camilla sprang to her feet and ran lightly to the Blue Salon, where the ladies were sitting.

'Mama, it occurs to me that if I were to return to Bath at once and speak to Mr Brooke myself it would be much easier than trying to arrange this all by letter—and quicker too. I do not like to think of poor Miss March worried by this after all the strain she has endured these past few months. And,' she added shrewdly, 'if I return and require a chaperon, then Marchy will *have* to leave her sister. I could go to Bath by way of Cheltenham; it would not be so very far out of my way. After all, the unfortunate woman will never gather up her nerves if Marchy is always there beside her.'

Mrs Knight's furrowed brow spoke of her doubts at the wisdom or propriety of this scheme, but her elder daughter added hastily, 'And I could set in train the orders for Ophelia's trousseau. Linen and so forth. There is much that will not need a particular decision by Ophelia...and I can ensure that Miss Forbes will be free to devote herself to Ophelia's gowns.'

It worked, as Camilla had known it would. Her mother's face brightened. 'What a good scheme, my dear. And if you could have a word with Madame Le Brun about hats…she is after all, the best in Bath.'

Lady Ellwood nodded encouragingly. 'We will, of course, place both the chaise and servants at your disposal for tomorrow, Camilla, if you are determined to go.'

'Tomorrow? I had thought to set off at once.' Her mind made up, this delay seemed intolerable.

'No, no, not to be thought of,' said Lord Ellwood, who had come into the room and overheard the plans. 'That heavy rainstorm last night has brought a tree down over the millstream. The road is flooded and although they are digging drainage channels to carry the water off on to the fields it is best to leave it to tomorrow and make an early start then.'

But Camilla, fired as she was by the desire to return home—and the desire not to think about Nicholas again—remained restless. After luncheon she donned stout walking shoes and her pelisse and set off across the park, determined to see the state of the mill and the river for herself.

Despite the storm of the previous night, the day had now become warm, and she quickly took off her bonnet, swinging it by the ribbons as she squelched across the grass of the park towards the mill which she could see beyond a distant stand of trees. Everything gleamed wet and green in the watery sunshine and the smell of burgeoning growth filled her nostrils with the restless scents of spring.

Finally, panting somewhat with the effort of walking across the heavy ground, Camilla arrived close to the riverbank. The area around the old mill was thronged with men and horse teams and she craned to see what they were doing. But the bank was too high and at her feet a small ditch, its bottom silted with wet mud and weeds, barred her way.

Clear water was running off the fields into the ditch, making it far too wet to ford. Camilla decided to follow its course, certain that somewhere she would be able to cross, and sure enough after a few minutes she came upon a crossing place where an old plank had been laid from bank to bank. The track to the mill lay beyond.

Picking up her skirts, Camilla set foot cautiously on the wood. It dipped, but seemed firm enough, so she edged out towards the middle of the eight-foot span. Half-way across she began to wonder at the wisdom of what she was doing. The plank was bowing and she cast an anxious eye at the distance which yet remained.

Gingerly, she stepped forward, testing the strength of her bridge. The clear spring air was suddenly full of the sound of powerful hoofbeats and instinctively Camilla looked up to see who the rider was. As she did so, she and the plank wobbled, her precarious foothold gave way, and she teetered wildly, arms spread out for balance.

She caught a glimpse of a great black horse, of a familiar figure astride it, and heard Nicholas's voice call her name. It completely destroyed both her concentration and equilibrium. The next moment Camilla was standing up to her knees in cold water. She gasped in shock and dismayed discomfort as her shoes filled with mud, seeping through her stockings and between her toes.

Seconds later she was being dragged, none too gently, on to dry land. Nicholas was grasping her arms above the elbow, his fingers hard even through the thick pelisse. And, despite the fact that she was now out of the ditch, he showed no inclination to release the hold.

Camilla, although she would have denied it vehemently, had cherished a very detailed fantasy about the circumstances under which she and Nicholas would have their next encounter. She would be exquisitely gowned and groomed and on the arm of some impossibly handsome and unimpeachably aristocratic gentleman who had just laid his heart and his fortune at her feet. She would be able to dismiss with a cold glance the presumptuous greetings of Lord Lovell, who would, by this time, have realised how mistaken he had been in her.

And instead she was wearing a very ordinary gown, a positively dowdy pelisse, her hair was in rats'-tails from the damp wind and her skirts were mired to the knees. She could have screamed with fury and humiliation.

'Unhand me, my lord!'

'Certainly, Miss Knight.' Nicholas let go of her as abruptly as he had seized her, causing Camilla to slide once more down the slippery grass slope.

'Oh! Help!' She flailed wildly for balance, caught his gloved hand and was hauled towards him, this time on to the hard surface of the track. Her cheeks flushing hotly, Camilla realised she had nowhere to go. She could hardly flounce off over that treacherous plank—even if one could flounce with one's boots full of ditchwater. And pushing past Nicholas towards the mill would only expose her to the interested gaze of a dozen yokels.

Defiantly she raised her eyes to meet his, as if

daring him to comment on her predicament. At her sides her fingers clenched tight until the seams of her kid gloves creaked. And Nicholas—Nicholas merely stood there, his horse's reins looped over negligent fingers, his clothing, despite his rescue of her, immaculate, his blue eyes dancing and at the corners of his mouth just the faintest twitch of amusement.

'Don't you dare laugh at me!' she stormed, stamping her foot. It was a mistake. There was an unpleasant squelching noise and mud oozed out of the lace holes of her boots. Nicholas, quite unforgivably, laughed out loud.

All the anger drained out of her, leaving her feeling cold, miserable and verging on the edge of tears. Camilla squinted furiously in an effort not to cry. She knew the end of her nose was going pink; all the better to match her cheeks, she thought in despair. Her skirts dragged coldly at her legs and she felt her stockings dragging too, dankly. 'Oh, just go away!' She averted her eyes quickly, determined that he should not see her tears.

'Oh, Camilla, don't cry!' His arms came round her, warm and comforting, and despite herself she melted into them.

'No, I'm all muddy,' she protested feebly, making no effort to free herself from the strength of him.

'I know, and very pathetic you look too,' Nicholas said, his voice warm.

'But someone will see us.' Her voice was muffled against his riding-coat.

Nicholas took a step back and held her at arms' length, looking into her face. His own had lost its amusement. 'Whatever is the matter, Camilla?

Worried that word might get back to Cousin Stephen and make him think twice about making you an offer?'

'Stephen?' Her cousin was the last thing on her mind. Camilla struggled to follow his train of thought. 'But Stephen has made an offer.'

'And it has been accepted?' Nicholas demanded abruptly.

'It has, my lord. And why should that be any of your business?' Ignoring her wet skirts and disarrayed hair, Camilla drew herself up and regarded him with some *hauteur*. 'Or is it your opinion that Mr Stephen Knight is too respectable to marry into our family?'

'Doubtless he feels that after his very public display of affection at the very end of the play he has little choice but to make you an offer.'

'Make *me* an offer?' Camilla regarded Nicholas as though he had run mad. 'My lord, you have quite mistaken the case. Stephen is engaged to marry Ophelia.'

For a long moment she could not read his face, then he said softly, 'Oh, poor Camilla.' His gloved finger traced her cheekbone. 'No wonder you want to cry. Is that what sent you out for a walk on this damp afternoon?'

Camilla was so furious that she was out of his grip and across the plank bridge before she was even aware of moving. Safe on the other side she stood, anger shaking her slender form, and stormed at him. 'You, sir, are presumptuous, impertinent and, and…jealous! How dare you speak of my cousin in those terms? I am delighted that he and Ophelia have found happiness together and I never want to see you again so long as I live!'

Nicholas swung up on to Thunderer's back, checking the horse's immediate inclination to canter off and his own to put the animal at the ditch, ride after Camilla and scoop her up on to the saddle in front of him. He watched the muddy figure stumble away across the wet, tussocky meadow, then pulled the horse's head around and rode off. He thought of her words all the way back to Freddie's. Jealous? Him? What a ludicrous notion. Why, dammit, he could have any woman he wanted—including the sanctimonious Miss Knight. But the pure and respectable Miss Knight had a double life, however reluctant she was to admit it. How dared she lecture him?

More and more furious, he dug his heels into Thunderer's black flanks and gave the stallion its head. He almost flattened Freddie as he came clattering into the yard, powerful emotion still coursing through his veins. Tossing the reins to the groom, who led away the sweating animal, he dragged off his tight gloves.

'You certainly put him through his paces, Nick,' Freddie remarked, sauntering over the cobbles to perch on the mounting block. 'Damn good animal, isn't he? Shame you'll never get to own him. I know it's not the end of the month, but surely you'll concede you've lost the wager?'

His friend's eyes when he looked at him were glittering strangely and Freddie had the uncanny feeling that it wasn't him that Nick was looking at. 'I wouldn't be too sure about that, my friend. I can take Thunderer off you any time I wish.'

Chapter Eleven

Camilla closed her book of tablets with a snap and threaded the pencil through its ribbon loops before tucking it into the reticule which sat on the carriage seat beside her. The sound of the horses' hooves changed as the chaise turned into the yard of the inn and she picked up her bonnet and replaced it on her head, tying the grosgrain ribbon in a bow.

'Oh! We're here, miss!' Mathilda the maid said with a squeak of excitement. 'Ooh, it does look *big* Miss. And aren't there a lot of people about?'

Camilla reflected wryly that virtually everything they had encountered along their route that day had seemed big to the little chambermaid. Mathilda had never set foot beyond the village before and was quivering with the excitement and the responsibility of being a *real* ladies' maid

Camilla, who had set herself resolutely to construct the most comprehensive list of personal and domestic linen that her sister could possibly require when married, had been constantly distracted from her task by cries of wonder and amazement from Mathilda. But that too had been a welcome distrac-

tion from thoughts of Nicholas and her own appallingly unladylike behaviour yesterday. The man
seemed to bring out the very worst in her, which
was a very lowering reflection.

The postillion had jumped down to open the carriage door for her, and as she stepped on to the cobbles Camilla realised that for once Mathilda had not
exaggerated. The yard was thronged with people of
every class and station and with vehicles ranging
from modest gigs to at least one elegant equipage
with a coat of arms emblazoned on its gleaming
black door.

Camilla lifted her skirts carefully to negotiate a
puddle and found herself the object of an unasham-
edly admiring member of the dandy set, his quizzing
glass trained upon her ankles. She shot him a frigid
glance, then, turning her head, realised that the interest was shared by a very down-at-heel ruffian, a
terrier under his arm, who was lounging against the
mounting block.

'Come, Mathilda, don't dawdle,' she said sharply,
leading the way towards the inn door. Lord Ellwood
had recommended this hostelry most particularly:
what on earth was afoot to transform it so?

The landlord was just inside, wiping his hands on
his vast white apron and looking harassed. Around
him there was a throng of potboys carrying out tank-
ards of ale to those waiting outside, a valet demanding assistance in getting his master's trunk
taken upstairs, and a small child wailing because its
kitten, taking fright, had dived under the oak settle.

The man saw Camilla and his expression changed
from harassment to dismay. 'Oh, I beg your pardon,
ma'am, but as you can see we're terrible busy today.

There's no private parlour left, I'm sorry to say, but if you would care to step through to the back room with your maid, my wife will attend you there.'

Camilla raised her eyebrows and began to draw off her gloves. A servant came in with her valise and waited at her side. 'I am Miss Knight. You should have a room for me, bespoken by Lord Ellwood's messenger this morning.'

The landlord looked even more flustered. 'Oh dear, ma'am. We did get the message, and there is one room for you, ma'am, because the gentleman who had ordered it was taken ill on the way here, but I don't know if you'll be wanting it, things being as they are.'

At that moment a somewhat boisterous group of young bucks swaggered in calling for ale and clapping one another on the shoulders as they shared a jest. The landlord hastily opened a door and ushered Camilla out of the passage. 'You see how it is, ma'am, no place for a lady.'

'Lord Ellwood assured me that the Black Horse was the most respectable hostelry in Buckingham. Are you telling me that this is not the case?'

'Well, ordinarily, ma'am,' he said with some pride, 'I wouldn't hesitate to make that claim myself. I say we keep the most comfortable house, the finest food and the best-kept ale for fifty miles around! But you see, it's the prize-fight over at Rickett's Farm tomorrow, and the town is packed out. It's a big fight, you see—the Slough Bull against a new Irish challenger.' He licked his lips eagerly. 'There's a lot of money riding on it, ma'am, and that's brought them all in from miles around.'

'So I see. I have no interest in such matters,'

Camilla replied with some asperity, but inwardly her heart was sinking. So much for setting out alone: at the first hurdle everything was going horribly wrong and for some reason she did not feel able to rise to the challenge with her usual confidence. 'Well, is there another inn you can recommend, somewhere quieter?'

The man shook his grizzled head. 'Not this side of Chipping Norton, ma'am. As I said, this is a big fight, they're coming from all over and putting up where they can.'

'*Chipping Norton!* Why, that must be all of twenty miles away! I have driven from Cambridge today and have no desire to drive any further than I have to.'

'It's nearer thirty mile, ma'am, to the Prince's Arms, which is the nearest I could recommend to a lady with any confidence under the circumstances,' the man said apologetically. 'Look, now, you sit down—you won't be disturbed here—and I'll get my wife to wait upon you. You can have a look at the bedchamber, ma'am, and see what you think. But you'll have to eat in your room. There's no private parlour to be had, and you'll not want to be seen in the public rooms.'

The landlord left to summon his wife. Camilla gazed around the little parlour, her spirits lowering by the minute. So much for independence, for activity to chase thoughts of Nicholas from her mind and make her feel in control of her life once more! Raucous laughter swelled from the public bar beyond and she clutched her reticule, her fingers tight on its handle. With long experience in the Green Room she had thought herself more than able to cope with any awkward situation: now, more than anything, she wanted the reassuring presence of a man, of Lord Ellwood, of Stephen, of Nicholas...

The door opened and Mathilda came in looking scared, her little face pinched with worry. 'I don't like it here, Miss Knight. It's full of undesirables, it is. Can we not find another lodging?'

With someone to look after, Camilla rallied her spirits. 'Now, Mathilda, don't look so afraid. The landlord's wife is coming to attend us and show us to our room. We will be confined to it until tomorrow morning, I am afraid, but we will be comfortable, I am sure. We must make the best of it,' she added briskly, and was rewarded by seeing the maidservant brighten at this show of confidence.

Mrs Whitwell, the landlord's wife, proved to be a cheerful little bird of a woman, very sensible of the delicacy of Camilla's position. 'Now, you just come along with me, ma'am, and we'll soon have you comfortable. A nice little room, if a little out of the way. Not that that's any bad thing today,' she added.

Loud voices echoed down the passage demanding, 'More ale, and hurry up about it!'

The Black Horse was a substantial, rambling establishment which appeared to have been added to almost by whim over the centuries. It fronted the main street of Buckingham, growing backwards and sideways to eat up the gaps between the other houses beside it and to surround the great stableyard.

Camilla's head spun as they went up and down short flights of steps, crossed landings and finally arrived at a large panelled door. Mrs Whitwell peered round it and then ushered Camilla and

Mathilda through and into a parlour with other doors leading off.

'I'm afraid the parlour won't be available to you, ma'am,' she apologised. 'And all the rooms off have been taken by a party of gentlemen,' she added warningly. 'But down here—' she disappeared down a narrow passage '—here's your chamber, ma'am. It's quiet—well, as quiet as anywhere will be in Buckingham tonight—and no one's any reason to come down here. There's a truckle bed for your maid, and a table and chairs over here by the window.' She bustled across and tugged back the curtains to let in more of the late evening light. 'Now, I'll bring you a nice cup of tea, and then when you want your dinner—or anything else—just you pull the bell over there, ma'am. I'll attend you myself, never fear.' She bobbed a curtsey and bustled out.

Camilla paced round the room slowly, watching her maid unpack her overnight valise. Mathilda, her spirits restored, went about her new duties with a pride and care that brought a small smile to Camilla's lips. The girl was rising to this challenge, and was probably even now constructing a dramatic retelling of that afternoon's events for the servants' hall.

They drank their tea when it arrived and Mrs Whitwell lit the fire. Seated by the window, Camilla gazed down into the alleyway below which was all the view the room afforded. The view of the crowns of a large number of hats, both smart and disreputable, was entertaining for a short while only, and Camilla was soon regretting being so forgetful as to fail to pack something to read. Sitting brooding, trying not to think about that last mortifying encounter with Nicholas, she was brought back to the present by a sharp pang of hunger.

Looking over her shoulder, Camilla realised that not only was the light in the room quite dim, but that Mathilda had curled up on the truckle bed and, her hand beneath her cheek, was fast asleep. The clock on the mantel shelf struck seven rather tinnily and Camilla tugged the bellpull. At least dinner would provide a welcome diversion and occupation, and she could retire to bed afterwards. Doubtless those attending the prizefight would set off at the crack of dawn, so she would find the inn more congenial in the morning.

The clock struck the quarter and she realised that no one had answered her summons. Impatiently she tugged at the cord again and was rewarded by the entire length falling at her feet, leaving a frayed end beyond reach above her head.

Camilla gave a sharp, exasperated sigh. Now what was she going to do? She thought briefly of rousing Mathilda, but the girl looked so young and so tired that she hadn't the heart to send her off into the noisy bustle of the inn. She turned the key and opened the door, listening. But there was no sound of movement or voices from the private parlour beyond, so she stepped out, closing the door behind her, and walked along the short stretch of corridor and into the room. The doors were all safely shut and the passage beyond empty.

Emboldened, Camilla walked across, and had nearly reached the far passage when she heard the sound of booted feet striding towards her and then taking the short flight of stairs two at a time. Her heart thudded, and she looked around wildly for somewhere to hide. A second later the man she least—and most—wanted to see in the world strode in to the parlour, his face alive and animated.

They stared for a long moment at each other and then almost as one they took a step forward and stopped. Camilla felt as though she was being torn in two: one part of her just wanted to throw herself into Nicholas's arms, but another part could recall only too clearly their angry exchanges over the past few days and Nicholas's mocking, bitter words on the riverbank. She stood watching him like a wary animal, ready to turn and run at the first sign of aggression.

'Camilla, my dear...'

His voice sounded so tender! Was he then so happy to see her? had he followed her? 'How did you know I was here?' she managed to say.

'I did not know. I had no idea you had even left Cambridgeshire. I left because I could not bear it there any longer. The thought of a bachelor party at my home following this prize-fight seemed an ideal distraction from what was ailing me.' His smile was rueful.

'I could not bear it either,' Camilla whispered. 'And, it seems wicked to say so, but the sight of Ophelia's happiness stung like a burn. I had to be busy and my old nurse needs me, so I left.'

Nicholas opened his arms and she walked into them instinctively, desiring only to be in his embrace.

'Camilla, darling, I cannot believe you are really here,' he whispered into the soft mass of her hair. 'Camilla, look at me...'

She raised her eyes to his and saw him smiling

down into her face. Her heart almost stopped in her breast as he lifted one finger to trace the full, sensual curve of her lower lip. 'Nicholas…I…'

'Shh.' He bent and swept her up in his arms, and in one stride had shouldered open a door. He set her down inside the room as he heeled the door closed behind him. Glancing round, Camilla realised she was in his bedchamber. His many-caped driving-coat had been thrown carelessly over a chair, but his valet had obviously already unpacked his valise and evening clothes lay out ready on the bed. Her heart gave a little thud of happiness mixed with fear at the realisation of what she was doing and where she was.

Camilla knew she ought to go now, this moment. If anyone saw her here she would be utterly compromised. But somehow she just did not care, because Nicholas had turned from the door and she was in his arms again. He was kissing her gently at first, then, as she responded, with increasing passion, his tongue exploring, demanding, sending wild thrilling urges coursing through her.

All the anger that had been between them had miraculously disappeared, without a word being said. The anger had become passion and Camilla realised hazily that that was what it had been all the time.

But thought was not easy, and sensible, prudent thought impossible. Nicholas's lips were moving down the column of her throat, kissing, nibbling, teasing the soft flesh there, the pulse throbbing against his lips. Camilla entwined her fingers in his hair, compelling his head down to the swell of her breasts. He pushed impatiently at the lace of her fichu until his lips rested hot on her skin.

With a groan he raised his head and, looking deep into her eyes, pushed her gently back on to the bed, quite heedless of the shirt, neckcloth and immaculate tailcoat which were crushed beneath their weight as he joined her there.

Camilla realized that somehow she had lost both her kid slippers and that Nicholas's fingers were trailing shockingly up her foot, her ankle, the curve of her calf to her knotted garter.

'Nicholas…darling…stop, we should not…' It was a terrible effort to say it, she felt as though she was fighting all her instincts, the clamouring desire of her body, and above all, the waves of happiness that they were together, that the anger had gone, that he needed to be with her.

'Camilla, hush.' He paused, his fingertips caressing the bare flesh of her thigh. 'Do not be afraid. I love you, I want to be with you, but I only want what you are willing to give me. You must know I want to be with you…always. Finding you here is like a miracle; I thought I had lost you for ever.' His lips dropped once more to her breast, teasing, licking the aroused tip.

Camilla stiffened at the shock, at the pleasure he was giving her, then his words struck home. This man she loved had just told her that he loved her too, that he wanted to be with her, always. He wanted her to be his wife, she realised deliriously, as his fingers moved once more to stroke the silky softness of her inner thigh.

Nicholas shifted his weight above her and for the first time she felt his arousal. The heat of him burned through the fine lawn of her gown and his breathing was ragged, catching in his throat. She gazed up into his face, saw his eyes intent with passion. She put up her hands and cradled his hot face tenderly. 'Nicholas...' She let her fingers stroke across his cheekbones, her heart brimming over with love for him.

She knew she should not be doing this, should not be here with him, but he loved her as she loved him, and they would be married. Driven by mutual passion, they were only anticipating the inevitable— and that could not be wrong, could it?

'Camilla...my darling, I love you, I want you, but only if you want me too. You know what I am asking, don't you?'

His fingers were doing things which made it difficult to think, to breathe, to do anything but arch gasping into his embrace. In answer to his question all she could do was seek his mouth blindly, clinging to him as he took her into realms of pleasure she had never known could exist.

Suddenly, shockingly, a chorus of male voices filled the air, shattering their hidden sensual world. Boots clattered on the parlour floor, chairs scraped, and the sound of valises being dropped on the boards reverberated through the unlocked door.

Nicholas swung off the bed and in one movement turned the key in the lock, standing listening intently with his back against the door panels. Camilla scrambled up against the pillows, instinctively gathering the disordered lace of her bodice together in one hand. 'What...?'

'Shh!' Nicholas whispered urgently. 'It is the others—my friends. They must not find you here.'

'Others? Which others?' she whispered back, dismayed, her heart thudding in her chest, her whole body aching with interrupted passion.

'Freddie Corsham, George Marlow and William Hendricks,' Nicholas murmured, crossing the room and tugging his neckcloth back into some semblance of order. He tucked his shirt-tails back into his breeches and shrugged into his jacket. Stooping to the mirror, he raked his fingers swiftly through his disordered hair where Camilla's searching fingers had locked in it. 'Are you here alone?'

'Yes, I have only my maid. I was on my way to Cheltenham,' she whispered. It seemed somewhat late in the day to be discussing whether she was chaperoned! 'Why…what are they doing here?' she whispered frantically. All it needed was for Mathilda to be awakened by the men's voices and come looking for her for all to be quite lost.

'They are here for the prize-fight and to meet me,' he murmured. 'Give me ten minutes and I'll get them downstairs.' He looked at her white face and crossed to kiss her reassuringly on the lips. 'Don't worry, my love. It will be all right. Trust me.'

'I trust you, Nicholas,' she whispered back against his lips, her eyes huge in her face.

'Stand behind the screen while I open the door,' he urged. 'Remember, give me ten minutes.'

Camilla stood behind the screen which surrounded the washstand and heard the door open and close. Nicholas's voice, raised in greeting came back clearly through the panels, as did the responses of his three friends. Camilla hastily retied her garters, pinned her fichu back into place and did what she could with her tousled coiffure.

Emerging from behind the screen, she saw her left slipper by the bed. She lifted the coverlet and peered underneath, but there was no sign of the other shoe. Puzzled, she cast around the room, but still could not find it. She would have to risk lighting one candle, for the room, lit only by the firelight and the reflected light from the yard, was very dim now. Groping on the mantel she found some spills which caught quickly from the smouldering fire. But even with the candle in her hand she could see no sign of her other kid slipper.

She was starting to panic when she heard Nicholas say rousingly, 'Come on, stop sitting around here in this fug. Let us go down to the saloon bar and see how the betting is going. I have sovereigns burning a hole in my pocket even if you do not.'

To her relief she could hear the sound of chairs being pushed back and of the men rising to leave. Then a voice she recognised as Lord Corsham's rang out. 'Here! What's this? Upon my oath, there's a pretty little slipper if ever I saw one! And where's the lady, eh? Nick, you dog, you've not been here an hour! That is good going even for you!'

This sally was greeted with laughter, a few spicy comments which brought the blush to Camilla's cheeks, and speculation about who the hidden beauty could be. A voice she had never heard before said, 'Come on, Nick, don't be greedy. Introduce us to the lady!'

Terror lent speed to her feet and she virtually ran across to the door and twisted the key in the lock. The click sounded awfully loud and was obviously audible to the men outside. A cheer went up, and the second voice said banteringly, 'A shy one, eh? Well, Nick, we aren't going to move from this room until we meet your ladybird. Come on, Hendricks, ring for dinner and a couple of bottles of claret: who knows how long Nick's modest companion will take to emerge?'

Nicholas's mind raced. If the hidden woman had been a member of the muslin company then he would have no reason to hide her; they were all men of the world. But by refusing to reveal his companion he was as good as admitting it was a lady of quality with a reputation to lose. If he told them this was the case they would behave like gentlemen and leave while she came out, but Freddie at least might put two and two together—he certainly would if he saw Camilla next morning about the inn. And how had she arrived at the inn? In Lord Ellwood's carriage? If that were the case, his coat-of-arms would be on the doors. Damn it! Was there no way out of this coil?

'Nick? Just who have you got in there?' George Marlow asked slyly, putting his feet up on the table with the unmistakable air of one who was going nowhere.

Inside the room Camilla had pulled herself together and was casting around for escape. She crossed to the window, but looking out realised it gave out on to the main inn yard, still thronged with coaches and ostlers. No escape that way, even if she could have climbed down the ivy which clustered around the casement.

She brought up her hands to her lips in a gesture of despair and then saw her fingertips were sooty from the taper she had lit at the fire. It seemed at that moment as though the plan arrived in her mind complete, without the need for further thought. She could not leave this room as Camilla Knight, but she could act her way out of it!

Frantically she threw open the clothes press doors, rummaging recklessly amongst the carefully folded garments. There, gleaming in the subdued light, was the answer to her prayers.

The dressing-gown was an extravaganza of oriental silk which would have pleased even the exotic tastes of the Prince Regent. Dragons writhed across it, breathing fire in slashes of colour. She pulled it out and held it up against her: it was long, it must be full-length on Nicholas—against her it pooled on the boards. Camilla pulled off her dress, heedless of the ripping sounds she created. She swathed the dressing-gown around her body, arranging the folds and securing it with the cord which had caught back the bed curtain. She had another use for the sash, long, wide as a cummerbund and lavishly fringed.

With a practised hand she wrapped it round her head, totally enveloping her blonde hair in its folds and with the help of a tiepin creating a perfect turban. She lit a second candle and blew out the first. As she'd hoped, the wick was charred enough to provide enough black to darken her brows and lashes dramatically. She cast round for further cosmetic aid and smelt, before she saw it, the pot of geraniums which rested on the window ledge, still warm from the evening sun. Two petals crushed against her lips reddened them outrageously and she was transformed from a demure young lady into an exotic creature.

Out in the parlour Nicholas's mind was racing

desperately. Appeals to his companions' better natures, bribery and outright threats had all failed. Pleading had merely made them more obdurate, and the arrival of the claret set the seal on their determination to enjoy themselves.

George waved the waiter away and poured the wine himself, pushing the glasses across the table to his seated companions in turn. 'Sit down, Nick, and relax: we are not going anywhere, so you may as well resign yourself to showing us your hidden beauty.'

'Over my dead body,' Nicholas responded grimly, taking the proffered glass and drinking deep. As he spoke the unmistakable sound of the key turning in the lock froze them all. Four pairs of eyes turned to the door of Nicholas's chamber. Three pairs were alight with mischievous curiosity, the fourth with appalled resignation. Well, they were all old friends of his: however much they might tease him they were gentlemen too. He knew he could rely on their discretion—but he was only too aware of what an ordeal this was going to be for Camilla.

The door swung open on to complete silence, broken only by the sound of four wine glasses being set down on the table and a hoarse whisper from George. 'By all that's holy—it's…it can't be…it's Mademoiselle Davide!'

'Nick! You lucky devil!' Sir William gulped, swinging his boots down off the table with a thud.

The apparition swayed languidly into the room. '*Oh, non monsieur.* I can assure you luck has nothing to do with it.' Mademoiselle Davide reached Nicholas's side, smiled up into his rigid face, then, with a sensual possessiveness which made Freddie moan faintly, ran her fingers down his cheekbone, along his jawline and let her hand rest lightly on his lapel.

He bent, appearing to nuzzle her ear furthest from the onlookers and whispered, 'You little witch. I've been dying a thousand deaths out here!'

All Camilla's nerves, her fears, had vanished. The parlour was the stage and she had a part to play, the most vital of her life. There was her reputation, her family's name to protect, but most of all there was Nicholas's good name. If she failed in this his friends would know that the woman he was intending to marry had made her living as an actress. And that would put her—and him—beyond the pale of polite society.

She turned, her hand still resting on Nicholas's shoulder, and shared a welcoming smile amongst the three men. 'Are you not going to introduce me to your friends, *chéri*? They look fun—and you.' She turned and pouted crimson lips at Nicholas. 'You I have not yet forgiven for shutting me away in that boring room instead of letting me share your company.'

Hendricks darted forward, his cheeks flushed. 'Mademoiselle, please take this chair. Let me offer you a glass of wine—George, ring for another glass!'

For once in his life George Marlow did as he was bid by his old schoolfellow, jerking the bellpull with such force that the waiter appeared at a run. 'Dammit, where have you been! Another glass for the lady, and more candles. And where's our dinner? Hang on, hang on,' he called to the lad's fast retreating back. 'Set a cover for the lady, and make sure there's something fit for her to eat!'

'Yes, sir—right away, sir!' the boy gasped, hurrying out. Cor! That was a prime article and no mistake—and you saw a few in this job! He could hardly wait to get down to the kitchen and tell them all about it. If Cook sent up something really special, there might be a good tip in it as well.

Camilla glanced from under her lashes at Freddie, the only man who had met her as Miss Knight and the only man who knew that Miss Knight was a good amateur actress. But there was no look of recognition on his face, nothing but admiration and envy that Nick had secured such a prize. Nonetheless, it would be best to keep him at a distance, especially as George Marlow had sent for more candles.

She patted the chair next to her and fluttered her sooty lashes at William Hendricks. 'Please, sit by me, sir. And you must introduce yourselves, as Nicholas seems determined not to do so.' She indicated the other chair and turned her attention to George. 'And you, sir, you have the advantage of me, for you know my name. Can it be that you have done me the honour of coming to see me act?'

They sat hurriedly, both flushed, and George began the introductions. 'Sir William Hendricks upon your right, ma'am. Lord Corsham—' Freddie bowed '—by the fireplace. And I am George Marlow, your most humble and devoted servant.' He bent over her hand. 'We are all firm devotees of your art, and all of us devastated by the suddenness of your retirement.'

'Yes, indeed, mademoiselle,' William almost gabbled, reduced to schoolboy gaucheness by the nearness of his goddess. 'Could we not beg you to reconsider? Is there nothing we could do to persuade you to return to the stage?'

Camilla reflected wryly that it was a good thing that none of them realised that they were indeed seeing Mademoiselle Davide's final performance! She lifted a hand and waved vaguely in Nicholas's direction. He came across and caught it in his, giving it a warning pressure which she completely ignored. The terror had gone, as stage fright always had, to be replaced by exhilaration, by the power she had over these four men.

'Nicholas, you are a very naughty boy not to introduce me to your friends before. I am quite cross with you. They are all so very charming!'

Nicholas circled the table to sit opposite her, shooting her a glance that suggested quite clearly that she was in danger of over-egging this particular pudding. Camilla, her eyes dancing wickedly, blew him a kiss and turned to George. 'Now, you will tell me all about this prize-fighting, because I do not know anything about it, except that it sounds very exciting, and Nicholas will not explain. I expect you understand it much better than he does...'

George coughed pompously and shot his cuffs. 'Well, it isn't really a subject for a lady, but I must admit it is by way of being a passion of mine and I am generally acknowledged to be somewhat of an expert on form.' Encouraged by her wide-eyed admiration, he continued. 'Now, the challenger is an unknown Irishman called Patrick Shaughnessy, who has been training with Thomas Cribb...'

Camilla clapped her hands. 'Oh, I have heard of him. He is very famous, is he not?'

'Clever girl. He was the champion heavyweight of all England.' George patted her hand. 'Now, the defender is known as the Slough Bull, and he has been undefeated for his last ten fights.'

'But which one is going to win? Will it be this *toreau*?'

'Ah ha!' George tapped the side of his nose knowingly. 'That is where the bets are going.'

Camilla put her hand on his sleeve and gazed at him admiringly. 'But you know better, do you not, *Georges*?'

George flushed and admitted that he flattered himself that indeed he had a better grasp of form than most gentlemen.

Two waiters appeared at that moment, and this prevented George from being soundly abused by his friends, who were becoming restive in the face of this shameless self-promotion.

Nicholas, joining in the general banter while the waiters unloaded their trays heaped with food, wine and more candles, reflected that Camilla was magnificent and that he had never been so scared in his life. Like riding a tiger, it was exhilarating while you were in motion, but the thought of what would happen if—when—you fell off was terrifying.

How Camilla thought she was going to bring this theatrical dinner party to an end he could not imagine. But suddenly he stopped worrying and allowed himself to be swept along with the animated talk and the pleasure of watching her perform.

* * *

The clock struck one. The plates had long been swept aside, more claret had been sent for and consumed, and the conversation had flowed freely from prize-fighting to the stage, to the latest French fashions—about which Freddie was surprisingly knowledgeable—and finally to the precarious health of the King.

'No, I have never acted before the Prince Regent, and now I never will. It would have been a great honour, of course. Oh, but *messieurs*, regard the clock. I must retire. I need my beauty sleep and *sans doute* you gentlemen will all be up at some ungodly hour making a great deal of noise.'

'Never say you need beauty sleep, mademoiselle—how could one improve upon perfection?'

'You are too gallant, Sir William,' Camilla responded gracefully as she got to her feet. 'No, no, there is no need to open that door for me. I shall go to my own chamber and leave you all to your brandy and your betting. Goodnight, gentlemen.'

Nicholas followed her down the corridor to her chamber. Once they were safely round the corner he took her in his arms and kissed her. 'My God, you were magnificent! I have never been so terrified in my life—or so excited.'

His breathing was ragged as he kissed her hard. Camilla, all the exhilaration ebbing from her body, suddenly felt very tired, but very happy. Gently she pushed Nicholas away. 'No, darling, go back to your friends. When will I see you again?'

Nicholas looked down into her face and smiled. 'Just as soon as you get back to Bath. I will be waiting. You know my sister's direction. You have only to send for me.'

Camilla watched his tall, elegant figure disappear

back towards the parlour. She leaned her aching shoulders against the wall, suddenly overcome by how much she loved him. She was tired, so tired, but also restless, as she had often been after a particularly draining performance. She could not go out, and if she went to her room her fidgeting would doubtless wake her maid. Instead, on silent bare feet, she began to pace up and down the empty passageway.

She reached the bend just before the parlour and stopped, safely out of sight. The men had fallen silent as she had left them, but now as Nicholas reappeared he was greeted by a chorus of admiration.

'She is more beautiful close up than she is on stage,' Sir William sighed moonily.

'You lucky dog, Nick,' George growled, draining his brandy.

'Luck has nothing to do with it,' Nicholas retorted. Camilla flushed at the note of triumph in his voice, then told herself that of course he too had a part to play in this charade.

'No, indeed it hasn't!' Freddie suddenly exclaimed. 'You know what this means, don't you? Nick's won the bet—he's won Thunderer!'

'He's run out of time,' George stated dogmatically.

'No, he hasn't,' Freddie said gloomily. 'We gave him to the end of this month, and it's the first of June tomorrow.'

'Sorry, old chap,' Hendricks agreed. 'I don't think there can be any doubt that Nick has succeeded in making the Unobtainable Mademoiselle Davide his mistress, just as we agreed that night in the theatre. Thunderer is his.'

George got up unsteadily, scraping his chair back, and raised his glass to Nick. 'Here's to you, Nick, and well earned, I say. A stallion for a stallion, what?'

The men's laughter rang mockingly in Camilla's ears as she ran back to her chamber.

Chapter Twelve

Mrs Babbage was perhaps the most lachrymose individual Camilla had ever had the misfortune to meet. She knew she should feel nothing but compassion towards Miss March's widowed sister, but she was finding it very hard indeed to deal with a woman whose only response to every question, every decision, was to dissolve into tears and wail, 'If only dearest Mr Babbage was here!'

Camilla refrained, with difficulty, from pointing out to the widow that if Mr Babbage was there the situation would not have arisen, and, further, from mentioning that the unfortunate gentleman had suffered a long and difficult illness, and that no charitable person could wish him to be other than at peace with his Maker.

Yet, whatever the provocation, she could not regret her decision to come to Cheltenham, for poor little Miss March was worn to a thread, as Camilla could see from the moment she set eyes on her old nurse.

'Marchy darling,' she had cried as she tumbled down the steps of the carriage into the outflung arms

of her oldest friend and ally. They had both burst
into tears: Miss March because she was tired,
drained and once more in the company of her dearest 'Lilla, Camilla because she was so shocked by
the sight of Miss March, suddenly old and helpless.

She had sat numbly in the carriage all the way
from Buckingham, forcing herself to make responses to Mathilda's eager questions, simply counting the minutes until she could fall into her old
nurse's arms and have it all made better. But the
miles passing by on the turnpike milestones had
brought her not someone who would pat her and
soothe her and tell her it was all going to be well,
as she had told a young Camilla so many times in
the past. Instead she found herself needing to support an old lady at the end of her tether, whose innocent mind could never have comprehended the
scandalous toils her charge had entangled herself in.

Miss March, who had never set foot in a theatre
in her life, had not quite understood what it was that
Camilla was about night after night as she changed
in her cottage and then slipped away with a kiss,
leaving her to her night-time indulgence of a cup of
chocolate. It seemed that darling 'Lilla was involved
with a group of like-minded friends who enjoyed
dramatics, and as this was a *slightly* daring thing to
do it was better if she returned via Miss March's.
After all, the old nurse had reasoned, if Mrs Knight
was complaisant about it, then it must be perfectly
all right, although it was a pity that dear 'Lilla
seemed so tired every evening.

So, exhausted, humiliated and with her life in tatters around her feet, Camilla had dismissed Mathilda
to unpack, drunk a strong cup of tea, pushed her

handkerchief firmly back into her reticule and set herself to discover how she could disentangle Miss March from Cheltenham before her health finally gave way.

If Mrs Babbage had been a torturer in full possession of Camilla's scandalous secrets she could not have inflicted more pain as she held forth to her enlarged audience. 'Dearest Mr Babbage, such a tower of strength for fifty years! I will not hide from you, Miss Knight, that I fell for him the moment I saw him! Oh, you do not yet know the felicity of falling in love with a fine gentleman, of receiving a declaration from his lips, of yielding your life and fortune into his hands, but you will, you will. And I pray you will never know the horror of seeing him snatched from you, leaving you all alone, alone...' And here she trailed off into tears again.

'Indeed I do not,' replied Camilla with such emphasis that Miss March looked startled and hurried to put right what she saw as her sister's tactlessness.

'You will do so, my dear Miss Knight, never fear! Somewhere there is the right gentleman for you. You have only to wait and he will come to you, rest assured.'

Neither lady was surprised when Camilla snatched her handkerchief from her reticule, burst into tears and fled from the room.

'Such sensibility, such a sympathetic understanding of your feelings,' cried Miss March.

'Indeed,' her sister sniffed. 'Dear child! So unlike so many young people of today!'

The Babbage house, although modest and neat, was well-appointed and the late Mr Babbage had allowed himself the indulgence of a small conservatory at the rear. Here Camilla took refuge and at last found the privacy and peace for a good cry. Last night she had been unable to sleep, lying awake and taut listening to Mathilda's snuffles and snores as the night became darker and the inn finally fell quiet.

Curled up in a tight ball of misery Camilla had crushed her handkerchief against her teeth to stifle her sobs and had lain silent while her thoughts whirled in a nightmare, mocking dance.

How *could* she have been so mistaken in Nicholas? How *could* she have believed him to love her when all he had wanted was her seduction? And for what? In order to win a horse! He must have known right from the beginning that she lived a double life. He must have sought her out cynically, intending her ruin simply for a bet. She had known of his reputation as a rake, but stupidly, innocently, she had also believed that he would treat her as a gentleman should a lady. She could only conclude that in his eyes, by following a career on the stage, she had forfeited that status and that protection. She had believed him when he said he loved her—perhaps he did, after his fashion, in perhaps the only way a rake could understand love. Doubtless he would have offered her a *carte blanche*: at least she had been spared the ordeal of discovering his intentions in his presence.

Her whirling thoughts had become no calmer as the inn had begun to come alive again. In the deep darkness before the dawn she'd heard the ostlers walking across the yard, the noise as stable half-doors swung open and horses whickered for their feed. From downstairs had come the rattle of grates being riddled and the clang of the pump-handle as chilled kitchen boys pumped the first buckets of water of the day.

All those people, awake and happy in their way. All knowing their role in life and what their expectations and dreams were. And in her chamber, gradually filling with light as the day dawned, Camilla had remained in a wretched huddle, swathed in the heavy silk of Nicholas's robe.

She'd stirred, and a waft of the sandalwood cologne he had sometimes used drifted up, warmed by her body. It had brought her to a recollection of how she must look, what she was wearing. Mathilda must not see her like this! She could not explain to the girl why she should preserve silence about such an odd occurrence, and the risk that she might innocently blurt something out was too great.

Cautiously Camilla had slipped out of bed and shed the robe, folding it as small as possible and tucking it into a calico bag she had brought to place linen in for laundering. The sash had swiftly followed, and the tiepin she'd tucked into her jewellery roll. That had just left the curtain cord, which she'd dropped on the floor by the window. Mathilda, sleeping the sleep of the very young, had slumbered on as Camilla wiped the soot from her brows and lashes with cold water from the washstand and scrubbed the geranium stain from her lips. The sting of the towel on her soft flesh had been a penance, and she'd scrubbed harder, trying to drive the memory of Nicholas's betraying mouth teasing those same lips.

The enormity of his betrayal flooded back to her now, as she sat in the respectable little glasshouse, unheedingly shredding the leaves of the fern which grew in a pot by her side. Nicholas had been so clever, so cynical, playing her like a fish on a line: alternately respectful and teasing, admiring and then apparently uninterested. He had kissed her, exploiting her innocence, her susceptibility to him.

And then how shocked and angry he had appeared to be after he 'discovered' her secret. And she had thought herself a good actress! Why, he was worth ten of her when it came to dissembling and deceit.

Not that she could accuse him of doing anything to damage Ophelia and Mama: no, he would not do that. They were *ladies*, and his code forbade him to do anything to hurt them. But she, Camilla, was another matter. She had forfeited his regard by her actions and so he could use her to his own ends as he chose. But to count her virtue as of less worth than the possession of a horse…

Suddenly angry, she sprang to her feet and began to pace up and down the short alleyway between the benches. What hypocrites men were! It was not just Nicholas: why, those three friends of his were the same—such fun to be with, so open, courteous and pleasant to her—but they would cut Mademoiselle Davide dead in the street if they met her when they were in company with their mothers or their sisters. Before they knew who she was they had bayed like hounds on the scent to discover her, for she had simply been Nicholas's 'bit of muslin' in their eyes.

Then her own innate honesty brought her to a standstill. No, she could not blame it all on Nicholas. What was he to make of a 'lady' who quivered at a touch from him, who returned kiss with kiss, who after a chance meeting in a strange inn was ready to surrender her virtue to him? Camilla closed her eyes in shame at the memory of how she must have looked, tumbled and half-clad on his bed.

She covered her eyes with her palms for a long moment until her breathing calmed a little and made herself think. Men had tried to kiss her before and some had almost succeeded. She had met many handsome, rich and eligible men in her time, had flirted and been flirted with, received admiring glances and even passionate poems. Yet not once had her heart been stirred, not once had her flesh quivered with response under a touch or a caress. Her dreams had been blameless, her imagination untouched by every man she had met.

Until she had met Nicholas. Yes, she could acquit herself of being an abandoned, over-sensual woman who would have responded like that to any passable man. She had been attracted to Nicholas from the first moment, had fallen in love with him long before she had allowed herself to acknowledge it with anything except her betraying body.

Camilla stared unseeingly through the glass to the small garden beyond. She loved Nicholas, loved him despite his betrayal. She knew she would never feel like this about any other man so long as she lived. Was the world full of foolish girls who had jeopardised their virtue for a rake and then spent the rest of their existence regretting it? She supposed she could not be the only one. Occasionally you heard the whispers.

'Lady Y has been a long time in the country— quite eight months, is it not…?'

'Young Miss B is looking very pale. Has not her engagement to Lord X been announced yet…?

Strange, is it not, that she fainted at the dance last night…?'

She should be grateful to Nicholas's boisterous friends. They had saved her from the ultimate folly as effectively as any three fierce chaperons could have done. How would she be feeling now, counting the days until she could be sure she was not carrying his child? How would she feel if those comforting signs did not come and her body told her that she was? Appalled, Camilla realised that she would be glad, not sorry to find that was the case. There was nothing for her now except the empty shell of her old life without even the stimulus of the stage: the thought of a little house in the country, a new identity as a young widow with her child was curiously attractive.

Carefully she smoothed down her gown, took a deep breath and made her way back to the front parlour. 'Shall I ring for tea? I am sure we would all feel better for some.'

What was Nicholas doing now, what was he thinking? Did he feel any qualms about his actions?

Nicholas was indeed feeling qualms, but not about Camilla. After a long and highly satisfactory day at the fight, where all four had reaped the benefit of George's advice and won handsomely on the Irish challenger, he was driving his curricle homewards with a deep furrow between his brows.

To his friends' surprise he had refused to ride Thunderer back to his estate but had left him to his groom to lead, choosing to drive off alone as soon as the last bout had finished. 'I will head back to Ashby now: you collect my winnings, Freddie; here are the slips. I will see you all in time for dinner, but I must have a word with my head keeper this afternoon if we are to have any sort of sport while we are there. It will only be pigeons, I expect.'

If Camilla had known the tenor of Nicholas's thoughts as he drove the fifteen miles back to his estates she would have been deeply wounded, seeing it as just another example of the hypocrisy of male 'honour'.

But Nicholas, his conscience quite clear as far as she was concerned, was acutely aware that he had just won Thunderer under false pretences and could see no way of getting out of it. The bet had been to seduce Mademoiselle Davide within two months, and not only did Mademoiselle Davide not exist, he had not seduced her either. Another five minutes in that bedroom… The match bays snorted and sidled as his hands tightened unconsciously on the reins, pulling his full attention back to the road.

Nicholas negotiated a tight bend, steadied the pair as he saw the mail coach ahead, then with a flick of the whip gave them their head and was round and away with a clear straight road ahead of him.

Three days at Ashby, then back to Bath and to Camilla: his mouth curved into a smile and Camilla would have recognised with a thudding heart the sensual droop of his eyelids. Meanwhile he supposed he *could* admit to Freddie that he had not actually seduced Mademoiselle Davide. Nicholas winced at the thought of Freddie's expression, let alone his likely comments. Or he could fabricate an opportunity to wager Thunderer again and lose him back to Freddie. A few really poor hands of whist ought to do it; Freddie was a good enough player to make that plausible if he thought Nick was off his game.

Camilla, meanwhile, by dint of agonising patience and persistence, had managed to establish which problems with Mr Babbage's will were causing such an upset. 'Yes, I see what you mean. How very worrying,' she agreed, after half an hour peering at the crabbed script. 'What a pity Mr Babbage did not see fit to place the making of his will in the hands of his solicitor but instead wrote it himself. I have no idea what the legal position might be, of course...'

Both older ladies nodded and clucked in agreement. After all, what mere female could understand these male mysteries. Men were so *clever* at business...

'*But*,' Camilla persisted, 'I think I understand the problem well enough to be able to explain to Mr Brooke, and I am sure he will be willing to act for you. After all, I am sure Mr Babbage cannot have intended to leave the house to the Home for Widows and Orphans and only fifty pounds to you, Mrs Babbage. He appears to have got the two things muddled up.'

'And Mr Brooke is so wise,' Miss March explained to her sister, for the fourth time. 'And yet still quite young. Most handsome and well set up, you know,' she added with a sideways glance at Camilla, who was trying to make a copy of the will to take to the lawyer and fortunately did not hear her.

'Indeed!' Mrs Babbage, finding a subject of interest at last, looked at Camilla with sudden attention. 'A younger son?'

'Oh, no…'

Camilla's hopes of bearing Miss March and the copied documents back to Bath the next day were foiled by both ladies, full of concern for her health. 'You look so tired, 'Lilla dear,' Miss March explained, slipping into using her nursery name the moment they were alone. 'Such dark shadows under your eyes. I am so grateful to you for coming all this distance out of your way for me; I do so hope you have not caught a chill.'

Camilla, casting round for excuses to escape the cloying atmosphere of Cheltenham, finally told Miss March about Ophelia's engagement. 'But please do not tell anyone, even dear Mrs Babbage. As she is not yet out, Mama does not wish it to be widely known.'

Miss March, happily assured that she had an explanation for Camilla's tiredness—excitement and late nights helping her dear mama make plans—stopped fussing and allowed Camilla to convince her that she had done her duty and that her sister would be the better for a few days by herself. 'And then that nice Mr Brooke will come and visit her, and perhaps once that worry with the will is straightened out she can go and stay for a month or two with dearest Cousin Emily…'

'And I do not know how I can go on in Bath if you do not come with me, Marchy, for I will need a chaperon, and there is so much I am charged with doing for Mama and Ophelia,' added Camilla mendaciously. 'We will have the Green Bedchamber made up for you, if you do not dislike that idea, and there will be no need for you to chaperon me to any sort of party you might not wish to attend while in mourning, for I am sure one of Mama's friends will be more than willing to do that.'

Miss March hurried away to supervise the packing of her best black silk, just the thing for a chaperon to wear. Whatever the sacrifice she would be at dear 'Lilla's side, even if it meant attending a ball at the Assembly Rooms!

Camilla was heartily glad to be home once more, but even the inescapable tasks that were waiting for her did nothing to soothe her mind or her aching heart. Cook, finding her absent-minded over the week's menus, was not to know that Miss Camilla had found a little cameo brooch in her jewellery box, or if she had, she could never have guessed it had been given to a certain Mademoiselle Davide in the Green Room of the Theatre Royal.

And Miss March, finding herself having to repeat for the second time her request for dear 'Lilla to pass her the blue embroidery silk, could not know that Camilla was looking bleakly into her heart at her image of Nicholas. Try as she might, she could not adjust her picture of him as strong and honest, wickedly funny, tender, sensual and exciting, and replace it with that of a heartless seducer, a man blinded by the conventions of the day to her love and to what she could bring him.

Mr Brooke, calling to peruse Camilla's copy of the Babbage will, thought her much changed, and of all her friends guessed most nearly at the cause. So, she had flown too near the sun and had her wings singed, he thought pityingly. Well-bred as Camilla was, it would be an ambitious step to aspire to marry an earl. Damn the man for leading her on! Mr Brooke was a patient man and, although not one given to deep passions, had been more cast down than Camilla realised when she had refused his first proposal. Perhaps if he were to wait a month or two, he mused, he could hazard his fortune again.

'This, I make no bones about telling you, Camilla, is a confused mess!' He poked with his quill pen at the sheets of paper covered in Camilla's flowing hand. 'However, there is some virtue in its very weakness. No judge, should it come to it, is going to believe that this was Mr Babbage's true intention. Leave it with me, for it is perfectly possible for a will to be amended after death provided all parties are willing. It will not look good for a charity devoted to widows to be seen to profit at the expense of just such an unfortunate person. I am sure, if Mrs Babbage is prepared to offer them a small additional sum, we can reach a satisfactory conclusion. I will leave for Cheltenham tomorrow and speak to her myself.'

He rose and unexpectedly took her hand in his, raising it to his lips. 'You are tired, my dear Camilla. Please look after yourself, for your friends do not care to see you so cast down.' The look he gave her was a speaking one, but she was hardly aware of it. 'I have acquired a new carriage: would you permit me to take you out in it soon? The fresh air and diversion will do you good.'

Camilla stood for a while after he had shown himself out, having reached agreement on the day for their drive. She raised the hand he had kissed to her cheek, unconsciously grateful for the comfort. Arthur was a good, caring friend. She looked out over the rooftops at the waters of the river below and remembered Nicholas staring out of this same window. It seemed very long ago. So much had happened between them since then.

After several minutes she gave a little start and walked determinedly into her bedchamber. Pulling out a stool, she reached up for a hatbox which she had pushed well to the back of the clothes press and lifted it down.

Inside were the folded dressing-gown and sash and Nicholas's tiepin. The heavy folds of silk felt alive and sensual under her hands and seemed to resist her efforts to fold them neatly and be trapped within the layers of brown paper she was parcelling them in. The scent of sandalwood rose rich and exotic to her nostrils, and she had to fight the urge to bury her face in the richness and drink in the scent of Nicholas for one last time.

Carefully she wrapped the tiepin in tissue paper and slipped it into the parcel, then she knotted the string and lit a candle. The hot red wax dripped onto the knot, sealing it with a dreadful finality.

She sat at her writing desk, pulled a sheet of paper towards her and began to write without hesitation or correction.

Miss Knight presents her compliments to the Earl of Ashby and takes the liberty of returning to him some items which have come into her possession during the course of a recent journey and which she believes belong to his lordship.

Miss Knight begs that the Earl will not trouble to acknowledge this trifling service and regrets that it is unlikely that she will be at home should his lordship call.

Miss Knight would like to take the opportunity to congratulate his lordship upon the acquisition of a very fine new horse and observes with interest what gratification his lordship's skill in games of chance gives his lordship's closest friends. Miss Knight will endeavour to learn from this example of the relative values placed upon friendship and the winning of a wager.

Camilla folded and sealed the envelope and rang for the footman. 'Please deliver this parcel and this letter to the residence of the Countess of Forres to await the arrival of the Earl of Ashby. There is no need to wait for a reply.'

The parcel and letter sat for two days upon the dresser in Nicholas's usual room in his sister's house. When he finally arrived from Ashby he was late for dinner and Georgiana, for once tolerant of informality, urged him to delay merely to wash. 'I will forgive you your riding-boots this once, Lovell,' she declared. 'You and I will be eating alone this evening. Henry has a bad head cold and has retired to bed so I have been forced to cancel this evening's visit to the theatre. Hurry down and tell me all the gossip from the country, for I swear not a thing of interest has occurred in Bath these two weeks past.'

The parcel was unnoticed in the shadows as Nicholas made himself respectable and ran downstairs again to join his sister. It suited him well enough to dine quietly at home that evening, for he was too late to visit the Paragon and Camilla. The delay added piquancy to his desire to see her and he was smiling as he entered the dining-room, wondering what she would be wearing next morning and whether she had managed to get all of the soot out of her eyebrows.

'You are looking very pleased with yourself, Lovell,' Georgiana observed tartly. 'Now tell me, how is my dear Lady Corsham? Not managed to marry off that scrapegrace son of hers yet, I see.'

Nicholas grinned. 'Poor Freddie, he was very much in his mama's bad books, I am afraid. Still, he has escaped once again, despite her best efforts. Lady Corsham is very well and begs to be remembered to you. So does Lady Ellwood. We attended a fine entertainment at their house one evening— amateur dramatics of a very high order. Lady Ellwood staged the whole thing outside on a grass stage: very effective, if unconventional.'

'Indeed? Pass me the gooseberry sauce, my dear. Really, I do feel this bird is a trifle tough. How is the salmon? And who was at Lady Ellwood's entertainment that I would know?'

Nicholas recalled a list of names, prompting a flow of reminiscence and faintly scandalous stories from his sister. 'And Mrs Knight with her daughters. One of them has become contracted to her cousin, who inherited the family estates, so there is much rejoicing as you may imagine.'

Georgiana looked up sharply. 'The Knights? The Knights from the Paragon? And which daughter has become betrothed?'

'The younger, Miss Ophelia.'

'Indeed!' Georgiana toyed with her meat, finally

pushing the plate away. 'Benton, you may tell Cook that this goose is tough.'

'Yes, my lady.' The butler removed her plate and left the room.

'And how does the elder Miss Knight take to her sister's engagement? I do not think that many would have wagered on her having her nose put out of joint by that child becoming betrothed before her.'

Nicholas shrugged and helped himself to burgundy. 'This is a fine bottle; remind me to ask Henry where he got it from. The Knight engagement is not yet announced, you understand. Miss Knight seems happy for her sister's good fortune, that is all I can discern.'

'Humph. When do they plan to return to Bath?'

'I cannot say when Mrs Knight and Miss Ophelia will come home, but I believe Miss Knight may have already returned.'

It was Georgiana's turn to smile. 'Unusual to have left her mother and sister and travelled alone. Shall I call upon her?'

Nicholas returned the look blandly. 'Just as you wish, sister dear. I am sure she would welcome your company. For myself, I shall call tomorrow morning.'

It was not until Nicholas was shrugging on his dressing-gown the next morning, after a belated and prolonged breakfast and was waiting for his valet to whisk his shaving soap into a rich foam, that he noticed the parcel on the dresser.

'What is that?'

'A parcel delivered a few days ago, my lord. There is a letter with it I understand.'

Nicholas picked up the letter and sat in the chair,

raising his chin to allow the valet to swathe him in a large towel. The man began to strop the razor as Nicholas broke the seal and opened the pages. His oath and the abruptness with which he sat up caused the startled man to leap backwards.

As he said afterwards to the butler, 'I'm still shaking now, Mr Benton. How I didn't take off his lordship's ear I'll never know, and my hands were all of a tremble. It's a miracle I didn't cut him shaving.'

'Years of experience,' the butler said graciously. 'Whatever it was, it's sent his lordship off with a rare scowl on his face, that's for sure.'

Chapter Thirteen

Nicholas's long legs and furious temper took him towards the long hill up to the Paragon without him even noticing the early morning scene around him. The smart set were out in their carriages or on foot, nodding and greeting each other as they went in and out of the many fashionable shops.

The pavements were newly swept and gleaming with wetness where shopkeepers had swilled them down. It was all lost on Nicholas as he wove his way through the crowds on the pavements, stopping occasionally to let a lady past, or nodding in acknowledgement of a 'good morning' called by a passing acquaintance.

He was walking around the Circus, heading towards Bennett Street, when there was a splintering crash as the owner of a sporting gig misjudged the angel at the corner and hit the kerb with one wheel. Chaos ensued; the horse got its legs over the traces, a sedan chair, cornering at the trot, collided with the rear, its Irish bearers filling the air with Hibernian oaths. All the traffic in the Circus ground to a halt, and Nicholas, unwilling to force his way through the throng of onlookers, found himself standing at the edge of the pavement.

Over the hubbub a feminine voice, carrying with the clarity of a performer, reached his ears. 'Oh, that poor bearer, I do hope he is not hurt!' It was Camilla, seated beside the driver of a very dashing tilbury.

Her attention was all on the accident, but Nicholas stepped back slightly behind a large matron wearing a toque and carrying a parasol. Through its silken fringe he could observe Camilla and her companion. Damn it! It was that sober-sided solicitor Brooke! Not, after all, quite such a puritan if he was prepared to splash out on such a sporting equipage.

Nicholas had thought how Camilla would look when he next saw her, but he was not prepared for just how very lovely she did look, perched up beside Arthur Brooke. Her slender form was sheathed in a fine wool walking-dress of spring green, with daffodil-yellow ribbons in her chip straw bonnet and yellow kid gloves on her hands, one of which carried a ridiculously small parasol, tilted rakishly over her shoulder.

She looked absolutely stunning, and was attracting the admiring attention of many of the gentlemen who had stopped to take in the scene. This attention had not been lost on Arthur Brooke, who could not but feel a certain smugness: not only was he driving the very latest sporting vehicle, but the lady beside him was a beauty of the very first water.

Neither he nor Nicholas could know what it had cost Camilla to rally her spirits and make the effort. But she was determined not to pine, and dear Arthur deserved that she made every effort to enjoy the treat he was offering her.

The blockage was cleared, the traffic moved on and Nicholas was left looking after the tilbury as it bowled once more towards the Paragon. 'Hell and damnation!' he swore, not quite enough under his breath to escape an outraged stare from the dowager behind whom he had been sheltering.

His expression by the time he reached the Knights' residence was still thunderous, a fact reflected on the footman's face as he answered the heavy knocking on the front door.

'I am sorry, my lord, but Miss Knight is not receiving today.'

'She will receive me.' Nicholas took a firm step over the threshold, thrust his hat, gloves and cane into the startled man's hands and opened the door into the salon. 'I will wait in here.'

He had a long wait. Finally, after the clock on the mantel had struck both the three-quarters and the hour, the footman returned. 'Miss Knight asks me to say she is not at home, my lord.' He held his breath for a long moment, wondering what he should do if Lord Lovell marched off to look for Miss Knight. It would no doubt be his duty to try and stop him, but he didn't fancy his chances...

'Indeed. Then please find me pen and ink.'

Relieved that the alarming visitor was showing signs of departing, the man hurried to obey. Nicholas took up the pen, scratched one line, signed it with a single initial and dusted it with sand. 'There. Take this to Miss Knight immediately, if you please.'

Camilla, sitting over her account books with Miss

March mending linen beside her, heard the footman return and saw with relief he was carrying a note. 'Has his lordship gone?'

'No, Miss Knight. He said to give you this.'

Camilla unfolded the note and spread it out on top of her accounts.

Come to me, or I will not leave this house until I have searched every room.

The bold arrogance of a single 'N' filled the rest of the sheet.

'Are you quite well, dear?' Miss March enquired. 'You have gone positively white.'

'Thank you, Marchy, I am quite well. There is a gentleman here to see me, and I am afraid that if I do not allow him to speak to me he is going to take up residence in the salon. Would you be so kind as to accompany me?'

Miss March exclaimed at the early hour, speculated as to what he might want and who it was, worried that it might be a message from Mrs Knight with bad news, and generally managed to prevent Camilla achieving a single coherent or helpful thought before they reached the salon.

Camilla let the footman open the door and dismissed him with a smile. 'Thank you, James. His lordship will not be staying long enough for us to require refreshments.'

Nicholas stood as she entered, his eyebrows raised somewhat at the sight of Miss March.

'Miss March, may I introduce the Earl of Ashby? My lord, Miss March—my companion.'

Nicholas threw Miss March into a tizzy by bowing over her hand with exquisite grace. He lifted her little paw in its lace mitten in his and led her to the door before she had a chance to protest. 'Miss March, I have long desired to meet you, and I trust I will have the opportunity before long of making your better acquaintance. However, I am afraid that I have a matter of the utmost discretion to discuss with Miss Knight and I simply cannot have another person present. I am sure you will understand.'

She was almost out of the door before she realised what was happening. 'But my lord! I must chaperon Miss Knight!'

'I promise I will not seduce her this morning,' Nicholas replied, with such sincerity that she was reassured and was half-way back to the parlour with the salon door firmly closed on her before what he had said penetrated her brain.

'How dare you say such a thing?' Camilla knew she was white. Her hands were shaking so much she had to clasp them tightly together.

'Surely you do not expect me to seduce you here; it would be most inappropriate.' He strolled across and stood very close to her. 'Will you not sit down and tell me the meaning of that letter you wrote me?'

For a moment Camilla found she had no power to move or speak. Whether it was anger or misery that froze her she had no idea. Finally she managed to sit down, still clasping her trembling hands tightly together and said, 'You should be more careful where you discuss your successful wagers, my lord. I overheard your friends in the inn congratulating you. Surely you cannot be surprised if I resent my virtue being the subject of a public bet?'

There was a long silence before Nicholas spoke.

'Miss Knight's virtue has never been in question, nor discussed,' Nicholas said quietly.

'You are playing with words, my lord,' she said sharply, looking up at him. There was nothing to read in his face except a mild regret at her anger. 'I am both Mademoiselle Davide and Camilla Knight. You have always known that. I realise it now. You have played with me, toyed with my affections, manipulated the way I felt about you—and all because you made a bet with your friends over a horse and an actress! Are you not ashamed of yourself?'

'I did not know who you were when I made that bet.'

'But you soon did, did you not? It would have been very easy to have walked away, Nicholas—I made it easy for you by vanishing as Mademoiselle Davide. No one would have thought anything of it if you had failed to find one actress who chose to retire completely. Your friends would have had no reason to mock your much vaunted virility and success with women, would they? Nick the stallion? Nick with the devil's own luck with women? Even he cannot be expected to seduce a woman who isn't there. But, no, you had to seek me out and play with me like a cat with a mouse.'

He walked away and stood with his back towards her, looking out of the long window. 'You seemed to welcome my company.'

Camilla bit her lip until the pain steadied her. 'You mean I appeared to welcome your embraces.' She managed to say it without blushing crimson, even when Nicholas turned to regard her steadily.

'Yes, those too.'

'It did not occur to you that I had fallen in love with you?'

He met the challenge in her eyes, returning her stare. 'Not at first. I did not know, you see, what experience you might have had in your other life.'

'You must think me a very good actress if you could not tell I was a virgin!'

'I do think you are a good actress. You proved it at Lady Ellwood's house.'

Camilla got to her feet with a jerk and took one angry pace towards him. 'And you decided to take the opportunity I so foolishly gave you to win your bet! You could have warned me you were expecting your friends the moment you saw me in that inn. At best I could have left the place, there and then. At worst I would have spent the night unseen in my room. But, oh no, it was too good a chance, was it not? You made love to me. You told me you loved me…'

Her voice cracked, but she steadied it with an effort, throwing up a hand to still the step he made towards her. 'I was such a fool I thought you meant to marry me. I suppose I am not the only woman who has made a fool of herself over a man. But I did believe, my lord, that you were a gentleman, that you would not split hairs to the point of protecting my mother and my sister but not caring what happened to me.'

Nicholas's face was dark, his mouth tight. He seemed to remain where he was by a great effort of will. 'You seem determined to think the worst of me.'

'I do,' she spat back. 'And do not think I do not

think badly of myself as well! Are you telling me that that horse is not in your stables now?'

'Yes, I am. It is in Freddie's.'

'How come?' Camilla raised a skeptical eyebrow.

'Because I could not accept it: I had not won the wager, so I lost to Freddie at cards that night—with Thunderer as my stake.'

Camilla sat down again, staring at him. 'Let me understand this aright. You gave the horse back. Not because it was an ungentlemanly thing to have done to have wagered my virtue on it or because you had betrayed me. You gave it back because you *failed* to seduce me and therefore you had won it under false pretences?'

'You really do not understand, Camilla. Now listen to me...' Nicholas raked his hand through his hair as if wrestling his words into an order which would convince her of what he was trying to say.

'I understand only too well, my lord!' Camilla was in no mood to be mollified.

'No, you do not.' He took two long strides towards her, then stopped at the look on her face. 'I had to make things right with that damned horse and Freddie, then I had to come and see you...'

'For what purpose? Do not try and pretend I have stung your *honour* to the point of feeling you need to buy me off! Well, my lord? What have you come to offer me?' Camilla sat back in the seat and regarded Nicholas with cold disdain, but her breathing was far from steady

'I came to offer you an apology, although quite frankly, Camilla, just at the moment all I feel inclined to do is box your ears!' He looked as though he might carry out the threat and Camilla sat upright with a grim determination not to give him the satisfaction of seeing her flinch. 'I also came in order to ask you to marry me,' he finished.

'To marry you!' She was on her feet again, face to face with him, eyes sparkling with fury. 'You ask me to marry you after what happened in Buckingham!'

'That seems a very good reason,' he retorted hotly. 'After all, I damned near took you…' He pulled himself up and added, 'I mean, I compromised you.'

'Took me! How dare you use such indelicate language to my face? And to marry you for *that*! It is the worst reason I can think of! Let us be quite clear about this: why did you not ask me to marry you before? In the inn you told me you loved me.'

'Lovells do not marry actresses. You may have kept your scandalous secret from all but your family but that is hardly the point: you have behaved in a way totally unfitting for the Countess of Ashby.' Nicholas had his temper on a tight rein again. It was obvious that he considered this to be an adequate explanation.

Two spots of colour burned high on Camilla's cheekbones.

'Oh, I see. Lovells do not marry actresses. Well, that is plain enough, my lord. How irritating I must be, confusing your rigid code of honour! Sometimes I am an actress, but I am always a lady. And now, because you made a botch of seducing the actress and your precious honour will not let you risk the lady being compromised, you have gritted your teeth and decided to make the best of it!' Camilla side-stepped neatly, away from the anger which burned in Nicholas's blue eyes. 'Well, my lord Earl, you may take your very gracious offer and remove yourself from this house! I never want to see you again!'

She swept over to the door, wrenched it open, and finally lost her composure. 'Oh, go away, I hate you!'

Faced with an interested audience of the footman, Miss March and Cook holding a rolling-pin, Nicholas produced an impeccable bow, snatched up his hat and cane and stalked through the front door.

Under Camilla's smouldering gaze the footman scurried to close the door, then removed himself swiftly through the green baize door.

Miss March, clutching Cook's arm, looked at her charge in astonishment, but words were beyond her. Camilla turned to the cook and addressed her loftily. 'Mrs Powes, I do not believe I have seen this week's menus as yet. Will you be so good as to bring them to the salon immediately? Oh, and I think Miss March will be better for a cup of camomile tea.'

She gathered her skirts and swept off to the salon, followed by Miss March in a state of great disarray and emitting faint clucks of disapproval. 'Dearest 'Lilla…that man…'

If Nicholas had thought about it at all he would have assumed that his sister would be out making morning calls, but Lady Forres, far more interested than she had let him guess in the progress of his relationship with Camilla, was hovering in the drawing room with the door ajar.

She heard his key in the lock and put down her tambour frame with a look of alert interest in her eyes. Now, how had her incorrigible brother gone on with the lovely Miss Knight? Then the sound of his cane and hat hitting the hall stand made her wince and she slowed in her eager advance to the door. The butler's voice as he arrived in the hall was faintly reproachful.

'I must apologise, my lord, for not being here to open the door to you. May I take your gloves, my lord? Is that your hat on the floor, my lord, doubtless your valet will be able to do something with it. Her ladyship is in the…'

'I have no need to disturb her ladyship at the moment, thank you, Benton. Please have my valet attend me in my chamber immediately: I will be leaving this morning.' The words were clipped and Georgiana came to a complete halt, her lower lip caught between her teeth.

So, his suit had not prospered. What on earth had happened to put him in such a temper? And how had he managed to fail with Miss Knight? Georgiana, having seen them together, was convinced that Miss Knight had a distinct partiality for her brother. What was the girl thinking of? He was the Earl of Ashby, after all!

Emerging into the hall, she followed the sound of his footsteps up the sweeping stairs and along the landing, pushing open his bedchamber door without ceremony. Her brother was sitting at his writing-table staring at a blank sheet of paper, the pen in his hand. Without turning his head he said curtly, 'Stevens, pack my things at once. We leave as soon as maybe.'

'Lovell, why are you in such a pet?' Georgiana demanded, sweeping into the room and sitting firmly on the end of the bed.

'I am not in a *pet* as you put it, my dear sister. I am just writing you a note: I find I have to return to Ashby urgently.'

'Nonsense. You have received no message from Buckinghamshire.' The door opened and the valet appeared, looking startled at the sight of the Countess perched unconventionally on the bed. 'You may go, Stevens. His lordship no longer requires you.'

The man effaced himself quickly and hurried off. Mr Benton's expression when he had given him his lordship's summons and the dented hat had spoken volumes: perhaps the butler could throw some light on his lordship's black mood.

'Georgiana, I would be obliged if you did not countermand my orders to my own servants.' Nicholas tossed down the quill and got to his feet.

'Sit down, Lovell, and stop pacing; you are making me feel tired. Now, what have you done to upset that lovely Miss Knight?'

Nicholas regarded his sister blankly, then his face relaxed and he laughed. 'I see you are taking your usual measured view of life, Georgiana dear! I beg you, never allow your ignorance of the facts to stand in the way of your opinions.'

The Countess flapped her hand at him irritably. 'Never mind all that! Now, I assume she has refused you?'

'And what makes you think I have made Miss Knight an offer?'

'You have been in love with her for weeks...'

'Have I?' her brother asked faintly.

'Of course, although no doubt your frivolous friends might not notice. And she, of course, is head over heels in love with you.'

'Is she?'

'Stop sounding like a parrot, Lovell. Despite the

fact that Miss Knight is an elegant, well-mannered and refined young woman, her true feelings cannot be hidden from an experienced woman of the world such as myself...'

'In that case,' Nicholas responded wryly, 'you may tell me why she has refused me, and why she is out and about with her damned man of business—who, if I'm not very much mistaken, aspires to be rather more than that to her.'

'Presumably because you have done something to upset her,' Georgiana declared. 'Really, Lovell, you men are so clumsy in matters of the heart.'

'If she loves me,' Nicholas asked, the wry smile still twisting his lips, 'would she not forgive me, whatever I have done?'

'It depends what she has to forgive you for.' Georgiana eyed him closely. 'And only you know what it is—and just how unforgivable you have been. Nick,' she said suddenly, seizing his hand and pulling him down to sit beside her, 'what has gone wrong?'

Nicholas stared down at his sister's heavily be-ringed hand clasping his and knew he could not begin to tell her of Camilla's double life. 'Nothing I can tell you about: it is not all my secret to tell. You are right. I have given Miss Knight quite unforgivable provocation.'

'Then,' Georgiana said gently, 'you may have to face the fact that for once in your life there is something which being the Earl of Ashby cannot secure you.'

Chapter Fourteen

Next morning Mr Brooke called at the house in the Paragon at the respectable hour of half past eleven and found Miss Knight, clad in a gown of soft sea-green, sitting alone in the salon with a book of poetry in her hand.

Camilla laid the volume aside as he came in and smiled with pleasure at the sight of her old and trusted friend. It was so good to see Arthur Brooke; she had always regarded him as a friend as well as her man of business, and now she wished they were on such terms that she could confide in him as a brother.

After they had exchanged greetings and he was sitting beside her on the sofa he enquired, 'A new volume? Would you recommend it?' He picked it up and scrutinised the spine.

'I really cannot say,' Camilla confessed. 'I intended to cut the pages, but as you can see I have been sitting here quite idle all morning.'

She spoke lightly, as though mocking her own indolence, but Mr Brooke could sense a falseness in her tone. Her skin was pale, there were slight shadows under her eyes as though she had not slept, yet her hair and grooming were, as always, impeccable. It was as though something—or someone—had sapped her spirits. Yet when he had left her yesterday she had been quite her old self.

'I have come to let you know what progress I have made with Mr Babbage's will,' he began, conscious that he was engaging only part of her attention. 'I believe you were quite correct in assuming he had simply confused his intentions when he began to write them down. I have consulted a colleague with much experience in this area of law and he says…'

Camilla listened dutifully, but the words washed over her and afterwards she could not have repeated what Mr Brooke had imparted.

'…no need for a judge to be involved at all,' he concluded. She looked at him blankly, so he added, 'Good news, do you not agree?'

'Oh, yes…thank you so much for all your trouble.'

Arthur Brooke cast round the room looking for inspiration. He could not think of a pretext to keep the conversation going but he did not want to get up and leave Camilla when she was so obviously out of spirits. Her eyes were cast down, the long lashes fanning her pale cheeks and he felt a sudden desire to take her in his arms, protect her from life's hazards.

'That is a pretty cameo,' he finally remarked for lack of something else to say—or do. 'Is it new? I do not think I have seen you wearing it before.'

'I…it was a present, given to me by…someone who was a friend but is no longer so. That made me reluctant to wear it, but I am trying to overcome such foolishness. It is a pretty thing, is it not?' Her tone was studiedly neutral, but knowing her as he did Arthur sensed deep pain, even betrayal, behind those few words. Betrayal? Was he becoming melodramatic? he chided himself. The atmosphere in the room was beginning to affect him with a sense that some catastrophe had taken place and Camilla was hiding it from him.

She gazed down at the cameo that Nicholas had given her that night in the Green Room and touched it with one fingertip. Mr Brooke could not see the expression in her downcast eyes, but he saw the soft curve of her lip tremble and he found he could be sensible no longer.

'Miss Knight…Camilla. I realise this is sudden, and that I should speak to your mama first, but you cannot be insensible of the regard in which I hold you and the strength of my feelings for you. Will you not be my wife, my dear Camilla?'

Camilla, finding her hands seized in his, looked up in astonishment. 'Mr Brooke—Arthur—this is indeed sudden. When you asked me this question before, did we not agree that we would be better remaining friends?'

'Yes, but my feelings for you have undergone a change. I find myself quite…enamoured of you.' His honest brown eyes looked earnestly into her face as if seeking her answer there. 'I cannot offer you luxury or a title, but I can promise you every comfort, a good home, my devoted protection.'

Camilla met his gaze for a long moment. She could accept him—and the marriage would be everything he said. He would be a good, affectionate husband and in time she would learn to be content, but the minute she thought it she rejected it as dishonest. She did not love Arthur, and what was more she loved Nicholas. She could not betray Arthur in that way by giving him second best, despite the fact she had been betrayed herself.

Gently Camilla disentangled her hands from his. 'Arthur, my dear, you are a very good friend to me and I know you would make a wonderful husband.' She saw hope dawning in his face and hurried on before he could misunderstand her. 'I hold you in high regard, Arthur, but I do not love you and I do not believe I ever can, not as a wife should. And,' she added with an attempt at lightness, 'I would make a very bad wife for a lawyer, you must admit!'

'You love someone else, do you not?' he asked soberly.

Camilla looked him straight in the face and said simply, 'Yes.'

'I think I can guess to whom you refer.' Camilla held up her hand as if to stop him saying the name. 'But you will not marry him either?'

'No. I will never marry, I think.'

'Then what will you do with your life, Camilla?' He was looking at her with concern and affection.

'What I always intended,' Camilla replied with a little shrug. 'Be a companion to Mama, a support to Ophelia. She is to marry our cousin Stephen Knight, so perhaps I will have an aunt's duties in the fullness of time.'

The small silence stretched on, then Arthur enquired gently, 'And that will be enough for you?'

'It will have to be,' Camilla said with sudden determination. 'I have no intention of moping, in fact

I have moped quite enough already. We will say no more about it. Let me call Miss March in and you can explain to her what you have achieved for her sister.'

'No!' To her consternation Arthur Brooke fell to his knees beside her. 'No, Camilla! I cannot permit you to sacrifice yourself in this way because some personable rake with charm and a title has toyed with your heart and then cast you aside.'

Camilla put out one hand and touched his shoulder. 'Please, Arthur, do not say any more.' This was hurting so much.

'I will say more! Your nobility of character, your generosity of spirit that would set aside your own hurts to support your mother and sister without thought for self, only serves to endear you even more to me. Please, please reconsider, Camilla. I only want to make you happy. You like me a little, do you not? We are friends, are we not? We can build love on that foundation—so many people go into marriage with far less, yet become happy!'

Camilla felt under siege, not only from Arthur Brooke's passionate declaration but also from her weaker self. How easy it would be to say yes. Arthur would always be a good husband, and he would make a good father too; she sensed that. Perhaps marriage to him would be the only chance she ever had to have a family of her own.

Overwhelmed by affection for him, and a deep sense of regret that she was going to have to disappoint him, Camilla took his earnest face in both her hands and leaned forwards to kiss him gently on the cheek. As her lips brushed his face she murmured, 'No, Arthur, I am sorry. You are my dearest friend; let us at least keep that.'

Arthur Brooke was too human not to turn his lips to meet hers. If this was going to be the only opportunity he ever had to hold her in his arms, then he was going to seize it. As his lips touched hers the door swung open and Nicholas strode in, his progress unimpeded by the protesting footman in his wake.

For a moment the four people in the room froze. It was Nicholas who spoke first, his words cutting across the silence.

'I will thank you, sir, to unhand Miss Knight!' Damn it! He had come to tell her he loved her, tell her he knew he had been an arrogant fool, to humble himself and lay his heart at her feet only to discover this! That bloody little solicitor, with his stiff disapproval and his dusty ways kissing her on the hearthrug!

There was a sharp click as the door shut behind the footman, for once showing admirable discretion and effacing himself.

Mr Brooke, his face flushed with anger and embarrassment, jumped to his feet, revealing himself as far from the little clerk that Nicholas had mentally labelled him. As tall as his lordship, in his dark, impeccably cut suiting he looked every bit as formidable in his anger as the Earl.

Camilla too jumped to her feet, 'My lord, Arthur...please...' They both completely disregarded her.

'How dare you burst in upon Miss Knight's private apartments in this way, my lord?' Arthur

Brooke's hands were clenched at his sides, his eyes locked with Nicholas's.

'It is a good thing for Miss Knight that I did. In the absence of her chaperon, who knows what liberties you would have taken next, sir!' To Camilla's frightened gaze Nicholas was looking extremely dangerous. His sword hand was flexing automatically, although naturally he wore no weapon; his face was set and hard, his eyes cold and glittering.

Hastily she stepped forward, placing herself between the two men, and said as steadily as she could to Nicholas, 'Your behaviour and your accusations are unwarranted, my lord. Mr Brooke has only the most honourable of intentions.' Nicholas's eyes narrowed at this palpable hit, but she swept on. 'Whom I choose to receive in my own house, with or without a chaperon, is my business and mine alone!'

'It strikes me, Miss Knight, that you should be thanking me for preserving your reputation, not roundly abusing me. What would your mama have said if she could have seen that pretty little tableau just now?'

'*You* speak to me of my reputation?' she stormed at him, completely forgetting the presence of Arthur Brooke. 'When has my reputation ever been of the slightest concern of yours? My mother would have no qualms about my receiving an *honourable* declaration, nor would she appreciate your interference in this family's affairs. You, my lord, are neither my father, my brother nor my husband, and as such have no influence or rights over me!'

Her breasts were rising and falling in the close-fitting gown with the strength of her emotions, her cheeks were flushed rose and her eyes sparked fire at him. Nicholas thought he had never seen her look more beautiful nor more desirable. 'For heaven's sake, Camilla, stop this nonsense. Dismiss this clerk. You know you are meant for me.'

Before she realised what he was about Nicholas had taken her by the shoulders, pulled her towards him and fastened his mouth on hers in a hard, urgent kiss.

The embrace lasted only seconds before Camilla found herself being lifted bodily out of the way and Arthur Brooke standing in her place, almost toe to toe with Nicholas. He drew back his clenched fist and, before she could cry out, drove it with punishing force straight at Nicholas's chin. He saw it coming, but the two men were far too close for him to avoid it connecting.

The blow sent Nicholas back a pace, then he recovered and threw an answering punch which sent the lawyer sprawling on the sofa. Camilla cast herself on Arthur's chest as the only way she could think of stopping Nicholas following up with another blow. 'Stop it—stop it both of you!'

Arthur shook his head as if to clear it, then put Camilla firmly on to the sofa beside him before getting to his feet. 'My lord, you will meet me for this.' Camilla was shocked by the cold menace in his voice: this was not the Arthur Brooke she knew.

'With pleasure,' Nicholas responded, equally coldly. He was massaging his bruised knuckles but his eyes were fixed on his opponent. 'Name your seconds, sir. Lord Forres will stand my friend.'

A fire of fury swept through Camilla from head to toe. How dared they brawl over her like this? She stood up and spoke sharply to both men. 'Stop this.

Stop it now! Both of you can take yourselves out of this house and agree your stupid duel somewhere else. I have had about as much of your male honour as I can take; it leads to nothing but grief and heart-ache. Now *go*!'

The two men, both still obviously in the grip of icy rage, bowed to her and left, punctiliously giving way to each other at the door.

They parted on the doorstep with a stiff bow, Arthur Brooke striding off up the hill, Nicholas, who had no wish to keep him company, going down to-wards the town. Mr Brooke reached Walcot church and turned blindly into the churchyard. He needed somewhere to sit and think, and the bench beside the aisle wall seemed as good a place as anywhere.

How the devil had he got himself into this coil? It was quite obvious that Nicholas was the man Camilla loved, and it seemed equally obvious that he was in love with her. He was certainly exhibiting violent possessiveness towards her. Killing or wounding the man she loved was hardly going to win over Camilla, he reflected, before common sense got the better of him and he had to admit to himself that if anyone was going to be hurt it was going to be him. The Earl, as the challenged party, had the choice of weapons, but whatever he decided upon he was going to be more than a match for his opponent. The best he could hope for was that the Earl would choose pistols. For himself, he would delope rather than risk hitting the man.

With a sigh Arthur Brooke got to his feet and set off to find a discreet friend to act as second for him, and to check that his will was up to date.

Four hours later, at the Forres house in the

Crescent, Nicholas was hardly having a more enjoyable time than his erstwhile opponent.

'You bloody idiot, Lovell!' his unsympathetic brother-in-law yelled. 'Georgiana is going to go mad when she hears of this.'

'We must make sure she doesn't,' Nicholas said firmly, jamming his bruised knuckles still further into his pockets. He had finally tracked down Lord Forres in his study, moodily contemplating a pile of bills, and had done nothing to improve his temper by informing him that he was to stand as his second in a duel with a respectable Bath solicitor.

Both men fell silent and were still contemplating the situation when there was a knock on the front door. A few moments later Benson came in with a card on a silver salver.

'A Mr Murray to see you, my lord.' Henry scooped up the card and scanned it swiftly.

'Ask him to wait in the front salon, Benson. Is her ladyship at home?'

'No, my lord, she asked me to say that she will not be in until after dinner. She is dining with Lady Richardson.'

Henry waited until the door closed behind the butler. 'Well, that's a small mercy at any rate. I wouldn't care to try and keep this from Georgiana with the house full of this other chap's seconds.'

Nicholas got to his feet. 'Is that who he is?' He flipped over the card and read,

"In the matter concerning Mr B."

'Well, how conciliatory do you want me to be?' Henry asked. 'Are you going to apologise?'

'Damn it, no! He was kissing her.'

Henry's eyebrows rose. 'So? You are not engaged to the lady. Was she in distress?'

Nicholas grimaced and raked his hand through his already unruly hair. 'No, she was kissing him back.'

'Then why did you hit him?' he asked with irritating reasonableness.

'Because I was going to ask her to marry me,' Nicholas said through gritted teeth.

'Sounds to me as though you should be apologising all round, old boy. Damn if I wouldn't have hit you myself in his shoes. Still, if you are determined to fight, what weapons do you want? I suppose it doesn't really matter. You can kill a provincial solicitor with either sword or pistol, I imagine.'

'Pistols. It will make it easier to delope.'

'Humph.' Henry got to his feet. 'Well, just hope your man hasn't a good eye, because while you are busily aiming over his head he could be winging you.'

The early-morning mist was still shrouding Claverton Down the next day as Nicholas and Lord Forres climbed out of their carriage and looked around. 'Six o'clock on the nose,' Henry remarked, consulting his pocket watch. 'There's the surgeon's gig. And here comes your man. He's not a shirker, that's for sure.'

Mr Brooke, looking unusually pale in his dark clothing, descended from his carriage accompanied by his second, Mr Murray, and waited while the two seconds came forward to discuss the field.

After a few minutes Lord Forres came back and indicated a flat area. 'That'll do. Now, I've brought my pistols. Which do you want?'

Nicholas took one at random and waited while Henry took the other over to Mr Brooke. In silence the two men obeyed the seconds' directions to turn and pace away from each other.

Waiting, the pistol held at his side, for Lord Forres to raise the white handkerchief, Nicholas looked at Arthur Brooke and wondered just how good a shot he was. He would not want to kill this man and find himself having to flee the country, but an inexperienced shot might well aim to wound and make too good a job of it. Would he ever see Camilla again?

Henry raised the white cloth and both duellists took aim. A vision of Camilla's face swam before Nicholas's eyes as he heard Henry call, 'In your own time!'

The still morning air was rent by two almost simultaneous cracks. Through the swirl of smoke from his own pistol, Nicholas could see from the angle of Arthur Brooke's arm that he too had deloped and fired well over his opponent's head.

Nicholas's heart was still beating loud in his ears as he walked slowly over to where Brooke was standing, one hand on the side of the carriage, a rueful grin on his very pale face.

'Mr Brooke, are you satisfied?'

'I am, my lord.' He cleared his throat. 'Not an experience I should wish to repeat, I must admit.'

Nicholas touched his shoulder. 'Nor I, sir, nor I. Come, there is a tavern down the hill; will you join me? There is a matter I would discuss with you.'

At the same time as the two duellists were talking over a glass of brandy in the Claverton Arms, Camilla was pacing her chamber. She had slept very little and now felt slightly sick as she contemplated the day before her. What was going on? She knew nothing—had never wanted to know anything—about the etiquette of duelling. How long would it take for the seconds to make the arrangements? A day or two, surely. Did she still have time to stop this madness? How could she? What could she say or do to change their minds once they set on a course of honour?

After a desultory breakfast, where she crumbled more bread than she ate, Camilla spent the morning pacing the drawing-room, driving Miss March to distraction by refusing to tell her what was the cause of her agitation. 'Oh dear, well if you will not tell me what is amiss, my dear, I will go and sort that old linen cupboard, for I declare I cannot sit here a moment longer,' she stated, as near to irritation as she ever got with her dear 'Lilla.

Fortunately for Camilla, a note arrived shortly afterwards in Mr Brooke's hand. For a long moment she stared at it. Was it to say he had killed Nicholas? Or had he written it before the two men had met, in case he was killed himself…?

It was pointless tormenting herself. Taking a deep breath, Camilla slit the seal and unfolded the stiff sheet.

My dear Miss Knight, I write to put your mind at rest. Both his lordship and I are unharmed, having met this morning and both fired into the air. Honour having been satisfied, I am now leaving for Cheltenham, but hope to call

on you as speedily as I can upon my return.
Believe me, I am, and will remain, your good
friend and servant Arthur Brooke.

Camilla's legs gave way and she dropped into the
chair, the letter crumpled in her hand. So that was
that. They were both safe, thank the Lord. It was
plain from Arthur's note that he had accepted that
she could never be his wife, but that he would remain her friend. That was good: she would have
hated to hurt him and she was going to need his
friendship now that she must give up all hope of
Nicholas. But he would remain in her heart and her
dreams and that must be enough. The future of spinsterhood that she had outlined to Arthur Brooke was
all that remained to her.

Two days later, as Camilla and Miss March were
sitting down to afternoon tea, Samuel came in with
a letter on a salver. 'For you, Miss Knight.'

The handwriting was familiar, and it was with a
slight frown that Camilla slit the seal. What could
Mr Porter of the Theatre Royal be writing to her
about now? Their connection was at an end, as he
knew only too well!

Mr Porter presents his compliments to
Mademoiselle Davide and requests the favour
of an interview with her upon a matter of some
urgency.

Mr Porter finds himself in possession of the
sole rights to a remarkable new play which he
has no hesitation in saying would be the the-
atrical sensation of the decade.

*The playwright has created the leading fe-
male role for Mademoiselle Davide and Mr
Porter considers that no other thespian could
undertake the role with such success as he an-
ticipates she could bring to it.*

Camilla, with mounting excitement, scanned the
rest of the letter. It did indeed sound a fascinating
role. She turned to the second page.

*Mr Porter requests a reply from Made-
moiselle Davide this very day. He apologises
for this unmannerly haste, but time is of the
essence if this manuscript is to be secured. Mr
Porter will be in his office between four
and six this afternoon, and can assure
Mademoiselle Davide of complete discretion if
she condescends to call upon him there.*

Her immediate instinct was to throw the paper in
the fire, but something stopped her. She spent half
an hour debating with herself, then, suddenly deci-
sive, she ran to her dressing-room.

As she tucked the last tendril of blonde hair under
the dark wig and fastened the long cloak around her
shoulders, Camilla felt the old excitement stirring.
This was madness; she had sworn to renounce the
theatre. But now what had she got to lose? Her life
was empty, Nicholas was gone, and at least she
could fill the emptiness with the hypnotic world of
make-believe.

With her hood pulled well up to hide her hair and
face, she asked the footman to call a sedan chair and

soon found herself outside the Theatre Royal stage door. Inside it was dark in the unwindowed corridors, the air heavy with the smell of dust, limelight and greasepaint. It was so familiar, so welcoming, she felt her blood stir in excitement.

But the silence was so odd and unsettling. She had never known the theatre without the bustle of stagehands, the banging of the scene-makers' hammers, the raised voices of rehearsals on stage.

The door at the foot of the stairs to Mr Porter's office was ajar and she began to climb. As she gained the landing, her heels sounding loud in the silence, a thought struck her. How had Mr Porter known where to send the letter and to whom to address it? She had never told him or anyone else at the theatre who she really was.

Camilla hesitated, suddenly very unsure of the wisdom of being there. But before she could turn and go the door in front of her opened inwards. Well, she could not go back now and never know who had discovered the key to her identity. Taking a deep breath, she stepped inside the theatre manager's office.

Of Mr Porter there was no sign, but the office was not empty.

'Hello, Camilla.' Nicholas stood up from the edge of the desk where he had been sitting. 'You came very promptly.'

'You! What are you doing here? And where is Mr Porter?'

Nicholas shrugged. 'Mr Porter is where I have paid him to be—in the local coffee-house, I suppose. Forget Mr Porter. Come to me, Camilla darling.'

Camilla, feeling as though she was in some sort of dream, walked forwards into his open arms and clung to him. 'Oh, Nicholas, what is this about?' But, in truth, for the moment she did not care why he had summoned her. She just wanted to be here, in his arms, her face pressed against his chest, drinking in the subtle smell of him.

She felt his hands on her head, then he had tugged off the wig and tossed it aside. 'It is about getting rid of this,' he murmured into her tumbled hair. 'It is about saying goodbye to Mademoiselle Davide, Camilla, my love.'

Camilla thrilled to his touch, to his endearments, but she still felt dizzily uncertain of what he intended. That searing scene in the Sydney Gardens when he had so angrily informed her that he had no intention of making her an offer of *any* kind still haunted her. 'Nicholas, what do you want from me?'

'I want you to be my wife, Camilla. I love you. I want to spend the rest of my life with you.'

Camilla pushed herself away from his chest and looked up into his face, lit with the light from the dusty window. 'But you told me that Lovells do not marry actresses. You are the Earl of Ashby!'

'And you are no longer an actress. But even if you were, I do not care. I love you. No one knows your secret, but that is neither here nor there—if the whole of polite society discovered that you were Mademoiselle Davide tomorrow I would not heed them. After all, I *am* the Earl of Ashby, and I do not give a damn what society thinks of me.'

Nicholas pulled her close again. 'Oh, I was so angry when we overheard those two old witches gossiping about us in the Sydney Gardens! Not angry with you—not particularly angry with them; they were only acting true to type—but so angry and ashamed at myself. I knew I should either have gone away, hugged my family pride to myself and forgotten all about you, or I should have told you that I knew your secret and that I did not care. Told you that I loved you and wanted to marry you...'

'Why then were you so cold, so angry with me?' she asked softly against his shirt-front.

'I do not think I have ever put myself quite so thoroughly in the wrong! I can only blame my damnable pride for what I said and how I said it. The other day when I found you with Arthur Brooke I was coming to tell you that. Coming to apologise for my arrogance, for hurting you so much. When I saw him kissing you I thought I had lost everything, every chance of happiness I could ever hope for.'

He buried his face in her sweet-smelling hair and said huskily, 'The morning of the duel, as I stood there waiting, all I could see was your face—all I could think of was that I might never see you again. Afterwards I spoke to Arthur Brooke, told him something of what a fool I had been. It was he who convinced me that I could still win you back, that he knew you loved me. He only proposed because he thought we would never marry.' A tinge of laughter touched his voice as he murmured, 'You made me so jealous, you know: your cousin Stephen, Arthur Brooke... I suffered torments imagining you with them. If nothing else, that pain should have told me all I needed to know about my feelings for you.'

Camilla clung to him. 'Nicholas, I was so frightened I was going to lose you. I love you so very much. I had made the decision that if I could not have you then I would have no one.'

Nicholas tipped up her face to his and she thought she had never seen his eyes look so tender.

'Camilla, tell me you will marry me. I want you to be my wife more than anything I have ever wanted in my life.'

'Oh, yes, Nicholas, I would very much like to marry you. Very much indeed.'

His kiss seemed to last for a lifetime. Finally, still holding her gently against him, Nicholas lifted his mouth from hers and smiled down into her happy face. Seeing him, seeing his look of love, she could not doubt he meant everything he said.

'Nicholas, why did you come back to me that day?'

'Because of something my infuriating sister Georgiana said. She told me that in you I had found the one thing that my rank, my fortune, my place in society could not secure for me. And at that moment I realised I cared nothing for any of them, that they were meaningless if I could not have you, Camilla.'

He kissed her again and she kissed him back with an intensity that convinced him that his love believed him, forgave him, and was his for ever.

* * * * *

The Gentleman's Demand
by
Meg Alexander

After living in southern Spain for many years, **Meg Alexander** now lives in East Sussex, although having been born in Lancashire, she feels that her roots are in the north of England. Meg's career has encompassed a wide variety of roles, from professional cook to assistant director of a conference centre. She has always been a voracious reader, and loves to write. Other loves include history, cats, gardening, cooking and travel. She has a son and two grandchildren.

Chapter One

1810

In the gathering dusk of a winter afternoon the long low parlour was filled with shadows. A few logs smouldered on the hearth, puffing out occasional gusts of acrid smoke. Neither of the occupants of the room appeared to notice. Then the man began to cough.

'For God's sake send for candles, girl!' he snapped. 'And send for someone to tend this fire before we choke to death.'

Such a fate might be better than further hours of argument, Sophie thought wearily. She kept that sentiment to herself as she rose to ring the bell.

'The wind must have changed direction,' she said quietly. 'We've always had a problem with this chimney…'

'Would that it were your only problem!' The man fell silent as a servant entered the room. It was but a momentary respite. As the door closed behind the boy he picked up the lighted candelabra and carried it over to his daughter's side, setting it on the table by her chair.

'Just look at you!' he snarled. 'To think that any child

of mine should be living under these conditions! I shouldn't have known you for the girl you were six years ago.'

'What did you expect?' Sophie cried in desperation. 'Have you no mercy, Father? It's but a month since I was widowed...'

For a moment there was silence. Then, with a visible effort to control his anger, Edward Leighton spoke in a softer tone.

'Forgive me for distressing you, my dear, but I can't see your loss as anything but a blessing. You are still young, and you have your life before you. Come home with me and make a fresh start. We shall find some way of glossing over your absence for these past years. A single mistake may be forgiven, serious though it was...'

'A serious mistake?' Sophie gave a bitter laugh. 'Father, you haven't changed. How lightly you dismiss my marriage...'

His face darkened. 'I never took it lightly. It was the worst blow of my life. I gave you too much freedom, Sophie. When you eloped you ruined all my hopes for you, and with such a man! You could scarce have chosen worse.'

'Stop!' she cried. 'You shan't disgrace Richard's memory.'

'Others did so long ago. You won't pretend that he was aught but a penniless nobody, possessed of neither character nor probity?'

Sophie's eyes flashed fire. 'How dare you say such things? You didn't know him.'

Her father gave an ironic laugh. 'I decided to forgo that honour. Others were not so fortunate. Why was he dismissed from the Revenue Service? Can you tell me that? I heard some talk of corruption.'

Sophie rose to her feet and eyed him with disdain. 'I never believed those lies. There was a plot against him.'

'Others believed it. The evidence was strong, and the authorities were in no doubt. You knew better, I suppose?'

'I refused to listen to rumour, or to believe those trumped-up charges.'

'Still as headstrong as ever, Sophie?' Edward Leighton sighed. 'I must admire your loyalty, even though it is misplaced.'

'You'll never understand, so there is no point in speaking of these things.'

'Very well. I haven't come to quarrel with you. My dear, nothing will restore your husband to you, but life must go on. It is early to speak of it, but in time you will remarry... With rest and an easier life you will regain your looks, and then we'll see. William, you know, has never married, and he is of a forgiving disposition.'

Sophie stared at him. 'So that's it!' she said slowly. 'I might have known that there would be some reason for your sudden change of heart. It wasn't concern for me that brought you here. Unwed, I am of use to you again.'

Her father was quick to rebut the charge. 'You are grown so hard,' he complained. 'Must you pick me up on every word? Your mother and I are thinking only of your happiness.'

'And that of Sir William Curtis too, no doubt. I'm sorry, but I don't believe you. You've always coveted his fortune and his lands.'

'Was it so wrong to want the best for you? I could never understand why you took against him.'

'A man with the reputation of a lecher? Father, you were blinded by his wealth.'

'No man is perfect, Sophie, as you must have learned by now. All this high-minded disregard for comfort and position proves to me that you are still a foolish girl. It is not the way of the world.'

Sophie did not answer him.

'There is no hurry for you to wed again,' he said in a coaxing tone. 'We shall not rush you into making a decision. William has shown great forbearance. He has forgiven you your—'

'My silly misdemeanour in marrying another man? How noble of him. I wonder, will he accept my son as well?'

Edward Leighton's face grew dark. 'Don't be a fool!' he snapped. 'I'm not suggesting that you bring the boy.'

Sophie looked at him in disbelief. 'What are you saying? You can't mean it! Christopher is your grandson.'

'No!' he cried. 'I'll have no whelp of Firle's beneath my roof. You must send him for adoption…'

It was enough. Sophie rose to her feet. 'I always thought you hard,' she said. 'But this is unbelievable!'

'You may believe it, my girl. Was I ever hard with you? I gave you everything—'

'Everything but understanding, Father—'

'Pah! A child should be dutiful and obedient to the wishes of its parents. You had no experience of the world. At seventeen, how could you decide where your best interests lay?'

'Not with Sir William, certainly…'

'Firle was a better choice? In my view he was lucky not to be transported.' A bitter laugh preceded his next words. 'You don't agree? Tell me, then, where did he find the money to buy this place? It is a well-known hostelry. Have you any idea how much it must have cost?'

Sophie shook her head and turned away. It was a subject which had often troubled her. 'He had friends…' she whispered.

'That, at least, is true, but who were they? Did you ever meet them?'

Her silence gave him his answer.

'I see that you did not. You didn't think to ask? Well, after all, it was not a woman's place to do so. I don't blame you for your ignorance, but you must face the truth. The man you married was a handsome weakling, seduced by the opportunity to make easy money.' Squire Leighton looked at his daughter and sighed. 'You aren't the first woman to be deceived by such a creature, and you won't be the last, more's the pity.'

Sophie began to tremble, but she faced him squarely. 'You shan't say those things of Richard—' She could not go on.

'Stuff! What do you know of men and their desires? Firle was on the make, my dear. His prayers were answered when an heiress fell into his lap. He must have thought that I'd forgive you once you were safely wed.'

'I know better!' Sophie was on her feet, her cheeks aflame. 'He wouldn't have touched a farthing of your money, and nor would I, even had you offered it.'

'There was no danger of that.'

'No, you made that all too clear. You cut me off completely, Father. In these last six years I haven't heard a word from you. I wrote to Mama, but I had no reply. Did you forbid her to answer me?'

'I did.' Edward Leighton looked about him in disgust. 'Would you have had her visit you here, in a common alehouse? How pleasant it would have been for her to see her daughter mixing with all and sundry!'

'I'm not ashamed of it. It is an honest living.'

'Bought with the proceeds of corruption?'

Sophie controlled her anger with an effort. Then, as the

gusting wind sent rain lashing against the window-panes, she changed the subject.

'The storm grows worse,' she observed quietly. 'Will you stay here tonight?'

'I must leave within the hour. Sophie, you haven't answered me. Come home to us. One mistake may be forgiven. It will soon be forgotten—'

'As I must forget my son?'

'I meant what I said.' Her father's lips tightened. 'I won't house that reminder of your folly.'

'Then there's no more to be said. I thank you, Father, but I can't accept your offer.' Sophie glanced through the window. 'Won't you stay?' she asked again. 'You won't wish to travel in this weather.'

'I'll be the judge of that. I may tell you that nothing would persuade me to remain beneath your roof. Of all the wicked, ungrateful girls...'

'I'm sorry you feel like that.'

'I do, and I wash my hands of you. You've made your bed. Now you must lie in it. It will break your mother's heart, but you must make no attempt to get in touch with her. From now on I have no daughter, and nor has she.' He pushed past her and stormed out of the room, calling for his carriage as he did so.

Sophie stood by the fire, listening to the bustle as his horses were put to. She felt sick at heart as the carriage rolled away, but he was asking the impossible. Nothing would have persuaded her to part with her son. Christopher was her life.

There had been no question of her falling in with his demands, but the stormy interview had shaken her to the core. The shock of seeing her father had unnerved her, but a feeling of desolation was soon followed by anger.

Then that too faded, giving way to despair. What was she to do?

On the day that Richard died she'd closed the inn, wanting only to be left alone. A dreadful lethargy had possessed her, and when her servants began to drift away she'd made no effort to stop them, knowing that she could not find their wages. Richard had left her penniless. It was but one more blow to add to those she had already suffered.

She felt very cold. Shivering, she moved closer to the glowing fire, standing before it with a hand on either side of the mantelshelf. At least her father's visit had succeeded in shaking her out of the apathy which seemed to have paralysed her will.

On the day of the tragedy she'd felt that she could not go on, struggling against the fates which seemed to delight in dealing her so many cruel blows. Had it not been for Kit...

Her lips curved in a faint smile. Thank God he was so young. He, at least, had been untouched by what had happened.

She glanced at the clock. Kit had been sleeping for an hour. He wouldn't wake just yet. Meantime, she must try to think of some solution to her problems.

Perhaps she could sell the inn. Then she'd be able to move from this isolated spot and make a new life for herself and her son in one of the larger coastal towns.

Absorbed in planning for the future she stood on tiptoe, studying her reflection in the mirror above the mantelshelf.

It wasn't surprising that her looks had shocked her father, she decided. Grief had taken its toll upon her face, and the grey eyes looked enormous against the ivory pallor of her skin. She twisted a lock of hair between her fingers. It felt lank. She couldn't remember when she had last washed it and the heavy mass of auburn curls no longer shone.

She wrinkled her nose. The smell from the burning logs was worse than ever. Then she gave a cry of terror. This was the smell of burning cloth. Glancing down, she saw that her skirts were badly singed and yellow tongues of flame were beginning to race upwards. She stepped back quickly, but it was too late. She was already ablaze.

Screaming, she beat wildly at her skirts, but to no avail. Then she was enveloped in folds of heavy cloth and thrown roughly to the ground. Strong hands beat none too gently at her garments as she was rolled back and forth.

Frantic with terror, Sophie struggled to free herself, but she was powerless in the iron grip of her rescuer.

'Lie still!' a deep voice ordered roughly. 'And for God's sake stop that squawking.'

Sophie had little option. The unceremonious handling of her person had left her breathless, but at last she managed to push away the cloth which covered her head. Then her eyes fell upon a kneeling figure who was still slapping at her skirts.

It was too dark to see him clearly, but when he picked her up and carried her over to the settle she realised that he was very large. He picked up the candelabra, knelt in front of her, and began to examine the damage to her gown.

'No harm done!' he said at last. 'You've lost a gown, but not your life. Have you no sense at all? Headstrong you may be, but I must doubt that you are fireproof.'

'I...I wasn't thinking...' she faltered weakly.

'I won't argue with that.' Satisfied that he had extinguished the flames, her rescuer tugged at the bell-pull and ordered brandy.

Sophie shook her head as he thrust a brimming glass towards her. 'I hate the taste,' she said.

'Drink it, ma'am! You've had a shock!' His tone brooked no argument. Certain that he would be obeyed, he turned away, filled his own glass, and sat down, studying her intently.

Sophie returned his gaze. She had never seen this man before and she felt a twinge of panic. The harsh features, thrown into strong relief by the faint glow of the candles, were forbidding. Deep lines seamed his face across the brow and beside his mouth and his dark eyes held no trace of warmth.

Sophie regained her composure slowly as she sipped at the brandy. She could not imagine what this man was doing here. The inn was closed.

'I must thank you, sir,' she said cautiously. 'I believe you saved my life.'

The stranger said nothing.

Sophie tried again. 'May I know your name?' she asked.

'I am Nicholas Hatton. The name can mean nothing to you.'

'How should it? We have not met before. I'm grateful for your help, but how came you to be here?'

She heard a short laugh. 'Why, ma'am, I am staying here. Is this not a public hostelry?'

'It is, but we are closed. I have few servants here...'

'No? Your man gave me a key...'

'Matthew should not have done so. I'm sorry, but you must leave...'

The man glanced towards the windows, which were rattling in their frames, obscured by the pelting rain.

'Come now,' he said smoothly. 'Will you turn me away on such a night?'

Sophie was alarmed by his persistence. Tall and broad, he might prove to be an ugly customer if thwarted, and Matthew would be no match for him.

Now she regretted her folly in admitting that most of her servants had left. Had this stranger come to rob her? If so, he would find little of value on the premises. There was nothing here worth taking, but she and Kit might be in danger if he didn't believe her. At best he might search the place, and at worst he might attack her.

The man seemed to read her mind.

'I don't have rape in mind,' he drawled.

Sophie blushed to the roots of her hair. 'I didn't think you had,' she lied.

'Then, Mistress Firle, you are a fool. You have no protection here. Your man looks none too strong to me.'

Stung by his words, Sophie leapt to Matthew's defence. 'He can still fire a gun,' she snapped.

'He will find no need to do so.' Nicholas Hatton leaned back, totally at ease. 'Is this a bad day, or do all your customers receive a similar welcome? You dispatched your last visitor with scant ceremony.'

Sophie glared at him. 'How dare you eavesdrop upon a private conversation? How long have you been sitting there? Why did you not reveal yourself?'

'Why, ma'am, I found it fascinating.' The hooded eyes held a mocking glint. 'Besides, I might have embarrassed you.' He grinned and she saw the gleam of perfect teeth.

Sophie could have struck him.

'My affairs are no concern of yours,' she retorted sharply.

'On the contrary, Mistress Firle, they concern me deeply...' His smile had vanished and she saw him then for what he was—a dangerous man. The hard lines of his mouth and jaw did nothing to reassure her.

'How do you know my name?' she demanded. 'And what do you want from me?' Poised for flight, she rose to her feet and seized the candelabra. If she could slip past him, she would barricade herself in Kit's room.

Hatton removed the lighted candle from her grasp. 'I must hope that you keep a salve for burns, my dear. Hot tallow on your hands can be extremely painful. You will sit down, if you please, and listen to what I have to say.'

'I have nothing to say to you. Please go. It isn't far to the nearest town...you would be more comfortable in Brighton—'

'I'll go when my business is concluded.' His tone did not brook argument.

'And what exactly *is* your business?' Sophie decided to humour him. She didn't expect to hear the truth, but she was beginning to suspect that her visitor must be connected to the smuggling fraternity. The inn lay on the route from the coast to London, but if he hoped to use it as a safe house she would have none of it.

'Why, Mistress Firle, it is with you.' His smile did not reach his eyes.

Sophie backed away, but he reached the door in a couple of strides, blocking all chance of escape.

'Don't be afraid!' he said more gently. 'I don't mean to harm you.'

'Then let me go,' she breathed.

'As soon as you've heard what I have to say...'

'Sir, you may save your breath. This inn will not be used by the "free traders", as they like to call themselves.'

'Now you are jumping to conclusions, ma'am. I thought merely that you might care to know exactly how your husband died...'

Sophie looked up at him. Then the world went dark.

* * *

When she recovered it was to find herself seated in a chair, with her head pressed firmly between her knees. A strong hand rested on her hair. Then a finger slid beneath her chin and dark eyes held her own.

'Better?' His voice was softer as he questioned her.

She nodded briefly, but she could not speak.

Hatton began to pace the room. 'Forgive me!' he said quietly. 'That was brutal, but I had to find some way of breaking your reserve.'

'You succeeded.' Her voice was barely above a whisper. 'Must you torture me? Richard's death was an accident. The cliffs are crumbling. In the darkness he didn't see the edge.'

'Not so! Is not the path always clearly marked with a line of painted stones? They are visible even through a mist.'

'What are you trying to say?' Sophie found that she was shaking uncontrollably.

He didn't answer her at once. Instead he offered her another glass of brandy. 'Drink this! I believe that you will need it.'

Sophie waved the glass aside. 'Go on!' she whispered.

Hatton hesitated, but there was no easy way of telling her. Best to get it over with at once.

'Richard Firle was murdered,' he said at last.

He thought that she would faint again. The huge grey eyes had closed and her pallor was alarming, but at length the shallow breathing eased. Sophie made an effort to regain her self-control.

'You can't know that,' she whispered. 'I won't believe it. My husband hadn't an enemy in the world. He fell…they found him on the rocks below…'

'You never wondered why he ventured out in such inclement weather?'

'There was a message. He was asked to help. Someone had been injured...'

'And was that person ever found?'

Her silence gave him his answer.

'It was a trap,' he continued calmly. 'The stones had been moved. They led him to his death.'

'But why?' Sophie looked up at her companion. It was becoming increasingly difficult to doubt him. If his words were true, they would answer many of the questions which had tormented her since the day of the tragedy.

Richard had known the cliffs so well. As a Revenue Officer he'd been well aware of the dangers of the Sussex coast. He'd ridden over the land for years, discovering every cove and possible landing place for the men who ran their illicit goods ashore, mostly at night, but sometimes in broad daylight.

In those days she'd feared often for his safety, though he tried to keep the worst excesses of the smugglers from her. It wasn't possible. Those stories were common knowledge. How often had she heard tales of blackmail, beatings, torture and even murder.

When two of his colleagues were discovered in a well, bound and stoned to death, she had begged him to resign, but he'd refused.

It had made it all the harder to believe the charges laid against him. Yet in a way she'd taken the news of his dismissal with a feeling of relief. At least he would be safe.

It had been hard for her, but she had chosen to share poverty with him since the day of their elopement.

Did she regret it now? Of course not. Yet even in those first few months of marriage a tiny worm of doubt had begun to eat away at her belief in him. There were too many mysteries…too many unexplained absences, accounted for by what she'd later found to be lies.

Then she had Kit, and that made up for everything.

Lost in thought, she became aware that her companion had not answered her.

'Why?' she repeated. 'Why should anyone wish to harm Richard? He left the Preventive Service long ago.'

'You are mistaken, ma'am. I can tell you that he did not.'

'But those charges…? I knew that they were lies, but somehow they were proven and he was dismissed.'

Hatton gave her a long look. 'You were unconvinced of the truth of it? I thought that we had done better.'

'What do you mean by that remark? What had it to do with you?'

'I organised it, Mistress Firle. Your husband was my man. We needed an informer. Who better than a disgraced Revenue Officer, accused of taking bribes?'

'So it was you? You were the cause of my husband's death?'

'Firle knew the risks,' Hatton told her coldly. 'He accepted them. He wasn't the first to die, as you must know. I want the men who killed him, and the others.'

'Why come to me?'

'I am convinced that you can help. I won't continue to send brave men to their deaths. Now, I too intend to lay a trap.'

'You shan't use me!' Sophie said firmly. 'My son comes first. I won't put him at risk. What do I care about a few kegs of brandy, or some packages of tobacco?'

'I hoped that you might care about murder.'

That silenced her.

'You won't be at risk, I promise. Who will suspect a

woman? I can give you a couple of bruisers for protection. Use them as ostlers if you wish.'

'I won't do it!' Sophie's mouth set in a mutinous line. 'You shan't use me in any of your plans. I intend to sell the inn and move away from here.'

'Unfortunately, you can't do so. The inn does not belong to you.'

'My husband left me everything in his will.'

'It wasn't his to leave. This inn belongs to the authorities. I put him in the place myself.'

'You are lying. I don't believe you. This is a trick. You would say anything to get your way…'

Hatton shrugged. 'Speak to your lawyer if you doubt me. The inn is in my name.'

'Are you telling me that you could turn me out?'

'I could, but I should be sorry to do so. All I ask is a few months of your time. Open up your doors again. If I'm not mistaken, your previous customers will return.'

'So I am to be the bait?'

'Those are crude terms, ma'am, but, to put it bluntly, that is so. Did you know any of your customers?'

'I did not!' she retorted. 'My husband did not wish me to enter the public rooms.'

'Did he say why?'

'He told me that for the most part they were unsavoury characters. He tolerated them for their lavish spending habits.'

'Quite! There were also other reasons. Now I suggest that in future you make yourself agreeable to these men, make yourself amenable to suggestions, plead poverty if you must…'

'That won't be difficult,' she assured him grimly. 'What else am I to do?'

'Keep your eyes and ears open. Men speak freely when

they are at their ease and primed with drink. Such talk will be of interest to me.'

'So I am to be your spy?'

'Dear me, what a way you have of speaking straight. Then, yes, if you will have it so…'

'How do I know that I can trust you? I've seen no proof of your identity. You could be a member of a rival gang.'

'Read this!' Hatton pulled a document from his pocket.

Sophie looked at him uncertainly. Then she began to read. The authorisation left her in no doubt of his probity.

'You could have stolen this,' she accused.

'Very true! But I did not. However, you are wise to doubt me. You have more sense than I imagined.'

'You are insulting, sir.' Sophie eyed him with acute dislike.

'Am I? I meant that as a compliment, but I have no notion of how to deal with women.'

'That, Mr Hatton, is all too obvious. You force your way in here with these preposterous suggestions, and expect me to fall in with your plans—'

'You have no choice,' he told her calmly.

'You are mistaken. I could leave this place.'

'Where would you go? Have you any money?'

Sophie did not answer him.

'I thought not. Firle was never the thriftiest of men. You could, of course, return to your father's home, but I think you will not leave your son.'

'You monster!' Sophie was ready to choke with rage. 'I see that spying is your forte. You listened on purpose to my conversation.'

'It was instructive.' He didn't trouble to deny it. 'I had to be sure of you.'

'So you would use my son to get your way? You disgust me! I owe you nothing, Mr Hatton. In fact, it would be a pleasure to trick you—'

'Others have tried it, ma'am. Let me assure you that the consequences would be unpleasant.'

'More threats? Why, you are naught but a common blackmailer—'

'We are wasting time.' Clearly Hatton was impervious to insult. 'I am waiting for your answer.'

Sophie thought quickly. There must be some way of outwitting him.

'I need more time to consider,' she said at last.

'You have an hour. When we dine tonight you will give me your decision.'

'You plan to dine here? That will not be possible. We have no food to spare.'

'So I understand, but I have no intention of going to bed upon an empty stomach. I sent out for provisions. If I'm not mistaken, Matthew's wife is already busy in the kitchen.'

'Sir, you take too much upon yourself. How dare you walk in here and give orders to my servants?'

'You prefer to starve?'

'There was no question of that,' she told him stiffly. 'I meant only that we should be unable to provide a meal which would satisfy your high standards.' She hoped that her sarcastic tone would anger him. To her fury he began to laugh.

'That's better!' he approved. 'I'm glad to see that you haven't lost your spirit. In the future it will serve you well.'

'And you?'

'I live in hope that it will serve me too. Now, ma'am, you will wish to change your gown before we dine.'

Sophie followed his eyes as he glanced down at her

shirt and saw to her horror that the singed cloth was in tatters, revealing a generous expanse of shapely leg.

Hot colour flooded her cheeks. What a spectacle she must present. She jumped up in confusion, expecting some sly remark, but Hatton had turned away.

'You must excuse me now,' he said. 'I have work to do. Shall we say in my rooms at seven?'

'Your rooms?' she echoed blankly. 'I thought I had explained. You can't stay here. The inn is closed.'

'But not to me, I think.' He held up a hand to still her protests. 'Must you always argue, woman? This place is mine, and for the present you are here on sufferance.'

Helpless and seething with outrage, Sophie pushed past him and went to find her son.

Chapter Two

Anger turned to panic when she found that Kit was not in his room. Hideous images filled her mind. Had Hatton already spirited him away, holding him hostage against her good behaviour? She wouldn't put anything past that ruthless creature.

Wildly, she searched the upper floor, but she could find no trace of the child. Then, as she hurried down the stairs she heard his gleeful laugh. Thank heavens! He was in the kitchen.

She burst into the room to find him seated at the old deal table, playing happily with a ball of grubby dough.

Half-fainting with relief, she caught him to her, raining kisses on his face and neck until he tried to wriggle free.

'You're squashing me!' he complained.

'I'm sorry, my pet. You gave me a fright. How did you get down here?'

'Mistress, I brought him down. He'd been calling for some time...' Matthew's wife gave Sophie a reproachful look.

'Oh, Bess, I'm sorry. I hadn't realised that it was so late. Our unexpected visitor kept me talking.' Sophie swallowed hard. 'He intends to stay, I fear. Have we food enough for a decent dinner?'

'Enough for a week, I shouldn't wonder. The gentleman sent round to the nearest farm as soon as he arrived, and without so much as a by-your-leave…' Bess gave her mistress a curious look. 'Do you know him, ma'am?'

'He convinced me that he is perfectly respectable.' Some inner voice warned Sophie not to mention Hatton's connection with the Preventive Service.

'That's as may be, but I thought that we were closed. Matt told him to go on to Brighton, but he wouldn't hear of it.'

'That's understandable. The storm is growing worse…'

'The weather weren't too bad when he arrived.' Bess was unconvinced. She gave her mistress a worried look. 'T'ain't right to have a stranger in the place when you have no one to protect you.'

'Mama has me!' Kit struggled from his chair and went to his mother's side.

'That's right, my love!' Sophie ruffled his hair. 'Now, Bess, can you manage? Mr Hatton wishes to dine with me at seven.'

'I'll do my best, but you should have warned me—'

'How could I warn you when I didn't know that he was coming?' Sophie said wearily.

'Well, mistress, be it on your own head. A gentleman yon customer may be, but there ain't no call for you to sit with him alone.'

'Nonsense, Bess! Pray don't allow your imagination to run away with you. If you must know, Mr Hatton has a proposition for me. He suggests that I re-open the inn.'

'Why would he do that?' Bess stood with arms akimbo, bristling with antagonism towards the stranger.

'I have no idea.' Sophie was losing patience. 'That is what I intend to find out.'

She rose to her feet, and froze as Bess gave a piercing shriek.

'Whatever is the matter?' she cried in alarm.

'Mistress, your gown! It's burned to shreds!'

'I stood too close to the fire, that's all.' Sophie looked down at the tattered garment. 'Don't worry, I am quite unharmed.' She glanced at Kit and then at Bess, warning the woman not to pursue the subject.

'No more!' she hissed into Bess's ear. 'If you throw your apron over your head and have a fit of the vapours, I shall slap you hard!'

Kit had returned to his pile of dough. Now he was sticking currants into the grubby mass, attempting to create a face.

Sophie held out her hand. 'Will you come with me, love, or are you happy here with Bess?'

'I'm busy!' The small boy bent over his task with an air of intense concentration. 'This is for your supper, Mama. Bobbo is helping me.'

'Then I shall look forward to enjoying it.' Sophie dropped a kiss upon his hair. She often worried about her son, believing that he needed playmates, but Kit was an inventive child. He was never bored, finding something of interest in everything about him, and clothing his little world in the vivid colours of a capricious imagination.

His best friend was Bobbo, a mysterious creature invisible to the human eye. Bobbo had appeared when Kit was three, and in the past two years he had become a part of the family.

Bobbo was a demanding creature. Sometimes he fitted happily into the routine of the household, but on occasion his ideas could be outrageous. In the usual way, Sophie found this figment of her son's imagination vastly entertaining, but now she was unable to raise a smile.

Hatton's story filled her mind to the exclusion of all else. Could it possibly be true? In the years since her marriage she and Richard had grown apart, but his death had been a crushing blow. She mourned for the love they had once known and agonised over the accident. Had he lain injured on the rocks below the cliffs, unable to move, and knowing that the incoming tide would drown him?

The men who found him had assured her that it wasn't so. Richard had been killed outright and his body had not been carried out to sea. She'd forced herself to believe that he hadn't suffered and she had come to accept the accident, tragic though it was. Murder was something else.

A tap at the door roused her from her dark imaginings.

'I've brought hot water, mistress. Will I help you change your gown?'

'Thank you, Abby. I haven't much time…'

'Mother says I am to serve you with your dinner.' Abby glowed with self-importance. 'And I'm to tell you that Father and Ben will be close at hand.' The girl gave her a curious look.

Sophie managed a faint smile as she slipped out of her damaged gown. 'Your mother is as bad as Kit,' she observed. 'They share a wild imagination…'

'She worries about you, Mistress Firle, left on your own like this.'

'I know it, Abby, but there is no need. Our visitor is perfectly respectable.'

'Well he frightens me,' the girl announced. 'He is that big, and my, don't he know how to give orders?'

'I think he means well.' Sophie was anxious to bring the conversation to an end. 'Will you fetch me a gown?'

'Which one, ma'am?'

The question brought a smile from Sophie. 'There isn't much choice,' she replied drily. 'The grey will do, and I'll wear my cap tonight.'

'It don't match,' Abby protested.

'That is the least of my worries!' Sophie washed her hands and face and allowed herself to be buttoned into a simple round dress, long-sleeved and cut high at the neck. 'Help me pin up my hair.'

With some difficulty she pushed the abundant locks beneath a modest widow's cap and glanced at herself in the mirror. Behind her Abby pulled a face.

'You look like one of they Puritan women in Kit's picture book...' Abby was clearly unimpressed by her mistress's toilette.

'I'm not attending a reception at the Prince's Pavilion in Brighton,' Sophie replied severely. 'You may put Kit to bed for me when he has had his supper. He'll want a story, but none of your ghosts and hobgoblins, if you please. I don't want him to have nightmares.'

'As if I would!' The girl threw her an injured look. Then she hesitated in the doorway.

'Yes, what is it?' Sophie picked up her reticule.

'Mistress, is it true that you'll stay here at the inn? We've been that worried. We've nowhere else to go, you see.'

'My dear child, I'm well aware of that, and I haven't forgotten how kind your mother and father have been to me. They have stayed on without wages...'

Abby blushed with embarrassment. 'They take no account of that, ma'am, being as they have a roof above their heads, and food enough to eat.'

'But I take account of it, Abby. If I'd sold the place, your father would have had his share, but...well...I haven't decided yet.'

In truth, her decision was already made. Hatton had been right. She had no choice but to fall in with his wishes. To do otherwise meant destitution, not only for Kit and herself, but for Matthew and his family.

All she could do now would be to hold out for the best conditions she could think of.

She hurried down to the kitchen, intending to bid her son goodnight, but was stopped on the threshold by Bess's look of amusement.

'Abby said that you was got up like a nun,' the older woman observed. 'Quite right too, if I may say so. No man in his right mind would—'

'Bess, that's quite enough!' Sophie was tempted into a sharp retort. 'I'm not expecting to be raped!'

'No chance of that!' Bess chortled. 'Take care, ma'am, or you'll get grease upon your gown. I'd say naught if it were to fall upon your cap.' She eyed the offending garment with disfavour.

'You know that I must wear it,' Sophie told her coldly. 'It is perfectly suitable…'

A snort of disgust was the only reply, and Sophie was not prepared to argue. Clearly she was in the way, and she was already late for her appointment with the dreaded Mr Hatton.

He was not in his rooms, so she sat by the fire, searching her mind for some solution to her problems. She could think of nothing.

'Brooding upon your sorry fate?' a deep voice enquired.

Sophie swung round to find Hatton standing in the doorway, a bottle of wine in either hand.

'I took it upon myself to inspect your cellars,' he explained. 'They are quite a revelation, ma'am. The Prince himself would be happy to own such a stock.'

Sophie glared at him as he walked towards her. Then he stopped.

'Dear God! What have you got upon your head?' A hand reached out and twitched the cap away, allowing the mass of auburn curls to fall upon her shoulders. 'That creation is enough to frighten the French!'

'How dare you!' Sophie tried to clutch at the cap, but Hatton held it out of her reach. 'I am a widow, and widows are supposed to wear such things.'

'Widows' weeds?' he mocked. 'Forget it!' He tossed the cap into the fire. 'Black ain't your colour, ma'am, and nor is grey. You'll be of no use to me if you insist on looking like a crow.'

Sophie's eyes flashed with anger. 'Don't you mean a crone?' she cried.

'No, I think not!' He gave her a long, considering look. 'You are too thin, of course, but you will pay for dressing. Blue, I think, or possibly green…?'

'If you think to dress me up as some alehouse strumpet you may forget it,' she cried hotly.

Her anger increased as she heard a low laugh. 'Not even I could manage that. You will always look the gentlewoman, Mistress Firle. It is no bad thing. Who is more likely to elicit sympathy than a pretty widow, fallen upon hard times?' He poured the wine and offered her a glass.

'I've had no sympathy from you, sir.'

'None whatever! But then you must remember that I am impervious to women's wiles. Stubborn hot-heads, most of them, and you are no exception.'

'Then I wonder that you should care to trust your plans to me.'

'Don't worry! I shall keep an eye on you.'

'Then kindly keep your opinions to yourself. I shall take no notice of them.'

'Oh, I think you must,' he answered cheerfully. 'They are so sensible, you see.'

For a moment this outrageous statement threatened to rob Sophie of the power of speech. Then she found her voice.

'How true! What could be more reasonable than an invitation to become your spy and put my life and that of my son in danger? Why, such suggestions must be commonplace in genteel circles!'

Hatton's eyes twinkled as he looked at her. 'So the kitten has claws? Well done, Mistress Firle!'

'Don't try to patronise me!' she snapped.

'I shouldn't dream of it. I am accustomed to respect my colleagues.' Hatton was grinning at her.

A sharp retort died upon her lips as Abby entered the room, carrying a laden tray.

With formal courtesy, Hatton drew out a chair for his bristling companion. Then he seated himself at the table with the resigned expression of a man expecting an indifferent dinner.

Sophie eyed him with malicious amusement as he bit into a fluffy golden omelette stuffed with mushrooms. He said nothing as he cleared his plate.

Then Abby served the fish which had been intended for Sophie's supper. Bess had cooked it in her special way, coating it with herbs and seasoning before rolling it in a muslin cloth and steaming it gently above a pan of boiling water. When it was unwrapped the skin came away with the cloth, leaving the flesh firm and white, and ready to be bathed in a delicate butter sauce of her own devising.

Hatton raised an eyebrow. 'Do you always dine like this?' he asked.

'Very rarely, Mr Hatton. At least, not in these past few weeks. We keep chickens and a pig, of course, and we grow our own vegetables. The goose, I fear, would have been beyond our resources... I understand that we have you to thank for that.'

'I like to eat well.' He brushed the implied thanks aside. 'Let us hope that Bess has done it justice.'

Sophie gave him an acid smile. 'You need have no fear. You won't go hungry, sir.'

When the bird arrived she was pleased to see that it had been roasted to perfection. The rich dish was accompanied by a sharp apple sauce, designed to clean the palate, and a selection of winter vegetables, including Sophie's favourite mixture of carrots and turnips, mashed together with pepper, salt and butter.

Hatton was won over when he tasted it. 'I wonder why I haven't sampled this before?' he said. 'It should be served with every meal.'

Sophie smiled. 'You sound like the man who ordered apricot tart with every meal, whether he ate it or not.'

Hatton pushed his chair back from the table. 'Let us hope that Bess has mercy on us,' he announced. 'I couldn't eat another bite.'

His hopes were dashed when Abby arrived with apple pie and some local cheese. He was about to wave it away when Sophie frowned at him.

'Try a little of it,' she insisted. 'Bess will be disappointed if you don't.'

Obediently, he inspected the tray. Then he held up a square of grubby pastry decorated with a large initial.

'What is this?' he demanded.

'Oh, dear, that offering is for me. Kit made it for my supper...'

Hatton's smile softened his harsh face. 'You are fortunate in your son, ma'am.'

'I believe so, Mr Hatton, and I will defend him with my life.'

'That won't be necessary, Mistress Firle. I have promised that you will be in no danger.'

'How can you promise that?' she cried in irritation. 'Unless this is a wild-goose chase? I believe it to be so. Why should the free traders choose to use this inn? You have been misinformed, I fear.'

'Have I? I think not! Be honest with me, ma'am. Have you noticed nothing amiss since you came to live here?'

'I have told you. I did not enter the public rooms.'

'I am aware of that, but you are not blind, my dear. Did you sleep well at nights?'

Sophie stared at him. 'I kept my shutters closed,' she admitted.

'Even in summer? Were you told to do so? And what reason were you given?'

Sophie lost all patience with her questioner. 'I didn't care to ask,' she cried. 'How well do you know this area, Mr Hatton? Smuggling takes place along the coast, but there is a reason for it. These fishermen have lost their livelihood due to the French war. They can earn as much in a night as they can in a month by other means. Must their families starve?'

'And what does it lead to?' he asked coldly. 'You have your own answer to that.'

'The government could stop the trade overnight,' she insisted. 'All they need to do is reduce the duty.'

'Is it so simple? Taxes are needed to run this country—'

'To subsidise a war?' Sophie regretted the words as soon as they were out.

'You disappoint me!' he told her sternly. 'Brave men have given their lives in the fight against Napoleon. Would you give up our hard-won freedom?'

Sophie hung her head. 'Of course not? Forgive me, I spoke in haste! If I were a man I should fight too.'

'You can still fight, ma'am, but in a different way. Well, will you give me your decision? We are to be colleagues, are we not?'

'Only if you agree to my conditions.'

'Go on!' Hatton prepared to listen.

'In the first place, I must have your assurance that my son will not be put at risk.'

'Agreed!'

'I hope so, sir.' Sophie gave him a dagger-look. 'Should any harm come to him I'll kill you myself.'

She had expected some sneering taunt in reply, but Hatton said nothing.

'Also, there must be a limit to this arrangement. You mentioned six months, I believe?'

'I did.'

'And then there is the matter of payment...'

'You have some figure in mind?'

Sophie named a figure so large as to force him to withdraw his offer. She was prepared for a refusal, but to her astonishment he nodded.

'Done! You'll earn it, never fear! Anything else?'

Sophie shook her head.

'Very well, then. Shall we shake hands upon our bargain?' He reached across to her, aware of her reluctance to allow him to touch her, and amused by it.

Sophie looked down at the clasped hands. Enclosed within the lean brown fingers, her own looked very white.

At least his grasp was warm and firm. To her surprise she realised that she had expected nothing else, but she drew her hand away as if she had been stung. There was something deeply disturbing about Nicholas Hatton, and it had nothing to do with the perilous adventure upon which they had embarked.

Her companion led her over to a seat beside the fire.

'Now to practicalities, Mistress Firle. Time is of the essence in this present matter. If we delay, the trail will grow cold.'

In spite of her misgivings, Sophie felt a sudden spurt of excitement. If Richard's murderers could be brought to justice her task would be worthwhile.

'What must I do?' she asked.

He didn't reply at once, frowning as he twirled the stem of his wine-glass between his fingers.

'How much do you know about the running of this place?' he asked at last. 'What were your duties here?'

'I thought I had explained. I didn't enter the public rooms, but there were the usual tasks such as cheese- and butter-making, brewing ale and putting up preserves. I'd hoped to make a flower garden, but it was always being trampled down.'

'By whom?'

Sophie hesitated. 'I don't know,' she admitted.

'I think you do,' he said sternly. 'If I'm not much mistaken, the damage always happened at night. Be honest with me, ma'am. You must have suspected something...'

'I may have had my suspicions, but I never saw anything. Richard always insisted that the shutters were closed at night.'

'You may have been blind, but you are not deaf, my dear. Tell me what you heard.' His eyes were hard, and faced with his implacable determination, Sophie felt constrained to tell the truth.

'I think there were ponies...many ponies,' she admitted reluctantly. 'Groups of men were with them, but they spoke in whispers. I couldn't hear their conversation.'

'But you knew they were smugglers?'

'I suspected it, but it was naught to do with me. There were always such men along this coast. For some it is the only way to feed their families.'

'Sheer folly!' he announced with contempt. 'Do you know the penalties for smuggling, ma'am? Transportation is the least of it. What of their families, then?'

'They know the risks,' she faltered.

'Possibly, but those risks have increased since the war with France. The south coast is almost an armed camp, with dragoons and militia everywhere in case of an invasion. The stakes are now so high that only the most ruthless continue with the trade. They will stop at nothing to protect their chosen territory. Now they have not only the authorities to fear, but also their competitors.'

'You mean the rival gangs?' Sophie looked perplexed. 'I've heard of them and the battles at Mayfield and Bexhill, but were they not broken many years ago?'

'They were...' A look which Sophie could not fathom crossed her companion's face. 'Others have taken their places.'

It was chilling news and Sophie's resolution wavered. 'Why should they come here?' she whispered faintly. 'The men I spoke of may not be the ones you want, but if you are right it would be sheer folly to return to the scene of their crime.'

She heard an ugly laugh. 'They think themselves to be untouchable,' he assured her. 'And especially since they have disposed of the informer in their midst.'

'Richard?'

Hatton nodded.

'But why here?'

'This was considered to be a safe house, isolated as it is. They will return, Mistress Firle. Nothing is more certain. The inn is on a convenient route between the coast and London and they won't expect trouble from a woman. You may expect an approach at any time…'

Sophie gave him a wavering smile. 'Sir, it is a terrifying thought.'

'You'll be in no danger if you keep your head,' he told her briefly. 'And I've promised you protection.'

'In what form?'

'I shall be here myself,' he said. 'I propose to appear as one of your former suitors, intent on resuming our acquaintance now that you are widowed…'

Alarm bells rang in Sophie's head. 'Why not my brother or my cousin?' she asked quickly.

'That might be too easily disproved. These men will take nothing on trust. Suspicion is their watchword. That is how they stay alive.'

'I see.' For some unaccountable reason Sophie found that she disliked his plan intensely. This charade was something she had not bargained for.

She looked at Hatton and coloured. Once again he read her mind correctly.

'Don't worry!' he mocked. 'My wooing will not be importunate. I believe I shall find it possible to resist your charms.'

'And I yours!' she cried hotly. 'More than any man alive!'

'Then we are in agreement, but you must learn to control your temper, my dear. It will not serve if you continue to look at me as if I had crawled from beneath a stone.'

'You have judged my opinion of you to perfection, sir.'

'Then perhaps I might ask you for some small example of your acting ability. Now, to business. To run this place successfully you will need more servants. I'll place some men with you—'

'That may arouse suspicion,' she told him in alarm. 'Country folk are wary of strangers. They'll expect me to employ local men.'

'And so you shall,' he soothed. 'The men I send will not alarm your clientele, and nor will you, I hope.'

Sophie stared at him. 'I don't know what you mean,' she said.

'Well, ma'am, can you unbend sufficiently to mix with the lower orders with any degree of civility?'

She eyed him coldly. 'If I can be civil to you, I should have no difficulty,' she replied in icy tones.

'Ouch!' He threw back his head and roared with laughter. 'Point taken, ma'am!'

Sophie ignored that comment. 'You spoke of haste. When must I reopen?'

'This week, I think. What will you need?'

'Servants, supplies of food and liquor…everything, in fact.' She went on to add to the list with abandon, hoping to dismay him, but he merely nodded.

'Very well, two of my own men should be enough. Hire others where you can. You made an excellent point. Too many strangers will frighten off our quarry.'

'You seem very sure that the men you seek will come here.' She gave him a curious look.

'Nothing is more certain if you play your part. How good an actress are you?'

'I can't see how that should signify.'

'Then let me explain. Suppose you should overhear some word about this recent tragedy? You strike me as a woman of some spirit. Could you keep your feelings to yourself?'

'Of course!'

'I must hope so, Mistress Firle. It might mean the difference between life and death. I want no heroics from you.'

'Must you try to frighten me?'

'Yes!' he told her bluntly. 'Try to understand what we are dealing with. These men would slit your throat without a second thought. There is too much at stake for them to show you any mercy.'

'I need no convincing, Mr Hatton.'

'Then heed my words. Dead, you are not of the slightest use to me. Alive, you are worth your weight in gold.'

'I still don't understand,' she said slowly. 'Why do you imagine that I'll succeed when your own trained men have failed?'

'They didn't fail altogether, ma'am. We have come close on more than one occasion, only to lose our quarry at the last, betrayed by an informer. The pattern has always been the same.'

'But you must have some inkling as to when and where illicit goods are landed…'

'We've had our successes, but goods, as you term them, are not my main concern. French spies arrive here on a regular basis. Worse, English gold is being smuggled from this country to pay Napoleon's troops.'

'Why gold?'

'For profit. An English guinea will sell for half as much again in Paris.'

'But fisherman have not the means to buy them.'

'Exactly. There are powerful men behind this trade, and they are the ones I want.'

'I see.' Sophie was beginning to understand the motive behind this single-minded pursuit of England's enemies. 'Do you know who they are?'

'I do, but I must have proof before they can be taken. In the meantime, my men are still at risk.'

Sophie detected a note of deep concern. 'So you *do* care about their safety?'

'They are my responsibility,' he said shortly.

'And that is all?'

'What else?' His words were a challenge, warning her to expect no softening in his attitude.

She decided to ignore the rebuff. In the course of their conversation she'd found herself in sympathy with his motives for involving her, but she could not like him.

'How long do you intend to stay here?' she asked casually. 'Surely your men will be able to give me protection enough?'

'Anxious to be rid of me?' His eyes were twinkling with amusement. 'What woman would turn down the attention of a devoted swain?'

Sophie did not reply. She was torn between a strong desire for his protection, and an even stronger dislike of his arrogance. This was a man accustomed to giving orders. It was clear that he expected them to be obeyed without delay.

This might work with his minions, she thought rebelliously, but he must learn that he could not rule her life.

'Perhaps your concern is for my safety?' he mocked. 'Pray don't worry about me, ma'am. I have the best of explanations for my presence here. Your charms are such that I could not stay away...'

Sophie rose to her feet, pink spots of colour in her cheeks. 'Another cheap gibe?' she said coldly. 'That remark is in the worst of taste.'

'Oh, do sit down!' he snapped. 'Damned if you aren't the prickliest female I have ever met! Good God, woman, can you think of a better story?'

'This story is ridiculous! No one will believe it!'

'Why not? For years I have loved you from afar. Even

when you refused my suit I never gave up hope, but when you eloped with Firle my friends feared for my sanity...'

'I'm not surprised, Mr Hatton. I have doubted it myself, but I see that it amuses you to make may-game of me.'

'This is no game, I can assure you. I thought I had made that clear. Now that you are widowed, will it be thought strange that I should wish to offer my heart once more?'

'Strange, indeed, since you don't appear to have one!' Sophie did not trouble to hide her contempt.

'Temper!' he reproved. 'Now, ma'am, you must be tired. You've had an exhausting day, which, you will admit, has been overfull of incident.'

'And what has that to do with you?'

'Forgive me! I am concerned about the health of my beloved, you see.' The dark eyes danced as he looked at her. 'Your father's offer of a home and your refusal will not have gone unnoticed in this household. Sir Edward has a penetrating voice. Then there was the unfortunate incident when you burned your gown, and finally you have been forced to listen to my outrageous suggestions. May I suggest that you retire?'

'You may not! I am no schoolgirl, sir, to be dismissed at will. Pray keep your opinions to yourself. If you must know, I am not tired in the least.'

It was true. For the first time in weeks, Sophie felt alive again. Now there was some purpose to her life. She could serve her country and help catch the men who had murdered Richard. Then, too, she would earn enough to secure a decent future for herself and Kit.

If she had to work with Nicholas Hatton to achieve those ends she would do so, but it would not be easy. The longer she was in his company, the more she found herself disliking him.

She watched him as he tugged at the bell-pull. When Abby arrived he asked to see her mother.

Sophie was mystified. 'What do you want with Bess?' she asked.

'I am minding my manners,' Hatton told her solemnly. 'Is it not usual to thank the cook for a good dinner?'

She looked at him in suspicion. This kindly gesture was surely out of character. This was a devious man. He must have some ulterior motive.

He didn't leave her in doubt for long. As Bess tapped at the door a large hand seized her own and raised it to his lips. She struggled to free it, but his fingers closed. Furious, she looked up at her companion, to find that he was regarding her with a tender smile.

Then, apparently, he became aware of Bess. In some confusion he dropped Sophie's hand, and stammered out some words of thanks.

'Why, sir, it was a pleasure.' Bess smiled, disarmed at once by his compliments. 'Abby tells me that the mistress has eaten well, and high time too.'

'I fear that she has been neglecting herself.' Hatton regarded Sophie with a fond expression. 'With your help, Bess, we shall restore her to the girl I knew so long ago.'

'Mistress, you should have told me,' Bess reproved. 'Here we were, all so worried about you dining with a stranger...and the gentleman ain't a stranger, after all.'

'I didn't say he was,' Sophie told her stiffly. 'I said that Mr Hatton was respectable—'

She ignored a choking sound from her companion, but as Bess whisked out of the room she rounded on her tormentor.

'Must you behave in this ridiculous way?' she asked.

'It served. If I am not mistaken, Bess is at this moment forecasting wedding bells for you... I hope I have convinced her. As I explained to you, my experience of women is somewhat lacking.'

Recalling his seductive tones, Sophie gave him a sour look. 'Don't take me for a fool!' she said. 'At a guess, I would say that your experience is vast.'

'Then you feel that Bess is convinced?'

'Bess is a foolish old woman. She believes that no woman can survive without a man to care for her.'

'And you do not?'

'No, I do not, and in the future I hope to prove it.'

'What an innkeeper you will make! Why, in a month or two you'll have the countryside agog. Men will flock to this place in droves—'

'Why so?' She saw his smile and realised that the question was a mistake.

'Think about it, Mistress Firle! A beautiful young widow in possession of a highly desirable property? What could be more tempting?'

'I shall not encourage them.'

'Oh, yes, you will.' His smile vanished as he leaned towards her. 'For a start, you will change your manner. That cool reserve is well enough in a girl, but you are a woman grown. You have had a husband and a child.'

'You suggest that I should flaunt myself? Low-cut gowns, perhaps?'

'Not necessarily, but you will need more suitable clothing. I'll drive you into Brighton in the morning.'

'I have no money for fripperies.'

'That need be no problem.' He took out a sheaf of banknotes and pushed them towards her.

Sophie was tempted to throw the money in his face, but common sense prevailed. 'I shall need some things for Christopher too,' she warned.

'Use it as you will,' he said indifferently. 'But use it. Don't think to set some part of it aside...'

Sophie coloured, wishing him to the Devil. He had the most uncanny ability to read her mind. She'd intended to start her nest-egg with some of the money.

'I shall inspect your bills,' he continued remorselessly. 'Nothing too fancy, mind. Your gowns must be such as would become a recent widow, but no black, I beg of you.'

'Perhaps you would care to choose them?' she asked sweetly.

'I'll do so if you wish, but I'm sure that I can rely upon your taste.'

'You are too kind!' To her annoyance the sarcasm failed to move him. He only laughed and shook his head.

'Temper again!' he teased. 'Take care, my dear, or Matthew and his family will not believe our story.'

'They are not to know anything of our plans? Mr Hatton, I would trust them with my life.'

He looked at her in silence. 'Let me ask you something,' he said at last. 'Let us suppose that you were in the possession of certain information. You refuse to tell. Then your son is held in front of you at knifepoint. What would you do?'

'You know what I would do. I'd tell at once.'

'But you believe that Mathew does not have the same regard for his wife and children?'

Sophie hung her head. 'I see what you mean,' she replied. 'They shall learn nothing from me.'

'Good! Now, ma'am, if I may see you to your door?'

'Certainly not!'

'Great heavens, can you still believe that I have designs upon your honour?'

'Of course not,' she retorted. 'But it will give rise to talk.'

'And was that not what we intended? Don't worry! I will leave you at your door—'

'You will leave me at Kit's door,' she told him firmly. 'I always look in upon him before I retire.'

Kit was asleep, but, as usual, he had cast aside his coverlet. Sophie replaced it. Then she bent to kiss him, resenting Hatton's presence as she did so.

'You may leave me now,' she said.

He bowed and allowed her to proceed him from the room.

'Brighton tomorrow, then?' he suggested. 'Shall we say at ten in the morning, after breakfast?'

She was about to agree when suddenly and without warning, he caught her to him.

'Don't struggle!' he hissed. 'We are being watched.' Then his mouth came down on hers.

Sophie stood rigidly within his grasp, but her senses quickened. To her dismay she found that her own body was betraying her. She was responding insensibly to the pressure of those warm lips. Long-forgotten emotions coursed through her body. Then she pulled away.

With an inarticulate exclamation she fled to the safety of her room.

Chapter Three

Abby had missed nothing of the exchange between her mistress and the stranger. She hadn't intended to spy on them as she went about her business of turning down the covers in the bedrooms and sliding warming-pans between the sheets, but the sight of their embrace transfixed her.

Now she thrust her candle into Nicholas Hatton's hand to light his way back to his rooms. Then, agog with curiosity, she hurried after Sophie.

'Is all well, mistress?' she asked as she entered the bedchamber.

'Of course!' Sophie was pale but composed. 'Why should you imagine that aught is amiss?'

Abby was disconcerted. 'Why, ma'am, I wondered if the gentleman was taking liberties, with him being a stranger an' all…'

'I have already explained to your mother that Mr Hatton is not a stranger to me,' Sophie said mendaciously. 'If you must know it, he made me an offer before I married Mr Firle. Now he is come to renew his suit.'

Colour suffused her face. Sophie was unaccustomed to

lying, but she knew that it was necessary, if only to allay the girl's suspicions.

Apparently she had succeeded. Abby beamed at her.

'Why, ma'am, it's like a fairy-tale!' she exclaimed. 'Shall you take him, do you think? We'd all be that pleased for you—'

'Great heavens, Abby, give me time! I have no thoughts of marriage at this moment. My husband has not been dead above a month…'

Her sad expression discouraged further questioning, but Abby's thoughts were racing as she helped her mistress into her night attire. Dismissed at last, she hurried down to the kitchen to relay her news.

Bess hushed her eager chatter sternly. 'You'd do well to keep a still tongue in your head,' she warned. 'If I'm not mistaken, yon Mr Nicholas Hatton ain't the man to cross.'

'I thought you liked him,' Abby protested.

'He's well enough, but I make naught of his thanking me for his dinner. That's the way of the gentry. Words cost nothing, but they'll use you if they can.'

'Then you think he's come to use the mistress?'

'I don't know. She's gentry too, of course. It may be as she says and he's hoping that she'll wed him.'

Abby whirled about the kitchen, her head filled with romantic fancies. 'I hope so, Mother. If you'd seen him reach for her… He kissed her like a starving man offered a meal at last.'

'Give over with your nonsense! Starving, indeed! Why, a man like that can take his pick of a dozen likely wenches.'

'I expect so, but the mistress is so beautiful.'

'She ain't the girl she was when I first knew her. These

days she's naught but skin and bone, eating nothing even when the food was there for her.'

'But she ate well this evening.'

'Yes!' her mother said grudgingly. 'I'll grant the gentleman that much. She must have been feeling better... Perhaps it's as you say and all may yet turn out well for her, poor lass! Lord knows, she could do with a turn up in her fortunes after all she's suffered.'

'Oh, Mother, you are right. To be widowed so young...'

'That, my girl, was a blessing!' Bess said firmly. 'That ain't what I meant at all. I've watched the mistress fading away before my eyes long before yon Firle was killed.'

'You never liked him, did you?'

'I did not! To my way of thinking, handsome is as handsome does. That so-called gentleman was a liar and a cheat. What did he want, I wonder? He had a beautiful wife and a healthy boy, and he paid no heed to either of them.'

'That doesn't make him a liar and a cheat.'

'No...? Well...best that you don't know the whole. I'll tell you only that he kept a close watch on your father and myself. We were advised to turn a blind eye to anything untoward around this place at night.'

Abby's eyes grew round. 'Free traders?'

Her mother hushed her quickly. 'Be quiet, you foolish creature! Carry on with your chatter and we are likely to get our throats cut!'

Abby shrieked with fright.

'Oh, get on with you! There is no danger now. For heaven's sake, go to bed—'

'I shan't sleep!' Abby wailed.

'Stuff!' her mother snorted. 'As always, it will take a gunshot to waken you come morning. Now take your candle and get to your bed. Your father won't be pleased to find you making a great goose of yourself.'

'It won't be the first time!' Matthew was standing in the doorway. 'What ails the girl, for heaven's sake?'

'Father, shall we be murdered in our beds?' Abby was still quaking.

'Lord, no! What gave you that idea? The place is locked and barred as usual.'

'And Mr Hatton is still here?'

'He is…if it is any comfort to you, and your brother sleeps here too. You have three men to guard you, you foolish creature.'

Abby was satisfied at last, but when she left them Matthew turned to his wife.

'What have you been saying to her?' he demanded.

'I warned her to keep a still tongue in her head, husband. Abby rattles on, as well you know.'

'She can do no harm. We've kept our secrets to ourselves.'

'Did you tell this Mr Hatton of our suspicions?'

'Of course not! Those cellars will stay locked. He won't find the hidden entrances however much he pokes about.'

'He has been searching?'

'I can't say. He was down there earlier this evening, choosing his wine, or so he said…' Matthew hesitated. 'Don't it seem strange to you…this notion that the mistress should open up again?'

'Perhaps. I shall never understand the gentry. Maybe the mistress has told him that it's too soon for her to wed again.'

'Perhaps!' Matthew grew thoughtful. 'He doesn't intend to waste much time. I'm to send to the village at first light tomorrow with an offer of work for those as wants it.'

'And who's to pay them? The mistress has no money.'

Matthew patted his breast pocket. 'We've had our wages, wife, and more beside. The gentleman is grateful for our care of Mistress Firle.'

'But extra men? I doubt that we shall need them. There will be no trade along these roads at this time of year.'

'Bess, it has naught to do with us. Let him waste his blunt if he should wish to do so. I doubt if it will trouble him. His carriage is plain enough, but his cattle are among the best I've seen.'

Bess sighed. 'I wish that we were out of this. Many's the time we've heard and seen too much...'

'That's foolish talk! Where would we go? We'd best stick it out and hope for the best. The mistress may yet sell this place, and she's promised us a share. A chance like that don't come along too often for the likes of us.'

'But, Matt, she must have agreed to stay, else why should she be taking on more men?'

'It may not be for long,' he soothed. 'Now stop your worrying, wife. We must be up betimes tomorrow.'

Bess sighed again. 'I'm glad the gentleman is here, for all that. Mistress Firle will sleep sounder in her bed with someone to protect her.'

She was mistaken. Sleep was far from Sophie's mind as she tossed upon her pillows. The day's events had been extraordinary. She'd been startled by the unexpected arrival of her father, and deeply saddened to find him in the same inflexible state of mind. He'd spurned her son as if the child had been a bastard.

It was little wonder that when he'd gone she'd been blind to the danger of standing too close to the fire. She shuddered. Without Hatton's intervention she might have burned to death, leaving her son an orphan. It was high time she pulled herself together.

Now, with the arrival of this mysterious stranger, it was essential that she did so. His mission might be worthy. That she could accept. But the man himself was ruthless. In any dealings with him she would need all her wits about her. He would use any means to achieve his object.

Her cheeks burned as she recalled his kiss, and she drew a hand across her lips as if to wipe away the memory of his mouth upon her own. The sensation had been disturbing, and her blush grew deeper as she remembered her own response.

What must he think of her? Would he see her as a lusty young widow, desperate to satisfy her physical needs? She hoped not, but the fact remained that she had melted in his arms.

Then she grew calmer, although it was with an effort. She had agreed to this elaborate charade, for that was all it was.

His own words gave her comfort. He'd told her in no uncertain terms that she held no charms for him. Her manner was too cold? It would remain so as far as he was concerned. It was just that…well, he had taken her by surprise. Next time she would have her own emotions well under control.

A faint smile touched her lips as she lay awake for hours, planning revenge not only upon the men who had killed Richard, but also upon the arrogant Mr Hatton.

Quite how this desirable state of affairs was to be achieved she couldn't decide. There would be danger, but to her own surprise she found that she wasn't afraid. After years of misery she felt alive again. Danger there might be, but beneath that awareness lay a strong current of excitement.

Still wondering at her own response, she fell asleep at last.

* * *

By the next day her mood had changed. She had planned to treat her unwelcome visitor with freezing dignity, but she quailed at the thought of meeting him again. The memory of his embrace still troubled her.

His brisk greeting set her mind at rest, though his casual manner piqued her. Clearly the events of the previous evening had not troubled him in the least. As he assured her, he had been merely acting.

Sophie did not care to examine too closely the reason why this should annoy her. Without a word she allowed him to hand her up into his carriage, and for the rest of the journey into Brighton she answered him in monosyllables.

'Are you always so silent in a morning?' he asked at last. 'You can't have a sore head, you didn't drink enough.'

'I see no need to chatter,' Sophie told him coldly. 'If you wish for entertainment, you must not look to me.'

'But I do!' He turned to her and grinned. 'I find you vastly entertaining, ma'am, even when you do not speak. There is something in your eyes which is a challenge, or could it be that charming curl of your lips? It must have reduced many a man to despair.'

'You are talking nonsense, Mr Hatton. I don't find it amusing—'

'No? You would have me think of something else?' His leer made her recoil.

'Keep your distance!' she cried sharply. 'We are unobserved. There is no need to pretend. You are...you are...'

'An affront to maidenly modesty?' he suggested smoothly. 'Will you tell me that no fire lies beneath that cool exterior? I won't believe you.'

At that moment Sophie could have struck him. He was taunting her, reminding her of their embrace and the way she had responded. She glared at him, disliking him more each time she was forced to endure his company.

He had claimed to be lacking in experience of women. She turned away in disgust. She had little experience herself, but enough to realise that Hatton was a skilful lover. His kiss, demanding and insistent, was something beyond her wildest imaginings. It had brought her to life again.

That unwelcome knowledge enraged her further.

'Sir, you are no gentleman!' she cried. 'If I were a man you would not insult me so.'

'If you were a man you'd be of no use to me,' he replied carelessly. 'I doubt if we'd have met.'

Sophie tried for a firm grip on her temper, and when she spoke again her voice was calm.

'Are you not forgetting our purpose, Mr Hatton? You do yourself no service. At this present time my dislike of you is so intense that I find it difficult to hide. That was not your intention, I believe?'

'Certainly not. You must forgive me, ma'am. I'm a plain man, and I fear that my manner is uncouth.'

Sophie gave him a dagger-look. He was laughing at her again and she found it maddening.

She maintained a haughty attitude until they reached the Steyne in Brighton. Then a lively interest overcame her feelings of resentment. She'd longed to visit the place, but Richard had never brought her here, although they lived so close.

Now she gazed out of the carriage window, hoping to see the parade of fashionable celebrities who frequented that famous thoroughfare. To her disappointment the place was almost empty.

Hatton saw her expression. 'The keen wind from the sea has cleared the streets,' he observed with a smile. 'Those around the Prince prefer the comforts of a hothouse atmosphere, and then, you know, it is much too early for a promenade.'

'And the Prince's cottage? Is it close by?'

'You shall see it later. Call it a cottage if you will. Inside it is a palace.'

'You have been inside?' Sophie's curiosity outweighed her determination to betray no interest in anything he might have to say.

'Upon occasion!' The curt reply discouraged further questioning as they turned into North Street.

'Now, ma'am, on your left is Hannington's. The shop is newly opened and you will find it useful for such purchases as reticules, gloves and scarves—'

'You recommend it, sir, from personal experience?' Sophie could not resist the opportunity to goad him.

Hatton refused to be drawn. 'I propose to leave you here for a time when we have completed our business with the mantua-maker. I have another appointment.'

Sophie was careful to betray no interest in this statement. Doubtless he was about to make further plans for her discomfiture, but she would not give him the pleasure of snubbing her again.

Hatton rapped sharply upon the roof of the carriage.

'Back into Kemp Town, Reuben,' he ordered.

'Oh!' Sophie could not hide her disappointment. 'I thought we were to stay in Brighton.'

'Kemp Town is a part of Brighton…the oldest part, in fact. It is but a few hundred yards away.' Hatton gave her a curious look. 'You have not been here before? I had thought that since you lived so close…?'

'There was never time enough,' she replied shortly. It was pointless to explain that when Richard was alive there was never money to spare for outings. 'As you know, we did not keep a carriage.'

'But before your marriage? Your father did not bring you for the Season? Young ladies have been known to make excellent matches here.'

'My father had other plans for me.'

'Ah, yes, the estimable William Curtis! How unfilial of you to spurn him!'

Sophie eyed him with contempt. 'Must you remind me of your eavesdropping? It is nothing to be proud of, sir.'

'No, I expect is isn't.' He was unrepentant. In fact, he was smiling as the coach drew to a halt in front of a modest terraced house.

'What is this place?' she asked as he stretched out an arm to help her down.

'The mantua-maker, of course. Did you suppose that I had brought you to a den of vice?' Hatton looked about him. 'I'll admit, however, that this is not the most salubrious of neighbourhoods.'

Sophie could only agree as she looked up at the dilapidated building with its peeling paintwork. She had never trusted Hatton. Was this suggested shopping expedition merely a ruse?

She hesitated on the doorstep, shivering as the icy wind tore at her shabby clothing.

Hatton hurried her indoors. 'I suggest that you make a warm cloak your first purchase,' he suggested not unkindly.

Sophie bridled. Was he sneering at her? She would not be patronised. Pride alone kept her head high as the maid showed them into a comfortable parlor.

Then her spirits sank as a tiny creature hurried towards them with hands outstretched. Her simple elegance put Sophie's toilette to shame.

'Welcome, my l...' The words died upon her lips as

Hatton gave an imperceptible shake of his head. He was quick to offer his own greeting.

'I'm glad to see that you haven't forgotten your old friend Nicholas Hatton, madame. May I present Mistress Firle to you? She has need of a new wardrobe.'

He turned to Sophie. 'Madame Arouet will take care of you. She has much experience of fashion. Perhaps you will allow her to guide your choice…'

Startled by these uncompromising words, Madame looked from one face to the other. She was no fool, and she sensed the hostility in Sophie's manner.

'I expect that Mistress Firle will have her own ideas,' she said agreeably. 'Perhaps if I were to show her certain patterns and fabrics…?' This suggestion was accompanied by a charming smile.

Sophie's manner softened a little, sensing that she had found an ally. She nodded her agreement.

'Then if madame would care to step into the workroom?' Claudine Arouet shot a warning look at the man who called himself Nicholas Hatton. There was some mystery here, but clearly the girl had spirit. Bullying would not ensure her co-operation.

Hatton's arrogant manner had surprised her. On previous occasions she had found him kind and courteous. Now she looked at him and raised an eyebrow.

Hatton smiled then. He knew her very well, and understood the unspoken question.

'Mistress Firle has been widowed recently,' he explained. 'She has been too distressed to care for her appearance.'

Madame threw her eyes to heaven. Men would do well to hold their tongues on these subjects, she thought decidedly. Was he trying to rob the girl of all her confidence?

She smiled again at Sophie. 'That is understandable,' she agreed in her prettily accented English. 'But Mistress Firle looks charmingly, in spite of all. It will be such a pleasure to dress a lady with the slender figure of a model, when so many of my customers show evidence of spending too much time at the dining-table.'

Even Sophie smiled at that.

'She'll pay for dressing,' Hatton admitted grudgingly. 'But you'll agree that she's too young for widow's weeds?'

Madame resolved to speak to him as soon as the opportunity arose. Now she hid her feelings.

'There is always a happy compromise,' she said bluntly as she led Sophie into the other room.

Sophie's purchases did not take long. She found that she and Madame were in complete agreement as to styles and colours. Madame summoned her head seamstress and, leaving Sophie to be measured, returned to the parlor to find Hatton gazing through her window. She attacked at once.

'My dear sir, what are you about?' she asked. 'This is no way to bend a lady to your will.'

Hatton took her hand and kissed it. 'Am I in your bad books, my dear? A bull in a china shop, perhaps?'

'Most certainly! Would you take one of your famous thoroughbreds, and try to break it with cruelty?'

'Was I cruel!' Hatton looked disconcerted. 'I didn't mean to be. It's just that...well...the lady hates me. I see no remedy for that.'

'You might try using some of your charm.'

'That would not serve,' he told her shortly.

'Well, at least refrain from these unfortunate comments. If the lady is recently widowed, as you say, she cannot be feeling herself again just yet.'

'I stand corrected, Madame. I'll try to mend my ways. Am I forgiven?'

'Always, you shocking creature! You will give my regards to your father?' A look of infinite sadness passed fleetingly across her face.

Hatton took both her hands in his. 'I promise,' he said quietly.

Madame was quite herself again when Sophie came to join them, and she responded quickly to the girl's unfeigned thanks. She was too well bred to betray unseemly curiosity about her customer, though she could only wonder at the connection between this young woman and Nicholas Hatton. The lady's shabby clothing did not trouble her. Since the troubles in France, some of her dearest friends had been reduced to abject penury…among them, some of the highest in the land.

But Mistress Firle was an Englishwoman, and obviously gently bred. Perhaps the lady had fallen upon hard times, but how had Hatton become involved?

Was this some affair of the heart? She thought not. She was fond of Hatton and she owed his family much, but she had never ceased to wonder why he was still unmarried. He seemed impervious to female charms, and in all their dealings she had never seen him with a woman. Possibly there had been some unfortunate incident in his past.

She brushed the thought aside. It was none of her concern. She returned to the business in hand.

'The garments will be ready in a day or so,' she promised. 'If you will give me your direction, madam, they shall be sent to you…'

Blushing, Sophie gave her the name of the inn.

'And the account is to go to Mr Hatton?' Madame realised that her question was indiscreet, but she was anxious to see the reaction of her customers.

'Certainly not!' Colour flooded Sophie's face as she opened her reticule and took out the roll of notes. 'Will you let me know the total, please?' Her cheeks were burning. Did Madame Arouet imagine that she was Hatton's light o' love?

Anger made her careless. 'I do not know this gentleman well,' she said coolly. 'I met him only yesterday.' She stopped in some confusion. Hatton had warned her to watch her tongue. Had she said too much?

Madame was quick to set her customer at ease. Her hearing was acute, but she assumed a sudden deafness.

Hatton was swift to cover Sophie's gaffe. 'The ladies of my family suggested that I recommend you to Mistress Firle,' he announced. 'I must hope that she is pleased with her purchases...'

Sophie was ashamed of the sudden spurt of anger which had led to her indiscretion.

'Madame has been most helpful.' Sophie smiled then and Madame Arouet was startled into silence. That smile lit up the room as the girl's face was transformed.

She revised her thoughts at once as to the strange connection between Hatton and her latest customer. The young man would be well advised to watch his step. Shabbily dressed though she was at present, this slender girl had a certain quality about her which was totally disarming. When dressed as Madame intended her to be, not only Hatton would be in danger of losing his heart.

Then she chuckled to herself. Match-making? She could be as guilty of it as many another lady of advancing years. Hatton was so eligible. Years ago she'd hoped of a match for her daughter, Eugenie, but her quarry had insisted on treating the girl as if she were a younger sister.

Hatton picked up his gloves and cane. 'We must go,' he said. 'We have much to do today.' Then a thought struck him and he turned to Sophie. 'You remembered to buy a cloak, I hope?'

Sophie nodded, annoyed once more by his arrogant manner. 'It was my first purchase,' she told him shortly.

'And an excellent choice, if I may say so.' Madame picked up the finely woven garment and settled it about Sophie's shoulders. 'Mr Hatton, I'm sure you will agree that the colour is becoming?'

Her eyes held his, daring him to disagree with her.

Hatton laughed, but he could not resist the chance to tease. 'Turn round,' he ordered.

Mute with resentment, Sophie did as she was bidden.

Then, to her astonishment, he bowed and kissed her hand. 'A delightful choice,' he agreed. 'That glowing shade of blue is quite your colour, Mistress Firle.'

Nonplussed by the compliment, Sophie could only stare at him. Then she remembered her manners. 'Thank you!' she said in some confusion.

Madame accompanied her customers to the door, shivering as a blast of icy wind swept in from the street.

''Tis a bitter day,' she complained. 'But then you English are a hardy race. For myself, I long for the south of France. Perhaps, one day…?'

Hatton threw a comforting arm about her shoulders. 'Claudine, your day will come,' he promised.

Settled once more in the carriage, with a rug about her knees, Sophie gave him a curious look.

'You know Madame well?' she asked.

'She is an old friend of my father…my family,' he amended hastily. 'What did you think of her?'

'I liked her very much,' Sophie told him frankly. 'She was so kind. I was at a loss to choose from all those wonderful fabrics, but she understood exactly what I needed.'

Hatton chuckled. 'Is anything left of your nest-egg?' he enquired.

'Of course. I told you. I need some things for Kit.' She hesitated. 'Mr Hatton, I know you said that I should spend the money, but I don't feel comfortable doing so.'

'And why is that?'

'Matthew and his family have not been paid for weeks,' she blurted out. 'Their wages must come first…'

'That matter is settled, Mistress Firle. I took care of it last night.'

'Oh, I see!' Sophie faltered out her thanks, wondering as she did so if this masterful stranger intended to take over her entire life. She returned to a less controversial subject.

'How came Madame Arouet to Brighton?' she asked. 'To me she seemed a most unlikely mantua-maker, although, of course, she has great expertise.'

'Need you ask? Like many another, she is an aristocrat driven from her home in France by the revolution.'

'And her husband?'

'Arouet was beaten to death before her eyes. She and her daughter were lodged in a French prison for some months.'

Sophie gasped. 'How brave she is! One would never imagine that such a tragedy had happened to her.'

'She is a courageous woman,' he agreed. 'There are many such, forced to use what skills they have simply to survive.'

Sophie fell silent.

'Something troubles you?' he asked.

'Not exactly, but I was thinking. It is very strange. When tragedy strikes…I mean, when Richard was killed it was a fearful shock. I was so overcome with what it would mean for me and Kit that I thought of no one else. I should have remembered that I was not the only woman in the world to suffer such a loss.'

She stole a look at her companion and was surprised to see an expression of compassion on his face.

'You are growing up, my dear,' he told her gently. 'Believe me, I was sorry to hear of your husband's death.'

'Yes,' she said thoughtfully. 'I do believe you. That's why I'll help you catch his killers.'

He handed her down as the coach drew up before Hannington's in North Street.

'You have an hour to make your purchases,' he announced. 'Don't keep me waiting, Mistress Firle.'

'I wouldn't dream of it,' she told him stiffly. She turned away and hurried into the store. Now that she was sure that Matthew's wages had been paid, she could use that comforting roll of bills to buy flannel for Kit's shirts and woollen cloth to make him a coat. Sophie had learned to grow clever with her needle. Without those skills she and her son would have been reduced to rags in this last year or so.

It was a sobering thought. Her fingers closed about the roll of 'soft' as Richard had called it. She hadn't seen so much money since that dreadful day when she'd opened Richard's desk in search of paper for Kit's painting.

She'd gazed at the bills in disbelief. Richard was always pleading poverty, but there was enough here to keep them in comfort for a year. When she'd questioned him he'd flown into a rage, accusing her of spying on him and a lack of trust.

Well, it was true. From that day on, she'd never trusted him completely. They had become estranged, though it had grieved her deeply.

She glanced at the clock across the street. She had an hour. Swiftly she moved from one department to another, ignoring the tempting fripperies on display. Then, hurrying past the gaily coloured ribbons, she bethought herself of Bess and Abby. Stuff for gowns would be more welcome, she decided. She added two lengths to her purchases of wool and flannel, and gained the entrance to the street before the appointed hour.

Hatton raised an eyebrow in surprise. 'Good God!' he exclaimed. 'A punctual woman? I can scarce believe it!'

Sophie ignored the gibe.

'Are you hungry?' he asked in a jovial tone.

'No, Mr Hatton. I don't eat luncheon.'

'Well, I do!' he replied. 'And you'd be better for it. With more flesh on your bones you wouldn't feel the cold so much.'

'Thank you for your concern!'

'Think nothing of it,' he answered in airy tones.

'I don't think anything of it, sir, knowing as I do that your concern is merely for your own ends.'

She heard a maddening chuckle. 'Still furious? Blest if you ain't the prickliest creature I ever met in my life.'

'But did you not say yourself that your experience is not vast?'

'Touché!' Hatton laughed aloud. 'I led with my chin on that one, did I not?'

'Fencing *and* boxing, my dear sir? What a marvel you are, to be sure!'

'Compliments, ma'am? I did not expect them, I'll confess... How do you come to know so much about these manly sports?'

'You forget...I have a son,' she told him coldly.

'I don't forget. He is a fortunate lad, though I must hope that you don't frown at him as you do at me. That slight furrow on your brow may become permanent, you know. It will do nothing for your looks.' A long finger reached out to trace the almost imperceptible line.

Sophie thrust his hand away and stared out of the window.

Then, as the carriage stopped at the Castle Hotel, she attempted to assert her independence.

'Sir, I explained to you that I was not hungry, but pray don't let that stop you from dining. I will take a turn about the Promenade for an hour or so.'

Hatton looked at her in disbelief. 'Are you mad?' he exclaimed. 'Look at that sea. A single wave could knock you off your feet and suck you under.'

Sophie followed his pointing finger. The leaden waters of the English Channel did indeed look threatening. Whipped up by the wind, great sheets of water crashed inland, submerging the Promenade.

'Very well! I will wait here in the carriage for you. You must know that I cannot dine alone with you in public.'

'Of course you can't!' His lips twitched. 'That is why I took the liberty of bespeaking a private parlour!' He clamped an arm about her waist and half-lifted her from her seat.

To struggle would have been both useless and undignified. Sophie suffered herself to be led indoors.

She wasn't surprised to find that the food which was set before her was excellent, and in spite of her protestations she found that she was very hungry.

Hatton helped her liberally to the oyster patties and the roast beef, making no comment as she began to eat with evident enjoyment.

He confined his conversation to the question of staffing at the inn.

'I suggest that you interview my men at the same time as any others who may apply for work. I'll give you their names beforehand. That way, they will not arouse suspicion.'

'*I* am to interview these men?'

'Of course! After all, you are to be their employer.'

'But what am I to ask them?'

'All the usual questions,' he said carelessly. 'You will ask for previous experience, reasons for leaving their last position, honesty, sobriety and so on...' His eyes were twinkling. 'I'm sure you'll think of many more.'

'They may not tell me the truth,' she objected.

'Of course they won't, but you must use your judgement. See them in the room where we first met. It's dark enough for me to sit quietly in the corner—'

'Spying on me again?' she said bitterly.

'Purely out of interest.' His voice was smooth. 'Now, ma'am, there is something else.' He took a small package from his pocket and gave it to her.

'What is this?' she cried.

'Why not open it and see?'

Sophie tore aside the wrapping to reveal a small square shagreen box. She opened the lid and gasped. Inside lay the most beautiful brooch she'd ever seen. The large and glittering jewel at its centre was exactly the same colour as her cloak.

Sophie was no expert, but she knew at once that this was no trumpery piece of paste. The sapphire alone must be worth a fortune.

She coloured. 'I can't take this!' she said stiffly.

'You must!'

'Well, I won't! You go beyond the terms of our agreement. When you said that you'd pretend to be my suitor

I did not expect you to give the impression that…that…
Well, Madame Arouet believes already that I am your—'

'My light o' love? That is certainly my intention,
Mistress Firle.'

Sophie pushed the box across the table. 'Keep it!' she
said. 'You cannot force me to wear it!'

Hatton's patience snapped at last. 'You will wear it,
madam, and you will wear it here, where it is in plain
sight!' He jabbed a finger at her bosom. 'Now let us have
no more of your nonsense. I am tired of it! Your ill temper
is the outside of enough. Any more of it and I will turn
you out, with your son and your baggage, before this day
is out.' His voice was silky with menace.

Sophie knew that she had gone too far, but she would
not apologise. She sat in silence for the whole of the return journey to the inn.

With cool courtesy, Hatton handed her down from the
carriage.

'I shan't dine here this evening,' he informed her.
Without another glance in her direction he stalked away.

Chapter Four

Sophie was shaken by the day's events, and Hatton's threats had terrified her. What a fool she was! She could not afford the risk of being turned out of her home, however much she disliked him. Above all, there was Kit to think about. What demon had persuaded her into behaving so badly?

She must keep a firm grip on her temper. Just let her gain her ends, and then she might enjoy the pleasure of telling the arrogant creature exactly what she thought of him. She doubted if it would make much difference. This man cared nothing for opinions other than his own. But I'll do it, she vowed to herself. If nothing else, it would give her so much satisfaction.

Refusing Bess's offer of a light supper, she went to find her son.

'Shall I read you a story, Kit?' She drew the boy on to her lap.

'Yes, please, Mama! I'd like the one about the pirates.'

Sophie began the oft-repeated tale. She deplored the violence and skirted around the worst excesses of those tigers of the seas.

Kit stopped her halfway through the tale. 'You've forgotten the blood on the deck,' he accused.

'Oh, dear, so I have!' Sophie smiled to herself. Her son could not yet read, but he remembered every word of the tales she told him.

She finished the story and tucked him into bed. 'Now I have a surprise for you,' she said.

The eager little face looked up at her. 'Is it something very nice, Mama?'

'I hope you'll think so. It's a fishing rod.'

Kit's look of rapture was reward enough for her. She'd stolen out of Hannington's and into the shop next door to make her purchase. An extravagance, perhaps? But then, Kit had so little.

Now he lay down with the rod beside him, his fingers curled about it. Within minutes he was fast asleep.

Sophie looked down at the impossibly long lashes curling against his cheeks. Kit was such a little boy. Asleep, he seemed so vulnerable. She bent and kissed him, vowing as she did so that she would protect him at whatever cost to herself.

What had she suffered, after all? Merely a day spent in the company of an unpleasant creature who seemed to take a positive delight in goading her. And she had risen to the bait, she thought in disgust. She, who had always prided herself upon her calm and her even temper. Hatton, alas, seemed to bring out the worst in her.

In future she must not allow herself to be teased into fighting with him. A dignified silence appeared to be the answer to his gibes. He would soon grow tired of the game if she did not respond.

Then she heard the sound of carriage wheels. Hurrying to the window she was in time to see her tormentor driving away, handling the ribbons himself. He'll never take the corner at that speed, she thought with some satisfaction.

She was mistaken. Driving to an inch, Hatton negotiated the bend in the lane in style.

Robbed of the pleasure of watching him overturn the coach, Sophie wandered down to the kitchen.

There she found a cosy scene. Matthew and his family were seated round the table, deep in conversation with Hatton's coachman.

The man was on his feet at once, and Sophie acknowledged his salute with the briefest inclination of her head. Doubtless he, too, regarded her as his master's latest bird of paradise.

She eyed him sharply, but in his demeanour she could find nothing but respect. Reuben was an unprepossessing fellow, in spite of that. Short and squat, his arms seemed to her to be unnaturally long. Without a hair on his gleaming pate, his head merged into a bull neck above a barrel chest.

Clearly Hatton did not require elegance in his servants.

'Mistress, won't you let me send you up some supper?' Bess coaxed. 'I could make you an omelette.'

'I have dined well today,' Sophie told her with a smile. 'I couldn't eat another bite. I believe I shall retire early tonight.'

'Abby has lit your fire already. Mr Hatton thought you might need it.'

Sophie bit back a sharp retort. The redoubtable Mr Hatton took far too much upon himself, but it would not do to let her servants see her annoyance. She bade them goodnight, and went up to her room.

It was pleasant, after all, to enjoy the unaccustomed luxury of such warmth. In the past she had wakened often to find ice encrusting the inside of her windows, and it could not be denied that the night was bitter.

Settling into her fireside chair, she picked up her book and tried to read without success. Her eyes were closing. At last she sent for Abby, slipped out of her gown, and sought the comfort of her bed.

Sophie slept late next day. It was full daylight when she awoke to the sound of Kit's voice in the stable-yard. Her fire had been replenished as she slept, so the room was warm.

She slipped on a robe over her night attire and hurried to the window. Peering out, she could see that Kit, muffled to the ears in scarves and a woollen hat, was absorbed in drawing a large circle on the frosty ground with a long stick. He seemed to be chanting some strange song.

Intrigued, she watched as he divided the circle into segments. Then he stood in the centre with closed eyes, and pointed the stick in each of four directions.

She smiled. The child must be absorbed in some mysterious game of his own. Then, as she turned away, she heard a bellow of rage.

'Stop it!' her son shouted. 'You are spoiling the magic!'

A glance was enough to show her that an older boy, almost into his teens, was scuffing the circle with his boots, jeering as he did so.

'Spoiling the magic?' he mimicked. 'Well, I don't mind spoiling your game.'

'You will! You will!' Almost as red as a turkey-cock, her son doubled up his fists.

Sophie gathered her robe about her. Kit would be no match for the older boy. Then she heard a leisurely voice.

'You're magic, aren't you?' Hatton enquired. 'Why not turn him into a frog?'

Kit stood very still. 'Yes,' he said thoughtfully. 'I might just do that.' He pointed his stick at the older boy who gave a cry of fright and ran away.

'You must be Kit,' the deep voice continued. 'Allow me to introduce myself. My name is Hatton.'

'Thank you, Hatton. Do you know my mother?'

'Indeed I do. I'm on my way to see her now. You might care to accompany me.'

Sophie hurried herself into the old grey gown. Then she ran downstairs to find her son and his mentor engaged in a serious discussion as to the relative merits of worms or maggots when engaged in the art of fishing.

'My dear Kit,' she reproved. 'Will you never learn that it simply is not wise to fight boys older than yourself?'

'I didn't fight him,' Kit said simply. 'I said I'd turn him into a frog. Hatton thought of it.'

'*Mr* Hatton, if you please,' Sophie said severely.

'He said his name was Hatton,' Kit replied in injured tones.

'It will do well enough, since it is my name. Kit, your mother and I have some matters to discuss. Shall you mind very much if I ask you to help Reuben with my horses? They need to be groomed and fed.'

'Will he let me drive them?'

'He'll show you how to handle the ribbons. Later, I may take you out myself.'

Kit made a headlong dash for the door.

'One moment, Kit. I need your promise first.'

'What's that?'

'Will you promise not to turn my horses into frogs?'

Kit came back to rest a grubby hand upon Hatton's immaculate buckskins.

Sophie winced, but her companion did not appear to recognise the threat to his appearance.

'I wouldn't do that,' her son said earnestly. 'I don't use magic on my friends.'

Hatton rose to his full height and bowed. Then he held out his hand. 'Thank you,' he said with dignity. 'Good friends are hard to come by.'

Kit took his hand and shook it warmly. 'May I go now?' he asked.

Hatton nodded. When he turned back to Sophie he found that she was smiling, but she shook her head in reproof.

'You shouldn't encourage him in such nonsense, Sir. Kit has too vivid an imagination.'

'Don't try to stifle it, ma'am. It is a gift not given to many.'

She gave him a curious look. 'Have you children of your own?' she asked.

'I am not married, Mistress Firle, and to my knowledge I haven't fathered any bastards.'

Sophie's cheeks grew pink with embarrassment. 'I didn't mean to pry,' she said with dignity. 'It is just that you seem to have a way with children.'

'I don't talk down to them, if that is what you mean. They are human beings, like the rest of us, and often possessed of far more sense than their elders.'

Sophie was aware of the implied criticism, but she let it go, mindful of her good resolutions.

'He has no notion of danger,' she replied in a worried tone. 'Without your intervention he would have tried to fight that young lout.'

Hatton laughed. 'Your little game-cock isn't short of spirit. In time he'll learn that there are other ways to skin a cat.'

'I suppose so, but I cannot like the notion of his helping

to groom your horses. They are thoroughbreds, are they not, and doubtless highly strung?'

'He'll come to no harm in Reuben's hands.' Hatton was growing impatient. 'You must not mollycoddle him, Mistress Firle. Let him try his wings a little.'

'He's only five years old!' Sophie cried indignantly. 'Besides, he's all I have!'

'Then get out of his way, ma'am. The lad has promise, but he must learn. You can't protect him from every bump and blow.' Brusquely he dismissed the subject. 'Are you ready to interview your new servants?' He laid a sheet of paper in front of her.

'What is this, Mr Hatton?'

'Just a reminder of the questions you should ask. You will take Besford and Fraddon, of course. They are my men. Besford will make a suitable ostler, and Fraddon is an experienced cellarman.'

Sophie hoped devoutly that the two men would be less frightening in appearance than the terrifying Reuben. Her heart misgave her at the thought of her precious Kit in that strange creature's company, but Hatton recalled her quickly to the task in hand.

'There are four others from the local villages,' he told her. 'I must hope that you won't allow yourself to be influenced by appearances.'

'I can't accuse *you* of that, Mr Hatton. I've seldom seen a more villainous-looking servant than your coachman.'

'Reuben? I'm sorry that he doesn't meet with your approval. I didn't choose him for his handsome face.' Hatton tossed aside his cloak. Then he rang the bell. 'Your mistress will see the men now,' he informed Matthew.

With that he walked over to the darkest corner of the room, turned the wing-chair away from the door, and became invisible to the casual observer.

Sophie saw his own men first. Each of them was powerfully built and roughly dressed, but somewhat to her surprise they were not ill spoken.

Knowing that the interviews were merely a formality, Sophie did not keep them long, explaining their duties as best she could. Having engaged them on the spot, she left them in Matthew's hands, with instructions to unload the cartload of supplies which had arrived that morning.

Then her next candidate sidled into the room. Sophie took him in dislike at once. For one thing, he bore a striking resemblance to the boy who had tormented Kit that morning.

Apparently respectful, there was a knowing look about him as he took in every detail of the room. Sophie suspected at once that he had an eye to the main chance. She would never rest easy with this creature about the premises. Thieving, she guessed, was already on his mind.

The next man was a surprise. 'Why, Ben!' she exclaimed. 'What are you doing here?'

'Bess sent word that you needed help, ma'am. I hope you'll consider me. My sister can vouch for me...'

'I'm sure of it,' she told him warmly. She'd met Bess's brother on several occasions and always found him willing to turn his hand to any task about the inn, even though she could not pay him.

Pleased that she was now able to do so, she offered him a generous wage and was rewarded with a look of gratitude. Then he hesitated.

'I hope you won't think me forward, Mistress Firle, but I've brought my son along o' me. He can't get work nowhere...'

'But why is that?'

'I'm sorry to say, ma'am, but he's an innocent.'

'What do you mean?'

'If you see him, you'll know what I mean. He's never been quite right in the head, but he's a strong lad, and he's willing.'

'Will you call him then? I'd like to speak to him.'

As Ben turned to the door Sophie heard a slight cough from the direction of the window. She decided to ignore it.

Hatton had told her to use her own judgement and she would do so.

'This 'ere is Jem.' Ben preceded his companion into the room. 'He don't say much, ma'am, but he can understand you.'

Sophie looked up and gasped. Ben's son was enormous. He had to bend his head to negotiate the doorway and his giant bulk seemed to fill the room. Now he stood in front of her, smiling shyly.

'Would you like to work here, Jem?' she asked. 'Your father could show you what to do.'

The lad's smile grew wider, and he nodded. His bright blue eyes were fixed upon her with a pleading look.

Sophie studied the guileless face, and was captivated. Jem might not be bright, but she knew at once that she could trust him.

'Very well!' she said. 'Ben, will you tell Matthew that I have engaged you both?'

'You won't be sorry, ma'am.' Ben's look showed her what her decision had meant to him, but she stilled his fervent thanks. 'Make yourselves known to the other men,' she told him. 'They are strangers hereabouts.'

'Aye! Fishermen in from the coast, so they tells me.' Ben shook his head. 'There's no work there, they says, since the war with France.'

'Will you send the last man in?' she asked. 'I doubt if I shall have work for him as well...' Hatton had told her to engage four men, and she had already done so. Now she was at a loss as to what to say to the last of the applicants.

'He's gone, ma'am. He went off with the one you turned away.'

Sophie felt relieved, guessing that he was likely to be another undesirable.

As the door closed on Ben and his son, Hatton rose from his chair.

'You did well!' he told her. 'Better than I expected.'

'Good heavens, don't tell me that you approved of my choice? When you coughed I thought that you were warning me against accepting Jem.'

'It had the opposite effect, I believe.' Hatton was laughing openly.

'What! Oh, you wretched creature! You meant me to take him all the time.'

'Why not? I had already spoken to all the applicants, you see. I saw them earlier this morning, when you were still asleep.'

Sophie stared at him. 'You were here? Oh, I thought…I mean, I saw your carriage leave the inn last night, and I had imagined that you had not slept here.' Hot colour flooded her face as she realised the implications of her words.

'Never judge by appearances, Mistress Firle. For the present I can control my vile male appetite for female company, if that is what is worrying you.'

'What you do does not concern me in the least,' Sophie said scornfully. 'In any case, my disapproval would not alter your behaviour.'

'No, it wouldn't!' he agreed with a cheerful smile. 'I'm sure you feel the same about your own behaviour.'

As this happened to be true, Sophie saw no point in denying it.

'I'm glad to see that you are wearing your brooch,' Hatton continued smoothly. 'It looks well on you.'

'I found it useful,' Sophie admitted with some reluctance. 'The man I turned away never took his eyes from it. If I'd engaged him, I am persuaded that it would have disappeared.'

'An ugly customer!' Hatton agreed. 'His friend was of the same ilk.'

'What would you have done if I'd engaged them?'

'I thought it unlikely, but the question doesn't arise. Are you pleased with your new staff?'

'With two of them, at least. I'll reserve my judgement about your men, but I can trust Ben and his son.'

'True, and the lad, in particular, will be an asset.'

'Why do you say that? He is said to be touched in the head, you know.'

'We are not looking for scholars, Mistress Firle. Jem's size alone is enough to discourage troublemakers, but there is no harm in him. He'll serve you well, I believe.'

Sophie looked her surprise. 'I shall never understand you, sir. I had not expected this from you.'

'Sympathy for a troubled mind? Well, ma'am, you do not know me well. Let us hope that your opinion of me will improve on further acquaintance.' He opened the door and sniffed the air in appreciation. 'Time for our nuncheon, I believe. May I persuade you to join me?'

Mollified by his good opinion of both Ben and his son, Sophie preceded him into the dining-room.

She was feeling confused. It was true. She would never understand this man. She'd been astonished by the way her son had accepted him without demur. Children, she knew, had an amazing way of sensing sincerity in adults.

Of course, Hatton had made it his business to be agreeable to Kit, entering into the spirit of his game and treating him with respect. She hadn't expected it.

Nor had she supposed that he would see beyond the childlike demeanour of Ben's son. Had she been asked beforehand she would have sworn that Hatton would have forbidden her to engage the lad. Now, apparently, he approved.

As he seated her at the table, she realised that she was looking forward to her meal. He looked on with approval as she allowed Abby to help her to a dish of mushrooms bubbling gently in a coating of cheese sauce.

'The outing to Brighton did you good,' he observed. 'Today you have more colour in your cheeks. With plenty of good food we'll soon turn you into a buxom wench.'

Sophie laid down her fork. 'I may not care to become a buxom wench,' she told him stiffly.

'You couldn't!' he teased. 'That racehorse build will never carry spare flesh. Eat up, my dear! You need not fear to rival the fat lady at the fair.'

Sophie ignored these pleasantries. She found that she was hungry, and Hatton's teasing would not stop her from enjoying her meal. She attacked a generous slice of ham braised in Madeira wine, and dared him to comment further.

He didn't do so. 'Shall you be ready to open the inn by the end of the week?' he asked.

'I think so, now that we have enough staff and plenty of stores,' Sophie told him thoughtfully. 'What will happen then?'

'Why, let us hope that you will attract some trade, ma'am.'

'At this time of year? Sir, you are an optimist. Who would venture on these roads in winter?'

'More folk than you may suppose,' came the smooth reply. 'This place is isolated. Nevertheless, it is on the main route into Brighton. Possibly you may be visited by some of the young bloods in the town. Not all of them have the means to keep up with the Prince and his entourage. They seek other diversions. A pretty widow may be just the bait to attract them.'

Sophie frowned, but she was not displeased by the compliment. 'Yet these are not the men you seek, surely?' she objected.

'No, they are not, but a busy inn provides better cover for our quarry than one which is almost empty. I think you may expect some unusual visitors within the next few weeks.'

Sophie shuddered, but Hatton did not appear to notice. He pushed back his chair and bowed to her.

'Will you forgive me if I leave you, Mistress Firle? I have urgent matters to attend.'

Leaving her to her thoughts he walked away, and within minutes she heard the sound of his carriage wheels upon the drive.

Oddly, Sophie felt at a loss without him. In just a day or two she had grown accustomed to countering his taunts, and she had enjoyed the challenge to her wits.

Of course, he was not the type of man she admired. Sophie knew her own weaknesses. She'd always been attracted by a handsome face and figure. In her late husband's case she had persuaded herself that his appearance cloaked a character of sterling worth. She couldn't have been more wrong, as she now knew to her cost.

Hatton, at least, would never be described as handsome. High cheekbones and a strong jaw gave him a predatory look. If she'd been asked for an adjective to describe him she would have chosen 'merciless'. A dangerous man, by any standards. With that dark hair and eyes, and his swarthy complexion, he might have been taken for a pirate.

Sophie smiled to herself. She was allowing her imagination to run away with her. Kit was not the only one at fault in that respect. Hatton was a gentleman, she told herself. That fact was apparent in his manner, his carriage, and his air of authority. On occasion his formal courtesy had confirmed these views.

It had not made her soften towards him. He had shown the most ruthless disregard for the situation in which she found herself through no fault of her own. For the moment, it suited her to agree to all his plans, but that agreement would not last for ever.

She made her way down to the kitchen, and was astonished to find her son seated upon the fearsome Reuben's lap, sharing his meal of bread and cheese and pickles. The new fishing rod lay in the place of honour on the table, and Kit was absorbed in discussing the relative merits of worms or maggots as bait.

The man rose to his feet as Sophie entered the room, his huge hands setting Kit aside with surprising gentleness. His manner was respectful, but without the least trace of subservience.

'I hope that Kit is not making a nuisance of himself?' she ventured. 'If he interferes with your work, you must send him back to me.'

'The young gentleman has been a help to me,' Reuben told her. 'He has a feel for horses...he ain't afraid of them.'

Sophie quailed. Hatton's team looked skittish to her inexperienced eye. Kit could be kicked, or bitten, or crushed against the wall of a stall.

Reuben smiled at her, and his ugly face was transformed.

'Don't you worry, ma'am,' he assured her. 'Master Kit pays heed to what I tells him. He'll come to no harm along o' me.'

Kit threw a chubby arm round Reuben's neck. 'We haven't finished our work, Mama. Reuben says that we must clean the tack. That means the saddles and the bridles of the horses, you know.'

'Very well, then, as long as you do what Reuben says, but you must come indoors before it gets dark.' Sophie smiled at the ill-assorted pair and left them.

Once again she had been guilty of judging by appearances. Reuben might be ill favoured, but in those few minutes he had warmed to his evident kindness to her son.

She mentioned it to Hatton when he returned late in the afternoon.

'You are learning fast, Mistress Firle,' he told her drily. 'It's always as well to watch what people do, rather than what they say or how they look.'

Sophie said nothing. There was much truth in his remarks, and she could not argue.

'Now I have a surprise for you,' he told her.

'A pleasant one, I hope?'

'I trust that you will think so.' He rang the bell to summon Matthew. 'You may send the girl in now,' he said.

Sophie stared at him in astonishment, but she was even more surprised by the appearance of a woman not much younger than herself. The newcomer was an enchanting creature, flaxen ringlets framing a little heart-shaped face. A pair of large blue eyes looked at her briefly. Then they were hidden by impossibly long lashes as the girl bobbed a curtsy and kept them fixed on the carpet.

Sophie stiffened in anger. If Hatton thought to install his mistress at the inn she would have none of it.

'What is this?' she said sharply. 'I do not know this person.'

She looked at Hatton and caught a flash of anger in his eyes. 'Of course you don't!' he said in a curt tone. 'Nancy is not a native of these parts, but she is a skilled serving wench.'

'Serving whom?' she snapped out without thinking.

Hatton turned to the girl. 'Will you wait outside for just a moment?' he asked. 'I'd like a private word with Mistress Firle.'

As the door closed behind her he rounded on Sophie.

'Does your folly know no bounds?' he demanded in a furious tone. 'Can you run this place unaided? Who is to serve your customers?'

'Abby has always done so.' Outwardly defiant, Sophie was quaking inwardly.

'I see. In addition to serving food and ale she will also clean the place, make the beds and see to the wants of yourself and your son?'

'She is a capable girl.' Sophie was still defiant.

'She will need to be a marvel. Twenty-four hours each day will scarce be enough for her to carry out her duties. Don't tell me that her mother will help her. Bess will have more than enough to do to feed the men and any travellers who stop here.'

'I shan't be idle myself,' Sophie cried. Her anger now threatened to match his own. 'Abby and I will work together.'

'Indeed? With your vast experience of a servant's duties you are certain to be a wonderful help to her...'

The biting sarcasm made Sophie flinch. She did not answer him.

'It will be difficult to carry out the task I asked of you if you spend your time in scrubbing floors and emptying slops.' Hatton's logic was relentless, and she could think of nothing to say to him.

She gave him a look of hatred, but his reply was a contemptuous laugh.

'More dagger-looks? They'll cut no ice with me. What is your objection to Nancy? She is a willing worker, I assure you.'

Willing to do what? Sophie was tempted to fling the question at him, but she thought better of it.

'I prefer to choose my own female servants,' she replied in icy tones. 'I'd have chosen a girl from the local village—'

'You would have found it difficult, ma'am. I have made enquiries. We are close enough to Brighton for the local girls to find well-paid employment and easier conditions there.'

'Then why has this…this Nancy chosen to come here? To martyr herself, perhaps?'

It was a gibe unworthy of her, and she expected to be punished for it, but Hatton had been studying her stubborn expression. A slight smile lifted the corners of his mouth.

'Are you being quite honest, Mistress Firle? I think not. You object to the girl because she is well favoured. Tell me, would some ancient crone attract more custom to this inn?'

'She'll cause trouble. Respectable, you say? With that face and figure I take leave to doubt it.'

'Jealous, my dear?'

Sophie jumped to her feet. Anger had driven all thoughts of caution from her mind. She lifted a hand to slap his face, but he caught her wrist in an iron grip.

'Don't try it!' he said grimly. 'Sit down, you little fool! Dear God, you must have had wenches working for you in the past. Were they all ill favoured?'

'No! They were not! That is why…why…' Her voice broke and she could not go on. Appalled, she realised that she was close to tears. It would be the ultimate humiliation to break down in front of this detestable man. She turned her face away.

'Look at me!' he said more gently. 'I can only guess at what has happened in the past. Am I to believe that your husband was unfaithful to you?'

A large hand covered her own and to her horror she saw that a tear had fallen upon his skin. She tried to brush it away, but a second fell and then another.

'It wasn't Richard's fault,' she whispered. 'He was so handsome. They threw themselves at his head…'

'He could have refused them, my dear.' Hatton thrust his handkerchief into her hand. 'And now, I suppose, you have no faith in any man?' He was tempted to slide a comforting arm about her slim shoulders, but he thought better of it. It would only confirm her poor opinion of his sex.

'Not all men are the same,' he assured her. 'But now I understand. You believed that Nancy was my mistress, did you not?'

Sophie nodded. She was still incapable of speech.

'I should be angry with you, Mistress Firle. She is not, but had she been a connection of mine I should not have insulted you by bringing her here. I know that your opinion of me is not high, but that you must believe, at least.'

'I'm sorry!' she said in muffled tones. She could no longer doubt his word. 'I'll speak to her if you will call her in.'

'One moment, then!' He took the handkerchief from her and dried her eyes. 'We mustn't allow her to think that I've been beating you, or she may flee back to Brighton.'

Sophie managed a watery smile.

'That's better!' Hatton lifted her face to his and looked into her eyes. 'I wish that you could learn to trust me,' he said in an altered tone. 'We could deal well together, you and I.'

Chapter Five

That night it wasn't only Hatton's words which robbed Sophie of her rest. After lying awake for hours, she'd fallen into an uneasy sleep only to be awakened by a fearful clap of thunder, so loud that it seemed to shake the very foundations of the inn.

Then a livid flash of lightning lit her room, to be followed within seconds by another thunderclap. She realised that the storm must be immediately overhead.

Jumping out of bed, she threw on her robe and hurried into Kit's room, fearing that the child would be terrified. Her worries were needless. Kit was fast asleep. As usual, he'd cast off his coverlet and lay with his arms above his head, oblivious to the raging elements which tore so fiercely at the countryside.

Sophie listened to his steady breathing as she covered him again. She dropped a kiss upon his cheek. Then she checked the oil-lamp which burned far out of his reach on top of a high chest. As an extra precaution she'd installed a metal cage about it, holding it firmly in place in case a sudden draught should blow it over.

The lamp had been a source of some contention between herself and Richard. Her late husband had accused her of mollycoddling their son, insisting that Kit must learn to sleep in the dark.

'You'll turn him into a coward,' he'd sneered.

'I could never do that! Kit has plenty of courage, but he also has a vivid imagination…'

'Monsters under his bed? I never heard such nonsense! Perhaps you'd prefer that he burns to death? If that lamp goes over…'

'I'll make sure that it doesn't!' Sophie had replied with spirit. She would not give way on this matter, but it was then that she'd asked Matthew to construct the metal guard.

'Is he all right?'

She heard a low voice in the doorway and turned to find Hatton watching her. Clad in a patterned dressing-gown of silk brocade, he looked larger than ever.

'He hasn't wakened, thank goodness!' Sophie jumped as yet another violent clap of thunder crashed overhead. Then she managed a wavering smile. 'Oh, dear! I am not usually so foolish. In the ordinary way I do not mind a storm, but this is exceptional, is it not?'

'It is, and it will last for some time yet, I fear. Sleep will be out of the question. Do you care to join me in a glass of wine?'

As another flash of lightning lit the room, Sophie saw that he was smiling. Then, as her eyes followed the direction of his own, she gasped. Not expecting to find any-one about at that hour of the night, she hadn't troubled to fasten her robe securely. Now she saw in dismay that it was open to the waist, revealing a thin nightgown which left little to the imagination.

Blushing, she buttoned up her robe. 'Thank you, but I intend to stay with Kit,' she said with what dignity she could summon. 'He may yet wake.'

'Then I'll make up the fire in here,' he told her easily. 'May I suggest that you fetch your slippers, Mistress Firle, otherwise your feet will freeze.'

Shocked, Sophie looked down at her bare feet. In her haste she hadn't thought to wear her slippers.

'I won't be above a moment,' she exclaimed. 'Will you stay with him?'

'Certainly!' Preoccupied with coaxing the dying embers of the fire into life, he did not look at her.

Sophie ran back along the passageway, gained her room, and thrust her feet into her slippers. As an after-thought she picked up a heavy woollen shawl. Then, as she was leaving the room she caught a glimpse of herself in the mirror. Dear heavens, she looked a positive fright! Déshabillé was not the word for it. She looked flushed and rumpled, and her hair was loose, lying in a tumbled mass about her shoulders. She snatched up a ribbon and tied it back.

When she reached Kit's room again the fire was burning brightly. Hatton was installed in a battered nursery chair, perfectly at ease as he stretched long legs towards the warmth.

'Thank you!' Sophie said briskly. 'The storm is moving away, I think. You may yet be able to sleep.'

'I doubt it! Just listen to the rain!'

Sophie looked up in alarm as a torrential downpour hammered against the roof.

'Don't worry!' he soothed. 'This place is in good repair. I insisted on it.' He rose and fetched another chair for her, setting it on the other side of the fireplace.

'Fires in bedrooms are one of life's pleasures, are they not?' he observed. 'As a child I used to lie and watch the flames and fancy that I could see faces in the embers. It was even better when the weather was inclement and it snowed.'

Sophie tried to hide her surprise. Somehow she had not thought of this sophisticated creature indulging in childish fancies.

Hatton read her expression correctly and his lips twitched. 'Is it a shock to find that I am human, ma'am?'

'You have succeeded in hiding that fact up to now, Mr Hatton.' Sophie smiled back at him. He was trying to be agreeable, and life would be much more comfortable if she met him halfway. 'I must confess that it is an unexpected pleasure to be able to have fires in all the rooms again. I hate the cold. It seems to freeze my brain.'

'Then we must keep you warm, ma'am. There is nothing of you, after all.' He leaned forward and pulled the ribbon from her hair, allowing it to fall about her shoulders. 'That's better!' he approved. 'Don't you value your crowning glory, my dear? Why must you try to hide it with a hideous cap, or scrape it back from your face behind a ribbon?'

'Oh, please!' Sophie's hands flew up to the errant curls. 'Mr Hatton, you must leave this room. We are both of us in—'

'In a state of undress? So we are! But is it not comfortable to be sitting here in the warmth, listening to the storm outside?'

It was both comfortable and reassuring, but Sophie did not care to admit it, even to herself.

'Bess or Abby could waken up at any time,' she pointed out. 'They might come to look at Kit.'

Hatton sighed. Then he rose to his feet with some reluctance. 'And we must not forget the proprieties,' he teased. 'Very well, ma'am, I will leave you. You will call on me if anything untoward should occur?'

'Such as what?' Sophie was perplexed. Then she realised that whilst apparently attending to their conversation, Hatton had been listening closely to the storm. Or was it to the storm?

He saw her look of alarm. 'Just a precaution,' he assured her. 'You'll have no unwelcome visitors tonight, if I'm not much mistaken. This weather will deter the hardiest of men. They won't be able to move their goods. This rain will have turned the clay to a morass. The lanes will be impassable.'

'Then let us hope that it continues,' Sophie said with feeling. 'I don't feel very brave tonight.'

He gave her a long look. 'You'll do well enough,' he said. Then he bowed and left her.

For some time Sophie sat lost in thought. What had persuaded Hatton to look in on her son? Was it simple kindness, or had he been alerted by the sound as she opened Kit's door? Then a more sinister reason crossed her mind. Perhaps he'd been expecting someone else to enter the inn at night.

She thrust the thought aside. Had he not assured her that on this, of all nights, no one would venture out into the storm? As she listened to the pattering of the rain it no longer seemed so threatening. She must think of it as protection for her little household, even as a few drops came down the chimney and hissed on the glowing embers of the fire. Lulled by its warmth, she fell asleep.

She awakened to find herself in her own bed. As small fingers attempted to prise her eyelids apart, she heard a whispered voice.

'Are you awake, Mama?'

'I am now!' Sophie looked up sleepily at her son.

'There, now! Didn't I say that you should let your

mother sleep?' Abby tried to pull the boy away from Sophie's bedside.

Kit wriggled out of her grasp. 'I did as you told me,' he said indignantly. 'I counted up to nine when the clock was striking. I *can* count, you know.'

'Heavens, is that the time? Abby, you should have wakened me—'

'I guessed you couldn't have had much sleep, what with the storm and all. I was frightened out of my wits. I hid beneath the bedclothes...'

'It *was* very wild,' Sophie admitted. She was not really attending to Abby's words. Her eye had fallen upon her robe, draped neatly over the back of a chair, with her folded shawl beneath it and her slippers arranged precisely at the side.

She could not have put them there herself. Her slippers lay always beside her bed, with her robe placed within easy reach across her counterpane. Then, if Kit wakened in the night and called to her, they were readily to hand.

'Will I fetch your breakfast, ma'am?' Abby had to repeat the question twice before her mistress answered her.

'Oh, yes...yes, thank you! Though I suppose I should get up at once...'

'No hurry, ma'am. There ain't much you can do, and blest if it ain't still raining. It's hard to tell night from day. Father is busy lighting all the lamps and finding extra candles.' With that she hurried away.

Sophie plumped up her pillows and settled Kit in the crook of her arm. He loved to snuggle close to her first thing in the morning.

'What will you do today?' she asked. 'I thought we'd go for a walk, but the weather is too wet. Perhaps we could have a reading lesson?'

'Could we do that later?' The eager little face looked

up at her. 'Reuben has promised to show me how to cast with my fishing rod.'

'Oh, my darling, he doesn't propose to go down to the river? The water was running high even before this storm and the banks were crumbling. It would be far too dangerous—'

'Oh, no, Reuben says that it would be a waste of time. We are going to practise in the barn. He's going to draw a line on the ground, and I'm to try and reach it.'

'Mr Hatton may have need of Reuben,' Sophie reminded him. 'You mustn't make a nuisance of yourself.'

'Hatton doesn't mind. I spoke to him this morning. He won't be going out today. Did you know that Reuben can bend a poker in his bare hands?'

'No, I didn't. He must be very strong.'

'Reuben says that it's because of all the good food he ate when he was as old as me. We had ham and eggs and kidneys for breakfast this morning…though I didn't like the kidneys much, but I did eat them up.'

It was becoming all too clear that Reuben was the oracle. His word was law as far as Kit was concerned. Sophie resigned herself to the fact that what Reuben said was likely to be her son's main topic of conversation in the coming weeks.

Sophie looked up as Abby entered the room, bearing a laden tray. In the usual way she would nibble at a roll as she sipped her chocolate. Today the covered dishes held a hearty breakfast. She was about to send it back when she saw Kit's solemn look. Apparently Reuben's dictum was to apply to her as well.

She did her best with the ham and eggs, and found to her surprise that she enjoyed it.

'I must go now,' her son remarked. 'Reuben says that it is rude to be late when one has made an appointment.'

Sophie chuckled to herself. Reuben was clearly a man of strong opinions, but to date she could not fault his observations of her son. Kit had been a poor eater. If Reuben could persuade him into enjoying his meals, she could only be grateful to the ugly little coachman.

She slipped out of bed, feeling for her slippers. Then she remembered. They were on the far side of the room.

Sophie frowned. She had no recollection of returning to her bedchamber on the previous night, but she must have got there somehow. A dreadful suspicion crossed her mind. Had Hatton returned when she was unaware of him? Who else had the strength to carry her sleeping form? Neither Bess, nor Abby, nor Nancy were capable of such a feat, and Matthew, she felt, would have considered it an impertinence to take her in his arms. Hatton would have had no such scruples.

She went downstairs to find him deep in conversation with Fraddon, the new cellarman.

Sophie's tone was brusque as she interrupted them.

'Mr Hatton, I'd like a private word with you,' she announced.

'Certainly, Mistress Firle. Shall we go into the snug?'

Once again, he'd taken the initiative, but Sophie would not be deterred. Her face was set as she looked at him.

'Did you return to Kit's room in the early hours?' she asked in icy tones.

'I did!' Hatton's eyes never left her face. 'You have some problem with that?'

'Merely that I found myself in my own room this morning. I have no recollection of returning there.'

'No, you would not!' he said agreeably. 'You were fast asleep.'

Sophie flushed to the roots of her hair. 'You admit, then, that you took me there yourself?'

'Why should I deny it? It seemed the sensible thing to do. You would have awakened cold and stiff, I can assure you.'

'That is none of your concern, though I accept that you meant well.'

Hatton bowed.

'Even so, I don't seem to be able to make you understand. My reputation means as much to me as it does to any other woman. Suppose you had been seen carrying me to my chamber? Only one conclusion would be drawn—'

'I think it unlikely. At a glance you were an unlikely subject for seduction. Not only were you unconscious of your surroundings, but your mouth was open and you were snoring.'

Sophie gave a shriek of dismay. 'You are lying! I don't snore, you hateful creature!'

Hatton grinned at her. 'How do you know?' Then he relented. 'I was teasing,' he admitted. 'No, ma'am, you do not snore. In truth, you looked quite charming as you lay there in my arms.'

'Spare me your compliments, sir. I am not joking when I tell you that you go too far. Is it your intention to destroy me? If you don't mend your behaviour, my servants will lose all respect for me.'

'They won't do that,' Hatton told her lightly. 'They think highly of you, Mistress Firle, as you must know.'

She looked at him. 'Then will you tell me that you did not…I mean…well, my robe and my slippers were not in their usual place?'

Hatton sighed. 'I did remove them, ma'am. I thought it unlikely that you were accustomed to sleeping in your shoes. Then I drew your coverlet over you. Believe me, I took no liberties with your person.'

Sophie wanted to believe him, but she had no recollection whatever as to what might have happened in her room.

He read her mind correctly, and his expression hardened.

'I am not in the habit of forcing my attentions upon helpless females, whatever else you may think of me. Had I made love to you, my dear, you would certainly have known about it. In view of your condition it seemed pointless. You are no virgin, Mistress Firle. Surely you must know that the participation of both partners is needed to obtain the fullest pleasure.'

Sophie was scarlet with embarrassment. She had not expected such forthright speaking from any man. Now she realised that Hatton was furious. His honour had been impugned. No gentleman would take advantage of a sleeping woman.

'Please stop!' she cried. She wanted to cover her ears, but she knew that it would bring fresh sarcasm upon her head. 'I've heard enough! I do believe you.'

Hatton was not finished. 'I suppose I should be flattered by your estimation of my prowess with the ladies. I'm sorry to disappoint you, but dalliance, I find, requires a disproportionate amount of energy. I have neither the time nor the inclination for it at the present time. There are more important matters to attend. May I suggest that you try to remember them?'

Sophie could have struck him. 'I do remember it,' she said in icy tones. 'Perhaps you have forgotten that I have been widowed and my son has lost his father?'

Hatton did not reply and her fury grew.

'What a creature you are!' she cried. 'I'm not surprised that you are still unwed. You are the most insulting, arrogant, selfish man I've ever known.'

Hatton bowed again. 'Your assessment of my character is not original, madam. My mother echoes your sentiments at frequent intervals.'

'I'm not surprised.' Sophie turned away.

'Where are you going?' he demanded.

'Do I need your permission to return to my room?'

'Feathers still ruffled?' Hatton was unperturbed. 'I think we must call a truce, my dear. I shall need your help this morning.'

'Whatever for?'

'I propose to try a certain experiment.' He strolled across the room and pulled at the bell-rope. When Matthew appeared he was asked for the keys to the cellar.

Sophie was only half-attending to the conversation. She'd planned to cut out flannel shirts for Kit as the weather was still too poor for her to take her daily walk.

She had no idea what Hatton had in mind, but if he wished to inspect the cellars he could do it without her. He must know the place quite well. After all, he owned it.

Then she heard an odd note in Matthew's voice. It was unlike him to prevaricate.

Sophie looked at his face and was surprised to see that he was very pale.

'If you should wish for a particular wine, sir, I'll fetch it for you at once,' he said uneasily.

'Just the key, Matthew, if you please.'

Still Matthew hesitated. The gentleman had paid his overdue wages, and for that he must be grateful, but what could he want in the cellars? Mr Hatton, to his knowledge, had no connection with the running of the inn. It was Mistress Firle to whom he was responsible. He threw her a pleading look.

'What is it, Matthew? Are you not well?' Sophie looked

at him more closely and was surprised to see a strange expression in his eyes. She could think of no reason for it, but the man was obviously terrified.

'Have you found rats down there?' she asked. 'We'll send down the terriers to clear them out if that is what is worrying you.'

'No, ma'am, it isn't that. Perhaps if the gentleman will tell me what he wants, I can get it for him.'

'Matthew, I asked you for the keys. Your mistress wishes to check the stock of wines and spirits. As you know, she intends to re-open the inn within a day or two.'

Matthew's sigh of relief was almost audible. 'If that's all, sir, I can give my mistress the cellar book. It's all in order. She won't find a single bottle missing…'

Hatton looked across at Sophie and she understood him at once. He intended to inspect the cellars in spite of Matthew's clear reluctance to hand over the keys, and his injured expression.

'You must not think that I don't trust you, Matthew,' she soothed. 'But Mr Hatton is concerned about the conditions under which we keep the wines. We've had such heavy rains, and there may be a danger of flooding. Now, bring me the keys and we'll go down together.'

Matthew dared not argue further, but he didn't return himself. It was Fraddon, the new cellarman, who brought the keys.

Hatton motioned to Sophie to accompany him. In his hand he held a lantern of curious appearance which he shone ahead of him as he descended the steep flight of steps down to the cellars. Then he nodded to his man to light the oil lamps set at frequent intervals in the walls.

As the clear light flooded the cellars, Sophie looked about her. She could see nothing to account for Matthew's uneasiness. The barrels were neatly stacked along three of the walls, whilst the fourth and longest held a series of wine racks which reached from floor to ceiling.

'All seems to be in order here,' she observed. 'There was no need for you to badger Matthew.'

'No?' Sophie heard an ugly laugh. 'Then let me show you!'

Hatton walked swiftly to the middle section of the racks, pulled out two of the bottles and slid his hand into the aperture.

Sophie gasped as a part of the high rack swung towards her revealing not the brickwork which she had expected to see, but a massive wooden door.

'The key?' Hatton looked at Fraddon.

The man removed another bottle, felt behind the rack and handed an iron key to his master.

Then Sophie heard an anguished cry as Matthew thrust her aside. With his back to the door he spun round to face Hatton.

'Don't open it!' With arms spread-eagled, he tried to cover the lock. 'You'll get us killed!'

Hatton put him aside without the slightest difficulty.

'Stand back!' he ordered sternly. 'You have much to answer for, I think.'

Matthew's face was working. 'What could I do?' he whispered. 'Master, you don't know—'

'Perhaps I don't, but I intend to find out!' Hatton inserted the key into the lock, and the door swung back on well-oiled hinges. Then he shone the lantern ahead of him.

Sophie was close upon his heels and she gasped in astonishment as they entered yet another cellar of which she'd had no previous knowledge. It was very large, and the goods which it contained were strange to her. Much of the floor space was piled high with oilskin bags, filled to capacity. The kegs which filled the rest of the store were much smaller than a beer barrel.

Long ropes with iron hooks attached hung from the walls, as did an implement which bore a close resemblance to Kit's fishing rod, apart from the odd-looking pincers at the tip.

Then she shuddered. Stacked in one corner lay a heap of cutlasses. Shining in the lamplight they looked well-greased and ready for their murderous task. There were firearms too, and a great pile of heavy wooden staves.

Sophie swallowed hard. 'I don't understand,' she faltered. 'Is this some kind of store?'

'You might say that!' Hatton told her grimly. He turned to the trembling Matthew. 'Where do the tunnels lead?'

Matthew's resistance was broken. 'As far as the first copse on the hill,' he muttered. 'That's the entrance.'

Sophie was horrified. 'Oh, Matthew, do you mean to say that anyone could have entered whilst we slept?'

'No, ma'am. All the doors are bolted from this side. It ain't possible to get in through the tunnels.'

'Then that must mean…?' Sophie was thinking fast. Someone from inside the inn must have opened up the entrance to allow the smugglers access to their store. 'Who could have—?'

Hatton cut her short. 'This is not the place for a discussion,' he said brusquely. He turned on his heel and led the way out of the cellars.

The others were subdued as he settled himself behind a table in the parlour, and Sophie was unaccountably annoyed. Hatton was not a magistrate, and he must not behave as such.

Her fears were confirmed when he spoke to the unfortunate Matthew.

'You have much to answer for, have you not?' he enquired coldly. 'Why did you not see fit to inform your mistress when you realised what was happening here?'

'That were down to me, sir!'

Sophie turned to find Bess standing in the doorway with arms akimbo. She looked fully capable of taking on the redoubtable Mr Hatton and a dozen like him.

'I see. Won't you sit down, Bess?' Hatton rose and indicated a chair.

'No, I won't, sir, if it's all the same to you.' Bess was not to be mollified by such courtesy. 'My Matthew had naught to do with any of this. It was me that found out what was going on.'

'How did you do that?'

'It was quite a while ago. Matt had a putrid throat. He was coughing, so I came down very late to fetch him a hot drink. I saw 'em then.'

'But, Bess, who did you see?' Sophie persisted. 'Was it someone who used to work for us?'

'No, ma'am, it weren't…' Some of Bess's belligerence had vanished. 'I'd rather not say…'

'Quite right, Bess!' Hatton was quick to intervene. 'You followed them, then, right into the cellars? That was a dangerous thing to do.'

'I know it, Master. A worse band o' cut-throats I never did see. I told Matt that we must never speak o' they cellars, but he would find out for hisself.'

Bess paused and then she turned to Sophie. 'If you think that we done wrong, Mistress Firle, you won't want us to stay. We can be out of here by morning.' Her lips were trembling, but she stood her ground.

'Oh, Bess, I wouldn't think of letting you go!' Sophie threw her arms about her servant. 'You were not to blame. You found out these things by chance, but I do wish that you would tell us the name of the person whom you saw that night.'

'I can't!' By now Bess was weeping openly.

Hatton signalled to Matthew to take his wife away.

'I hope you are satisfied,' Sophie gritted out as the door closed behind them. 'You have succeeded in upsetting two kindly people who have become involved through no fault of their own. In future you will leave my servants alone.'

She had expected a sharp retort, but as Hatton looked at her she saw a curious expression in his eyes. Could it be sadness? Surely not? To hide her perplexity she picked up the oddly-shaped lantern.

'How did you know of the hidden cellar?' she continued. 'Was it because of this strange object? I imagine it is something to do with the smuggling fraternity, for I have not seen its like before. It looks more like a watering-can than a lamp and for all the light it sheds it might as well be so.'

Hatton took it from her. 'It serves its purpose well,' he told her. 'This is a spout lantern, used for signalling out to sea. The long spout prevents the light from being seen on land. The opening at the end is uncovered briefly to send messages in code.'

'Where did you find it? Did it lead you to look for the second cellar?'

'Fraddon found it hidden behind some barrels, but I've always known of the second cellar. Don't forget that I own this place.'

'I'm unlikely to forget it, since you lose no opportunity to remind me,' Sophie replied bitterly. 'If you knew of the secret place, why did you feel the need to torment Matthew? Did it give you pleasure to frighten him?'

'It gave me not the slightest pleasure,' came the cool

reply. 'But I had to know if Matthew was involved with the smuggling gangs. He was hiding something. That was obvious. He was already badly scared. I had to know why.'

'Well, now you *do* know!' Sophie said with some asperity. 'I hope you're satisfied.'

'Your loyalty does you credit, ma'am. It does not encourage me to trust you. In defence of your friends, you would help them bury a body, I believe.'

'Yes, I would!' she told him boldly. 'But this is nonsense. There is no question of burying a body—'

'As a mere figure of speech!' Hatton said in some amusement. He pulled at the bell-rope to summon Matthew once again.

'Tell me what you wish to know and I will question Matthew.' Sophie was determined to save her servant from further brutal interrogation.

'With your permission, I will speak to him alone. I think that you should leave us, Mistress Firle—'

'Certainly not! I shouldn't think of it.'

'Very well, if that is your decision. I hope you won't regret it.'

Matthew entered the room before she could reply. She looked at him in alarm. Matthew seemed to have aged before her eyes.

Hatton spoke without preamble. 'I want the truth from you,' he said. 'When was this last cargo delivered to the cellar? Don't try to gammon me by saying you knew nothing of it. I won't believe you.'

Matthew crumpled. 'I ain't a free trader,' he whispered. 'It was naught to do wi' me.'

'Of course it wasn't,' Sophie intervened. 'We don't suspect you, Matthew, but you must tell Mr Hatton everything you know.'

'Well, ma'am, once I knew of the cellar I kept an eye on it. Sometimes it was empty, and sometimes full. I 'ad to be careful, you understand, but the place was quiet in day time.'

'You haven't answered my question,' Hatton said coldly. 'That last cargo…when was it delivered?'

Matthew looked at Sophie and encouraged by her nod he was persuaded to reply.

'It was just afore the Master died, begging your pardon, ma'am, for reminding you of your trouble. That cellar had been empty for weeks aforehand, as if it had been cleared a-purpose for something special.'

'Special indeed!' Hatton muttered almost to himself. He turned again to Matthew. 'Since then you have not been approached?'

Matthew looked baffled. 'Approached, sir? You mean—?'

'I mean has anyone requested to inspect the cellars, perhaps on the pretext of buying up your stocks of wines and spirits?'

Matthew frowned as he tried to recollect. 'We've had one gentleman,' he admitted. 'Don't you remember, Mistress Firle? You refused to see him…'

'Yes, I recall. I had no interest in his offer. Matthew, is this all you know? As I understand it, the door of the cellar can only be opened from inside the inn. You must have seen who used the key?'

For some reason this question troubled Matthew more than any that had gone before. He kept his eyes fixed on the carpet and his mouth was set in a tight line, but his hands were shaking.

'Won't you tell me, please?' Sophie pleaded.

Matthew shook his head.

'I'll tell you, ma'am!' Again, Bess was standing in the doorway. 'Sorry I am to say it, but it were the Master.'

Sophie glanced at Hatton and knew what she had to do.

'Oh, no!' she cried. 'That can't be true!'

'As true as I'm standing here, Mistress Firle. Yon gentleman weren't all you thought him, though I know it's wrong to speak ill of the dead.'

Sophie turned away as Hatton dismissed her servants, on the pretext that she had suffered serious shock.

'Well?' he asked.

'Of course Richard let the smugglers in,' Sophie insisted. 'Was he not supposed to be a member of their gang?'

'He was!' Hatton did not look at her. 'Have you any idea of the value of that cargo in the cellar?'

'I couldn't begin to guess, since I don't know what it is. Those bundles wrapped in oilskin? What were they?'

'That was tobacco, ma'am, protected from immersion in the sea. Did you not see the grappling hooks? Our friends are in the habit of "sowing a crop" as they term it. They sink the cargo beneath a marked spot when threatened by the preventive officers. Then they collect it later. They do the same with the ankers.'

'Ankers? I do not know that term.'

'You saw them in the cellar. They are the small tubs of wines and spirits.'

'There were so many of them,' Sophie mused. 'The cargo must have been huge…worth many thousands of pounds?'

'A fair assessment, madam.'

Sophie had been thinking fast. 'I understand you now,' she said. 'The goods in the cellar are the bait, are they not? You believe that the smugglers won't give up the opportunity to continue with their operation?'

'Something like that,' Hatton agreed. 'Too much money is at stake here. They won't let it go.'

Sophie stared at him. 'What will happen now?' she asked.

'I think you may expect an approach. I can't tell you from which direction, or how it will be phrased. All I ask is that you be on your guard. Whatever is suggested to you, you will show reluctance to agree.'

'That won't be difficult!' she told him grimly.

'I don't expect it will, but remember, you will be surprised and shocked to learn that goods have been stored here in a cellar of which you had no previous knowledge. You will protest that it can't possibly be so. When it is proved to you, you will be terrified, fearing that the authorities will learn of the contraband. As you know, the penalties for smuggling are savage.'

Sophie swallowed hard. 'Transportation?' she breathed.

'That, or death! Your terror will seem natural enough.'

'You are convinced that they will come here?'

'Nothing is more certain. Someone made a serious mistake in killing your husband before the goods could be moved. If I'm not mistaken, there are certain gentlemen in London impatient for their profits on that cargo. Their initial outlay would have been enormous.'

Sophie was very pale. 'Would it not be simpler for them to kill me too?'

Hatton's smile transfigured his face. 'And lose a possible ally? No, my dear! They will know you to be in need of money. If they can get you on their side with soft words and promises, so much the better for them. The trade will resume as if nothing had happened.'

His hands rested lightly on her shoulders as he turned

her to face him. 'Above all, you must be on your guard. They must not suspect a trap. Can you do it?'

'I can...if you...'

'Yes, Mistress Firle. I shall be here.'

Chapter Six

In spite of Hatton's reassurance, Sophie felt deeply troubled as she went back to her room. She'd had no alternative but to agree to his scheme, but the thought of the coming ordeal filled her with dread.

Could she play her part? He'd made it all too clear that the slightest slip would mean disaster. She could recall every word of their conversation and now it seemed to her that he was asking far too much of her.

She'd been shocked by the discovery of the second cellar and its content, and Matthew's terror had added to her own.

How could she succeed in acting as Hatton's spy when his own men, highly trained and experienced, had lost their lives in the attempt?

She caught a glimpse of her face in the mirror, expecting to see panic written there. True, she was pale and the great grey eyes seemed larger than ever, yet her inner turmoil did not show. She took a turn about the room in an effort to calm herself. She must remember Hatton's purpose and her own.

He'd been clever, she thought ruefully. Not only had he promised that Richard's killers would be brought to justice, but he had offered her the chance to help her country. Could she do less than the men who were dying in their thousands on the continent of Europe in an effort to defeat Napoleon? It would be craven to even think of it.

With an effort she thrust her misgivings from her mind. The thing to do was to occupy herself, taking one day at a time.

She looked at the bolt of flannel cloth which she'd bought at Hannington's, and the pieces of Kit's shirt, carefully unpicked to act as a pattern. Then she laid out the flannel on the carpet, trying her pattern first one way and then another so as to make the best use of her purchase. Heaven knew when she would have the means to buy such cloth again.

Satisfied at last, she began to pin the pieces down. If she cut wide of the seams and extended the length of the garment at the sleeves and tail, her son would be well clad for the rest of the winter.

Her mouth was full of pins when she heard a tap at the door. In response to a mumbled command to enter, Nancy came towards her, bearing a number of boxes.

'The carrier brought your purchases from Brighton, ma'am,' she said.

Sophie was puzzled. Then she remembered. 'The gowns? I had forgot! Will you help me unpack them?'

Nancy lifted out the garments one by one, laying them on the bed, and Sophie quailed. She could not recall having ordered so many. She recognised the green with the black stripe, and the blue with its matching pelisse, but the bronze?

'How beautiful!' Nancy said softly. 'It is almost the colour of your hair, Mistress Firle—the same shade as autumn leaves. Must I put them away?'

'Please do!' Sophie's eyes had fallen upon an expensive

dark-green redingote and a number of spencers. Long-sleeved and waist-length with revers and a collar, they were designed to provide extra warmth, but she had not ordered them.

Nor did she recognise a braided pelisse in french merino cloth. There were a number of scarves in printed, knitted silk and yet another gown in dark blue kerseymere, buttoned high at the throat. Sophie picked up a tippet edged with fur.

'What is this?' she demanded.

Nancy looked her surprise. 'You didn't order it, ma'am? Perhaps there has been a mistake.' She smiled at Sophie. 'I believe it is known as a Bosom Friend because it protects the throat and chest...must I leave it aside to be returned?'

'I think so.' Sophie picked out the garments which had been her choice. 'These may be put away. Please leave the others on the bed.'

She was seething. Her order had been more than doubled. Hatton must have had a private word with Madame Arouet. Well, she would not allow him to dictate her choice of clothing. Nor would she allow him to pay for it.

'Where is Mr Hatton?' she asked.

'He left here at first light, Mistress Firle.'

'I see!' Sophie tried to contain her fury. 'When he returns, will you tell him that I wish to see him?'

'Yes, ma'am!' Nancy glanced at the pattern laid out on the floor. 'Would you like me to help you with that? I'm handy with my needle...'

'Why, yes, of course, if you'd like to do so.' Sophie was surprised, as much by the fact that Nancy's rich Sussex burr seemed to have vanished, as by her offer of help.

Nancy knelt down and began to pin the pattern with skilful fingers.

Then she saw the ring on Nancy's hand.

'A wedding ring?' she exclaimed. 'Nancy, you did not wear that when you came to see me first of all.' Then realisation dawned. 'Oh, I see! When we re-open it will serve to keep away the most importunate of our customers?'

She could not blame the girl. Nancy was quite lovely. She would be the target of every man who fancied himself as a devil with the ladies.

'The ring is my own,' Nancy told her quietly. 'I am a widow, ma'am.'

Sophie's heart went out to her. 'Oh, my dear, I am so sorry. You are young to suffer such grief…'

'I had been married six months.' Lost in memory, Nancy seemed to have forgotten the presence of her listener. 'They tortured him, you know. Then they threw him down a well, and stoned him to death.'

Sophie's blood ran cold. Wide-eyed with horror, she stared at her companion.

'But why? And who would do such a dreadful thing?' She had already guessed at the answer, and it terrified her.

'The same man who killed your husband, Mistress Firle.' Nancy's voice betrayed no trace of emotion and that deadly calm chilled Sophie to the heart.

'Who…who are you?' she whispered.

'I was Nancy Welbeck, the daughter of one of the Collectors on the Kentish coast. Then I met John Tyler. He was one of my father's Riding Officers. We married less than a twelve-month ago…'

Impulsively, Sophie reached out and took the girl's hand in her own.

'Then this is why you are here. You seek justice, just as I do?'

'Justice?' Nancy looked at her then and something moved in the depths of her eyes. They were swiftly veiled, but Sophie was undeceived. For this fragile-looking girl justice would not be enough. In her implacable hatred she sought nothing less than revenge.

'Justice?' she repeated. 'They owe me more than that. They took two lives when they killed John. I lost my unborn child when the news was brought to me.'

Sophie slipped an arm about the slender shoulders.

'Won't you try to remember the happy times?' she urged. 'Your husband would have wished that for you. The memory of those months, short as they were, will stay with you always.'

Nancy did not reply. She sat as if turned to stone. Her sorrow was too deep for any words of comfort to reach her. Vengeance was her overriding passion, and Sophie sensed its corroding influence.

'Did you mean it when you said that you would help me with this pattern?' she asked as she returned to the task of pinning the cloth. 'Can you think of a better way to arrange the pieces? I must not cut the flannel to waste.'

In silence Nancy knelt beside her, swift fingers laying out the pieces of Kit's shirt to best advantage.

Sophie was appalled by the story she'd just heard, but she hid her feelings well. Nancy needed help to recover from the tragedy which had overtaken her. It would be best to keep her busy.

Perhaps it was not tactful to engage the girl in cutting out garments for her own child, but Nancy seemed to be absorbed in her task. The sight of any child must sadden her, but Kit was an affectionate little soul. His unerring instinct led him always to offer love where it was needed. Nancy might yet find comfort in his company.

With the cutting-out completed, Sophie smiled at her companion. 'How skilled you are,' she said in admiration. 'You have done this before, I think.'

'I enjoy it, ma'am. I had some hopes of setting up a business…that is…before I married. I was often asked for copies of my gowns.'

'You designed them?'

Nancy managed a faint smile. 'They had a particular advantage, Mistress Firle, which I did not advertise to everyone. I chose always the best cloth, but the garments were put together with running stitches. That meant that they were easily taken apart, and the material re-used.'

'What an economy! I must remember it. And, Nancy, there is only one other thing. Pray do not call me ma'am, or Mistress Firle. My given name is Sophie.'

'Thank you!' the girl said gravely. 'It is kind in you to suggest it. Perhaps when we are alone? Otherwise it will give rise to comment in the kitchen.'

'Oh, I had not thought of that.' Sophie's face fell. 'I have so much to learn about the spying game.'

'You must be cautious at all times,' Nancy warned. 'It will become a habit.'

With those parting words she returned to her duties below stairs.

Sophie was anxious to make full use of the remaining hours of daylight, so she spent the rest of the afternoon stitching together the pieces of Kit's shirt. When he popped his head round the door she suggested that he try it on.

Kit pulled a face. 'Must I, Mama?'

'It won't take a moment. Then, if you like, I'll tell you a story…'

This promise kept Kit still for long enough for her to make sure that the garment fitted him. Then she laid it aside.

The parlour was already filled with shadows, but the fire provided enough light without the need to send for candles as Kit climbed on to her lap.

'Have you had a busy day?' she asked tenderly.

Kit gave a sigh of deep content. 'Yes,' he told her. 'We've been tying flies.'

'Tying flies?' Sophie was perplexed. 'How do you catch them, darling?'

Her son's laughter echoed about the room. 'Not those kind of flies, Mama. We were making fishing flies. Reuben says that they are better than worms for catching trout.'

'I see. Is it difficult to make them?'

'*Very* difficult. Reuben says that what is needed is dex…dex…'

'Dexterity?' Sophie supplied helpfully.

'Something like that. They are so pretty. I'll bring one to show you when we've finished them.' Kit snuggled closer. 'You smell good,' he announced.

Sophie hugged him close. 'Which story would you like?' she asked.

Kit's reply was prompt. 'The one about the pirates, please.'

Sophie smiled to herself. It was what she had expected. Kit never tired of her tales of adventure upon the high seas, the running up of the skull-and-crossbones when a prize was sighted, and the hoards of treasure to be found upon the Caribbean islands.

Blackbeard was his favourite. The exploits of the infamous Captain Teach fascinated him, and he tried to excuse the worse excesses of his hero.

'Did he *always* make his prisoners walk the plank?' he asked anxiously.

'Not always, I expect, especially if they begged for mercy. Besides, you know, most probably they could swim.'

'But what about the sharks, Mama?' Kit gave a delicious shudder. 'I'd have been so frightened.'

Sophie laughed. 'I doubt if you'll meet a shark, my love...'

'But I might find buried treasure,' Kit insisted. 'You promised that we should go down to the coast.'

'And so we shall when the weather improves. Sometimes the storms uncover treasure upon the beaches, though it isn't always gold and jewels.'

'Tell me about the jewels...' Kit fingered Sophie's brooch. 'Did they look like this? It's beautiful!'

'Blackbeard had chests full of such things, but he buried them far away, in the Indies.'

Kit would not give up his cherished hopes. 'You said he was an Englishman,' he insisted. 'He may have brought some back with him.'

'Perhaps he did.' She kept her thoughts to herself. No amount of treasure would have been much comfort to the famous tiger of the seas as he stood upon Execution Dock with a rope around his neck. He had taken his secrets with him to his Maker.

'If I dig deep enough I'll find it.' Kit was growing drowsy. The warmth of the fire and the comfort of his mother's arms finally overcame his efforts to keep his eyes open and he fell sound asleep.

Sophie looked down at him. She ought to rouse herself and put him to bed, but the moment was too precious.

This vulnerable little creature was her entire world. She would protect him with her life.

Carefully she moved her arm to settle him more comfortably. Then she leaned back and closed her eyes. After a succession of troubled nights a lack of sleep was beginning to tell on her. She did not stir as Hatton entered the room. Then, suddenly, she was wide awake, aware that she was being watched.

'No, don't get up!' His hand rested lightly on her shoulder. 'You must be much in need of rest.'

There was a note in his voice which she had not heard before and she looked up quickly. As the flickering firelight played upon the harsh planes of his face she thought she detected an expression which astonished her. In another man she would have described it as tenderness. It vanished quickly, confirming her belief that she must have been mistaken. Once more his look was unfathomable.

'Nancy informs me that you wish to see me,' he continued. 'How can I serve you, Mistress Firle?'

The mention of Nancy brought Sophie's concerns to the forefront of her mind.

'Mr Hatton, I feel that you are making a mistake,' she said earnestly.

'Another one? What do you have in mind?'

'How well do you know Nancy?'

'Well enough! Don't tell me that you are still convinced that she will be unsuitable? Too young? Too beautiful? Such sentiments are unworthy of you.'

'Those are not my main concerns. Why did you not tell me who she was? I learned today that her husband has been murdered. Is she yet another woman whom you seek to use for your own ends?'

Even in the dim light Sophie could see that his face

had hardened. 'It may surprise you to know that I did not seek her out. Nancy came to me.'

Sophie was silent for a time. 'No, it doesn't surprise me,' she said at last.

'Well, then, what is worrying you? You must believe that she will play her part in apprehending her husband's murderers.'

'My dear sir, you told me once that you have no great understanding of a woman's heart. I must tell you now that you are playing with fire.'

She heard a snort of disgust. 'Dramatics, Mistress Firle? I can well do without them.'

'You would do well to listen to me. Nancy is beyond your control. She is obsessed by hatred.'

'You think that a bad thing?'

'I can understand it, but I think it dangerous. She could put us all in jeopardy. If she finds the men who killed her husband and robbed her of her unborn child, I shouldn't like to be responsible for her actions. No words of yours will sway her.'

Hatton regarded her in silence. 'You may be right,' he admitted reluctantly. 'I'll watch her closely.'

Privately, Sophie thought that it would take more than that. Nancy was adept at concealing her true feelings. It had taken another woman to discover them.

'So you won't send her away?' she asked.

'I think not. If you are right, she might take matters into her own hands and ruin our entire operation. Better to keep her here. Don't you agree? Of course, if you and she are at daggers' drawn…?'

'We are not!' Sophie told him sharply. 'I like her very much. I'm sorry only that she is so obsessed. Hatred is the most corrosive of emotions. It harms the person who feels it far more than the object of their loathing.'

'You are right.' Hatton sank into the armchair opposite. 'I have often felt the same. In one way we play into the hands of our enemies by hating them. It can cripple a person for life, robbing them of normal pleasures.'

Sophie was surprised to find that he was in agreement with her. His philosophy was unexpected. She had imagined that this ruthless creature was no stranger to the worst excesses of hatred.

Now she looked down at the sleeping child upon her lap. 'I must put Kit to bed,' she said. 'Will you excuse me, sir?'

'Let me!' With astonishing gentleness he took Kit from her, bending so close that his lips almost brushed her cheek.

Sophie turned her head away. For some unaccountable reason she was disturbed by his nearness as an unfamiliar scent of tobacco, clean linen, soap and the outdoors assailed her nostrils. It was not unpleasant, and it stirred long-forgotten feelings in her breast.

What must it be like to feel those massive arms about her once more? The memory of his bruising kiss returned to trouble her. Her response had been immediate. He had sensed it immediately, as he had reminded her. It was humiliating to find that she had so little control over her natural instincts.

Now she held out her arms for Kit, but Hatton nodded to her to precede him from the room. If she tried to argue she would waken the child, so she led the way to Kit's chamber.

Hatton laid him on the bed, and proceeded to unfasten his shoes.

'What a family you are!' he joked, 'I seem always to be removing shoes from sleeping figures...'

The colour rose to Sophie's cheeks. 'There is not the

least need for you to do so, sir. I am perfectly capable of undressing my son.'

She was seething with indignation. It was ungallant of him to remind her of the previous night when he'd carried her to her own bed and removed her clothing.

Now he seemed to have read her mind. 'Forget it!' he advised. 'Now, if you'll lift the lad I'll slip him out of his coat and breeches.'

He was surprisingly deft and Kit showed no signs of awakening even as Hatton eased him into his nightshirt.

'There, ma'am!' he said with satisfaction. 'You'll hear no more of him before morning. He has become Reuben's shadow, and the pair of them are busy from morn till night.'

Sophie hesitated. 'Your man is very good to him,' she admitted.

'Why not? The boy is quick to learn and interested in everything about him. Besides, Reuben has no objection to being regarded as some kind of demi-god.'

Sophie saw the gleam of perfect teeth, and she laughed in spite of herself. 'I'm afraid he takes up far too much of Reuben's time, Mr Hatton. I wonder that you allow it.'

'It is no great problem at the moment,' he replied with a dismissive gesture. 'Now, ma'am, since your son is safely bestowed in his bed, I hope that you'll agree to dine with me?'

Alarm filled Sophie's head. Had she not decided to keep Hatton at a distance? She searched her mind to think of a plausible excuse to refuse him. She could not plead a previous engagement. The very idea was ludicrous. She had no friends in the locality. Nor had she any transport.

Hatton noticed her indecision. 'Come, you won't tell me that you prefer to dine alone? That is bad for the digestion, ma'am. Companionship is essential for full en-joyment—of a meal, I mean of course!'

He was teasing her again, and to her annoyance Sophie found that she was blushing furiously.

'Quite charming!' he announced with a twinkle. 'And rare indeed in a wife and a mother... Naturally, if you feel that you can't trust yourself to my company I shall understand.'

Hatton was enjoying himself and Sophie determined to give him a sharp set-down. Anything to wipe that infuri-ating smile from his lips.

'Were we not agreed that your understanding of women is limited, sir? I shall be happy to dine with you.'

She heard a shout of laughter.

'What a fib! Unconvincing, my dear, when that look would turn a man to stone. Shall we say at seven, then?'

Sophie could not bring herself to speak. She swept past him with her head held high.

She reached her room to find that Abby had put away all the garments which she had intended to return, leaving out only the bronze gown.

'I won't wear that!' she said. Her tone was sharper than she had intended and Abby looked surprised.

'Why, ma'am, is something wrong with it? I thought it quite the prettiest of all.'

Sophie saw the girl's downcast look and was ashamed of her ill-temper. 'You are right,' she admitted. 'The dif-ficulty is that I did not order it. The garments left on the bed were to be returned. There must have been some mis-take.'

Abby's face cleared. 'I'd keep them if it were me,' she told her mistress with a mischievous look. 'Oh, ma'am, you won't send back the fur-lined tippet? It's fit for a queen!'

'And I am not a queen, Abby.' Sophie was strongly tempted to change into her drab black gown, but she could imagine Hatton's reaction. He would realise at once that it was a childish attempt to annoy him. She would not give him that satisfaction.

'You may bring me the blue which is buttoned to the neck,' she said.

Abby brightened. 'It will go well with your brooch, Mistress Firle. My, that's a fine piece of jewellery! Mother says that it's high time a gentleman took care of you.'

This remark did nothing for Sophie's state of mind. She was almost tempted into another sharp retort, but she bit her tongue. She walked over to the wash-stand and poured some water into the basin.

'Is it still hot?' Abby asked anxiously. 'Mr Hatton told me to bring it up for six o'clock...'

'Did he, indeed?' Sophie's feelings threatened to overcome her. She washed and dressed quickly. She had had more than enough of Hatton's arrogance. This evening she would make it clear that she would brook no further interference.

He needed her to help him carry out his plans. He had made that clear enough. She was beginning to suspect that his threats to turn her out were simply an attempt to ensure her co-operation. Now she sensed that he would never do so.

She couldn't quite decide why she felt so certain of that fact, but tonight she would test out her belief. The challenge excited her and she made her way to his private parlour relishing the battle of wills ahead.

He was standing by the fireplace, but he turned as she entered the room, immaculate as always in a well-cut coat of the finest broadcloth, snowy linen and tight pantaloons with gleaming Hessian boots pulled over them. He had an excellent leg for the prevailing fashions, she noted grudgingly.

Sophie walked towards him with a smile which would have graced a crocodile, and his eyes narrowed.

'You are in looks tonight, Mistress Firle. Is this one of Madame Arouet's gowns?'

'It is.' Sophie's smile did not waver.

Hatton bowed. 'It is most becoming. The woman is a genius. Don't you agree?'

'I do, but sadly, her accounting system leaves much to be desired. I had not ordered more than one half of the goods which I received.'

'Really? Perhaps it is no great matter, ma'am. Can you make use of them?'

'Possibly...if I could afford them. Mr Hatton, please don't try to gammon me. This is your doing, is it not?'

'I may have suggested a few additions...'

'You had no right to do so. I won't accept them, sir!'

'Very well then, send them back!' he said indifferently. 'It does not matter to me.'

Sophie was nonplussed. She had expected a fierce argument.

'On the other hand, you could pay me for them when this sorry business is ended,' he continued smoothly. 'You may find them useful at some later date.'

'Possibly!'

He had cut the ground from under Sophie's feet and she knew it. She ground her teeth in frustration. It was impossible to get the better of him.

Now he looked up with pleased anticipation as Abby entered the room bearing a tray. He seated Sophie at the table with his usual formality, and favoured Abby with a smile.

'I'm starving!' he announced. 'What does your mother offer us this evening?'

'Dressed lobster, sir. It was brought up from the coast today. Mistress Firle will enjoy it—it's one of her favourites.'

'Your mother spoils us, Abby, with gourmet foods. How can she top that?'

'You are to have broiled fowl with mushrooms, Mr Hatton, and then a Celerata cream.'

'No apple pie?'

Abby looked confused. 'We finished it off,' she said timidly. 'The men were that hungry, but Mother will make another for you if you wish it.'

'No, you shall not worry her. Let us enjoy the Celerata cream, possibly with some cheese to follow. With that I shall hope to survive till morning.'

As Abby scurried from the room, Sophie gave him a look of reproach.

'You must not tease her, Mr Hatton. Now she will go back to the kitchen and tell Bess that you are not satisfied with your meal.'

'I doubt that, ma'am. Bess knows that I appreciate her cooking. I have been at some pains to get her on my side, you know.'

'I wonder that you bothered.'

'I had my reasons. Bess's opinion goes for much among the servants. I'm relying on her to back up my cover story. I wish her to consider me a suitable candidate for your hand...'

'You ask too much of her, Mr Hatton. With your lack of concern for the properties, it may have escaped your notice that a recent widow would be in mourning for at least a year. Most certainly no lady in that situation would think of offering encouragement to another man...

however charming.' She gave him a smile which would have frozen daffodils.

Hatton grinned at her. 'Compliments, ma'am? That is a pleasant change. At the risk of causing you some distress, I should inform you that Bess had no time for your late husband. She will not find it strange that you would seek for happiness so soon.'

Sophie glared at him. 'Have you been gossiping behind my back, and with the servants too?'

'No, I have not! My information comes from Reuben. Bess does not speak out in front of Kit, of course, but when the child is absent she makes no secret of her opinions. She feels that you were cheated by a man unworthy of you.'

'Richard's behaviour was none of her concern,' Sophie replied stiffly.

'You are mistaken, Mistress Firle. Your servants are fond of you. They did not care to see you duped. You were kept in ignorance of much that was happening here.'

'Then why did they not tell me?'

'Would you have believed them? Loyalty alone would have prevented it, and you say yourself that you will not listen to gossip.'

Sophie was silent.

'Or was it loyalty?' he continued inexorably. 'I find it astonishing that you did not question your husband's frequent absences, or the reasons for his tolerance of a clientele too dangerous for you to meet them.'

'He did not say that they were dangerous,' she replied. 'Just that they were rough and noisy.'

'You have not answered my question, ma'am. Perhaps you did not care to know the answer…?'

'Oh!' she cried. 'You shall not blacken his name. He

was your own man, after all. I had thought you must be proud of him. He died in a worthy cause.'

'Your loyalty to a man you did not love is admirable, my dear, but it is misplaced. It is high time you knew the truth. Firle was a double agent.'

Sophie stared at him. 'I don't know what you mean,' she whispered.

'Then let me explain. He fed us a certain amount of information, most of it useless. However, the information he supplied to his friends was of great value to them. They were warned well in advance of possible seizures, or a long-planned ambush at their landing beaches.'

Sophie felt that her throat had closed. It was almost impossible to breathe. She shut her eyes as the full implications of his words came home to her.

'You can't mean it!' she whispered at last. 'Do you tell me that he was working with the smugglers?'

'Beyond a doubt, ma'am. For a time we could not understand why our most secret plans appeared to be known to them. It became clear that we had an informer in our midst. The trail led to your husband.'

'I can't believe it! You must be mistaken. Why, that would mean that he was privy to the deaths of some of your own men...his friends...'

Hatton said nothing.

'I can't accept that you are right,' Sophie said more firmly. 'What possible reason could he have for agreeing to such a betrayal?'

A grim smile crossed her companion's face. 'Money, Mistress Firle! His share of the trade would have been substantial, but he must have realised that fortunes were being made by the men who backed the smugglers. I suspect that he tried to blackmail them, and in doing so he signed his own death warrant. They would not have hesitated to remove the danger.'

'But Richard had no money. We had no carriage and we lived so sparingly...' Then Sophie remembered the huge sum she had found in Richard's desk, and her face clouded.

'Yes?' Hatton prompted.

'Why would he need so much?' she pleaded. 'I did not ask for it.'

Her pitiful expression wrenched at Hatton's heart. The girl had courage, but she had borne enough. He would not explain that a womaniser such as Richard Firle would need bottomless pockets to keep his birds of paradise in luxury.

'Perhaps we shall never know,' he told her gently. 'It may be that he hoped to save enough to take you and Kit away from here.'

Tears gleamed upon her lashes, but she shook her head.

'You don't believe that, and nor do I. You said that I did not love him. That is true, but I thought I loved him once, and I thought he loved me. I soon learned the truth of it. My father was right. Richard was a fortune-hunter. When my father cast me off he had no further use for me.' She bent her head, but Hatton cupped her chin in his huge hand and forced her to look up at him.

'Don't fail me now!' he urged. 'You have your son to think about, remember?' He strode over to the bell-pull and summoned Abby. Then he took Sophie's hands and drew her to her feet.

'Can I persuade you to sit upon my lap, my dear? I feel that Abby needs convincing of my ardour.'

Sophie was too shocked by his revelations to put up

much resistance. It was oddly comforting to feel his massive arms about her, but it was also embarrassing.

'There is no need, I'm sure...' she said half-heartedly.

Hatton settled her more comfortably. 'This is no hardship, ma'am. Of that I can assure you.'

Chapter Seven

As Sophie lay inert within his arms, Hatton showed no disposition to release her, even when Abby had left the room.

She was very pale, and he looked down at her in some concern, aware that she was trembling uncontrollably. He picked her up and moved closer to the fire.

'Are you all right?' he asked. 'My apologies, ma'am. Perhaps I should not have told you of your husband's perfidy.'

'I prefer to know the truth,' she whispered through chattering teeth. 'It's just that I seem to be so very cold.'

'That is shock, my dear.' He reached out a long arm to the tray on the table beside him and poured her a glass of brandy. 'Drink this! I know you hate the taste, but it will warm you.'

Obediently, she sipped at the fiery spirit. As it coursed through her body she began to regain some semblance of composure. For a time she had seemed to lose all power of thought, but now her mind was racing. Her son was her first concern.

'Kit must not know of this. Please, I beg that you will never tell him.'

Hatton's lips tightened. 'Nothing was further from my mind,' he said abruptly. 'No child should carry such a burden.'

Sophie nodded. Then she remembered Nancy. If the girl should ever learn that it was Richard who had betrayed his colleagues...

She shuddered as she recalled the hatred in the girl's eyes. Revenge was an obsession with Nancy, and who knew where her vengeance might fall? Kit would be an easy victim.

Hatton held her closer, chafing her hands in an effort to warm them. 'What is it?' he asked quietly.

'I was thinking of Nancy. Does she know of any of this?'

'Of course not. Why do you ask?'

'She might harm Kit if she should ever learn that his father was the cause of her husband's murder. I fear that she is unbalanced.'

'How could she hear of it? No one in this household knows, apart from you and myself.'

Suddenly, Sophie became aware that she was resting comfortably against Hatton's massive chest. She coloured deeply as she attempted to struggle to her feet. He made no attempt to stop her.

'Better now?' he enquired.

'Thank you. I do feel warmer...' She managed a wavering smile as she took the opposite chair. 'It must be the brandy, I imagine. Is it your answer to all ills?'

'Only to some of them.' The hooded eyes regarded her intently. 'You have my admiration, ma'am—'

'Oh—why is that?'

'You are honest, Mistress Firle, especially with yourself. You do not seek to play the part of the grieving widow.'

'I can't,' she told him simply. 'I won't pretend to grief because I have lost my love. Richard was no longer that. Yet I do grieve in another way, for a life cut short by evil men. My son has lost his father, and Richard, whatever his failings, was our sole support. For that, at least, I must be thankful.'

'You are generous, ma'am.' Hatton's admiration grew. This gently nurtured girl had paid dearly for her one mistake in marrying Richard Firle. He could only guess at her agonies of mind when she realized that fact. The years must have worn away at her hopes, her dreams, her confidence and her faith in her fellow human-beings, but none of it had crushed her.

'You don't regret your marriage, then?' He was surprised at his own need to hear her reply, though he knew the answer before she spoke.

Sophie gave him a radiant smile. 'Of course not! I have Kit...'

Hatton turned away. Her courage shamed him. He was beginning to regret ever having considered drawing her into his plans. She had done nothing to deserve it. There must have been some other way to gain his ends without the need to involve this girl and her young son in such danger.

He was under no illusions. Sophie's life and that of the boy could be snuffed out like candles in the wind if anything went wrong. Only days ago he had thought the price worth paying. Now he knew that it was not. The realisation hit him hard. Hatton was no fool. He knew that he was growing dangerously fond of both Sophie and her son.

The knowledge shook him badly. It could put all his plans at risk. His expression was carefully controlled when he turned back to her.

'Will you open the inn tomorrow, Mistress Firle?' he asked. 'You have everything you need?'

'I believe so. We are well stocked, though I can't imagine that in the depths of winter we shall have much trade.'

'Then we must try to encourage it. Lamps in all the windows to offer a welcome to the traveller, and roaring fires. Bess may possibly wish to do some cooking…. There is nothing like the smell of fresh-baked bread, or the prospect of a juicy roast…'

Sophie shook her head at him. 'Mr Hatton, you are an optimist. Sometimes in the past we have gone for weeks without a single customer. I cannot think that it will change.'

Sophie was wrong. By noon on the following day she was surprised to hear the sound of carriage wheels. Glancing through the window, she saw six young men striding towards her door.

Hurrying down the stairs, she moved to greet them, warmed by the admiration in their eyes. Clearly her bronze gown was a great success.

'Gentlemen, what may we do for you?'

'Why, ma'am, we are in need of sustenance. The drive from Brighton has given us an appetite. What can you offer us?'

The man who spoke was in his early twenties. Tall and dark, he reminded her of someone, though she could not think why.

Sophie recited the menu quickly and was vastly amused when her customers ordered everything from soup through turbot to chicken, ham and mutton. She doubted if they would be able to eat one half of it, but she hadn't reckoned on a young man's hearty appetite. The food vanished like snow in summer. Then her customers set about Bess's apple pie with evident enjoyment.

Sophie was intrigued. 'How did you hear about the inn?' she asked as she served them with a sixth bottle of wine. 'We have only just reopened.'

They all beamed at her. 'Word gets about, ma'am.' The speaker's eyes had strayed to Nancy, who was engaged in clearing the tables. 'I suspect that we shall become your most faithful customers. Brighton can be dull, you know.'

Sophie laughed at him. 'Surely not? There are so many diversions…'

'But none that include the company of the most beautiful women in this part of Sussex.' The speaker gave her a gallant bow.

'Nonsense, sir! I suspect that your stomachs are your main concern. Have you enjoyed your meal?'

A chorus of approval convinced her, and Sophie beamed at them. 'We had not expected company today,' she told them. 'Next time you must let us know your wishes.'

'Ma'am, they have been more than fulfilled.' The young man bowed again. 'The Prince himself could not have dined with more pleasure.'

Sophie laughed. 'I doubt if his Royal Highness will venture along these country lanes in winter. You may not know that Sussex roads are said to be the worst in England.'

'And why is that, ma'am?'

'The county lies on clay. You were fortunate that we had frost last night, so that the ground is firm.'

'How true, Mistress Firle!' Hatton had entered the room. 'Yet this weather cannot hold. The wind is bringing rain from the west.'

The six young men looked up at him and he favoured

them with a pleasant smile. 'Just a warning, gentlemen,' he told them smoothly. 'The clay is a serious hazard. In summer it bakes to the consistency of rock, but rain turns it into a morass. In the past it has taken as many as twenty oxen to drag a wagon free.'

The young men looked at each other. They seemed reluctant to leave the comfort of the inn. One of them walked over to the window.

'No rain as yet,' he announced. 'Sir, won't you join us in a game of cards before we leave?'

Hatton nodded. 'As you wish. You stay in Brighton, so I hear. What brought you out into the country?'

Their leader grinned at him. 'My dear sir, it was a need to practise our driving skills. Ned there almost overturned the mail coach last time he took the ribbons. It cost him a small fortune to soothe the driver's feelings.'

His friend objected strongly to this slur upon his abilities. 'His lead horse was almost blind,' he insisted.

'And so were you when you took that corner, Ned,' the man beside him teased.

Ned maintained a dignified silence as he shuffled the cards. Then there was a pause as each man studied his hand.

Sophie left them to their game. She had enjoyed the company of these unexpected customers, feeling quite at ease with them. They had reminded her of the sons of family friends known to her since childhood. How long ago it all seemed now, the parties, the picnics, the village fêtes and the balls when young men such as these had presented themselves at her father's house, all vying for her attention.

She'd lost her heart to none of them, much to her father's satisfaction. His choice for her was William Curtis, the neighbouring landowner, whom Sophie had always held in keen dislike. For a time she had had an ally in her mother who pleaded Sophie's youth, but that excuse had worn thin as the months passed and she reached her seventeenth birthday.

Then she had met Richard. It was just a random trick of fate that he'd been sent to ask her father, a local magistrate, for a date when certain captured smugglers might be tried.

And my head was full of nonsense at that time, Sophie thought sadly. She'd been reading about the Vikings, half-thrilled and half-repelled by their exploits, but always intrigued. The splendid creature who rode up to her father's door might more fittingly have stepped ashore from a Norwegian galley.

She could remember every detail of that first encounter. She'd been standing at the foot of the steps about to mount her horse. The groom was already bending with locked hands to help her into the saddle. Then he'd been thrust aside, and Sophie turned to look into the bluest eyes she'd ever seen.

And I behaved like an idiot, Sophie thought bitterly. Richard must have found her the easiest of conquests. She had positively gaped at the impossibly handsome vision before her, marvelling at the sculptured perfection of his face, the wonderful curves of a mobile mouth, and the way the sunlight gleamed upon his blond head. She had discounted Viking ancestry immediately. This man looked more like a Greek god.

A wry smile lifted the corners of her mouth. Susceptibility to good looks had always been a weakness in her character, but from that day she had never looked at another man.

She'd braved her father's wrath, the indignity of being locked in her room and even threats of a diet of bread and water and serious beatings, until Richard had come for her that fateful night.

She'd gone with him without a backward glance, untroubled by the fact that she scarcely knew him. Their meetings had been few and, of necessity, fleeting. Love at first sight was true romance, as he had assured her, and she hadn't doubted the truth of it.

They had married on the day of her escape and, lost in dreams of happiness, Sophie could see no clouds upon the horizon.

Had not Richard assured her that once they were wed her father would relent? If she showed herself penitent and begged the forgiveness of both her parents, she would be restored to the bosom of her family.

It had not happened. Richard had reckoned without her father's implacable opposition to the match. It had been a body blow to him. Sophie had been the child of his heart, but she had spurned his wishes and his love. Even the thought of her was like a dagger-thrust. His only solace was to forget that she existed.

Richard had refused to believe at first that he had married a pauper, rather than an heiress, but as the truth came home to him, his manner towards Sophie changed. She'd been terrified by his coldness. How was she to live if he decided to abandon her? She loved him still, rejoicing when she found that she was pregnant. That, surely, would bring him back to her.

It didn't. Only when disgrace and dismissal from the Revenue Service threatened to crush him had he turned to her. She had stood by him, refusing to believe the accusations levelled against him, but troubled even as she defended him.

Richard seemed to lead a life apart from her, marked by mysterious meetings and frequent absences. When she'd tried to question him he'd frown, surly and abusive. On that last day of his life she had looked at him clear-eyed, wondering, not for the first time, how this man, handsome beyond belief and with the physique of an ath-lete, could have failed to live up to all she had expected of him.

Sophie shook her head, as if to rid it of troublesome thoughts. She could not change the past. Now she must think about the future. She looked up as Hatton entered the room.

'Your game is over?' she asked in surprise.

'Yes, your guests are leaving. I told them again that they must not underestimate the poor state of the roads. I reminded them that the oxen, the swine, the women and all the other animals in Sussex are noted for the length of their legs. It is said to be from the difficulty of pulling their feet from the mud... It is thought to strengthen the muscles and lengthen the bones.'

Sophie laughed in spite of herself. 'I had best come and bid them farewell,' she said. 'I enjoyed their company, and they enjoyed their meal. We shall have made a splen-did profit.'

'Congratulations!'

Sophie detected a sardonic undertone and she stared at him.

'Mr Hatton, you can't suspect these young men. I should have thought them harmless.'

'But then, you are easily deceived, are you not, Mistress Firle?' Hatton saw her angry look and relented. 'No, you are right. These puppies are not the men we seek.'

Sophie saw to her surprise that he was booted and spurred. Over his arm he carried a cloak with many capes.

'Do you go with them to Brighton?' she asked.

'No, my dear. My duties take me elsewhere. I shan't be away above a day or two.'

Sophie was horrified. 'No!' she cried. 'You can't! You promised us your protection. You shall not leave us now.'

'Your concern for me is touching…' Hatton's tone was sarcastic. 'Do you believe that I shall be lost upon the roads?'

'I don't care about you,' she cried wildly. 'I am thinking of my servants and my son.'

Hatton took her hand and drew her down to sit beside him. 'I wish that you could learn to trust me, ma'am. Believe me, you are not in danger for these next few days. With all this rain upon the western wind the roads will be a quagmire within hours. Wagons cannot move in such conditions, and the consignment in your cellar is too large to be carried by packhorses. In any case, some approach is certain to be made to you beforehand.'

Sophie was unconvinced, and her pallor alarmed him.

Hatton took her hands in his once more. 'You have done so well,' he told her gently. Absentmindedly, he was stroking the back of her hand with his thumb and she found the sensation disturbing. She drew her hand away as if she had been stung.

'When…when will you return?' she cried. She was torn between her dislike of him and an urgent wish for his protection.

'As soon as possible!' Unexpectedly he raised her fingers to his lips and kissed them. 'You are not without protection, Mistress Firle. You have both my men and your own. Jem is someone to be reckoned with, I feel…' He was smiling down at her.

Pride stiffened Sophie's resolve. 'Very well, then, go if you must,' she snapped.

'Sophie, please!'

'I don't recall giving you leave to use my given name, Mr Hatton. I see your promises now for what they are…completely worthless!' She turned on her heel and left him.

It was but the work of a moment to bid farewell to her guests. Then she stalked away without another glance at Hatton.

She heard the carriage leaving, to be followed by a single horseman, and she felt bereft. Beneath a ridiculous temptation to burst into tears she was furious. Hatton had drawn her into his plans, ignoring all her objections. Now, when it suited him, he was quite willing to leave her alone to face whatever dangers might be in store, and she was terrified.

It was all very well for him to claim that the servants would protect her. They might be willing to do so, but they knew no better than she did herself from which direction that threat might come.

Now she could only hope that he'd been right about the weather. For the next three days she blessed the leaden skies and the constant rain. Not a single customer had crossed her threshold. The greyness was depressing, but she could cope with that. What she feared most was the sudden arrival of strangers.

She tried to banish Hatton from her mind, telling herself that he wasn't worth a thought, but she found it difficult. She had grown accustomed to his teasing and that lazy smile and the comforting sight of his enormous figure about the place.

On several occasions during those few days she was tempted to pack her bags and leave with Kit, but where could she go? She had no money, and with a small child at her heels she would find it difficult to gain employment.

Try as she might, she could see no way out of her predicament, other than to stay where she was. Oh, if only Hatton would return! As the days passed she missed him more and more.

Of course, it was simply that he had promised to protect her. On this occasion, at least, she could not berate herself for being swayed by a handsome face. Hatton was no Adonis. His features were too strong for that. In repose his expression could be daunting. Not a person to whom one would readily apply for mercy, she thought rebelliously.

Well, she, at least, was not afraid of him, and when he returned she would give him a piece of her mind. Sophie spent much of her time thinking of sharp set-downs and crushing retorts which would reduce him to abject apology for his ill behaviour. That is, if he ever came back again. The sudden notion that he might not do so filled her with despair. Then common sense returned. Hatton had laid his plans with care. He would not abandon them now, however little he cared for her own welfare, or that of her child. It would be duty alone which drew him back to the inn, and she should admire him for his dedication.

But she didn't…at least, not altogether. Duty was important, naturally, and she would be the first to admit it, but other things were important too, such as consideration and affection.

Alarmed at the direction which her thoughts were taking, Sophie picked up her book. The small volume of poems had been left behind by a casual visitor some months ago. The beauty of the language, the various rhythms and the rich imagery of the work had proved to be a solace in the past, and now she knew many of the poems by heart, reciting them to herself as she went about her daily routine.

Her eye fell upon some lines penned by William Blake, an author new to her:

Tyger, Tyger, burning bright
In the forests of the night.
What immortal hand or eye
Could frame their fearful symmetry?

In the past the raw power of the poem had delighted her, but now it brought Nicholas Hatton forcibly to mind. Man and animal seemed as one in their predatory quest.

Sophie thrust the book aside. She must be losing her sense of proportion. Most probably the poem was not about an animal at all, but a symbol of some deeper meaning.

As for Hatton? He was just a man, possibly more ruthless than most, but a man for all that, and not a wild animal.

Yet the image stayed with her and she could not shake it off. That night she dreamed that she was running through a jungle, with some beast in hot pursuit.

She wakened with a cry, to find that her room was flooded with moonlight. The skies had cleared, and the rain had stopped at last.

Sophie lay there trembling. Now Hatton *must* return. He would know, even better than she, that once the roads were passable his quarry would return to the inn to collect the contents of her cellars.

The London men behind the trade would be growing impatient. They'd wait no longer for their profits on the vast cargo.

Further sleep was impossible. She waited until the first grey fingers of dawn had lightened the eastern sky and then she summoned Abby to fetch her water and help her dress.

'You are up betimes, Mistress Firle.' Abby was still half-asleep, and clearly unappreciative of Sophie's sudden desire to be up before the birds.

'I thought I'd go for a walk,' Sophie told her. 'I'm tired of being forced to stay indoors.'

'Can I come too?' A small face peeped around her door.

'Of course you may,' Sophie corrected. 'But first you must eat a good hot breakfast and let Abby dress you in your warmest clothes.'

'You'll catch your death,' Abby predicted in gloomy tones. 'There's been a frost, and the ground's like iron.'

This statement did nothing for Sophie's peace of mind, but she thrust aside her fears. Perhaps they would have no customers today.

When the sun was up she took Kit by the hand and set off down the lane. It was good to be out of doors on such a perfect winter's morning. A white rime clung to the verges of the road, untouched as yet by the weak rays of the sun as it glanced off trees and hedgerows bejewelled by the frost.

Sophie pointed to a solitary robin which regarded them with interest. Now she handed a bag of crumbs to Kit. The bird seemed almost tame. He hopped towards them, pecking eagerly at the bread.

'I bet I could train him to sit upon my hand. That is, if we could catch him, Mama.'

'No, we can't do that. He's a wild creature. It would be cruel to put him in a cage. Why not look for him when you are out of doors? He may stay close if you feed him every day.'

'That's a good idea!' Kit looked up at the sky. 'Will it snow, do you suppose? Reuben is making me a sledge.'

'I think it is too cold for snow. See how the ice has formed upon this pond. No, my dear, don't put your weight on it. It is too thin, as yet.'

'If it gets *really* thick, Hatton has promised to teach me how to skate,' Kit said with pride. 'He's very good, you know, he can do twirls and jumps, and he can skate backwards...' Clearly, this last astonishing achievement outweighed all the others in Kit's mind.

'Good gracious, how do you know all this?'

'He told me,' Kit said simply. 'He showed me, too. Just watch!' Kit ran along the icy lane and jumped in the air with his arms spread wide.

Sophie's lips twitched at the thought of the redoubtable Mr Hatton displaying his skating skills on dry land for the benefit of her son. She would have given much to have seen it.

'Of course, it's easier on the ground,' Kit told her gravely. 'The ice is slippery and first I have to learn to balance.'

'I expect it's rather like learning to walk,' she agreed.

'Well, I did that, didn't I?' Kit chuckled at his own joke and ran ahead of her.

She didn't keep him out of doors for long. The east wind was too cold, and she might have been naked for all the protection her warm clothing offered.

She hurried indoors to the comfort of a roaring fire, praying that the change in the weather had come too suddenly for the smugglers to have made their plans.

She had few customers that day. A carrier selling fish from the coast stopped by to ask for trade. Bess bought generously, knowing that the fish would keep well in the icy temperature of her food cellar. The man stayed only long enough to drink a tankard of mulled ale. Then he pushed on, clearly anxious to be rid of his load before nightfall.

Sophie ran to the window as a single horseman rode up to her door, but it was only a stranger, asking the way to Brighton. He was followed by the occupants of a carriage. A lady and two gentlemen came in to warm themselves and take refreshment, debating as they did so whether or not to continue with their journey.

'We might stay here, Matilda,' one of the men suggested. 'The food is excellent, and it will be much cheaper than the town.'

'Penny-pinching again, husband?' the lady sniffed. 'I *must* be at Brighton. My doctor insists upon it.'

'My dear, you can't intend to go on with his nonsensical suggestion of winter bathing? In this weather? Why, it is like to kill you.'

The lady would not be swayed. 'Much you would care,' she snapped. 'Dr Deaton has a splendid reputation and he knows my condition well.'

'Be it on your own head!' Her husband threw up his hands. He was not prepared to argue further. Then the other gentleman intervened.

'It may be as well to go on,' he suggested. 'If it should snow we might be trapped here for a sennight.'

'A week in this place?' the woman cried in anger. 'I won't have it! We must leave at once.'

Sophie saw them off without regret. She was in full agreement with the sentiments of the lady's husband. Anyone foolish enough to immerse themselves in the icy waters of the English Channel in the dead of winter was asking for trouble, whatever their doctor's orders.

Then she smiled. The woman might try the treatment

once, but she doubted if the experiment would be repeated. There were other diversions in Brighton which would be much more to her taste and would provide a more agreeable cure for her ailments, real or imaginary.

So far things were going well, but one hour later a coach driver came in with news that his coach had overturned a mile away. The horses were down and the vehicle had toppled into a deep ditch with the passengers trapped inside.

The driver was badly shaken, half-blinded as he was by blood pouring from an ugly cut across his brow.

Sophie dispatched Hatton's coach, with Reuben at the reins. She sent the rest of her male servants with him, laden with ropes and chains. Then she turned her attention to the injured driver.

The wound was not as deep as she had at first suspected, but she bathed it carefully before winding a bandage about the pad she'd used to staunch the blood.

Preoccupied with her task she hadn't noticed that she was no longer alone. Mindful of Hatton's sovereign remedy for shock, she reached for a bottle of brandy. Then she gasped. Behind her the room had filled with a group of silent men.

Sophie smiled at them uncertainly. They were too quiet and unlike any customers she had seen before. All of them wore loose clothing, but beneath it she could see that they were heavily armed.

'I'll be with you in a moment,' she promised. 'This man has been injured in an accident. I'll ring for someone to take care of him.' Despairingly she reached out towards the bell-pull, knowing full well that only Nancy or Abby would be likely to appear. She herself had sent her menfolk away.

'No need for that. Yon chap has fainted.' One of the men twitched the bell-rope away from her. 'Bad luck to have an accident like that!' He gave his companions a knowing wink.

Sniggers were followed by loud guffaws. Then one of the men walked past her, taking bottles of spirits from the shelves and handing them to his companions.

'Just saving you the trouble of having to serve us, ma'am!' he leered.

Sophie was thinking fast. She had no weapon with her. In any case, a single pistol would be useless against this mob. She must rely on her own wits. Pray heaven that Nancy did not come to find her. The men were downing gin and brandy as if it were water. At this rate they would be intoxicated within the next half-hour. She knew what that could mean. Both she and Nancy would be at risk, and Abby too.

'You are welcome to help yourselves,' she said pleasantly. Nothing in her voice betrayed her terror. 'Would you like some food?' It was all she could think of. Food might help to keep them sober.

'It wouldn't come amiss!' The man who had handed out the bottles reached out to finger her brooch. 'That's a nice piece, mistress. Did you get it from your fancy-man?'

Sophie's anger made her incautious. 'No!' she snapped. 'I am a widow.'

'Now there's a shame!' A dirty hand caressed her cheek. 'A good woman going to waste, I call it!' The hand strayed to the bodice of her gown, tugging it so that the buttons flew in all directions.

Sophie slapped his hand away, to the accompaniment of a shout of laughter from his friends.

Her anger seemed to inflame him further. He slipped an arm about her waist, drawing her close. His fingers were entwined in her hair, forcing back her head as he bent to kiss her.

Sophie lost all her fear of him. Now she fought him like a cat, biting and scratching at his eyes, but she was no match for his superior strength. He forced her back until she was laying across a table. Then his hands tore at her skirts.

Suddenly, Sophie heard a grunt and a dull thud. She struggled upright to find her attacker lying at her feet as if he had been pole-axed.

'My apologies, ma'am,' a cultured voice remarked. 'This was an unfortunate incident. The shock must have been severe. Won't you sit down whilst I fetch you a restorative?'

Still dazed, Sophie looked at the speaker. She saw a man not much above middle height and no longer young. Silver-haired, and thin to the point of emaciation, he had the face of an ascetic or some tortured mediaeval saint.

Now the blue eyes smiled encouragement at her. 'You are quite safe,' he said. 'Those animals are gone.'

Sophie looked beyond him to find that the room was indeed empty, apart from her companion. 'I have to thank you,' she said weakly. 'Foolishly, I left myself without protection. My men are attending some accident further up the road.'

Then she remembered the smiles and winks when the accident was mentioned. 'I think they caused it,' she said heavily. 'But why, I can't imagine.'

'Possibly they hoped to commit a robbery?' he suggested.

'Then why come here?'

'The arrival of your men must have frightened them away. This inn must have seemed the next best target.'

It all sounded very plausible, but Sophie was unconvinced. She sensed that her unwelcome visitors were members of the smuggling fraternity, but no approach had been made to her about the disposal of the goods still hidden in her cellar.

Her rescuer handed her a glass of brandy, and Sophie pulled a wry face. If gentlemen continued to ply her with drinks in this way, she might get a taste for the spirit which she disliked so much. Still, she could not refuse such a kindly act, and she took a sip to please him.

'Well done!' He bent to retrieve the brooch which was lying at her feet. 'This is yours, I believe?' He was careful to avert his eyes and looking down, Sophie could understand why.

Stripped of its buttons, the front of her gown was gaping wide, revealing an expanse of snowy chemise. She jumped to her feet, holding the edges of the cloth together.

'Excuse me!' she murmured in confusion as she fled the room.

Chapter Eight

Unwilling to explain the damage to her gown, Sophie didn't summon Abby to help her change. It was but the work of a moment to slip out of the ruined garment.

She had selected another one and was fastening the buttons at her wrists when she heard a sudden scream. It came from the stable-yard and her first thought was for Kit.

She dashed to the window and caught her breath in horror. Her gentlemanly rescuer was thrashing the man who had attacked her with appalling ferocity.

A bloody weal ran across the victim's face. It had narrowly missed his eyes, and he'd put up his hands to protect them. It didn't save him. Even as she watched a second savage blow drove him to his knees.

Sophie didn't hesitate. She fled down the stairs and out into the yard, catching at the upraised arm as the whip threatened to come down again.

'No!' she cried. 'Please stop! You shall not do this, sir!'

With his arm still raised, the man swung round and Sophie flinched away in terror as she waited for the blow to fall on her defenceless head.

It did not, but her terror did not lessen as she looked

up into the gaunt face. The blue eyes were empty of expression. She might have been looking through a pane of glass into the void beyond. This was the true face of evil, and she knew in her heart that this was one of the men whom Hatton sought.

Without another glance at the bleeding wretch upon the ground, he took Sophie's arm and led her indoors.

'I am sorry that you had to witness that, ma'am. A beating is all that these animals understand...' He was all solicitude as he helped her to a chair.

'There was no need for it,' she whispered faintly. 'I was unharmed.'

'The creature needed a sharp lesson,' he told her. His eyes had never left her face. 'May I make a suggestion?' He didn't wait for her reply. 'Don't leave yourself without protection. You must have men about the place.'

'I have,' she said weakly. 'But there has been an accident. They are gone to help.'

'All of them?'

She nodded. Then she realised the folly of that admission. 'They will soon return,' she said quickly.

The gentleman studied his perfectly manicured hands. Then he looked up and smiled. 'I must be on my way, ma'am. I stopped only to bait my horse, but I am glad to have been of service to you.'

Sophie tried to detain him. If she was right and this was Hatton's quarry, she should try to question him.

'I am so grateful to you, sir. Won't you take some refreshment before you leave? It is a bitter day.'

He bowed. 'Too kind! I have my failings, Mistress Firle, but a fondness for alcohol is not one of them.'

'Then a dish of tea, perhaps?'

'I thank you, but I must refuse. I have some way to go today.'

Sophie followed him along the passageway which led out to the stables, still intent on persuading him to change his mind. She was very much afraid of the strange visitor, but she had promised to help Hatton and she would keep her word.

Then an arm slid about her waist and a large hand covered her mouth to stifle a shriek, as she was drawn into the shadow of a dark recess.

'No,' a deep voice whispered. 'Let him go! He will be back, you may be sure.'

'You?' Sophie swung round to find herself face to face with Hatton. 'When did you return?'

'Some few hours ago,' he told her carelessly. 'You seemed to be handling matters well, so I did not show myself.'

Sophie was speechless with indignation, and in the darkness she saw the gleam of white teeth as he grinned at her.

'Why, you—' she began.

'Hush, and listen…'

The stranger was evidently speaking to his so-called groom. 'I blame you, Welbeck,' he said in glacial tones. 'Had it not been for that drunken fool, we might have been loaded and away by now. How came you to let the men indoors?'

'They were all but frozen, master,' came the abject apology. 'There ain't much traffic on this road. We had to wait for hours for a coach to come along, but we over-turned it with a rope across the road, just as you said.'

'And you expect congratulations? Why, you lout, for all the good it did we need not have troubled. I needed time to make my case for the removal of our goods, and that you did not give me.'

'Yon's nobbut a girl,' the man said scornfully. 'You could have knocked her on the head.'

Sophie heard a chilling laugh and then a yelp as the whip was used again. 'Watch your mouth, Welbeck,' his employer advised. 'You are speaking of a lady…and a lady whose help we shall need in future operations. Now fetch my horse.'

'Must Walt go with us, master? He's bleeding bad and almost blind.'

'I should have killed him,' came the brief reply. 'Knife him or bring him with you. Either way he can't be left here. I don't trust a drunkard.'

Sophie turned and buried her face in Hatton's coat. She was appalled by the raw ferocity in the speaker's tone.

'He seemed so kind at first,' she whispered. 'I didn't suspect him in the least…'

Hatton found himself stroking her hair. 'Don't worry,' he said. 'I'm here. You are quite safe.'

Sophie bristled as memory flooded back. 'You weren't here when I needed you,' she accused. 'And what did you mean when you said that I was handling matters well? I was attacked and might well have been raped—'

'I think not,' he said lightly. He did not mention how close he'd come to rushing to her rescue, and ruining his own plans.

'You seem very sure of that,' she told him bitterly. 'Am I so ill favoured that no man would touch me?'

He hugged her to him then and she could feel the laughter bubbling in his chest.

'Typically feminine!' he teased. 'No, my dear, you are not ill favoured and you know it well enough. Allow me to tell you that it is a privilege for any man to hold you.'

Sophie struggled out of his grasp. 'I hate you!' she cried. 'I wish that I might never see you again…'

Hatton followed her into the parlor. 'That's sad,' he observed with a twinkle. 'I was hoping that my reappearance might be welcome. Must I go away again?'

'No!' she exclaimed in alarm. 'I mean, it is your duty to stay until the danger is over.'

'Quite right, ma'am! Well, then, let us get down to business. What have you discovered?'

'Nothing!' she told him flatly. 'I am useless as a spy. They tricked me all too easily. I let all the menfolk go to help out with this so-called accident—'

'Not quite all of them. My own men were undeceived. They were hiding in the barn in case of trouble.'

'And what do you call trouble, Mr Hatton? It seems to me that your idea of danger is curious to say the least.'

'Had you proved recalcitrant, you might have been abducted—that is, until you came to your senses and agreed to their demands.'

'And that would have been acceptable to you?'

'No, it would not!' Hatton had reached the limits of his endurance. Now he walked towards her and lifted her face to his. Then he kissed her long and tenderly.

'Does that answer your question?' he asked in a low voice.

Sophie broke away from him in a panic, drawing her hand across her mouth as if to wipe away the touch of his lips.

'Despicable!' she cried. 'How dare you insult me so? If I were a man I'd call you out!'

Hatton regarded her for a long moment. 'If you were a man I should not have kissed you,' he said reasonably. 'Have you forgotten our plan?'

'Who were you convincing of your ardour this time?' she snapped. 'No one is observing us.'

'I thought I heard approaching footsteps, ma'am.' His

eyes were dancing. 'Anyone might have entered the room.'

'Liar!' Her anger was directed as much against herself as at him. With his mouth on hers she had wanted to throw her arms about his neck and hold him close as long-forgotten passions fired her blood. Such weakness was humiliating.

'Take care!' she cried. 'After today's experiences it would not take much to persuade me to take my son and leave this place, whatever the consequences.'

'Would you be so foolish?' he enquired mildly. 'I think not. Some of your experiences have been unpleasant, but not all of them, I trust. You seem to be none the worse for them.'

A glance at her face showed him her heightened colour, but at least she'd lost that look of terror which the stranger had inspired in her, and Hatton was satisfied.

'Now, let us a call a truce,' he cried. 'Can you tell me nothing more?'

'No! I had no time to move among the men on the chance of discovering their destination.'

'It is no matter,' he mused. 'The first approach has been made. When our friend returns he will have some plausible reason as to why his goods are stored in the cellar here. Don't be too eager to believe him…'

'You mean I should ask him for some proof of ownership?'

Hatton laughed. 'He will have nothing in writing, Mistress Firle, but he's no fool. As we heard, he would rather have you with him than against him. I would expect him to counter your objections with some hints as to how a penniless widow might provide herself with a comfortable living.'

'But what shall I say?' she cried in desperation.

'Let us play it by ear. The important thing is that you allow him to persuade you to let him move the cargo.'

'And then?'

'Then I shall follow him to his destination.'

'Suppose he should recognise you, sir? Clearly, you have been connected with the authorities for some time.'

'Worried about me, ma'am? I am flattered.' Hatton saw the glowering look upon her face and laughed. 'The gentleman does not know me by sight. It is only in this past year or so that I have taken on these duties.'

'And before then?'

'I was with Wellington in Spain, Mistress Firle. My brothers are still there.'

Sophie was surprised. It was the first time Hatton had spoken of his family. 'That must be a worry for you,' she told him with quick sympathy. 'The campaign is said to have been hard-fought...'

'It isn't over yet,' he told her grimly. 'I had no wish to leave, but it was felt that I could be of more use here.'

'But why you?'

'There are family reasons. My grandfather was instrumental in breaking up the Hawkhurst Gang. You will have heard of them?'

Sophie shuddered. 'Were they not murderers to a man?' she asked in faint tones. 'But that was fifty years ago.'

'Little has changed. My father carried on the work, but he has paid for it. When his house was fired he suffered serious injury.'

Sophie tried to swallow, but her mouth was dry. She stretched out a hand to her companion. 'Forgive me!' she whispered. 'I didn't understand. You have the best of reasons to pursue these men, apart from a wish to serve your country.'

Hatton took her hand in his and kissed it, but whatever

he had been about to say was interrupted when Kit rushed into the room.

'Hatton, Hatton, you are back! The pond is frozen hard. Will you teach me to skate? You promised…'

Laughing, Hatton took the child upon his knee. 'I don't skate in the dark…but tomorrow… Shall we say at ten o'clock?'

'If it rains the ice will melt.' Kit looked crestfallen.

'We'll face that dreadful calamity when it happens. Meantime, you might like to try your skates. Do you see that parcel in the corner? Open it and see what you can find.'

As Kit flew across the room and tore at the wrapping of his parcel, Sophie shook her head.

'You spoil him, sir. You are too indulgent.' Her smile left him in no doubt that she was pleased.

He shrugged her thanks aside. The expression on the child's face was reward enough.

Kit came towards them, carrying a pair of sturdy leather boots with long blades screwed into the soles. He might have been carrying the Holy Grail.

Sophie knelt beside him to help him lace them up. She was unsurprised to find that they were a perfect fit. Now she knew the reason for the sudden disappearance of a pair of Kit's old boots.

Hatton held out his hands to help the child to his feet.

'Comfortable?' he asked.

Kit nodded. 'I'm a bit wobbly, sir.'

'You will be so at first, until you find your balance, and the boots may be a little stiff. Try them for a while, but don't wear them for too long today, or you may get a blister.'

Both he and Sophie hid their amusement as Kit tottered away, doubtless to show Reuben his new treasures.

'I hope he doesn't fall and hurt himself,' she said anxiously.

'He'll have worse falls upon the ice. Are you sure that you wish to trust him to my tender care?'

'Kit has set his heart on it. Besides, Mr Hatton, I have no fear that you will let him come to any harm.'

For the first time in their acquaintance Hatton looked embarrassed, but he made a quick recovery.

'You mollycoddle him!' he told her roughly, expecting a furious retort. It did not come.

Sophie rose to her feet. She did not trouble to hide her amusement. 'And you are worse,' she told him. 'Kit has only to express a wish to you, and it is granted. Dear me, what a father you would make!'

The implications of this remark were not lost on either of them, and Sophie hurried away before she could compound her error further.

For the next few hours she was fully occupied in caring for the unfortunate occupants of the overturned coach. One of the gentlemen had suffered a broken arm, whilst the other was nursing various cuts and bruises. Only the woman had escaped with little more than a severe shaking. The experience had done nothing to improve her temper. Demands that their coachman be dismissed without a character were interspersed with bouts of strong hysterics.

Sophie lost all patience. She ordered a hot toddy and added a couple of extra measures of strong rum. With any luck the woman would fall into a drunken stupor and could then be carried to her bed.

'Why, Mistress Firle, you shock me!' Hatton was at her elbow, grinning broadly. 'I thought you despised hard liquor.'

'I am come to the conclusion that it has its uses,' she replied with feeling as she thrust the tankard into the woman's hand. 'Drink this, ma'am! It is a powerful restorative.'

She heard a choking sound beside her. 'Powerful indeed!' Hatton whispered. 'That potion is enough to fell a horse!'

Sophie did not deign to answer him. She moved away to enquire about the condition of the others. The man with the broken arm was not complaining, but his face was twisted in agony.

'The surgeon will soon be here,' she comforted. 'Then you will be more comfortable.'

'Ma'am, will you see to my friend?' he asked. 'I fear that he is bleeding badly.'

Sophie called for hot water and bandages. Then she set about treating his companion's wounds. She was still working on them when the surgeon arrived. He set her aside at once.

'No great harm done,' he announced. 'You have stopped the bleeding, ma'am. Now let us see to this gentleman here.'

Sophie fled. She could cope with bleeding, but she could not face the thought of standing by whilst the broken arm was set.

'Squeamish?' a deep voice enquired.

Sophie turned to find Hatton looking down at her.

'I suppose so,' she admitted with some reluctance. 'It will hurt quite dreadfully.'

Hatton threw his arm about her shoulders. 'You have done enough,' he announced. 'Those travellers need rest. Leave them to their slumbers and come and dine with me.'

'No!' she told him firmly. 'There is too much to do, I have not yet enquired about the groom—'

'Thrown clear, and quite unharmed,' he assured her.

'Well, the damaged coach will need repair. I must send for the wheelwright—'

'Already done! Anything else?' She saw the challenge in his eyes and thought she knew the reason for it. 'Perhaps you do not care to be alone with me. Could that be the motive for your unwillingness to give me the pleasure of your company.'

'Of course not!' Sophie stiffened. As usual he seemed to have this curious ability to read her mind, but she would not admit to the truth. 'I am not aware that you found pleasure in my company,' she told him coldly.

'No? Then I must be slipping, ma'am. I thought I had made it clear.'

Sophie backed away from him, suspecting that he intended to kiss her again, but he laughed and held out his hand to her.

'May we not be friends for this one evening at least? Let us forget our problems for these next few hours and dine like civilised people. You shall tell me of your life before you married Firle and I will entertain you with the gossip from Brighton.'

Sophie looked at him uncertainly, drawn to him like a moth to a flame. He was a disturbing being, dangerous to her peace of mind. In his company she felt fully alive, piqued on some occasions and furious on others, but always excited for some reason she could not fathom.

And then there was his kindness to Kit. That she could not forget. It would be churlish to refuse this simple request to dine with him.

At last she held out her hand. 'Very well,' she demurred. 'But on one condition, sir...'

'And what is that, Mistress Firle?'

'My servants need no further convincing that you…I mean…they all believe by now that you are come to…to offer me your hand.'

'Do they, ma'am? I must take leave to doubt it. Matthew and his wife both know full well that I have another purpose here. That is unfortunate, but once we entered the cellars it was inevitable. Let us hope that they did not share that knowledge with the others.'

'Matthew is no fool,' she told him quickly. 'He would not tell Abby. Nor will Bess speak of it to her brother and his son…'

'Good! I trust that you are right. It means, of course, that I must continue to pursue you.' Hatton's eyes were dancing.

'From a distance, sir. I must have your word on that.'

'Agreed!' He gave her a solemn bow. 'I must not kiss you, nor may I hold you in my arms, unless, of course, Abby should chance to enter the room.'

'Even then,' she told him solemnly. 'It is unseemly.'

'Suppose you trip or faint?' he teased. 'Am I to let you fall to the ground?'

'I shall not faint, Mr Hatton. And if you continue to annoy me, you may be the person who falls to the ground.'

'Threats, my dear?' Hatton shuddered in mock terror. 'You are a modern Boudicca…'

'Then you would do well to remember that the Queen of the Iceni was said to have scythes upon her chariot wheels. They cut away the legs from her opponents.'

'Touché.' He grinned. 'A truce then, ma'am?'

'A truce!' Sophie gave him her hand. 'Now, sir, I must change my gown. Bess does not care to have her cooking spoiled by laggardly diners.'

Hatton let her go, well satisfied with her complaisance. He'd determined not to allow her to dine alone, knowing that, if she were left to her own thoughts, Sophie would continue to reflect upon the dangers of her situation.

Was that why he had kissed her? If so, it had served its purpose in diverting her attention from the ugly scene she'd witnessed. She could no longer be in any doubt as to the ruthless nature of the men he sought.

Then he cursed softly under his breath. He was deluding himself. He'd kissed her because his passion for her could no longer be denied, and it was madness to fall into this easiest of traps. What was happening to him? Every instinct warned him to stay away from her...to keep her at a distance...but it needed only the sight of her to set his blood afire. Such folly was unlike him.

In the past he'd felt contempt for those who'd been so easily led astray by a pair of fine eyes or a charming smile, combined with a winning disposition. Now he was caught in the same toils. Perhaps it was not too late to extricate himself.

He grimaced in some amusement. Sophie's disposition most certainly could not be described as winning. She'd fought him every step of the way since the moment of their meeting. She was no milk-and-water miss, fierce as a tigress in defence of her young so he could do no other than admire her.

And that had led to...what? There had been no need to make a parade of his devotion. An arm flung carelessly across the back of a lady's chair was enough to cause a scandal in his circles. He'd kissed her to annoy her, as he now admitted to himself. Well, he had been hoist with his own petard. Her response had startled him.

At first he'd thought that he must have been mistaken, but when he had repeated the experiment he could no longer be in any doubt. This was a woman worthy of capture. At another time, and in another place, he would not have hesitated, but now his hands were tied.

Nothing of this showed in his manner as he rose to greet her later in the evening. Gravely, he led her to a chair and offered her a glass of Madeira.

Sophie shook her head. She had no intention of lowering her guard. Long reflection had persuaded her that, in agreeing to dine alone with Hatton, she was playing with fire. Long months as belle of the county before her marriage had given her a certain insight into gentlemen's intentions. Now she knew that Hatton wanted her, in spite of his protestations that he was playing a part.

Strangely, the knowledge pleased her. It gave her a degree of power over him, but she could not guess at its extent. That she would only learn by trial and error.

As they sat down to dine the tension in the room was palpable. Hatton addressed himself to a dish of turbot in sauce with every appearance of enjoyment, but Sophie seemed to have lost her appetite.

'Do try this macaroni *à la napolitaine*,' he coaxed. 'The Prince's chef could not better it.'

Sophie took a bite or two to please him.

He bent a critical gaze upon her. 'Let me ask you something, ma'am. Have you ever seen a racehorse?'

'Why, yes, of course.'

'Then you will have noticed their fine condition, with gleaming coats, and every muscle in perfect harmony?'

Sophie stared at him. She could not imagine where the conversation was leading.

'That is so,' she agreed.

'And are we any different, Mistress Firle? Racehorses

are fed with care, and that is the reason for their success. Human beings are no different.'

'Quite possibly. I cannot think why this should concern you.'

'It should concern you…' he said with meaning. 'You don't eat enough. It will tell on you in time, believe me. We humans have survived across the centuries because of our willingness to eat a varied diet.'

'You would have me make my way through seven courses?'

'No, ma'am, there is a happy medium. Now try these collops…' He helped her to a couple of chops, neatly trimmed of fat. 'You will find them light enough to leave room for the next course.'

Sophie was tempted to remonstrate. Instead she changed the subject. 'You promised to tell me all the Brighton gossip,' she reminded him.

'You sound like your son, ma'am.' Hatton chuckled.

'I must suppose I do, but I have always longed to hear of the doings of the great and good—'

'Or even the doings of the great and not so good?'

'Even that.' Sophie could not hide her curiosity. 'My father spoke often of the Prince and what a pleasure it was to see him strolling about the town, so popular and so much at ease with the common folk.'

'That, I fear, is somewhat changed since your father's day, though Prince George is still more popular in Brighton than he is in London.'

'Have you met him?' she asked eagerly. 'One hears so many rumours that it is difficult to judge of his character with any truth.'

'He is a curious mixture, much more so than other men. Obstinate, vain, highly strung and over-emotional, he is quick to take offence, sometimes where none is intended. He never forgives a slight to his person...'

'Then it is easy to dislike him?'

'It is almost impossible, Mistress Firle. You have not studied the other side of the coin. I think I never met a man with so much charm, when he chooses to exert it. He can be witty and entertaining, with an affability which disarms his enemies. I have seen them change their opinion of him in the course of a few moments.'

'You sound as if you admire him.'

'I do. He is greatly gifted. Did you know that he speaks four languages as fluently as English? He is fond of music, as are all the Hanoverians, and we have not had such a patron of the arts since the first King Charles.'

'But?' Sophie had sensed a certain reservation in his tone.

'But he is his own worst enemy. The people have no quarrel with his fondness for the ladies, to put the matter delicately. What they won't forgive is his treatment of his wife...his second wife, I mean.'

'Oh!' Sophie's cheeks were pink. 'You cannot mean that this story of a marriage to Mrs Fitzherbert can be true?'

'I'm afraid it is beyond doubt.'

'But that would make him a bigamist. I did not hear of a divorce before he married Caroline of Brunswick.'

'There was none. He never admitted to that first marriage.'

'But the child...the heiress to the throne? Surely that would make the Princess Charlotte illegitimate?'

'It is not spoken of. Now let us end this treasonable talk. You have told me nothing of yourself.'

'I think I should not like the Prince,' Sophie said with great finality. 'That is a pity. I always longed to see him.

As a child, you know, I always imagined Brighton to be a golden city, floating in the air, with Prince George at its heart, beloved by everyone.'

'Don't give up your dreams so easily,' he teased. 'The Prince would most certainly be beloved by you. He has one great quality which would cause you to forgive all else.'

'And what is that?' Sophie looked doubtful.

'He loves children, and he is adored by them. There seems to be a mutual and instant understanding. With the young, one sees him at his best. One cannot fail to think him a kindly and good-hearted man.'

'You are generous, Mr Hatton.'

'No, I speak merely as I find. Did your father know the Prince?'

'He didn't aspire to such heights,' Sophie told him in amusement. 'Even so, he had plans for me, that is, before Sir William Curtis was widowed and he saw the opportunity to join his lands to ours.'

'You were never tempted by the offer?'

'I was not!' Sophie's reply was curt and did not invite further questioning on the subject. Then she softened. 'Even so, I should like to have come to Brighton for the season. I'd heard of the balls, the concerts, the parties and the picnics, as well as the racing on the Downs.'

'But you married Firle instead?'

'Yes!'

Her wistful expression tugged at Hatton's heart-strings. That ill-advised match had robbed her of a large part of her girlhood. Far from leading the life to which she had been bred she'd found herself in this isolated spot, bereft of friends and family and tied to a man unworthy of her, with only her son for consolation.

Sophie saw his expression. She could not bear to be pitied.

'You must not think that I regretted my decision,' she told him stiffly.

'I did not think it for a moment. Kit, after all, is not to be regretted...'

Her smile transfigured her face and Hatton's heart turned over. The temptation to take her in his arms was overwhelming, and it took all his self-control to resist it. He tried to give the conversation a lighter turn.

'I think we must be thankful that you did not arrive in Brighton some six years ago,' he said. 'You would have broken many a heart among the 10th Dragoons.'

'The Prince's regiment?' Sophie dimpled. 'Mr Hatton, are you trying to flatter me?'

'Not in the least. Those susceptible young men would have been swooning at your feet.'

'Do spare my blushes, sir. You are talking nonsense.'

Hatton tried to pour her another glass of wine, delighted to see her restored to some remembrance of her girlhood, but she covered the glass with her hand.

'No!' she said. 'You shall not persuade me into further foolish chatter.' She glanced at the clock and rose with a sharp exclamation. 'Great heavens, how the time has flown! I had no idea that it was so late. You must excuse me, sir.'

He didn't attempt to detain her. Silently he held out his hand, and when she took it he raised her fingers to his lips.

'Our truce still holds?' he asked.

'It does, sir, and I must thank you for a pleasant evening.' For once, Sophie felt much in charity with him. Entertained by his conversation, she had forgotten all her fears for those few hours.

She fell asleep almost at once that night.

By the following morning she was much refreshed. The winter sun was pouring through her windows, but the frost still held the countryside in its iron grip. She could see the starry patterns against the glass.

Kit's voice sent her hurrying to look into the stable-yard. Hatton was already with him; as she watched, he lifted the child on to his great stallion, leading the beast with one hand as he supported her son with the other.

It wasn't only the Prince who had a great rapport with children, she thought wryly. Not for the first time she wondered why Hatton had not set up his own nursery. He must be in his thirties, but perhaps those years in Spain had given him no opportunity to choose a suitable bride.

Sophie sipped at her chocolate and nibbled at a roll. Then she went downstairs to enquire about the welfare of her unexpected guests. They were still bruised, but much recovered, and the gentlemen, at least, offered their thanks for all her kindness. Their female companion was anxious to be away, chivvying her husband to expedite the repairs to their coach whilst complaining of a sore head.

'Such an experience!' she moaned. 'I fear I have suffered serious injury. My head is like to burst.'

Privately, Sophie thought it far more likely that the woman was suffering from the effects of the several rum-laced toddies which she had consumed the day before, but she made sympathetic noises.

Then she looked up as a cheerful party of young bloods erupted into the room. She recognised them at once as previous customers. These were the men who had arrived on the day of her re-opening.

Now she eyed their costume in amusement. Broad-brimmed hats and long drab coats were, she guessed, intended to mark them out as grooms, rather than the aristocrats they were. Hatton had told her that it was a popular conceit, but Sophie found it something of a mystery.

Even more mysterious was the fact that they were all carrying skates. Now they clustered about her, vying for her attention, but their leader stilled the clamour with an imperious gesture.

'We are come to beg your indulgence, Mistress Firle,' he told her with a winning smile. 'Will you allow us to skate upon your lake? It is the only stretch of unblemished ice for miles around. We've tried elsewhere, but Ned here has already come to grief through reeds frozen into surface ice.'

Sophie glanced at the unfortunate Ned. He certainly seemed to be accident-prone, and was, at that moment, nursing a bleeding nose. It had not dampened his enthusiasm for the sport.

'My lake, as you are pleased to call it, is naught but a large pond swollen by the recent rains, sir, but you are welcome to skate upon it if you wish to do so.'

'Shall you care to join us, ma'am?' the young man continued as a chorus of thanks rose about her. 'We carry spare blades in case of breakages. It would be but the work of a moment to fix them to your boots.'

Sophie was flattered by his offer, but she felt obliged to decline. 'I have never skated in my life,' she protested. 'I should be certain to break a limb.'

'Not with someone to support you on either side.' The speaker was surprisingly persistent. 'Do say you'll come. It is quite the most delightful sensation in the world.'

Sophie hesitated and was lost. A spirit of rebellion seized her. She was tired of thinking about her present worries. Why shouldn't she have some fun? Hatton might have offered to teach her, but he hadn't done so. She would show him that others were not so laggardly. Her eyes sparkled with excitement as she hurried away to fetch her boots.

Chapter Nine

They heard the others long before they reached the pond. Kit, as always, was talking twenty to the dozen as Hatton helped him into his skates. Then he fell silent, frowning in concentration as they took to the ice with Hatton skating backwards and holding both his hands.

Sophie watched as Kit made his first attempts, trying to walk rather than to glide. Then he got the hang of it and began to shout with glee.

'Watch me, Mama!' he cried. 'I'm skating!'

'There now, Mistress Firle…you see how easy it is?' The young man, who had introduced himself simply as Wentworth, held out his hands to help her to her feet. 'Just trust yourself to Jack and me. We shan't allow you to fall.'

As Sophie stood upon the narrow blades she was tempted to refuse the offer, but all eyes were upon her, and she could not act the coward in front of Kit.

Wentworth was as good as his word, so with Jack holding on to her other arm she ventured out upon the slippery surface. It soon became clear that the two young men were experts, and after the first few anxious moments Sophie began to enjoy herself as she skimmed along between them.

A keen wind brought the colour to her cheeks, but it had no power to chill her as her companions increased their speed.

'Whoa! You will make the lady dizzy!' Hatton skidded to a halt beside them, with Kit holding tightly to his hand.

'Nonsense!' Sophie told him. 'I haven't had so much fun in years. I won't stop now, just when I feel more confident.'

'I wasn't suggesting that you stop, Mistress Firle... merely that we change partners.'

Sophie's companions seemed about to protest, but a glance at Hatton's face persuaded them otherwise. It was, therefore, with good grace that they glided away with Kit between them, and, much to his delight, increasing their speed as they did so.

'You are too high-handed, sir.' Sophie wasn't pleased. 'What right have you to dictate my actions, or the company I choose?'

'None whatever, my dear. I thought merely that you might like to try your new-found skills with a single partner?' He slid an arm around her waist and, taking her other hand in his, moved across the ice with an ease that communicated itself to her.

'Relax!' he advised. 'You hold yourself too stiffly. Put yourself in my hands. I shall not let you come to harm.'

At the end of a half-hour she had acquired a certain degree of proficiency, helped by his words of advice. Then he led her off the ice. 'That is enough for today. If this weather holds we shall have you skating on your own.' Raising his voice, he called to Kit, but for once the child was unwilling to obey his instructions to remove his skates.

Hatton's frown was enough to bring the child to his side, though he looked despondent.

'I wanted to practise,' he complained. 'Ned says that the best skaters always practise.'

'So they do, but not for so long that their legs grow stiff and their feet begin to bleed. Now sit down, Kit, and let us see what these young men can do.' He made a place beside him on the fallen log where they had left their things.

With the ice to themselves the young men treated them to a dazzling display of jumps and spins. Kit applauded them, but he was strangely silent.

'What is it, Kit? I hope you are not sulking...' Sophie reproved.

'No, Mama, but Hatton said that *he* could jump.'

Sophie chuckled as she looked at her companion. 'How fortunate that you have not removed your skates, Mr Hatton! I trust you will not disappoint us!'

She was rewarded with an answering grin as Hatton got to his feet. 'Anything for a quiet life,' he teased. Then he moved out to join the others.

To Sophie's surprise they cleared the ice for him, but in a moment she understood the reason for it. Moving at great speed, Hatton executed a startling number of difficult jumps and spins which left her breathless with admiration. The sheer beauty of the movements found her clapping wildly, and Kit was open-mouthed.

Then the others joined him. They did not have his skills, but Wentworth's movements struck a chord in Sophie's mind. As the young man turned in profile, her suspicions were confirmed.

'Why have you found it necessary to deceive me?' she demanded as she walked back to the inn with Hatton by her side.

'Ma'am?'

'Mr Wentworth is a relative of yours, I think. I cannot be mistaken. The resemblance is too strong.'

'He is my cousin.'

'Indeed? And his companions? Are they your cousins too?'

'Only two of them. The others are just friends.'

'I see. We are indebted to you for their presence here, I imagine. I wonder that you did not think to tell me of the relationship.'

'It didn't seem important at the time. Does it matter to you?'

'Of course it does not matter, Mr Hatton, but I dislike mysteries, and most of all I hate deceit.'

'My apologies, ma'am. You needed customers. I mentioned merely that a drive into the country might amuse these bucks, and that Bess's food was better than most. Does that displease you? It seems innocent enough to me.'

'I have learned that nothing is innocent in your actions, sir. There is always an ulterior motive.'

'Dear me! What can it be on this occasion? A delightful skating party? You said yourself that you have enjoyed it.'

'You are impossible!' she said with feeling as she stalked indoors.

Matthew came to her at once. 'Two gentlemen have been asking to see you, ma'am. I've put them in the snug.'

'Very well.' Caught off guard, Sophie was untroubled by this news. The damaged coach must have been repaired and the gentlemen had come to settle their account.

She set aside her bonnet, her tippet and her gloves, straightening her hair as she walked towards the snug. Then she stopped short at the mention of her own name.

'This Mistress Firle? Can you trust her?' a harsh voice enquired.

'It is unnecessary. I don't trust any woman. Sufficient to say that we persuade her to fall in with our plans.'

'I don't like it. You should not have brought me here. This is no part of our agreement.'

'You are happy enough to share in the profits,' his companion observed. 'Remember, no investment is without some risk.'

'Risk? What risk? You said there was none. Certainly I won't risk my neck—'

'You have already done so, my dear sir. There is but one penalty for treason.'

'And you have brought me down here? Our friends won't like it.'

'Our friends will understand the reason for it when I explain. I need you here today to lend a certain air of authenticity to my claim to own the cargo stored here. If I'm not mistaken, Mistress Firle is not a fool. She will need convincing.'

'You are very nice with your dealings with a slip of a girl,' his companion growled. 'If this place had been as empty as you promised, we might have been away by now.'

Sophie heard a sigh of exasperation. 'In broad daylight? Sometimes I think that you don't understand that nature of our business. Secrecy is essential.'

'I know it well. My name must be kept out of this. I may already have been recognised.'

'By whom? Our injured travellers in the parlour? I doubt if they move in our circles.' His sarcastic tone goaded his companion into a furious reply.

'You think yourself mighty clever, don't you, Harward? Don't it strike you as strange that two young women, both widows of Revenue Men, should be living under the same roof?'

'Not in the least. Many of these people know each other. Most probably they sought comfort in each other's company. I am surprised that you recognised Tyler's wife…er…widow. Are you acquainted with her?'

'I met her years ago, at her father's house in Dover. She was a child then, but that face is not easily forgotten.'

'I doubt if she'd remember you, and if she did, what can it signify? Why should she suspect a respectable businessman of dealings in illicit goods? You note that I am describing your activities in the kindest light?'

His companion was unconvinced. 'There are others here. Listen to the commotion! The noise is like to deafen a quiet man—'

'Come now, let us be done with this.' The man known as Harward was losing patience. 'You will not tell me that you fear young bucks, scarce out of leading strings? They frequent this place, merely because it is so close to Brighton.'

Sophie began to breathe more easily. Hatton had been wise to encourage the party of young bloods to visit the inn. In their midst, his own presence would be less conspicuous.

'I hope you may be right. Now, where is this Mistress Firle of yours? I'll do what you require of me. Then I must be away.'

'Leaving others to protect your back?' his companion suggested smoothly.

Sophie judged it time to enter the room before a serious quarrel could result. As she did so, Harward rose to his feet and came towards her with a concerned expression. He made her a deep bow.

'Mistress Firle, you remember me, I trust. Simon Harward, at your service.'

'I do, sir.' Sophie's heart was pounding as she faced the man she feared so much. 'I trust I find you well?'

'Well enough, I thank you, but it is your own health which concerns me. You have recovered from that unfortunate incident? I confess it has been much upon my mind…'

'It is forgotten, but I thank you for your interest, Mr Harward. Will you not present your friend?'

'Ah, yes, I had quite forgot my manners, ma'am. This is Mr Horace Sayles, a merchant and one of those gentlemen who keeps the wheels of commerce turning in the city.'

Sophie found herself under inspection from a pair of eyes which would not have shamed Caligula. Pebble-hard, they fixed her with a basilisk gaze. The man himself was short and squat, almost as broad as he was tall, but she guessed that the expensive coat hid muscle rather than fat.

His bow was perfunctory and he did not speak.

Harward took Sophie's hand and led her to a chair.

'My dear ma'am, pray don't think me forward, but I meant it when I mentioned my concern for you. I know of your sad loss…a tragedy for one so young…but is it wise for you to stay here alone, exposed to such unwelcome attentions as befell you the other day?'

'Sir, I have no choice.' Sophie was very much on her dignity. 'This is my home and also my livelihood. Where else would I go?'

'May I offer the suggestion that you sell the inn? Mr Sayles here might possibly be interested. His property investments are extensive.'

Sophie was silent. Three weeks ago she would have jumped at the chance to sell, but since then she had learned that the inn was not hers to dispose of. She became aware that both men were awaiting her answer.

'I...had not thought of it,' she faltered. 'I have no one to advise me. Will you give me time to consider your proposition?'

Sayles rose to his feet and walked over to the window. His impatience was evident, but Harward's manner did not change.

'Of course, my dear. This is a big decision for you. Naturally, you are wondering why we have approached you quite so soon?' He paused, and Sophie realised that he was weighing his words with care. 'The thing is, Mistress Firle, that we had an arrangement with your late husband. For a consideration he allowed us to store our surplus cargoes in your cellars.'

Sophie managed to look suitably astonished. 'We keep our ales and spirits in the cellars, sir. I have seen nothing else...'

'I don't expect you would,' he said agreeably. 'The entrance is concealed. Your husband insisted that it should be so. There is always the danger of pilfering, as he knew.'

'He said nothing of this to me,' she protested. 'Do you tell me that you have goods there at this moment?'

'We have!' The blue eyes rested earnestly upon her face. 'There is a danger that some of it may perish if it is left too long. Lace, for example, may rot in damp conditions.'

'I wonder that you should have chosen our cellars, Mr Harward. More suitable warehousing might have been found elsewhere.'

'You are quite right.' Harward sighed heavily. 'Sadly, Brighton is so overcrowded that every inch of space is taken. This is one reason why Mr Sayles proposes to buy the inn. There is little point in importing goods if one cannot store them safely.'

Sophie looked at the bland face. This was a clever man. He was so plausible. If Hatton had not warned her, she might have believed his every word.

An exclamation from his friend drew him to the window, but Sophie could not hear the whispered words which passed between them.

'Who is the tall gentleman?' Harward asked in casual tones. 'I think that I may know him.'

Sophie's blood ran cold. Almost paralysed with fright, she forced herself to join him at the window, knowing full well that Hatton must be the object of his interest.

That gentleman was strolling across the stable-yard with Kit settled happily on his shoulders.

'Do you think so, sir?' Her voice was surprisingly calm. 'Mr Hatton has but recently returned from the Peninsular War. You must have known him years ago.'

'A soldier, and one of our brave lads? I must be mistaken, ma'am. What a charming sight, to be sure. The gentleman looks very much at home here...' The keen eyes scanned her face.

Sophie willed herself to blush, but she could manage only a demure expression. 'I refused him then, but now that I am widowed he hopes...that is...' Her voice died away in confusion.

'Most understandable,' Harvard comforted her. 'Am I to wish you happy, ma'am?'

'Oh, no! Not yet! It is too soon. A widow cannot...I mean, I must not offer him encouragement before the year is out.'

'And then?'

'I am not sure, sir. It may be that I shall have no option.'

'On the contrary, my dear there is always an option, if one wishes to take advantage of it.'

Sophie stared at him. 'I don't know what you mean,' she said.

'Let me assure you, ma'am, it is nearly always a mistake to enter into wedlock merely to secure one's future. There are other ways for a sensible woman to earn a comfortable living.'

'Perhaps so, but I do not know of them.'

'Why, it is simple, Mistress Firle. If you decide to stay on here, we could pay you rent for the use of your cellars. We ship only the most valuable of cargoes, so the rent would be correspondingly high. Indeed, we owe you money at this present time.'

He drew out a large roll of notes and laid them upon the table.

Sophie gasped. 'Great heavens! Surely that is far too much?'

'Not at all, my dear. Now, if we might make some arrangements to move the goods?'

Sophie was seized with a spirit of mischief.

'Certainly, Mr Harward. I must imagine that you will wish to arrange for wagons immediately. They can't move when the ground is sodden. Shall we say tomorrow morning?'

For the first time Harward looked non-plussed. Then he recovered himself.

'You are right about the roads,' he agreed. 'I believe we should move whilst this frost holds. Darkness is not ideal for travelling, but we may have rain by morning.'

'Will you show me the entrance to this cellar?' Sophie asked in apparent innocence. 'I find it difficult to believe that it exists when I did not know of it.'

As she had expected, Harward was fully conversant

with the layout of the cellars. As she watched, he strode towards the hidden entrance and motioned her inside.

'You see the value of these goods, ma'am? Believe me, we have not overpaid you.'

'Will it not be difficult for you to carry them up the staircase and through the inn?'

'I think not, Mistress Firle. There is another exit some few hundred yards beyond the inn. All that we ask is that you allow one man entry to this cellar. He will unbolt the doors beyond.'

'I see.'

'I felt sure you would. Now you shall not trouble yourself further. Leave the rest to us. We have no wish to disturb your slumbers tonight.'

Sophie found that her hands were trembling. The man must think her a fool. What woman would accept such a cock-and-bull story? It must be clear to anyone of intelligence that this was a smuggling operation.

Sophie fingered the roll of notes in her pocket, and then she understood. Harward was under no illusions. If she had guessed at the truth of the matter, she had been paid to hold her tongue. Whether or not she believed him was not of any importance.

She led the way out of the cellars to find Matthew waiting for her. He was trembling with anxiety.

Sophie frowned a warning at him. At the sight of her companions he looked like a rabbit transfixed by a snake. Strangely, his terror stiffened her own resolve.

'Yes?' she said sharply. 'What is it, Matthew?'

'It's the folk in the parlour, mistress. Their coach has been repaired and they are wishing to be on their way after settling their account.'

'Tell them I'll be with them in a moment.' Sophie

turned back to her companions to find Harward gazing thoughtfully at the retreating Matthew.

'Your servant seems to be of a nervous disposition,' he observed.

To her own great relief, Sophie managed a girlish laugh.

'My dear sir, you must know what country people are like. They are suspicious of all strangers.'

'An unfortunate characteristic in his circumstances, ma'am.'

Sophie was on her dignity at once. 'Mr Harward, I cannot run this place alone. Help is not readily available. Both Matthew and his wife are loyal to me.'

Harward was all apologies. 'Pray forgive me, madam. I did not mean to criticise. It is just that…well…one wonders if the man would defend you should the need arise?'

'Now I see what you are about!' Sophie's glance was coy. 'You are trying to frighten me in the hope that I will sell to you…'

She heard a jovial laugh. 'You are too shrewd for me, my dear young lady. Now, are we agreed that you will open the cellar doors tonight?'

Sophie made a pretty show of hesitation. 'I don't know what to say,' she admitted in apparent confusion. 'Oh, dear! You will think me as suspicious as my servant, but do you have some paper to show your title to these goods?'

She heard a snort of anger from his companion.

'No, ma'am.' Harward's look was enough to put a stop to any further demonstration of ill will. 'Your late husband did not think it necessary. We had a gentleman's agreement.'

Gentlemen indeed! Sophie almost choked with indignation.

'Then I suppose I must take your word for it,' she told him grudgingly.

'I cannot blame you for your caution,' Harward continued. 'But consider, Mistress Firle. How could I know of the entrance to the cellar or find the key to the door if we had not used the place before?'

'Of course! I had not thought of that. How foolish you must think me.'

Harward bowed. 'Not at all. Caution is an admirable quality. It must always serve you well.'

Sophie appeared to be satisfied. 'When shall you wish the outer door to be opened?' she asked.

'Shall we say…at any time after six this evening. It will take us some time to arrange for wagons and ponies.'

And it will also be full dark by then and the moon will not be up, Sophie thought to herself. 'Anything else?' she enquired. 'Shall you wish that my servants help you?'

Pure mischief had caused her to ask the question and his answer did not surprise her.

'We should not dream of troubling you or them,' came the smooth reply. 'We have men enough of our own. There is, however, one further matter…'

'Yes, Mr Harward?'

'May I stress the need for discretion? This arrangement with your husband was not known to others…not even to your servants, I believe. We thought it better so. Word gets about in the most curious ways and we do not care to offer a target to any of the lawless bands who roam the countryside. Best to keep all your shutters closed tonight.'

Sophie was staggered by his effrontery, but she kept her countenance.

'Then, gentlemen, if you will excuse me? My customers are waiting.'

Harward made her a deep bow. 'A pleasure to do business with you, Mistress Firle. We shall not bid you good-bye, but merely *au revoir*.' With that he took his companion by the arm and strode away.

Sophie's eyes were sparkling with excitement. Now, at last, she had news for Hatton, but first she must see her customers on their way. She was too absorbed to notice that the partially opened door at the far end of the smug now closed without a sound.

The injured travellers were generous in their thanks, and also with their tips. Sophie tried to hide her impatience for them to be gone. Then she summoned Matthew.

'Will you find Mr Hatton for me?' she asked.

'No need! Matthew came to fetch me when you went into the cellars...' Hatton's expression was a curious mixture of pride and anxiety. 'Are you all right, my dear?'

'Of course I am!' Sophie could not wait to tell him her news. 'You were right! They plan to move the goods tonight.'

'So soon?' Hatton grew thoughtful. 'Matthew said that there were two of them. Who was our friend's companion?'

'Harward introduced him as a Mr Horace Sayles.'

Hatton gave a low whistle of surprise. 'Indeed? Now we are getting somewhere. What could have brought him into the open?'

'He offered to buy the inn.' Sophie gave him a mischievous look. 'I almost sold it to him.'

Hatton chuckled as he looked down at the vivid little face. 'Now you are making game of me,' he accused. 'What did you say to him?'

'I told both gentlemen that it was too serious a decision for a foolish little woman, with no one to advise her.'

She heard a shout of laughter. 'Did they believe you? If so, they can't be much of a judge of character.'

'Why, thank you, Mr Hatton!' Sophie dimpled at him. 'To be honest, I don't know if they believed me, but they made me another offer.'

'And what was that?'

'They wished to make me their associate. You were seen, you know, and they questioned me about you. I explained your lovelorn condition, but Mr Harward was at some pains to assure me that to marry for security alone was always a mistake. There were other ways for a lady to secure her future.'

Hatton's face darkened. 'They insulted you?'

'Of course not!' Sophie was puzzled. Then she understood him. 'Neither gentleman was looking for a companion, sir. They suggested that I continue the so-called "gentleman's agreement" which they had enjoyed before...before...'

'Before Firle was killed?'

Sophie swallowed hard and nodded.

'And what did you say?'

'I did as you suggested and was not too eager to fall in with their plans. I made a number of objections, but Harward was most persuasive. He even gave me this!' She took out the roll of notes and laid it on the table. 'It is a large amount of money. I don't know what to do with it.'

'Keep it! You have earned it!' Hatton was surprisingly abrupt.

'Is something wrong? I thought you'd be pleased.' Sophie's sense of achievement vanished.

'Of course I'm pleased. You have done well. I am only sorry that you had to be the one to deal with them.'

'I'm not!' Her tone was defiant. 'If you must know, I

enjoyed it. Oh, I was afraid at first, but it was not so difficult to play the part of a nincompoop.'

'Try not to get a taste for danger, Mistress Firle. These men are ruthless. From what I know of Harward, he is not easily taken in, and nor is Sayles. It may have suited them to appear to believe you.'

'Well, sir, I am glad to hear that you don't believe that I can play the part of a nitwit!' Sophie's tone was acid. She'd been proud of the way she'd played her part, but Hatton had dismissed her efforts out of hand.

'On the contrary...sometimes you play it to perfection, ma'am...and not always when you intend to do so.'

He was teasing her again and Sophie bristled. 'You are the most ungrateful wretch I know,' she cried.

'Am I?' He reached out and took her hands in his. 'Never think that of me. I am in your debt for life.'

The warmth in his voice brought hot colour flooding to her cheeks and she drew her hands away.

'What will you do now?' she said in a low voice.

'I think we must be ready for them. They will be allowed to get away from here. Then we will follow them to London. Sayles and his friends will be anxious to reap the rewards of this consignment after all these weeks. I shall hope to attend their meeting.'

Sophie's hand flew to her mouth. 'Will that not be much too dangerous?'

'It won't be without risk,' he agreed. 'But with any luck we shall catch all our birds in the same trap.'

'Is...is there anything I can do?'

'No, my dear. Your part in this is finished. Just do as they suggested. Say nothing to any of your servants, and keep all the shutters closed tonight.'

Sophie felt deflated. The part she'd played in Hatton's plans now seemed insignificant. His quarry would be caught, then tried and sentenced, and she might never know the outcome.

'You feel, then, that nothing will go wrong?' she asked.

'One can never be sure. There is always the chance of the unexpected...'

Suddenly she was seized with terror. 'Suppose you should lose them?' she cried.

'Then we must try again, but this is a huge consignment, Sophie. Neither men nor wagons will be easy to conceal upon the road.'

This time she did not reprove him for the use of her given name. Indeed, she barely noticed.

'That is not to say that they won't know they are being followed,' she insisted. 'At the first sign of danger Harward and Sayles will disappear. Dear God, they may come back to find out how they were betrayed.'

Hatton rested his hands upon her shoulders and shook her gently. 'Do you suppose that I haven't considered the possibility, my dear? Each of them will have two men to watch him at all times.'

'But they are clever. They could still elude you.' Sophie looked up at him and suddenly she was in his arms, held close against his chest.

'Would I let harm come to you?' Hatton's voice was raw with passion, muffled against her hair. 'Look at me, Sophie! Surely you must know by now...' His mouth came down on hers.

This time she could not doubt him. This was no part played to deceive her servants. His lips were warm against her own, at first gentle, and then insistent, willing her to respond to him.

Sophie melted into the spell of that embrace. Her arms reached up to circle his neck as she gave herself without restraint. Their mutual passion was dizzying in its strength, and she was breathless when he released her.

It was only to hold her away from him as he looked long into her eyes. Then he began to kiss her again, caressing her eyelids and the corners of her mouth with the lightest of a butterfly touch.

Sophie turned her head to find his lips again, but he held her at arm's length.

'Well, now you know, my love!' he told her in mock despair. 'I had hoped to wait until a more suitable time before declaring myself.'

Radiant with happiness, Sophie could not resist the chance to tease him. 'You have not done so, sir. I am at a loss to understand your strange behaviour.'

'Witch!' he tugged at a straying curl. 'What of your own, you shameless hussy? It was unkind in you to lead me on—'

'*I* led *you* on? Why, you wicked wretch! You kissed me without a by-your-leave.'

'So I did. It had escaped my notice, ma'am, that I should ask your permission first. But now I have another question for you. Will you be my wife?'

Too overcome to speak, she held out her hands to him and he saw the tears sparkling on her lashes.

'My dearest love?' he protested as he wiped them away.

'They are tears of happiness,' she assured him.

Chapter Ten

Still uncertain whether to laugh or cry, Sophie looked deep into Hatton's eyes.

'This can't be happening!' she whispered. 'I don't believe it. Am I dreaming, or have I really agreed to become your wife?'

'I hope so, my dear.' Hatton held her closer to his heart. 'Otherwise I shall be deeply shocked. Seated upon my knee, and with your arms about my neck, you are in a most compromising situation.' He chuckled as he nuzzled his lips to her cheek.

Sophie blushed as she struggled to free herself. 'We must be mad!' she cried.

'Of course we are! But love is sweet madness, is it not?' His arm stayed firmly about her waist.

'But I did not think that you…I mean, I had no idea that—?'

'That I cared for you, my darling? Sophie, you must be blind!' He began to laugh. 'There isn't a soul within this place who hasn't been convinced of it for days.'

'But you said that you were play-acting…'

'I lied, my love.'

'Oh! When did you first realise…that it wasn't simply a part of your plan?'

'It was never part of my plan to fall in love with you, and I struggled against it mightily, but to no avail. I was lost from the first moment I saw you, though I did not know it at the time.'

'I thought that you disliked me,' she said in a small voice.

'Then I must be a better actor than I had imagined. I was unsure of you, my darling, and, speaking of dislike, I did not dare to hope that you could ever care for me. I have treated you so ill…' His face grew sombre.

Shyly, Sophie reached up and pressed her lips into the hollow of his neck. 'That isn't true! I didn't understand at first, and that was why I fought you. Now I know that you only did your duty.'

'Drawing a woman…any woman…into danger is a most unpleasant duty. I hated threatening to turn you out of your home, and playing upon your fears for Kit. I'm not proud of my actions.'

'You should be, sir, especially as they must have cost you dear.'

A large hand ruffled her hair. 'Sophie, do you feel that you could unbend sufficiently to call me Nicholas? It is my given name, you know, and we cannot continue to stand upon formality.'

'I'll try!' The colour flooded her face once more. 'It will seem strange. I know so little about you.'

'Not true! Aside from the fact that I have three cousins, you are well aware that I am an unfeeling, deceitful and arrogant brute. In fact, the ideal husband!'

Laughing, Sophie hid her face in his coat. 'Did I really say all that?' she whispered.

'You did, and more besides. I wonder that I had the

temerity to make you an offer. It took some courage, I can tell you.'

'What persuaded you to speak?' she asked in muffled tones.

'Sheer desperation, my love. I'd resisted it so often, believing that you'd laugh me to scorn, but today, when I took you in my arms, I thought there might be hope for me.'

'You know it, Nicholas. When you kissed me…well…I too was lost. Oh, my dear, is this not sheer folly? You have given me no time to think…to consider…'

'What is there to consider? If we love each other, that should be enough. Do you love me, Sophie?'

'I do, with all my heart, but it has come as a shock. I might have suspected, if I'd had any sense at all, but I never thought of it. I missed you dreadfully when you went away, but I told myself that it was because I'd been left without protection.'

'You had my men here,' he protested with a smile.

'It wasn't the same. I needed to see you, to be with you, and to know that you were close at hand.' She gave a rueful sigh. 'In these matters, Kit is wiser than I am myself. He thinks the world of you.'

'I am the luckiest man alive!' Hatton raised her hand to his lips. 'Sophie, this must be our secret for the moment. If Harward were to hear of our betrothal, you might be in danger.'

'How so?' Sophie was puzzled.

'At this present time he believes you to be without protection and vulnerable. With no one to advise you, you have fallen in with all his plans. The prospect of an imminent marriage for you will not suit him in the least.'

'But I'd still allow him to move his cargo,' she objected.

'A husband might not be so gullible.'

'I could promise not to speak of it.'

'You think he would believe you? You must have heard of pillow-talk, my dear. Harward would think it more than likely that you would confide in your beloved. He won't risk it.'

Sophie's eyes widened. 'You believe that he might try to stop me?'

'You know too much, my darling. Let him continue to believe that you have not thought of marriage. All that concerns you is a secure future for yourself and Kit.'

'Are you talking about me?' Kit came into the room and stared. 'Hatton, why do you hug Mama? Has she given you a present?'

'The best present in the world, Kit, but it is a secret. We shall tell you of it in a day or two.'

Kit was too full of his own concerns to object. He walked towards Sophie with his arms stretched out before him. In his upturned hands he held a box.

'I have a present for you, Mama. I made it myself.'

Sophie looked down at the jewel-like object resting in the folds of paper. It was a brightly coloured fishing fly.

'This is truly beautiful,' she exclaimed. 'Did you really make it, Kit? It must have been very difficult.'

'It was,' he admitted. 'Reuben made me do it six times. I nearly gave up, but he said—'

'Yes?' Hatton prompted.

'He said I'd do it in the end, and I did.'

'You did indeed, my darling, and I shall treasure it.'

'It might make a brooch, Mama, or you could wear it in your hat.' Kit climbed on Hatton's knee and dropped a kiss upon his cheek.

'I'd like another one of those,' Hatton told him.

Chubby arms encircled his neck as Kit obliged. Then he looked at his mother. 'I love Hatton,' he said.

'Better than Reuben?' Sophie teased.

Kit's reply required long and careful thought. 'Both the same,' he said at last.

'I see that I am promoted,' Hatton chuckled.

'Then you must take care that you are worthy of your god-like status,' Sophie joined in the joke.

It warmed her heart to see the loving relationship between her son and this stranger who had appeared so unexpectedly in their midst.

Not for the first time she mused on the caprice of fate. Three weeks ago she'd had no idea that Hatton existed. Almost crushed by the blows that life had dealt her she'd felt numb with misery and only half-alive. Now she contemplated her future in a daze of happiness. All her doubts were stilled.

What she had mistaken for dislike had been an unwillingness to commit herself to love for a second time. How she'd fought against it, refusing to see any merit in this man who now possessed her soul.

When had she changed? She couldn't quite decide. She'd even suspected Hatton's kindness to her child, believing that he must have some ulterior motive. It had taken time to convince her that this apparently unfeeling brute had a gentler side to his nature.

Now Kit was playing with the fobs on his watch-chain. 'Could you skate when you were as old as me?' he asked.

'No! I learned later when I went to Holland. The men there race each other along the frozen canals in winter. I wanted to try it.'

'I'd like to see them. Will you take me one day?'

'One day. You have my word on it.'

'Promise?' Kit's face was solemn.

'It's a promise.' Hatton set the child down. 'Sophie, I must go. There is much to do before tonight. We can't risk mistakes. I may not see you for some time.'

Sophie couldn't hide her dismay. So much had been left unsaid. She wanted to assure him of her love once more, to say that he would be always in her thoughts, and to beg him to be careful. She turned to Kit.

'Will you ask Bess if she has some food for us, my pet? Mr Hatton has to leave quite soon. He must not be delayed.'

Kit's face fell. 'Hatton, you *will* come back, won't you?' His lower lip was trembling.

'Nothing is more certain.' Hatton held out his hand to the child. 'Take care of your mother, Kit. I shall be back before you know it.'

'Must you take Reuben too?'

'Yes, but we shan't be gone for long. For the time being you must rely on Bobbo to keep you company.'

Kit's face cleared. Then, humming a little tune, he hopped out of the room on one foot.

Troubled though she was, Sophie was forced to smile.

'That's the sign of a particularly happy day for Kit, my dear.'

'The hopping and the singing? Perhaps I should follow his example. It is certainly a particularly happy day for me.' His expression was quizzical as he looked at her.

'I beg that you will not. There are many fragile objects in this room. I should not care to see them broken.' Sophie's laughter did not reach her eyes. She knew what he was about. The joke was an effort to lift the tension in the air.

Now she wanted to throw herself into his arms and beg him not to leave her. It took all her self-control not to do so. Her throat was dry and she found it difficult to speak, but she managed it at last.

'I was surprised to hear you speak of Bobbo. When did Kit tell you of his imaginary friend?'

'It was at our first meeting. Since then he joins us every day. A difficult chap, this Bobbo! He and I do argue on occasion. He has some curious notions as to what is best for Kit, but between us Reuben and I have Bobbo well in hand.'

Sophie burst into tears.

'What is it, my love?' Tenderly, Hatton took her in his arms. 'Are my jokes as bad as that?'

'Don't!' she sobbed. 'Pray don't make light of what you are about to do. I'm so afraid for you...'

'I shan't be alone, Sophie, and you've seen my bruisers. Don't they give you pause? Personally, I shouldn't care to meet them in a dark alley if they were my enemies.' He slipped a finger beneath her chin and raised her face to his. 'They'd lay down their lives for me, you know, but hopefully that won't be necessary.'

'But you will be careful?' she pleaded.

'Yes!' His ardent gaze brought the colour to her cheeks. 'I have much to live for. Don't trouble your head about me. Now, for your own part, you will remember my instructions?'

Too overcome to speak, she nodded.

'No heroics, mind! Follow Harward's plan to the letter. It will take courage to go into the cellars and open the outer door, but you alone can do it. You may be under observation and Matthew must not be seen to have any knowledge of the store. Everyone must be warned beforehand to keep their shutters closed. They must be blind and deaf to any sound outside the inn in the early hours. We have come too far to risk a mishap now.'

He took Sophie in his arms once more. 'Don't be afraid!' he urged. 'These men need you, Sophie. They have no reason to distrust you. They believe you to be a willing accomplice. You won't be in the slightest danger as long as you follow their instructions. Open the outer door, don't look back, and then go to your room.'

Then his mouth found hers and she melted into his embrace, her arms about his neck.

'Come back to me!' she whispered. 'I couldn't live without you.'

'You worry too much!' He dropped a kiss upon the tip of her nose. 'Take heart, my love. All this will soon be over. Then it will fade from your memory like a bad dream.'

'I pray that you are right.' She clung to him once more in a last embrace. Then she disengaged herself. 'Come,' she said. 'You must eat before you leave. You shall not go away unfed.'

Her smile was uncertain, and, looking at her, Hatton knew that she was trying to bring her courage to the sticking point.

'The sooner I go, the quicker I shall return,' he told her lightly. 'Shall we join the others?'

They found a merry party at the dining-table and Sophie saw to her surprise that Kit was with them, propped up on several cushions to bring him level with his plate.

Any fears she might have had about his normally finicky appetite were soon dispelled. Too absorbed in chatter to quibble, he demolished a bowl of mutton stew almost without noticing.

So much for coaxing him into eating just another mouthful, she thought wryly. Evidently the thing to do was to ignore the problem and leave him to it. Her son was leading a most unusual life. Other children of his age would have been banished to a nursery and warned that they might be seen but not heard at a set time each day.

Well, it would not do for her, no matter how unconventional her treatment of her son might appear to others. These years of childhood were too precious. Kit must feel always that he could come to her and join in whatever life she could offer him.

She looked at Hatton, half-fearing to see a look of disapproval, but he was smiling broadly at Kit.

'You've joined the other men, I see.' He drew out a chair for Sophie. 'Are you keeping them in order?'

'We are thinking of making Kit the president of our club,' the man named Wentworth told him. 'A magician must take first place. Don't you agree?'

'Undoubtedly!' Hatton peered at his plate. 'This stew now. It could be from an ancient recipe. What do you say, Kit? Will it turn us into tadpoles?'

Kit was too convulsed with glee to answer him. It was Wentworth who replied.

'My dear sir, you need not fear to eat the dish. Kit murmured an incantation before we took a bite. Any spell there may have been is broken.'

Hatton looked at the grave face and his shoulders began to shake. He bent his head and began to eat.

Sophie too was trying hard to hide her laughter. At the same time she was warmed by the kindness of the young men about her table. Clearly, they had made it their business to take an interest in her son, and she liked them for it.

Their banter was both witty and entertaining, and gradually she was persuaded to join in. Later she was surprised to find that she too had cleared her plate almost without noticing.

Slowly and imperceptibly her spirits lifted, and by the time they took their leave of her she was able to return their thanks with the assurance that she had enjoyed their company.

Hatton, she noticed with a pang, had decided to leave with them. Throughout the meal she had watched him closely as he spoke to the other men. He'd given no indication that Wentworth and two of the others were his cousins. As far as her servants were concerned the gentlemen were travellers met together in the casual way of customers at any hostelry.

She schooled her own expression to no more than friendliness as she watched the little party ride away. Then she went back to the parlour.

As always the place seemed empty without Hatton. Life was very strange, she mused. Call it fate, or luck, or chance…whatever it was, she could only wonder at the quirk of fortune which had led her to this point in her circumstances. A delay of only half an hour would have caused her to miss the visit of Richard Firle to her father's home all those years ago.

If she hadn't fallen in love with him on sight, she might have married any one of half a dozen suitors for her hand. Somewhere she had read that human beings were no more than playthings of the gods. They had been more than ordinarily capricious in her own case if that were so.

Then she dismissed the thought. Chance might play a part in determining one's future, she decided, but human beings always had a choice. She'd chosen Richard, and it had been a mistake, but now she had been given a second chance to find happiness. She would not let it go.

Her ill-starred marriage had brought her to this place, but without it she would not have had Kit, nor would she have met Hatton. Perhaps in time the gods grew tired of cruelty and decided to relent.

She was still lost in thought when Abby came to find her.

'Will you come to the kitchen, Mistress Firle? Me and Mother...well...we're that worried!'

'What is it, Abby? Everyone enjoyed their meal. No one found fault with it, though mutton stew is not a favourite of mine. Only your mother can make it taste delicious.'

Abby did not answer her question. She shook her head and set off for the kitchen without further comment. There she walked over to her mother's side and both women turned to face their mistress.

Sophie knew at once that there was something sadly wrong.

'Has someone been hurt?' she asked anxiously. 'What is it, Bess? Pray don't keep me in suspense.'

'You'd best sit down,' the woman told her bluntly. 'What I have to say won't please you.'

'Very well. I'm waiting...'

'It's Nancy Tyler, mistress.'

Sophie sighed with relief. 'Is that all? Have you quarrelled with her? If she isn't doing her work, I'll speak to her myself.'

'That isn't all, ma'am. She works too hard if anything. Fair runs herself into the ground, she does. 'Tis the nights, you see.'

'What on earth do you mean? Does Nancy go out at night? She needs no permission to do so...she may like to walk.'

'She don't go out.' Bess's mouth set in a tight line. 'She locks herself in her room.'

'Bess, she is entitled to some privacy. I wonder that you begrudge it to her.'

Bess shook her head. 'You don't understand. Abby, you had best tell the mistress what you saw.'

'I weren't spying, Mistress Firle,' the girl said in her own defence, 'but Nancy's room is next to mine. She talks all night, and I can't sleep.'

Sophie frowned at her. 'Nancy has had a tragic life. No doubt she has bad dreams. Won't you be patient for a while? In time she may not suffer so—'

'She weren't dreaming, ma'am. She were quieter when she came here, but I could hear her clearly. At first I thought she had someone in the room with her…it were like…well, like a conversation with another person.'

'That can't be so,' Sophie protested. 'Nancy has no friends here whom she might ask to visit her.'

'No, ma'am, I know that.' Abby was clearly uncomfortable, but a look from her mother urged her on. 'I didn't know what she were up to, so I…well, I took the knot out of the wall.'

'You did what? Must you speak in riddles, Abby. I don't know what you mean.'

''Tis a loose knot in the wooden panelling.' Bess answered for her daughter. 'It gives a sight of the other room.'

'I wonder that it was not sealed long ago,' Sophie cried in indignation. 'Anyone might have watched the maids if they knew of it.'

Bess avoided Sophie's eye. 'Well, it weren't sealed up,' she said. 'And now, when you hear what Abby has to say, you might think it for the best.'

Sophie felt sickened and disgusted. It did not need Bess to tell her for whose benefit the peephole had remained unsealed. Richard must have watched the girls dressing and undressing as the fancy took him.

'Go on!' she said faintly.

'Well, ma'am, I were that surprised. Nancy had a table laid for two, but there was no one there but her. She were talking to an empty chair as if it were a person, pouring wine and serving food. I thought it were some fancy game of hers, but then she began to cry and hold out her arms...I didn't watch no more.'

'I see. Has this happened more than once?'

''Tis every night now, mistress, and it's getting louder. She shouts and screams and cries and last night... well...she has a pistol. Waving it in the air, she was.'

'You should have told me of this before,' Sophie said sternly. 'I won't have firearms in the house. They could prove a danger to all of us.'

She was at pains to hide her anxiety about Nancy's state of mind. Those conversations seemed likely to be with the girl's dead husband and Sophie felt sick with horror. Clearly, Nancy fancied him to be still alive.

Now she blamed herself for this tragedy. She should have concerned herself far more with Nancy and less with her own problems. Hopefully, it was not too late to bring the girl back to reality. She smiled at Bess and Abby.

'I'm glad you told me. Nancy is in need of help. I'll speak to her today.' She rose as if to go, but Bess stayed her with a gesture.

'I'm sorry, ma'am, but you ain't heard the worst of it. There's more...' She signed to her daughter to go on.

By now the excitable Abby was subdued. 'Nancy has changed, ma'am. Last night the table wasn't laid and she didn't pour the wine. She sat by the fire with a bundle in her arms, and she was singing lullabies. Then she laid the bundle in a drawer, made up like a cot. She seems to think she has a baby now.'

Sophie's blood ran cold. This was a step too far. Nancy sounded seriously unhinged, and it would take someone far better qualified than Sophie to help her. Meantime, she could prove to be a danger to all of them, especially as she knew of Hatton's true identity. She might prove to be the ruin of his plans.

Drawing on all her courage, she made her way to Nancy's room to find the girl engaged in sewing.

'Leave that, Nancy, please!' she said. 'We need to talk.'

'Yes, Sophie?' The great blue eyes looked up at her with guileless innocence.

Sophie did not know where to start. 'Are you sleeping well?' she said lamely.

'I don't sleep! There is no need!' came the startling reply.

'Nancy, we all need to sleep, otherwise we get so tired. Then we begin to imagine things. Suppose we call the doctor. He will give you something to help you.'

'No! I need to keep my wits about me.' Nancy's look was furtive. 'I mustn't lower my guard.'

Sophie adopted a coaxing tone. 'Well, then, won't you come and sit with me? You might help me with my sewing.'

Nancy shook her head. 'I can't do that today. I mustn't leave my baby.' She gestured towards a shapeless bundle lying on blankets in a drawer beside the fire.

Sophie felt close to tears. The bundle bore no resemblance to a child. She swallowed hard.

'You might…you might bring the child with you,' she suggested. Nancy must not be left alone again in her present state of mind.

'No! He's safer here.' Nancy took the bundle in her

arms and began to croon a lullaby. 'Poor little one! He cried so hard last night, but he's quiet now.'

Sophie made a desperate effort to hide her alarm. It was clear that Nancy's mind had given way under the pressure of her grief at the loss of both her husband and her unborn child. She tried again.

'Come down to my room,' she urged. 'It's much too cold for you in here. You will take a chill.'

'Do you find it cold?' Nancy began to throw sticks upon the fire, smiling as it blazed. 'There, that's better! We shall be cosy now, won't we, my pet?' She looked down at the shapeless bundle with such tenderness that Sophie felt stricken to the heart.

She forced a smile. 'You are quite right, my dear. It's warmer now. May I come and share your fire with you?'

'If you like, but you won't harm my baby, will you?'

'Of course not, Nancy, I want to help you. Now I must fetch my things. Will you promise not to lock your door against me?'

A look of cunning flickered across the girl's face, but it vanished so quickly that Sophie wondered if she had imagined it. A nod was the only indication that Nancy had heard her.

Sophie was torn between unwillingness to leave her alone and the knowledge that she must summon the doctor without delay. Nancy's condition was beyond the help of a lay person.

Swiftly she ran down to the kitchen to find Matthew talking to his wife and daughter. She saw real anxiety in his eyes.

'How is she?' he asked.

'Nancy is very ill, I believe. Matthew, will you fetch the doctor?'

'I will if I can find him, mistress, but it is getting dark. Sometimes they comes for him at night.'

'They...who are they?' she cried impatiently.

'Why, the...free traders, ma'am.'

'You mean he treats these men? You surprise me. Surely a man in his position should inform the authorities as to their whereabouts?'

'They takes care that he can't do that, ma'am. He's always blindfolded before they leads him away.'

'He could still inform on them. It might be possible to set a trap.'

'He won't do that,' Matthew told her firmly. 'Not if a man is wounded.'

'Indeed!' Sophie was furious. 'A nice distinction, I must say. I wonder if he knows that a deranged mind is the result of the activities of his villainous patients.'

Bess stepped forward then and laid a hand on Sophie's arm. 'Ma'am, you are upset and its not to be wondered at. Matthew will fetch the doctor, as you say...' She jerked her head towards the door, but Matthew hesitated. Then he cast a look of appeal at Sophie.

'Mistress Firle, you will take care? If the girl is as sick as you say, she may be dangerous. Abby tells me that she has a gun... Mayhap you shouldn't be alone with her. We could lock her in her room.'

'I won't do that!' Sophie said with decision. 'Just be as quick as you can. The inn must be secured as soon as possible, with the shutters drawn and the doors bolted.'

Looking at her companions, she realised that these instructions came as no surprise to them. Hatton must have made his wishes clear before he left. Bess looked anxious and clearly Abby was terrified.

'Off you go!' she ordered as Matthew lingered by his womenfolk. 'Ben and his son may sleep indoors tonight.'

A look of gratitude was her reward. In the normal way of things the two men slept above the stables. Now even Abby looked relieved.

'Must I come with you to sit with Nancy?' she asked with some reluctance.

'I think not, Abby, though it is kind of you to offer. Later you may bring us something light for supper...perhaps a little broth? Has Nancy eaten anything today?'

'She ain't been out of her room all day,' Bess told her. 'I thought she must be sick. A girl like that...well, she wears a wedding ring but that's not to say she has a husband. Some man may have got her into trouble...'

'Nancy isn't pregnant, if that is what you're suggesting, Bess. If you must know it, she was widowed and the shock caused her to lose her unborn child.'

Bess flushed. 'We was not to know it,' she said defensively. 'She ain't spoken more than a word or two to any of us.'

'Why didn't you tell me?' Sophie cried. 'You must have sensed that there was something wrong.'

''Tweren't none of our affair if she chose to keep herself to herself. She did her work and that was good enough for me.'

Sophie stifled further reproach, knowing that she was more to blame than her servants. Hatton had accused her of being blind as far as his own feelings were concerned. She had been blind in regard to Nancy too. Now she must try to put things right as far as she was able.

She hurried back to the snug, only to find Nancy wasn't there. She went back upstairs and found Nancy sitting by the fire. Then she noticed that the bundle was still in its makeshift cot tucked up beneath a blanket.

Sophie sighed with relief. Nancy seemed much calmer

and her eyes were closed. The girl must be exhausted. Sleep might possibly restore her to a more rational frame of mind, Sophie thought without conviction.

Well aware that she was clutching at straws, she walked over to the window and stared out into the darkness. There was no sign of Matthew yet. Now she prayed that he would find the doctor. Tonight, above any other, she didn't need a sick woman upon her hands.

Too much lay ahead of her. Under other circumstances she would have sat with Nancy through the night, but if she were to play her part in Hatton's plan she would be forced to leave the girl for a time. When the doctor came she would insist upon a sedative for Nancy.

Wearily she reached out to close the shutters, but a voice at her shoulder made her jump.

'Don't!' Nancy cried sharply. 'I must watch for them.'

Startled almost out of her wits by the girl's stealthy approach, Sophie stepped back and collided with her. Then she froze. Nancy's hands were hidden within the folds of her skirt, but there could be no mistaking the fact that she was holding a pistol.

'Please give me that!' Sophie held out a shaking hand for the gun.

The girl seemed not to have heard her. 'They'll come tonight, you know. I listened to them talk…' Her voice was dreamy and her smile struck terror into Sophie's heart.

'Listen to me, Nancy! You are imagining things. A snatch of conversation can be misleading. It could have referred to anything.'

The glittering eyes rested on her with a look of pity. 'You didn't think so, Sophie. You agreed to all they said.'

Sophie stared at her. These flashes of lucidity made the girl's condition all the more frightening. It wouldn't be easy to deceive her, but how could she have known of Harward's plans?

Then she remembered the door at the far end of the snug. It had closed almost imperceptibly as she'd left the room with Harward and his companion. She'd paid no attention. If she'd thought of it at all, she'd have imagined that it had swung to of its own accord. She hadn't considered an eavesdropper.

Now she came to a quick decision. She laid a gentle hand on Nancy's arm. 'Let us sit down,' she said. 'I think we need to talk... I'll leave these shutters open for the moment. Then, if we hear anything untoward, we can look out through the window.'

Nancy appeared to be satisfied by this concession, but her hands remained hidden in her skirts, as Sophie busied herself with building up the fire.

It threw out little warmth as the grate was too small to hold more than a lump or two of coal and a few sticks. Comfort, as Sophie realised to her shame, had not been the first consideration in a servant's bedroom. Looking about her, she saw that it was bleak in the extreme, furnished only with a wooden-slatted bed covered by a thin mattress and a couple of worn blankets. The chair on which she sat had a broken strut and the chest in the corner leaned drunkenly on missing feet.

This miserable abode was where Nancy had been left to cope with her grief. It was little wonder that she had found no solace here.

'I'm sorry that you've been living under these conditions,' Sophie said gently. 'Why did you not tell me, Nancy? We could have made you much more comfortable.'

'I thought you knew. In any case, it did not matter. I

had a fire. At my last place the servants were forbidden to take fuel. You could freeze, however sick you were.'

I could have given her a room on the floor below, Sophie thought miserably, though it would have given rise to speculation by the other servants. Nancy's part in Hatton's scheme might have come to light if she'd been treated in a different way.

Sophie thrust aside her troubling regrets. It was important now to gain Nancy's trust, and every minute counted. The hours were passing quickly. It would not be long before she must go into the cellars to do Harward's bidding. She dared not risk the chance that Nancy might follow her.

'If you overheard our conversation, you will know that Mr Harward had an arrangement with my husband,' she said steadily. 'Some of his goods are stored in the cellars beneath the inn. He has asked if he might move this cargo. Is there anything strange in that?'

Nancy laughed in her face. 'Do you think me a fool?' she cried. 'I had not thought you stupid, Sophie. Why the secrecy? Why must they move these goods at night?'

'They are afraid of being ambushed,' Sophie faltered.

'By smugglers?' Nancy was growing hysterical. Her voice had risen to a shriek. Now she caught at Sophie's hands, crushing them in her own so hard that she threatened to break the bones.

'The truth now?' she demanded harshly. 'These men are the smugglers themselves, and you know it.'

Sophie disengaged herself with difficulty. There was little point in attempting to dissemble further.

'I suspect it,' she said carefully. 'But we can't be sure. That is why Mr Hatton intends to watch them—'

She heard a contemptuous laugh. 'His lordship is convinced, if you are not—'

'His lordship?' Sophie stared at her. 'I was speaking of Mr Hatton.'

'So was I? Didn't you know that he was heir to the Earl of Brandon? I thought he must have told you.'

Chapter Eleven

Sophie looked at the girl with pitying eyes. How on earth had Nicholas come to play a part in her strange fancies? Now she was at a loss as to what to say or do. Would it be best to appear to agree with her wild imaginings? There seemed little point in attempts to reason with her, but she could try.

'Perhaps you are thinking of someone else?' she suggested gently. 'What gave you the idea that Mr Hatton is a lord?'

'My father knew the Earl quite well before the old man was injured. They worked together for years to stop the smuggling trade.'

'That may be so, but why do you imagine that Mr Hatton is the Earl's heir?'

'I met him long ago in Kent. He came with Claudine and his father…'

'Claudine? Do you mean Madame Arouet?'

Nancy shrugged. 'I had forgot her other name. Now that the Countess is dead, it's said that she will marry the old Earl. She's been his friend for years.'

Sophie was seized with a feeling of dread. Nancy's story sounded plausible…too plausible…but she'd heard that the deranged could be extremely cunning. There might be some obscure motive behind these ridiculous suggestions, but for the moment Nancy sounded perfectly rational.

'I think you should rest,' she said firmly. 'Won't you lie down upon your bed? Give me your gun. I'll keep it safe for you.'

The faintest of smiles lifted the corners of Nancy's lips.

'You don't believe me, do you?' she challenged.

'I don't know what to believe, and nor, I suspect, do you. Now let us have an end to this nonsense, Nancy. Give me the gun...'

Very slowly, Nancy's hand appeared from within her skirts. As Sophie had guessed, she was holding a serviceable pistol. Sophie reached out to take it from her, but the girl's fingers closed convulsively about the weapon.

'No!' She shook her head. 'I need it. You must ask his lordship if you want one of your own.'

'I shouldn't dream of asking for a gun,' Sophie told her sharply. 'I've never fired a weapon in my life. Have you?'

The girl ignored her.

'Nancy, I think you have forgot. We have men here to protect us if danger threatens, though I think it is most unlikely.'

She heard a low chuckle, and the sound was chilling. 'They'll come tonight, but I'm ready for them. Listen!' She raised the pistol with a steady hand and aimed it at the door.

'No!' Sophie too had heard the approaching footsteps. Now her voice cracked on a high note of panic. 'That will be Abby with your supper. Let me talk to her!'

To her great relief, it was Abby who replied to her whispered question. She had brought the doctor.

'Wait, please!' Sophie was terrified as she turned to

face the upraised weapon. Nancy might fire at any man who entered the room. It took all her self-control to speak quietly and persuasively. Her mouth was so dry that she had to swallow several times before the words came out.

'The doctor is here,' she said. 'I hurt my ankle on the pond this morning. It's so painful, Nancy. You won't mind if he looks at it?'

'Is this a trick? These men are clever.'

'It's no trick. Come now, you know the doctor, my dear. He came to Bess when she burned her hand. Don't you remember?'

Nancy nodded. She lowered the gun, but she would not relinquish it. It stayed hidden in the pocket of her skirt.

Very slowly Sophie opened the door. Something in her face must have warned the doctor. He hesitated on the threshold.

'Thank heavens you are here,' Sophie felt that she was babbling. 'My ankle is so badly swollen. Can you give me something for the pain?'

He saw the desperation in her eyes and was quick to understand the reason for it. He didn't look at Nancy as he walked into the room.

'Sit down, Mistress Firle!' he said. 'Let us see if the ankle is broken.' He signalled to Abby to bring the candles closer. Then he placed a chair for Sophie so that he could study her companion whilst pretending to examine the foot.

Nancy turned her head away, but he didn't need to see her face to realise that she was close to breaking point. Her body was as taut as a bowstring.

Sophie gave an artistic wince as she removed her shoe. Then he examined her foot with every appearance of concern.

'Nothing broken, ma'am,' he told her cheerfully. 'But

this is a bad case. You must be very careful...' It was the clearest possible warning that Nancy was in a most dangerous state of mind.

Sophie's look was pleading. 'What must I do?' she asked.

'Rest is what is needed here, Mistress Firle. Rest and complete quiet. I'll give you a sedative. You won't find it unpleasant. Taken in a hot drink it is unnoticeable. You will sleep for hours.'

He rose to his feet and turned to Nancy. 'Is this your room?' he asked.

Nancy didn't answer him.

'What a pleasure it is to see a cosy fire,' he continued, apparently untroubled by her rudeness. 'Now, Mistress Firle, I must be on my way. I am called to a sick woman in the village. The poor wretched creature is without a single covering for her bed.'

Sophie understood him at once. 'We have bedding and to spare,' she cried. 'Let me find it for you. Abby, will you stay here to make up the fire again? I shall only be a moment.'

Abby looked about to refuse, but a stern glance from her mistress caused her to think better of it.

Sophie slipped out of the door and drew the doctor away to the far end of the landing.

'She mustn't hear us whispering. Oh, what am I to do? Doctor Hill, she has a gun...'

'I saw it, ma'am. Abby told me what has happened. Nancy's mind has gone, I fear. Without the gun we might have overpowered her, but the risk is now too great. She could fire at random. In any case, we cannot move her at this time of night.'

'This time of night?' Sophie glanced at the clock in the

hall below and realised to her horror that in less than an hour she must open the cellar doors.

'Will you give me the sedative?' she asked. 'I'll try to get her to take it at once.'

He opened his bag and thrust the preparation into her hand. 'The doses are made up, but don't give her more than one, ma'am. They are very strong. Too much can be dangerous.' His face was grave. 'Have you no one with you other than the servants? You are taking a serious risk. I think we should move the girl without delay. I'll try to arrange it for tomorrow.'

'Must you?' Sophie's look was pitiful. 'I couldn't bear to think of her confined to a madhouse. With care she may recover…'

He shook his head as he took his leave of her, and she hurried back to Nancy's room.

Abby was standing by the door, and, as Sophie reappeared, she shot out of the room. Sophie called her back again.

'Did I not mention that we'd like some broth? Please bring it up at once.'

Sophie awaited Abby's return with ill-concealed impatience. Time was running out. If Hatton's plan was to succeed she must make her way to the cellars within minutes.

'What took you so long?' she cried as she snatched the tray from her servant's hands.

'The broth wasn't ready, mistress. Mother made it fresh for you.' Abby was startled by the unexpected sharpness in Sophie's tone.

Turning her back on her companions, Sophie slipped the sedative into one of the bowls of steaming liquid.

'Now, Nancy, won't you try to eat?' she coaxed. 'You

will feel so much better if you do. Come now, just a sip or two to please me?'

Obediently, Nancy picked up her spoon. Then she cried out as her lips touched the scalding broth. 'It's too hot!' she whispered.

Sophie gave a despairing glance at the clock. If she hurried, she need not be away for more than a few minutes.

'Then let it cool. Abby, do you stay with Nancy. I shall be back at once, but I must see your father.'

Matthew was not far to seek. He was waiting for her by the cellar door.

'Give me the keys,' she demanded, 'then please go up to Nancy's room. You need not enter. Just stay by the door. Abby may have need of you.'

Matthew was torn with indecision, wondering whether Sophie or his daughter would be in the greatest danger.

'Nancy is quieter now,' Sophie comforted. 'I think you need not fear for Abby's safety. This is a precaution.'

'But what of you, ma'am?' he protested. 'Won't you go back upstairs? I will open the cellars. It's no task for a woman.'

'Do as you are bidden!' Sophie snapped. 'You know that this is all arranged.' She looked at his worried face and softened her tone. 'Think about it, Matthew! These men may be waiting by the entrance to the tunnel. They are expecting me, but no one else is supposed to know of their cargo. They might kill you on sight.'

Matthew paled, but he persisted. 'It's too dangerous. Why should they not kill you?'

'They need me. Besides, they think that I'm their ally. Now, Matthew, Mr Hatton has arranged this scheme. Do you believe that he would allow me to put myself in peril of my life?'

'I suppose not, but...well...we can't be certain what they'll do.'

'Nothing is certain in this life.' Sophie spoke with a lightness she was far from feeling. 'Now give me the keys! Do you have the lantern?'

His silence spoke volumes as he obeyed her.

'Remember now, you must not follow me!' Sophie's heart was pounding as she made her way down the cellar steps.

The light from the lantern was of little comfort to her. It served only to emphasise the shadows which closed in on her from either side. Following the single beam, she hurried to the hidden entrance to find that Matthew had already pulled the shelves aside and unlocked the door.

Ahead of her the huge cellar lay in darkness, and she was seized with terror.

She could only hope that Matthew hadn't taken it upon himself to open the doors at the far end of the tunnel, otherwise her unwelcome visitors might already be awaiting her.

She stopped and listened, but there was no sound. Reluctantly, she moved into the tunnel, knowing that she was now beneath the hillside behind the inn. The place was damp and at once she had to fight a sense of claustrophobia. If the walls caved in, she would be buried alive.

Fearfully, she raised the lantern to examine her surroundings. Then she noticed with relief that the passageway was shored up with heavy baulks of timber. Evidently it had been found worthwhile to construct it with great care. These men must make a handsome profit, she thought bitterly, if they could sanction such an outlay. How long had it taken them?

Her hands shook as she examined the bunch of keys that had been hidden behind the shelves. There was no indication as to which of them she needed. The first two would not turn in the lock, and she began to despair. Perhaps the metal had rusted from lack of use over these past months.

In her frustration she kicked angrily at the door. If the third key did not fit, Hatton's plan would be ruined.

To her relief it slid smoothly into the lock. She turned it and pulled at the doors. They swung open as if on oiled hinges.

Sophie peered out into the darkness, holding the lantern high above her head. She could see nothing outside the pool of light. She listened in silence, but nothing stirred in the blackness. What had she expected? Wagons, ponies, groups of men? Possibly they were hidden in the copse of trees.

Well, she had played her part. It was over, much to her relief. She turned away. Then she screamed aloud as a figure appeared beside her, and she almost dropped the lantern.

'No, don't raise it!' a conversational voice advised.

Sophie knew at once that it was Harward. Furious with him for giving her such a fright she disobeyed his order, thrusting the lantern towards him. Then she quailed.

In that shadowy light the sharp planes of his features were thrown into relief, giving him a predatory look. His smile did nothing to reassure her. He resembled nothing so much as a savage wolf, his lips curled into a snarl.

Now he took the lantern from her hand and set it on the ground.

'You have been fortunate tonight, my dear,' he observed. 'You did not follow orders, Mistress Firle. That was a mistake…'

'I…I don't know what you mean.' Sophie's voice was little more than a croak.

'Were you not advised to keep your premises locked, with shutters closed and your servants in their beds?'

'I did as you told me.'

'Then how is it that one of your men was allowed to ride into the village this evening?'

'Matthew? He went to fetch the doctor. One of my girls was taken ill.' Sophie's teeth were chattering with fright.

There was a silence. Then Harward bowed. 'Fortunately, ma'am, we know the doctor. It is, perhaps, as well…'

Suddenly, Sophie lost her temper. 'You have been spying on us?' she accused.

'Just a sensible precaution, Mistress Firle. We could not risk betrayal.'

'To one of your so-called bandits?' In her fury, Sophie threw caution to the winds. 'Do you imagine I believe that cock-and-bull story?'

'I never did.' Harward observed mildly. 'I don't regard you as a fool. You know quite well what we are about.'

Sophie tried to recover her position. 'It does not signify to me,' she said. 'I am looking for security, Mr Harward. You have promised me that.'

'And I'll keep my word.'

'Well, then, I shall leave you to go about your business. It is dark enough, God knows. You will be undisturbed this night.'

She heard a low laugh. 'You underestimate me, ma'am. We did not intend to move tonight. We needed to be sure of you. Had your servant visited anyone other than the doctor…well…we might have wondered if you were indeed a friend.'

Sophie shuddered. Matthew had come so close to death that night. She was thankful that her voice was steady when she spoke again.

'I trust that you are satisfied,' she said in haughty tones. 'Let me remind you, sir, that I am taking all the risks here. If this cargo is discovered on my premises I face imprisonment, transportation, or even death. I want it moved without delay.'

'Of course you do, and so do we. Shall we say tomorrow evening, then?'

'Certainly! That is, I suppose, unless I have need for a further visit from the doctor...'

'Ah, now you are offended.' Harward sounded regretful. 'I am sorry for it, ma'am, but you must understand that a degree of caution is as much in your interest as in our own.'

Sophie nodded stiffly.

'Then may I suggest that you lock the door behind me? Until tomorrow, then?' With an exquisite bow Harward turned and disappeared into the darkness.

Breathing hard, Sophie closed the heavy door, slamming home the bolts and turning the key in the lock. Then she hurried back along the tunnel and through the cellars, bruising her ankles on crates and boxes in her haste.

She found Matthew waiting for her.

'Didn't I tell you to look out for Abby?' she cried. 'She might have had need of you.'

Matthew shook his head. 'My girl is in no danger, ma'am. Nancy is asleep.'

'Thank heavens for that!' Sophie's sense of relief was overwhelming. Nancy must have drunk the broth containing the sedative. She questioned Abby at once.

'She ain't eaten much of it,' the girl informed her, indicating the half-empty bowl. 'She wanted to wait for you. I set the dishes beside the fire to keep them warm.'

Sophie was in a quandary. Had Nancy taken enough of the sedative to quieten her for hours, or would it be best to persuade her to finish off the broth? Nancy stirred then and Sophie decided on the latter course.

'I'm sorry I was so long, my dear. I was looking forward to sharing this meal with you. See, Abby has kept our food warm. Won't you try a little more?' She picked up her own bowl.

Rather to her surprise, Nancy made no objection. She took the proffered dish and sipped slowly at the contents.

Sophie decided on a little encouragement. Food was the last thing on her mind, but Nancy was regarding her intently, so she began to eat with apparent relish.

'Abby, you need not wait to clear away,' she said. 'It is very late. Do you go to bed. The dishes can wait until morning.'

Nancy had stopped eating.

'Finish it up,' Sophie urged. 'See, my own bowl is almost empty.'

Nancy picked up her spoon again, much to Sophie's relief. Aside from the necessary sedative, the broth would do her good. Heaven alone knew when she had last eaten. Now, with food inside her and a roaring fire to warm her through, the girl should fall into a sound sleep.

'Won't you lie down upon your bed?' she suggested. 'I'll help you to undress.'

Nancy baulked at the suggestion. 'May I not sit here by the fire?' she whispered.

'Of course you may!' Sophie was determined to avoid a confrontation. 'I thought only that you would be more comfortable…'

Nancy smiled, gazing at the leaping flames as if she were in a trance-like state. Then she turned her head and Sophie was startled by the look of triumph in her eyes.

Something was wrong. Sophie attempted to get to her feet, but her limbs would not support her. Overcome by an appalling sense of lassitude, she tried to move her leaden body.

'Sit down!' Firm hands pushed her back into her chair. 'You shouldn't have tried to drug me, Sophie. I watched you through the mirror.'

'It was only to help you sleep...' Sophie could barely recognise her own voice. Her words were slurred and now the smiling face above her seemed to be changing, dissolving into a whirling mist.

'What have you done to me?' she whispered.

'I changed my bowl for yours. Now *you* will sleep. I couldn't let you stop me, Sophie...I know what I must do.'

'Oh, please! You must not. You could ruin—!' Sophie closed her eyes and fell into darkness.

When she awoke it was to find herself in her own bed, with Hatton at her side. His face was grim.

'Nicholas?' She reached out a hand to him. 'What are doing here?'

'Thank God!' He gathered her to him with a groan. 'I thought she might have poisoned you.'

'It was only a sleeping draught,' she said with some difficulty. She still felt heavy-eyed and lethargic. 'She changed the dishes, giving hers to me.'

'I should have listened to you.' Hatton was filled with self-reproach. 'I had no idea that she was so close to breaking point.'

'Nor had I. I knew she was disturbed, but I didn't realise how badly until Abby told me that she'd been holding conversations with her dead husband. Worst of all, she believed she had a child...' Two large tears rolled slowly down Sophie's cheeks.

Hatton kissed them away. 'Don't worry!' he soothed. 'When we find her she shall have the best of care—'

'*When* you find her? Oh, no! Do you tell me that she is gone?'

'She won't have gone far. Her quarry is here. I thank heavens that you kept her close last evening, else all might have been lost. Can you tell me what went wrong?'

'I sent Matthew for the doctor,' Sophie told him miserably. 'It didn't occur to me that the inn might have been watched. He was followed. They suspected betrayal, you see. It was only when he came back with the doctor that they trusted me again.'

'So that was why they didn't move the goods last night?'

'No! They had no intention of doing so. Harward is a careful man. He wanted to be sure of me.' She heard a sharp intake of breath.

'You mean you actually spoke to him last night?'

'He was waiting for me by the entrance to the tunnel.'

Hatton held her close. 'I should never have let you take such risks.' His face was muffled against her hair. 'Can you ever forgive me?'

'There was no risk,' she answered lightly. 'He even apologised when I flew at him—'

'You flew at him?' he echoed in disbelief. 'Sophie, why must you take such chances? Were you not afraid?'

'I was terrified at first,' she told him frankly. 'But then he made me angry. He looked so smug...so sure that he had me in his power. I didn't take kindly to his threats, especially when he spoke of Matthew.' She shuddered. 'I hadn't realised that he would watch the inn so closely. If Matthew had gone anywhere other than to the doctor's house, they would have killed him.'

'Matthew was in no danger,' Hatton told her. 'We were

watching too. He was followed by one of my men both into the village and back again.'

'Then you were close at hand? I wish I'd known it.'

Hatton kissed her gently. 'You are the most precious thing in life to me, my darling. Would I leave you before our enemies are gone from here?'

Sophie rested her head against his chest. 'I'm so glad,' she whispered. 'Yesterday was one of the worst days of my life. Oh, Nicholas, I needed you so badly. I didn't know what to do, with Nancy half-demented. I tried to reason with her, but it was useless. She has a gun, you know.'

'Yes, Matthew told me.' Hatton's face was sombre. 'We must find her quickly. She could be in great danger.'

'You didn't see her leave the inn?'

'No, my dear, but it was dark, and we were some little distance away, hiding in the woods.'

Sophie thought for a moment. 'She wouldn't go far, I think. She knows now that Harward gives the orders and must have been responsible for her husband's death. He is her target. I am certain of it.'

'I wonder. She has had other opportunities to kill him, Sophie.'

'I think she wanted to be sure. I didn't know it at the time, but she was listening when Harward and his friend made their proposition to me. Then, as you know, they went away before she could take action.'

'We must find her. This could mean the ruin of all our plans. She could remove our only lead with a single shot. Have you any idea where she could be?'

'I don't know.' Sophie thought hard. 'It is full daylight now. You might search the outbuildings…'

'That has been done.' He hesitated. 'You must not think me unsympathetic to her plight, my darling. I can scarce imagine what she must have suffered in these last few months. I am not thinking only of our present operation, but Nancy is a danger to herself as well as others.'

Sophie held his hand against her cheek. 'I don't think you hard, my love, and if you had seen her yesterday… well, I hope never to witness such a tragedy again.'

'It must have been very bad.' Hatton held her closer.

'It was horrendous. Perhaps I shouldn't have sent for Dr Hill, but I felt that Nancy needed some expert help. She wouldn't allow me to take the pistol from her. All I could think of was the sedative. It didn't occur to me that she could be so cunning. She watched me through the mirror when I slipped it into the bowl of broth.'

'You have little experience of madness, Sophie. I have met with it only once myself. The most frightening aspects are these sudden flashes of apparent lucidity. They put everyone off guard, but the dementia is always there.'

'She wasn't violent,' Sophie said defensively.

'That was because she saw a simpler way of outwitting you. Thank God that you didn't attempt to restrain her by force. I dare not think what might have happened.'

'Doctor Hill advised against it, and she did seem quieter after he had gone. She was still rambling, of course. She even mentioned you…'

The arms about her tightened. 'How was that?'

'Oh, she had some wild idea that she had met you long ago, with Madame Arouet. It must have been a childish fancy. The Earl of Brandon was part of this strange dream. She said that you were his heir.'

Sophie did not know what she had expected. Perhaps some further words of sympathy for the demented girl, or even an expression of surprise. She heard none of these.

Hatton stiffened, and as she looked up at him her heart turned over.

'What is it?' she asked quickly. 'Why should this non-sense trouble you? Oh, I've been so foolish. I should not have told you of these crazy fancies.'

Hatton was silent for so long that Sophie was seized with dread. He had grown very pale.

'They are not fancies,' he said at last. 'Nancy told you the truth.'

'No!' she cried. 'I won't believe it! Could you not trust me enough to reveal your true identity? You said you loved me. You even asked me to become your wife. Tell me it isn't true!'

'It's true,' he answered stubbornly. 'How could I tell you, Sophie? I had several reasons for keeping my identity a secret. My father is known to be the scourge of the smugglers. His name is known to every villain in the land. Would they overlook the sudden appearance of his son on this part of the coast?'

Sophie turned her head away. 'You deceived me,' she said coldly. 'Did you think that I, who loved you, would be likely to betray you? I was the one person you might have taken into your confidence.'

Hatton's face grew harsh. 'I thought I had explained,' he said. 'Anyone can be forced into betrayal. With a knife at Kit's throat would you have given me away?'

Her face gave him his answer, but she refused to be mollified.

'I was never questioned, Nicholas. There was no question of betrayal.'

'We could not be sure of that.'

Sophie disengaged herself from his embrace. 'You said that there were other reasons,' she challenged. 'Will you go on? I'd like to know exactly why and when you decided to continue in this deception.'

Hatton put his head in his hands. 'Does it matter, Sophie? You say you love me. Isn't that enough?'

Sophie stared at him. 'Of course it matters,' she replied. 'When I was a girl I married a man whose life was based upon deception, whether it was concerned with money or...or other women. I can't allow it to happen to me again.'

'I should have told you, my darling.' Hatton's face was a study in misery. 'But I wanted to be sure that you loved me for myself alone.'

'I see.' Sophie might have turned to stone. 'You felt that the prospect of wealth and a title might have persuaded me into marriage, however much I disliked you?'

Hatton did not reply.

'I suppose it is understandable.' Now Sophie's tone was cutting. 'You must have been the catch of several London Seasons. How many match-making mamas have you managed to fend off, to say nothing of their hopeful daughters? It has given you a biased impression of the female sex.'

Again he said nothing.

'Will you please go now?' she said in a high, clear voice. 'We can have nothing more to say to each other. I was mistaken in you and, clearly, you do not know me at all.'

Hatton attempted to take her hands. 'Don't send me away like this,' he pleaded. 'I love you, Sophie, and I thought you loved me.'

'I thought so too, but now it is over. I won't be misled again. Now you had best find Nancy. Harward intends to move his cargo tonight. You won't wish for anything to go wrong.'

'Don't you mean anything else?' His look was ghastly. 'Sophie, please! I beg you to reconsider—'

'No!' She would not look at him. 'There is nothing more to say.'

Chapter Twelve

Hatton went without another word, leaving Sophie numb with misery. Happiness had come so close, only to be snatched away again.

She had loved Nicholas with all her heart, and she'd trusted him implicitly, only to be deceived once more.

Had she been unreasonable? She thought not. She could understand his reasoning in part. Harward would have found no difficulty in forcing her to betray her lover's true identity if his suspicions had been aroused. A threat to Kit would have been enough. Then his carefully planned operation would have failed, with dire consequences for her country.

Worse, Nicholas would have been murdered out of hand, as others had been before him. As for herself and Kit? She understood Harward well enough to know that he would leave no witnesses. No one able to identify him would be left alive. He would not hesitate to order a wholesale massacre. Betrayal would not have saved her.

She found that she was shaking with terror, but she made a supreme effort to regain her composure. What was done was done. She could not unsay the words which had hurt her lover so deeply. Nor did she wish to do so. Her own common sense told her that he had been right to hide his identity when they first met.

What she could not forgive was his assumption that the prospect of wealth and a title would influence her decision to accept his offer of marriage.

How could she have been so mistaken in him? Clearly, he didn't know her at all. A moment's thought would have reminded him that her first marriage had been to a penniless Revenue Officer. Then, she had not hesitated to put love before possessions.

But Nicholas knew that the scars of that marriage were not yet completely healed. Perhaps he had believed that she would not care to repeat the experiment. The man is a fool, she thought with a spurt of anger. Surely he could have trusted her enough to believe that she loved him for himself alone.

A little worm of doubt assailed her. Others had not done so. For years he had been the target of every match-making mama in London. He spoke of them with cold contempt, knowing the reasons for their overtures.

Sophie felt very cold. Now she found that she was rocking back and forth, rubbing her arms in an effort to restore some warmth to her icy limbs. She needed to think and her thoughts were not encouraging.

Was she behaving like some silly schoolgirl? She'd already admitted to herself that in some respects his decision to use an assumed name had been the right one. Why could she not accept it?

She knew the answer well enough. She'd lived with deceit for too many years ever to wish to become a victim again, but she might have forgiven even that, once she knew a valid reason for it.

What had shocked her to the core was the feeling that she and Nicholas were strangers to each other. She'd believed that they had grown so close, but his doubting her integrity had killed that belief.

She could not know it, but he too was regretting his explanations to her. What demon had persuaded him to tell her of that final reason for hiding his identity? He'd known at once that it was a mistake. He'd seen the closed expression on her face, and who could wonder at it?

Even to suggest that wealth and a title would sway a woman of character such as Sophie was an unforgivable insult. Well, it served him right. At the last, his pride had been his undoing. He'd wanted only to be honest with her. Instead, he'd driven her away.

Now he cursed himself. For a time it had been sensible to conceal his identity from her, if only to ensure that his plans would not be put in danger. Now, when his quarry was almost in the trap, he should have trusted her.

She had loved him enough to agree to become his wife, knowing almost nothing about him, he thought in anguish. Today, when she'd accepted him, he should have revealed that final secret. At this stage, no harm could come to her. Instead, she'd been forced to learn it from another. The agony of his loss was almost too much to bear.

Then Matthew entered the room.

'Have you found Nancy?' Hatton asked.

'No, sir. The men have searched the outbuildings and the wood, but there's no sign of her.'

'And indoors?'

Matthew shook his head. 'She could be anywhere. There are places enough to hide.'

Hatton nodded his agreement. The inn had been used for years by the smuggling fraternity. Even he did not know the full extent of the alterations which he suspected had been made to the building. If the rooms were mea-

sured against each other and compared with the walls outside he would have wagered on discrepancies in those
measurements. A man might disappear within the walls
simply by pressing a certain section of the wooden panelling to give access to the space behind.

'Nancy may have found such a place,' he ordered. 'She
cannot stay concealed for long, so you must continue to
keep watch. It's important that we find her.'

'And if we do?'

'I think you should pass the word that no one must
attempt to take her on their own. She has a gun, as you
well know, and at this present time she can't be held responsible for her actions. An accident now would mean
disaster.'

'So what must we do, sir?'

'Go on looking. If you find her, keep her under observation. We mustn't lose her again. I must away for a short
time, but I'll return as soon as possible.'

Hatton picked up his gloves and his riding crop, flung
his many-caped coat about his shoulders, and set off for
the stables.

Seated by the window of her bedchamber, Sophie
watched him ride away. She felt that her heart was breaking. Was this the last that she would ever see of him?
Without him her future seemed bleak indeed, but it had
been her own decision. She would not, could not, change
her mind. Fighting the overwhelming urge to open the
window and call him back to her, she turned away.

As she made her way down the stairs she became aware
that the atmosphere within the inn had changed. There
was a curious air of tension about the place.

With every sense alert she walked into the kitchen to
find her fears confirmed. Bess and her daughter were very

pale. Neither looked as if they had slept, and their eyes were haunted.

Sophie sank into a chair. 'Bess, I'd like some chocolate, if you please, and I think I might eat a roll.'

Bess looked startled by this apparent return to normality, but she bestirred herself to do Sophie's bidding. Then she flung her apron over her head and began to wail. Abby looked about to do the same.

'Stop that at once!' Sophie ordered. 'What good will it serve? I had thought better of you.'

Beth's wails changed to gasping sobs. 'We thought she'd murdered you,' she whimpered. 'When Mr Hatton could not rouse you we thought you must be poisoned, ma'am.'

'What nonsense! Where would Nancy find the means to poison me? She hasn't left the inn.'

'There are certain plants—'

'None of which can be found in winter, especially with snow upon the ground. Now, do be sensible, Bess. All that happened was that Nancy gave me the sedative intended for herself. It was a sleeping draught.'

'Wicked creature! I don't know how she durst do that.'

'Nancy's mind is sick. You know that well enough. Now, tell me exactly what happened yesterday. I have no recollection of it. At what hour did you find me?'

'Mistress, it was late. We'd none of us closed our eyes. What with the orders to keep the shutters closed, and all the men on edge, we were afeared. It must have been in the early hours when Mr Hatton came to find you. He looked that worried...'

Sophie eyed her servant coolly. Hatton's worry was not for her, she imagined, but for the failure of his plans. At that hour he would have expected to be on his way to London, following Harward to his destination.

'What then?' she demanded.

'Well, ma'am, he was like a man demented. He looked ready to kill us all for leaving you alone with Nancy, especially when he heard about the pistol.'

'I hope you told him that it was my decision.'

'He wouldn't listen!' Abby began to weep again. 'I thought that he would strike me. He said...he said...'

'Never mind what he said!' Sophie answered briskly. 'I have not suffered any harm. Now, listen to me carefully. Have you any idea where we might find Nancy?'

Both women shook their heads.

'I doubt if she'll be out of doors,' Sophie considered. 'In this weather she would freeze to death.'

Abby could not repress a scream. 'Oh, Mistress Firle, don't say that she's still here?' She turned to her mother. 'I won't stay!' she cried in panic. 'I want to go back to the village. My aunt will take me in.'

'Abby, you are a fool!' Sophie did not trouble to hide her anger. 'You are in no danger. Has Nancy ever tried to harm you?'

Wild-eyed with terror though she was, Abby shook her head.

'She had opportunity enough,' Sophie continued calmly. 'She could have threatened you with the pistol, or even knocked you on the head, but she did neither.'

'You say that, ma'am, begging your pardon, but my girl did not try to cross her.' Bess came at once to her daughter's defence.

'Nor will she do so now. Good heavens, Bess, I'm not asking either of you to stand up to Nancy. All I ask is that you tell me if you catch sight of her.'

Bess was growing calmer. Now she nodded her agreement. 'Mr Hatton said the same, even to the men. Even so, ma'am, we can't stay. I said as much to Matthew. We'd like to leave as soon as it's convenient.'

'It's never likely to be convenient,' Sophie told her in despair. 'Oh, Bess, I had such faith in you! You and Matthew have supported me even in the worst of times. Will you leave me now?'

'I'm sorry, ma'am!' Bess was adamant. 'I know that you promised us a share whenever you came to sell the inn, but our lives are more important than the money.'

'You are in no danger,' Sophie cried. 'Mr Hatton must have told you—'

'We don't believe him, ma'am. Things are happening here which none of us can understand. The gentleman may be powerful, but maybe he ain't a match for those agin him.'

Sophie was silent. She could no longer argue. For one thing, she had been deceiving these good people for the past few weeks. If the inn was not hers to sell, she could not give them a share of the proceeds.

She'd placed her faith in Hatton. He would not see them destitute, but now that she had broken with him she could no longer ask him for any favours on behalf of her servants.

Her shoulders drooped. 'You must do as you think best,' she said at last. 'Meantime, Bess, I suppose that we must think about provisions?'

Bess would not meet her eyes. 'We've enough and to spare for the present, ma'am. The men must be fed, but I doubt if we'll get any passing trade.'

She was wrong. At noon the door to the inn flew open and a noisy group of customers trooped indoors.

Sophie recognised them at once. The skating party had returned, with Hatton's cousins among them.

With an effort, she forced a smile. 'Do you skate again today?' she asked.

'No, ma'am.' The young man known as Wentworth bowed politely and gave her an engaging grin. 'Today we have brought some other of our friends. We are in search of sustenance…'

'Oh, dear! My cook may be at a pass to feed you all. You are eight in number, are you not? Let us see what we can do…'

Sophie hurried back into the kitchen. 'Bess, must we give them bread and cheese?' she asked.

'No, ma'am!' Bess was on her mettle at once. 'In this weather that won't do. The young gentlemen will be cold and hungry.' She thought for a moment. 'Give me an hour, Mistress Firle. They may pass the time with their wine or ale. Then we'll give them something for their bellies.'

She was as good as her word. Within the hour the company was sitting at table with expectant faces and Sophie was amused to see that Kit was among them, seated on a pile of cushions. He smiled at her, and then returned to a serious discussion with one of his companions on the merits of different fishing flies.

Bess had excelled herself, perhaps ashamed of her decision to abandon Sophie in her hour of need. A creamy leek and potato soup was accompanied by crusty bread. It vanished like snow in summer. This was followed by a dish of trout cooked in wine and butter.

Sophie had been surprised. 'How did you keep this fish?' she asked Bess. 'We could not have bought it recently.'

'It was packed in ice, ma'am, and then stored in the cellar. As long as the ice don't melt, it won't go off.'

Bess busied herself with the final touches to the dish, pounding up a mixture of herbs, capers, anchovy fillets and garlic with mustard and the juice of lemons. Then she mixed together butter and flour. Removing the trout from the baking dish, she heated up the remaining liquor and added the flour and butter paste. When it thickened she threw in the herb mixture and poured it over the fish.

Up to this moment Sophie believed that she had lost her appetite, but the delicious aroma was tempting. At Wentworth's insistence she sat down beside him and tasted a mouthful of the dish.

'You must pray that the Prince never visits you, ma'am,' he told her with a smile. 'Most certainly he would try to take your cook away.'

'You are very kind, sir. Bess will be delighted by that compliment. I must hope that your appetite is not flagging. You are to have ham braised in Madeira wine to follow.'

'Splendid!' Wentworth looked about him. 'Yet we are your only customers, Mistress Firle. Why is that? With food such as you provide I had thought that your tables would be filled each day.'

'We had been closed for several weeks,' Sophie told him briefly. Though Hatton had claimed to be his cousin, the young man did not appear to have been taken into his confidence. Was that claim yet another attempt to deceive her?

She could be sure of nothing, except that the very ground beneath her feet seemed to shift with every hour that passed.

Then Hatton entered the room, nodding an acknowledgement to the assembled company. As he took a vacant chair, Kit slid down from his high perch and climbed upon his knee.

The tiny gesture of affection was too much for Sophie.

With a muttered excuse she rose to seek the sanctuary of the snug. Once there, she gazed out at the winter landscape with unseeing eyes, aware only of the anguish in her heart, and the ruin of all her hopes and dreams.

She and Nicholas could have been so happy, especially as Kit adored him so. Then his arms were round her, his cheek resting against her hair. She must have left the door ajar as she hadn't heard his quiet approach.

For one unguarded moment she melted into his embrace, enveloped in the animal magnetism that was so particularly his own. Then she stiffened and pulled away.

'My darling, won't you reconsider?' he pleaded. 'Say that you forgive me...'

Sophie turned to face him, aware that the agony in his eyes must match her own. 'There is nothing to forgive,' she told him quietly. 'We were mistaken in each other, that is all.'

'Will you throw away our happiness because of a few words spoken in haste?'

'I hope I should not be so foolish,' she said with dignity. Suddenly she felt very calm. 'Let me try to make you understand. I have had time to think, and I believe that events have overtaken us. We have been thrown together in unusual circumstances. Perhaps it is no wonder that we have fallen victim to illusion.'

'That isn't true!' he groaned.

'Isn't it? Have we not each seen in the other some ideal, to be found only in a world of fantasy? I don't know you, Nicholas. Everything has happened much too fast. Even now, I do not know your name.'

'There, at least, I did not lie to you,' he muttered. 'My given names are Crispin Nicholas. I am the Viscount Hatton.'

'I thank you for your honesty.' Sophie's face was grave.

'I can only wish you well, my lord.' She held out her hand. 'Let us not part in anger. I must thank you for many kindnesses.'

'I don't want your thanks!' he cried in desperation. 'Sophie, I want your love. Don't tell me that it is too late.' He reached out his arms to draw her to him, but she moved away.

'Must you make this so painful?' she whispered as she moved towards the door. Her words were a mistake. She knew it when he stayed her with a hand upon her arm. Then he looked deep into her eyes.

'Would it be painful if you didn't love me still?' he asked.

Gently she disengaged herself. 'I won't lie to you, my dear. I hadn't thought to know such pain, but I shall learn to live with it. We should never suit, you know.' With that she hurried back to the dining-room to join the others.

As they entered the room together, Wentworth's gaze flickered from one face to the other. Then, without comment, he addressed himself to his meal once more.

Hatton took Kit upon his knee. 'Will you do something for me?' he asked easily.

'Of course I will.' The child beamed up at him.

'Then find Reuben and the other men. Tell them I wish to see them on a matter of importance.'

He waited until Kit had skipped away. Then he rapped on the table for silence.

'We go tonight,' he said.

'You are sure this time?' Wentworth turned to face him.

'I think it certain that our quarry will wait no longer. These are careful men. The inn has been under close observation. It was unfortunate that Matthew rode out to fetch the doctor yesterday, but no harm was done. They didn't intend to move their cargo until they could be sure that Mistress Firle had not betrayed them.'

Wentworth glanced at Sophie with admiration in his eyes. 'I salute your courage, ma'am. You have played no small part in this.' He looked across at Hatton. 'Cousin, is there no alternative? Surely someone else could open the outer door tonight. Mistress Firle has done enough. Must we ask more of her?'

'The choice is hers.' Hatton kept his brooding gaze fixed firmly on the table. Duty demanded that he should insist upon her participation, but he could not ask her to put herself in danger once again, even though it meant that all his plans might fail.

Sophie made the decision for him. 'I shall open the door,' she announced. 'I am in no danger, Mr Wentworth. The leader of these men believes that I am his willing accomplice, motivated only by a greed for gold. He judges others by his own desires.'

Wentworth smiled at her. Then he turned back to Hatton. 'What of the girl?' he asked. 'I take it that Nancy has not been found?'

'Not yet. My greatest fear is that she will appear from hiding and take action on her own, but I have ordered certain measures. All the servants will keep watch indoors, especially on this floor. She won't be allowed to gain the doors.' His face was grim.

'Nicholas, you will not harm her?' Sophie asked in dismay.

'She must be restrained, ma'am.' He would go no further and Sophie was reduced to silence.

Looking round the table at the circle of eager faces, she was forced to admit that he'd been clever.

Now she understood the reason for the frequent visits of this party of apparently carefree young bucks. Hatton would use only men that he could trust, and who better than his own flesh and blood.

But there were so few of them, she thought in anguish—even with Reuben and his bruisers added to their number they would be less than a dozen. She thought again of the silent crowd of smugglers who had trooped into the inn on the day she had first met Harward. There must have been thirty or more and she had no doubt that they were well able to call upon others.

Hatton sensed her disquiet. 'Don't worry!' he soothed. 'We are not planning on a pitched battle. We intend to follow them to London. We believe they unload on this side of the river. Hopefully, their backers will be waiting for them.'

'There are not enough of you!' she cried. 'You cannot fight a mob of murderous ruffians!'

'We shall have support,' he comforted. 'At Southwark others will join us when we give the signal. It is all arranged.'

'Oh, you will take care?' she breathed.

It was Wentworth who took her hand. 'Believe me, ma'am, we all value our worthless hides,' he told her with a twinkle. 'We shall proceed with the utmost caution.'

A general shout of amusement greeted this remark, and Hatton felt obliged to explain it.

'My cousin is not noted for his caution,' he said gravely. 'On this occasion I am hoping that he will follow his instructions.'

Wentworth gave him a mock salute. 'Certainly, my lord! I shall follow them to the letter. Who am I to question the orders of my superior officer?'

The conversation deteriorated quickly into a bout of chaffing which threatened to develop into horseplay.

Sophie looked in wonder at the laughing party. Within

hours these gay young men would be putting their very lives in danger. That prospect seemed to be the last thing on their minds.

She turned to Hatton. 'You are sure that Nancy is still within these walls?' she asked.

'She must be, Sophie. Most certainly she did not leave the inn last night. We should have seen her.'

'So you were watching too?'

'Naturally. We were hidden in the woods.'

'You were sure you were not seen?' she asked anxiously.

'I'm certain of it. Harward would not have planned to move the goods tonight if he's suspected a trap.'

'I wish it were all over,' she whispered. 'How I hate that tunnel! It is so dark and dank.'

Hatton took her hand in his. 'No one will blame you in the least if you feel that you can't go on,' he told her gently. 'We all admire your bravery.'

'Brave? I don't feel brave at all,' she admitted.

'Then, Sophie, you must not feel obliged—'

She stopped him with a look. 'I want to draw back, but I can't,' she told him. 'We've come too far to give up now. If I didn't open those doors tonight I could never forgive myself for my cowardice.'

The look in his eyes was reward enough for her. 'Then we must try to match your courage,' he told her very softly. 'Sophie, I still intend to try to win you. Will you give me leave to see you again?'

She was about to answer him when the hubbub in the room was stilled. All eyes rested upon the gentleman standing in the doorway. Dressed in the height of fashion, he presented a striking figure, though not in his first youth.

Sophie repressed an inward groan as she sank down in her chair. Even Hatton's massive figure could not hide her from the searching gaze which scanned the room. This was all she needed. Urged on, no doubt, by her own father, Sir William Curtis had come to call.

He came towards her at once, ignoring the assembled company.

'There you are, my dear!' he said in jovial tones. 'And quite as lovely as ever, if I may be permitted to say so.'

With hands outstretched he drew her to her feet and slipped a proprietorial arm about her waist. Then, with total disregard for her evident distaste, he kissed her full upon the lips.

Sophie was strongly tempted to box his ears. When she was under her father's protection he would not have dared to take such a liberty. Now, apparently, he regarded her as fair game. She was wise enough to school her expression into one of complaisance. At the first sign of her displeasure this unwelcome visitor would have found himself run through by one of the gentlemen who now looked their surprise at this unexpected turn of events.

Hatton looked like thunder.

'Sir William, allow me to make these gentlemen known to you,' she said hastily. His bow was perfunctory to the point of insolence until she came to Hatton.

'The Viscount Hatton, do you say?' Sir William pursed his lips. 'I had not heard that you were returned from the Peninsula, my lord—'

'How should you?' Hatton's reply was curt. 'We are not acquainted, sir. Nor are we like to be.'

It was a sharp set-down, and Sir William crimsoned. He seemed about to retort, but a strange glint in his lordship's eye warned him against it. Clearly, the gentleman was spoiling for a fight.

Sir William turned his back. The younger man was of an athletic build. Doubtless he was able to give a good account of himself in a bout of fisticuffs, and he himself had no desire for a bloody nose.

Then his eye fell upon Kit. The child had run his errand. Now he was standing close to Hatton.

'I told them, sir,' he whispered. 'They are waiting for you.'

'Sophie, is this your son?' Sir William asked. 'The boy is not unlike you.'

'Yes, this is Kit.'

'I see. Come here, my lad! Let's have a look at you!' He advanced towards the child, but Kit retreated behind Hatton.

'Disobedient? Hmm! The lad lacks discipline. Your father was right. He should be sent away to school—'

'He's only five!' Sophie exclaimed in anger. She might have said more, but Hatton forestalled her.

He bent down, picked up Kit and set the child upon his shoulder. Then, without a backward glance, he walked out of the room.

Sir William did not trouble to hide his rage. 'Upon my word!' he blustered. 'There would appear to be no limit to the insolence of some members of the *ton*. Strange company you keep, my dear! The man is a perfect lout!'

Sophie heard the scrape of a chair, and peering round Sir William's bulky figure she saw Wentworth advancing towards them with a purposeful tread. She caught his eye and shook her head. This was no time for a private fight. She caught at her companion's sleeve.

'We need to speak in private,' she insisted. 'Have you a message from my father?'

Sir William looked at the circle of hostile faces, and made no objection to being led away. Sophie took him into the snug and closed the door, though she was careful to keep her hand upon the latch.

'You wish to be private with me?' her companion leered. 'Let me tell you, Sophie, your father hopes that we shall make a match of it. Then he will be happy to receive you again.' He walked towards her with arms outstretched.

'Keep your distance, sir!' she cried. 'I have not the least wish to be private with you. If you must know it, I have just saved your skin. My friends do not care to see me offered insult.'

Curtis stared at her. 'Insult?' he echoed. 'How have I insulted you? I came to make you an offer.'

'You may keep your offer to yourself. You have just behaved as if you owned me. I have never offered you encouragement, even as a girl. In my father's house you would not have dared to take such liberties with my person, or to use my given name without permission.'

'Ah, but matters are different now, I think.' He gave her a crafty smile. 'You have no protector, unless, of course, you have allowed the estimable Viscount to bed you. He seems very much at home here.'

'If you think that, I wonder that you should consider offering for me,' Sophie gritted out the words. She was too angry to say more.

'I don't mind another man's leavings,' he informed her. 'In certain matters experience is of much value. Pray don't pretend that you cannot understand me. You are no longer an innocent girl.'

Sophie looked long and hard at him until his eyes fell before her own. The years had not been kind to her former suitor, and dissipation had taken its toll. He was now grossly fat, his bulk confirmed to some extent by stays. She could hear them creaking as he moved. She stared at the loose-lipped mouth and the little pig-like eyes. Even now they glittered with lust.

'I am sorry that you have come so far upon a fruitless errand,' she said at last. 'I should warn you, sir, that the roads about this place are not safe after dusk. You had best leave now.'

To her horror he advanced upon her once again. 'Still teasing me, my dear? It will be a pleasure to tame you.'

'Don't touch me!' Sophie made as if to open the door. 'Lay a hand on me and my friends will give you the thrashing of your life.'

He was forced to believe her then, and his face grew dark with rage. Bending towards her, he whispered such a stream of filth into her ear that she was nauseated. He left her in no doubt as to what he would like to do to her if the opportunity arose.

Her hand flew to her mouth. 'Vile!' she cried. 'How vile you are! You have always disgusted me. Now I know that I was right.'

She flung the door wide and ran to join the others.

Hatton had returned. When he saw her face, he tried to brush past her in pursuit of her tormentor.

'No!' she whispered. 'Let him go! He taints the air I breathe.'

'He won't come back?'

'No, he won't come back.'

Hatton's expression did not change. 'You are un-harmed, I hope?'

'Yes, my lord. He did not dare to press his suit much further.' In spite of her ordeal, Sophie's eyes began to twinkle. 'You were extremely rude to him, you know. I think your manner frightened him.'

'What a toad! I should have horsewhipped him.' He took her hand and kissed it. 'We must leave you now, my dear, but will you give me an answer?'

'To what?'

He looked at her in despair. 'Have you forgot so soon? When our friend arrived you were about to give me leave to return to you.'

'I can think of no way of stopping you from returning to this inn,' she said demurely. 'It is, after all, your own property.'

'And you?'

She would not answer him, but he gave a joyous laugh. Then, at his signal, the others left the room.

Hatton gathered Sophie to him. Slipping a finger beneath her chin, he raised her face to his. Then his mouth came down upon her own in a dizzying kiss which left her breathless.

'I shall return to claim you,' he promised. 'I won't take no for an answer.' Then he was gone, with a last injunction to follow his instructions to the letter, and to take no chances. 'I love you more than life,' he told her. 'Take great care, my dear. We shall be close by.'

Sophie glanced at the clock. It was already growing dark and in her mind's eye she could see that hateful tunnel beneath the inn. She sent for Matthew.

'Do you think we might light the staircase leading to the cellar, and possibly the wine cellar itself?' she asked.

He shook his head. 'The lights would be seen from the tunnel, ma'am. The doors ain't that good a fit.' His face was a picture of apprehension. 'Will this be the end of it tonight?' he asked. 'Me and Bess...well...we can't take much more of this.'

'It will be over very soon,' she soothed. 'Then, perhaps, you will change your mind about leaving me?'

He looked uncomfortable. 'It ain't our wish, ma'am, but we ain't keen to lose our lives.'

'I know, but I think that we may put our trust in Mr Hatton, don't you?'

He gave her a look of reluctant acquiescence. 'I'd best go,' he said. 'We ain't found Nancy yet.'

That was a worry which haunted Sophie in the hours that followed. Then, as the clock struck midnight, she made her way into the cellars. She'd be fine if she didn't think of what might lie beyond the outer door.

When at last she flung it open she sighed with relief. In the cellars and even in the tunnel she had sensed another presence close upon her heels. She'd swung round once or twice, holding her lantern high, but there was silence. She was being fanciful. Her nerves were playing tricks upon her.

Then Harward stepped into the circle of light.

'You don't need me now,' she told him hurriedly. 'I had best get back.'

He didn't answer her. He was looking beyond her, and something in his face alerted Sophie to danger. She swung round and gasped. Nancy stood behind her with her pistol trained upon the smuggler's head.

'Stand aside, Sophie,' the girl ordered. 'You are in my line of fire. This is the man who killed my husband. Now I'll send him to the fires of hell.'

Before she could utter a word of protest, Sophie was seized from behind. Using her as a shield, Harward drew his pistol and fired it in one swift movement, shooting Nancy through the heart. She fell without a sound.

Chapter Thirteen

Faint with horror, Sophie slumped against her captor, but Harward thrust her to one side, pinning her against the wall of the tunnel with an outstretched arm. Then he motioned his men forward.

'Get rid of that!' he ordered, pointing to the prone figure lying at his feet.

Sophie closed her eyes as two of the men seized Nancy's arms and dragged her away.

'What must we do with her?'

'There's a lake, I believe, or you might bury her, but be quick about it. We can't afford to waste much time.'

'The lake is frozen, mester, and the ground…well…it's too hard to dig—'

'For God's sake!' Harward cried impatiently. 'Must I do all your thinking for you? You'd best hide the body in the woods, then, and cover it with brushwood.'

'And this one?' The man gestured towards Sophie. 'You can't leave her here. She could get you hanged.'

'So she could!'

There was a long silence and Sophie closed her eyes as she waited for the shot which would end her life. She could think only of her son.

Now she prayed with all her heart that Hatton would take care of him.

Then Harward came to a decision. 'There's no hurry!' he announced. 'We'll take her with us. She may prove to be a useful bargaining counter if aught goes wrong.'

Sophie's entire body was shaking, but she found her voice at last.

'You...you said that we were partners...' Her voice was unrecognisable, even to her. 'Why must you treat me so?'

Harward took her arm and dragged her back along the tunnel until they reached the cellar. Making his way past the groups of men already at work upon the cargo, he drew her to one side.

'You must not take me for a fool, my dear.' His expression was almost kindly. 'You have been careless, Mistress Firle, and that I cannot tolerate. Your servant might have killed me.'

'She was sick. I told you of it yesterday. That was why we sent for Dr Hill. Then she disappeared. Believe me, we have tried to find her.'

'Apparently, with singular lack of success,' he drawled. 'Well, it is no matter, since the girl is dead...'

'There was no need to kill her,' Sophie whispered. 'You might have shot her in the arm—'

She heard a low laugh. 'Dear me! What a sentimentalist you are! Alas, it is as I feared! You have no stomach for this business.'

'At least I can use my head!' she cried. 'What have you gained by this...this murder?'

'Only a certain degree of satisfaction. I had not allowed for this unfortunate incident. Now it must change our plans, which does not please me.'

'I don't see why it need change anything,' she told him in despair.

'Don't you, Mistress Firle? You surprise me, since you have claimed to be able to use your head.'

Sophie looked at him. He was smiling, but the smile did not reach his eyes. They were as hard as sea-washed pebbles.

'Perhaps I should explain, since you seem unable to understand me. I no longer trust you, madam. Are you about to assure me that you will overlook this unfortunate occurrence? That you will find some reason for the disappearance of your servant? That our partnership will continue in an amicable fashion? I think not, my dear. I can see it in your face.'

'Won't you give me time to think about it? It has been a shock to me...' Sophie was playing for time, but even as she spoke she knew that her pleas were useless.

'Don't waste your breath!' Harward turned away. 'We cannot use this place again. Now you will go back with us. I suspect that we may have need of you. Every instinct tells me that here is something havey-cavey about this business.'

Sophie was close to breaking point. She caught at Harward's sleeve. 'I won't!' she shrieked. 'You shall not take me from my son.'

For answer he signalled to the nearest man, and Sophie shrank away. She knew the creature by the ugly weal which disfigured the left side of his face. This was the man who had attacked her and received a beating for his pains.

Sophie screamed aloud. Then a fist connected with the point of her jaw and she fell into darkness.

When she came round it was to find herself beneath a pile of packages. Her head was pounding, and her jaw was so painful that she thought it must be broken.

So much for Hatton's assurances, she thought bitterly. Surely he'd heard the shot which had killed Nancy? The sound must have carried clearly in the still night air. Then she recalled that the tunnel was deep underground. The earth must have muffled the gunfire.

But he and his men were keeping watch. He'd told her so himself. Perhaps they hadn't been close enough to see her being carried to this cart. One bundle would look much like another.

She shifted her position slightly in an effort to ease her aching limbs. Then she realised that her hands and feet had been securely bound. Harward was taking no chances. If she escaped, he must know that it would be all up with him.

She groaned as the cart rumbled over a patch of stony ground. Before their journey was over the violent shocks were likely to break every bone in her body. It could not matter now, she thought in despair. She was being taken to her death. Harward would never let her go, knowing that her testimony could convict him of murder.

The tears rolled down her cheeks as she thought of Kit. The child would have no one now.

'Hush up!' a gruff voice mumbled. 'I don't want to be told to knock you out again...'

'Why not, you pig?' She recognised the voice at once as that of the man with the scar across his face.

'I could have hit you harder, ma'am. And 'twas me as wrapped you in the blanket and settled you on these soft bundles.'

'Am I supposed to be grateful to you?'

'You might well be. I left your brooch in the cellar, so's they'd know as we'd taken you.'

Sophie was silent. She was thinking hard. The man sounded almost apologetic, but she didn't allow herself to hope. He was an unlikely ally.

'Why did you do that?' she asked at last.

'I owes you one. Yon Mester Harward would have blinded me, if you hadn't stopped him.'

'Will you release me?' she whispered.

'No, ma'am, I can't do that. He'd kill me for sure.'

'Then will you loosen my bonds? They are much too tight.'

'Aye! Give us your hands!' He hugged at the ropes which bound her.

Sophie repressed a cry of pain as her circulation was restored. 'And my feet?'

Again he loosened her bonds. 'Don't let on if he comes back,' he warned. 'There's many another as will be glad to take my place in the cart and you know what that could mean.'

Sophie shuddered. Harward might consider that rape was no more than suitable repayment for her failure at the inn.

Now she resolved to try to make a friend of her companion.

'Why do you stay with him?' she asked. 'You know that you risk imprisonment and transportation, and even, in the worst case, death?'

'Ain't got no choice, ma'am. There's no work for such as we. The fishing's gone, and mining too. My bairns had empty bellies...'

'You do this for your children?' Sophie warmed towards the man.

'Yes, ma'am.' He seemed to be struggling for words. 'That night...when I came at you...well, I'm sorry for it. I'd taken too much drink.'

'You have already made amends,' she told him. 'Do you know where we are going?'

'Lunnon, Mistress Firle. But I don't know where...I ain't been this way afore.'

'So this is your first run...your first attempt at smuggling goods?'

'Aye, and it's like to be my last. I hadn't reckoned on murder.'

'Poor Nancy!' Sophie's voice broke on a sob. 'It was a wicked thing to do.'

'Yes, ma'am.' Her companion did not argue.

'What is your name?' she asked.

'It's Walter, Mistress Firle, but they call me Wat.'

'Well then, Wat, how long will it be before we reach the city?'

'They wuz reckonin' on many hours, with maybe a stop or two along the way.'

'Will you stay by me?' Sophie was clutching at straws. Wat was her only hope of rescue.

'If I can. You'd best get some sleep.' It was clear that the conversation was at an end.

Sophie didn't argue further. The man had taken a fearful chance in leaving her brooch behind, and also in loosening her bonds, in spite of his fear of Harward. She must not antagonise him. Wat had given her one small glimmer of hope. Later she would speak to him again.

She burrowed deeper among the oiled silk bags. It was bitterly cold and the rising wind was merciless. It sought out every crack in the wooden sides of the wagon, but at least the packages gave her some protection.

Her head still ached, and her jaw was tender, but at least the shaking which had rocked the whole of her body had stopped. She tried to take deep breaths, willing herself to be calm.

As long as Harward thought she might be useful to him, she was in no immediate danger, but if Nicholas tried to rush the wagons in a bid to rescue her, Harward would despatch her out of hand. She was too dangerous a witness to be left alive to send him to the gallows.

She wondered if Nancy's body had been found. The pool of blood at the entrance to the tunnel was clear evidence that someone had been killed or injured.

Now she prayed that in his agony of mind her lover would do nothing foolish. She'd had no time to count the numbers of men within the cellar, but they could not be less than fifty. Others had awaited them outside, loading the wagons and holding the heads of the ponies.

With every mile that passed, others came to join them. She'd heard the whispered greetings and she marvelled at their disregard of danger. A band as large as this could not pass through the Sussex countryside unnoticed, even at night. Perhaps their strength was such that no one dared attack them.

She tried to comfort herself with the thought that Nicholas too was expecting reinforcements, but not until they reached the outskirts of the capital. That might be too late for her, especially if he lost their trail.

She didn't know London well, and she had no wish to know it better. On her rare visits she'd been appalled by the stench of refuse mixed with the horse droppings which littered the streets. She and her mother had carried pomanders, but even at the time she'd wondered if those small bags of aromatic herbs were of much use as a guard against infection.

Then there was the noise. How her ears had rung with the clanging bells of the muffin-men and the pie-sellers and the shouts of the beggars who pressed in upon their carriage.

She tried to remember if they'd passed through Southwark. She knew that it was south of the river and that it was an insalubrious area. Her mother had pulled down the leather curtains to shield her from the gaze of the blowsy strumpets who called from every window. It had seemed to Sophie to be a warren of narrow streets and alleyways.

Here, she guessed, the band of smugglers might break up, making their way to their destination in small groups, so as not to attract attention. Other than the Bow Street Runners, there was no organised force of men to halt them, but the authorities in the city could call upon the Militia or the Dragoons. Harward would know this well enough, and he would take no chances.

Then a thought occurred to her. Suppose her enemy had decided to use decoys? Some of the wagons might not carry contraband. How would Nicholas know which ones to follow?

If only she could think of a way to help him. Careful to make no sound, she began to tear at the lace upon her petticoat. She might be able to thrust a part of it through one of the gaps in the sides of the wagon. It would flutter in the wind.

She had got no further with this plan when the vehicles drew to a halt. Then she heard Harward's voice. He was speaking to one of his companions.

'I'd best check on her,' he announced. 'If I'm not mistaken, our little Mistress Firle has a quick mind. She may be plotting mischief at this moment.'

'What can she do?' a deep voice growled. 'She's bound tight, but if you like I'll take Wat's place to keep an eye on her.'

Sophie heard a low laugh of amusement. 'That won't

be necessary,' Harward said. 'I chose my man with care. Wat, above anyone, has no love for her.'

'Don't stir!' the man beside her warned. 'Pretend to be asleep.'

Sophie was happy to obey him. She froze as the covering of the wagon was drawn back, and a light illuminated the interior.

Harward studied her prone figure for what seemed an eternity.

'You must have hit her harder than I thought,' he said with satisfaction. 'Well done, Wat! Don't take any chances with her. She caused you a severe beating.'

The covering was drawn back, and Sophie was plunged into darkness once more.

'Aye!' the man beside her muttered beneath his breath. 'But she ain't the one who gave me a scar I'll carry till I die.'

Sophie waited until the wagons began to roll once more. Then she spoke to her companion. 'Thank you!' she said quietly.

His only reply was a grunt.

'How many children do you have, Wat?' she asked. 'Won't you tell me their names?'

'What do you want to know for?' He sounded surly, but she guessed correctly that any encounter with Harward terrified him.

'I thought it would pass the time if we spoke of them. I have a young son of my own.'

'I seen 'im,' he offered. 'Bright little lad he is, an' all. You should never 'ave taken up wi' Mester Harward, ma'am. Didn't you know the danger?'

'I had no choice,' she told him. 'He isn't the easiest person to refuse.'

'That's true!' he said with feeling. 'Well, what's done is done. There's no use crying over spilt milk.'

'You were going to tell me about your children.'

The man's voice softened. 'There's Em'ly, and my little Amy. My lad is the youngest. 'E's just a babe.'

Sophie couldn't hide her dismay. 'Oh, Wat, you asked why I had put myself in danger. What of you?'

'I told you, ma'am. Did you ever 'ear your child crying wi' 'unger? I couldn't stand it no more...'

'But, Wat, suppose that you were taken? What would happen to them then?'

'They'd starve!' came the grim reply. 'Don't worry, I won't be taken...'

A silence fell between them.

Then, greatly daring, Sophie spoke again. 'There may be another way,' she said cautiously. 'If you were to help me, I could speak out for you. I have powerful friends.'

'They wouldn't be no use to a dead man. I can't do it, ma'am. You wouldn't get six paces afore 'e shot you down, an' me as well.'

'He's going to kill me, anyway. You know that, don't you?'

'Don't talk like that,' he muttered. 'You be useful to 'im, Mistress Firle.'

'For how long?'

When he did not reply, she turned away and closed her eyes. Now that it seemed that her last hope was gone, she tried to help herself. She tore at the lace again, and the stitches gave at last, leaving a length of the fabric in her hand. Now she was in a quandary. Did she dare to use it?

Men were trudging along beside the wagon. She could hear their muttered conversation. A single glimpse of her signal would be enough to bring Harward back. He was on edge already. She'd heard it in his voice, beneath the smooth attempt at a confident tone. He'd realise at once that someone must be following. For all she knew he might halt to arrange an ambush. Either way, it would be the end for both herself and Wat.

She must think of something, but her brain refused to function. All she could see in her mind's eye was the image of Nicholas, with Kit upon his knee, laughing and secure in their mutual affection.

What a fool she'd been. Nicholas loved her truly. In her heart she'd known it all along. Why, then, had she sent him away with some trumped-up charge of an insult to her character? She knew the answer. It was cowardice. After her experience with Richard, she'd been unwilling to trust any man. Her heart had pulled her one way, and her head another.

A sob escaped her lips. She'd seized upon the first excuse to avoid another commitment. Now her darling would never know the depth of her regret. She'd left him without a word of love, and it was too late now to make amends.

'Now, ma'am, don't 'ee take on.' Wat's tone was kindly. 'I ain't said that I won't 'elp 'ee, if I can see my way to it.'

'You've just told me that I can't escape,' she told him in despair.

'Not 'ere, ma'am, and not at this particular minute, but there's a ways to go. They'll be that busy when we reaches Lunnon... Maybe we'll see a chance...'

Sophie reached out for his hand. 'I won't forget your kindness, whatever happens, Wat.'

'T'weren't nothing, ma'am. As I told you, I don't 'old wi' murder.'

The next few hours seemed endless, but as they reached the outskirts of the capital the roads were better. Soon they were rattling over cobblestones, and Sophie knew that they must be near their destination.

'Now don't you go a-doin' nothin' stupid,' her companion warned. 'Leave it to me to take a look about.'

Sophie was aware that they had slowed down almost to a crawl, and there was something else. The wind had died away and the noise from the street seemed to be curiously muffled.

She raised herself a little and tried to move her limbs. Stiff from many hours of lying bound in the bottom of the wagon, she could scarcely move. How long had their journey taken? Surely it must be daylight?

'Where are we?' she whispered. 'Can you see anything?'

Her companion seemed to be enveloped in a haze of yellow mist. Now he loosened the covering at the rear of the wagon and peered out. She heard a muttered exclamation.

'Danged if I can see a thing. In this fog you couldn't find your hand in front of your face.'

Hope flared high in Sophie's breast. 'This may be our chance,' she urged. 'Come with me, Wat! We could slip away without being seen. I'll make sure that you don't suffer for your part in this.'

'Where would we go, ma'am? I ain't been 'ere afore, but I 'eard tell that the streets ain't safe, especially in these fogs. We'd be knocked on the 'ead and robbed for sure.'

Sophie coughed as the acrid vapour caught at her throat. Her eyes were streaming, and she found it difficult to breathe, but still she tried to persuade him.

'That may be better than what may lie ahead of us. Harward cannot allow me to live. You know that as well as I do myself, but won't you think of what may happen to you?'

Wat didn't answer her.

'Suppose the Runners are waiting for you?' she continued. 'There's always the danger of a trap.'

'Mester Harward will see 'em off. There's too many of us for they Redbreasts.'

'But not too many to fight off a company of Militia, or a troop of Dragoons. Do you want to sit in the dock at Newgate, with your coffin in front of you, listening to a person preaching a last sermon, before they take you out and hang you?'

She heard a sharp intake of breath, but Wat had hesitated just too long. Fog billowed into the wagon as Harward raised the covering at the back.

'Awake, my dear?' he enquired. 'I thought I heard you coughing. This fog is so unpleasant, is it not, but it is quite a feature of the London scene. I confess that I enjoy my trips into the country.'

'I'm sure you do,' she told him bitterly. 'They must show a handsome profit.'

'Oh, they do, my dear! They do! Bear up, Mistress Firle. We are almost at our destination. We shall have you safe indoors before too long.'

Sophie was silent, but despair engulfed her. If Wat had acted quickly they might have escaped into the fog. She'd welcomed it at first, but now it was her enemy. Even if her rescuers were close at hand they would find it almost impossible to follow the different groups of smugglers as they made their way towards the river.

They were now close to the Thames. Sophie could hear the hollow boom of the warnings from the mass of shipping which thronged the busy waterway.

She guessed that they were making for one of the warehouses which lined the river banks. Then the wagon stopped. At some prearranged signal great doors swung open upon their hinges and they moved inside, out of the all-pervasive choking mist.

The thud of the closing doors sounded to Sophie like a death knell, but she was given no time to think. Rough hands reached out for her and dragged her from the wagon. Then Harward produced a wicked-looking knife and sliced through the ropes which bound her feet. She held out her hands, but he shook his head.

'Not yet, I think! Now come with me!'

As he took her arm she tried to move, but her legs would not support her. She heard an exclamation of impatience, and then she was flung over the shoulder of one of his companions.

At the head of a flight of steps, Harward led the way into a well-furnished room. Sophie was surprised. It might have been the setting for a business meeting. Then she realised that that was exactly what it was.

Half a dozen men were seated around a long mahogany table. As she was thrust into a chair, they looked up in astonishment.

'What's this then, Harward?' one of the men enquired. 'Have you taken leave of your senses?'

'No, sir! I have an excellent reason for bringing this woman here...'

For the first time in their acquaintance, Sophie detected a note of deference in his voice and she looked at his questioner with interest. This was clearly a man of substance, as were his companions.

'Well, man, out with it! What has gone wrong now?'

'A minor incident, my lord. Unfortunate, but necessary. The lady was a witness.'

'Another killing! Will you never learn? The last one

caused a serious delay in realising our profits, or had that escaped your notice?'

Harward flushed. 'We had no choice. None of you gentlemen would care to be the victim of a blackmailer, I fancy.'

He had courage in speaking as he did, as Sophie quickly realised. The men around the table were unaccustomed to being threatened. Their expressions were murderous.

Then one of the others spoke. 'We don't quarrel with your methods, Harward, but we do object to inefficiency. If aught else goes wrong we may have to look elsewhere for co-operation...'

Harward had regained his composure. Now he bowed. 'You will not find it necessary, my dear sir. The goods have been retrieved and it is a large consignment. Shall we get down to business?' He moved to take a seat at the table, but one of his companions stayed him with an upraised hand.

'What of the woman?' he demanded.

'Why, sir, she presents no problem. You need not fear that she will speak.'

Sophie lifted her head and looked at them, but none of the men would meet her eyes. They knew Harward's intention as well as she did herself.

'I don't like it!' One face at least was twisted in distaste. 'Is there no other way?'

'We could let her go, of course.' Harward glanced at Sophie and she shuddered. He looked like some predatory animal, tensing for the kill. 'But remember, gentlemen, she has seen you, and the lady is no fool. Given the opportunity, she will be happy to destroy you.'

'This girl?' The speaker sounded incredulous. 'Offer her money, man! That should silence her!'

Harward took his time, anxious that his next words should carry maximum effect.

'This, gentlemen, is Mistress Richard Firle!' he said.

For Sophie, the silence which followed this statement could only be interpreted as a death sentence. Each of them had been party to the killing of her husband, if not in fact, certainly in their acquiescence. Her fate was sealed.

'Why bring her here?' one of the men enquired. 'You are not infallible, Harward, as we know to our cost. If she should chance to escape, all our lives are forfeit.'

'I think not!' Harward looked at her as a cat might look at an injured mouse. He was toying with her before the kill. 'I believe that she will serve another purpose.'

'We've had enough of your mysteries, man!' an irritated voice announced. 'As for myself, I have no time to waste. We've struggled here through the worst of the weather. Forget the woman! She has naught to do with us.'

'On the contrary, sir, you may find that her presence here will prove to be invaluable. We may not have long to wait...' With great deliberation he drew out his pistol and laid it on the table.

Sophie closed her eyes. Was he planning to murder her here, in front of his companions? She wouldn't put it past him. It would implicate them all—a useful consideration for a man like Harward.

'Spare us the melodrama!' the previous speaker snapped. 'Save your posturings for those who will appreciate them. We have no need of weapons here, though I don't doubt that you flourish them among your men. Kindly remember where you are!'

Harward reddened at the contemptuous tone. It goaded him into a sharp reply. 'Does the thought of violence trouble you, my lord? Perhaps you should consider more carefully exactly what is involved in these operations which bring you so much profit. My hands may be dirty, but your own are none too clean.'

Sophie heard the scrape of a chair, and she opened a cautious eye. One of the men was on his feet, his face a mask of anger.

'Damn your insolence, you dog! You will keep a civil tongue in the presence of your betters. Have you forgotten who I am?'

'No, I have not forgotten you...any of you...' Harward's gaze rested on each man in turn. 'My betters, you say? Tell me, who is more at fault—the man who kills when necessary, or the traitor whose gold has brought about the deaths of many thousands of his own countrymen?'

There was an ominous silence, but Sophie could sense the tension in the still figures of the men who sat around the table. An explosion of some kind seemed imminent, and as she watched, Harward laid a careless hand upon his pistol.

'I suggest that you mind your own manners, gentlemen,' he continued. 'Let me assure you that we sink or swim together.'

A murmur of rage greeted his words. It was left to one of the older men to save the situation.

'Gentlemen! Gentlemen!' he pleaded. 'Where is the sense in quarrelling among ourselves? We are wasting time. Now let us forget our differences. Perhaps our friend here will give us an account of the profits we have made. It was the usual fifty per cent, I hope.'

Harward thrust the pistol into his capacious pocket. Then he bowed, and when he spoke it was in a more agreeable tone. He'd made his point. He had them in his power and they knew it. He was tempted to inform them that those who ride the wind must reap the whirlwind, but he thought better of it. If ever he decided to give up the dangerous occupation of free trading, each of these men would provide him with a handsome income for the rest of his life. They had delivered themselves into his hands. The late Richard Firle was not the only one who had considered the possibilities of blackmail.

He drew out a chair and sat down at the table. 'We have taken the usual profits,' he informed them. 'As always, they are returned to you in the form of goods.'

'Most satisfactory!' The peacemaker beamed his approval. 'We should be able to increase that profit by half as much again if we choose our markets carefully.' He nodded at Harward. 'Will you give me a hand, sir?'

He reached beneath the table and, with Harward's help, lifted up a strongbox. As he raised the lid, Sophie stared, wide-eyed. The box was filled with golden guineas.

'This is the next consignment,' the older man announced. 'Let us hope that in future we meet with no further difficulties such as those we experienced on this last occasion.' He lifted out a small leather sack and pushed it across the table. 'Perhaps you would care to count your share, Mr Harward?' he suggested.

'Not at all, my dear sir! I trust you implicitly.' Harward's tone was ironic as he laid his hand upon the sack. Then, quite suddenly, he motioned the others to silence and jerked his head towards the door.

Sophie's heart was pounding as she followed the direction of his gaze. Then she cried out as Hatton stepped into the room.

'Welcome, my lord!' Harward murmured smoothly. 'We have been expecting you. Gentlemen, pray allow me to introduce our visitor! The Viscount Hatton is the son of the Earl of Brandon.'

The panic on the faces of his companions was unmistakable, but Harward appeared to be enjoying the situation. 'How right I was!' he observed. 'I was persuaded that the presence of the lady must bring you to us.'

Hatton did not answer him, though he kept his enemy firmly in his sights as he moved to Sophie's side. His pistol did not waver.

'Can you stand?' he asked her briefly.

Sophie could hear the emotion in his voice. She knew then that he had not expected to find her still alive.

She nodded, too overcome to speak. Mutely, she held out her bound hands.

'My apologies, Mistress Firle!' Harward rose and walked towards her. 'An oversight on my part! Pray allow me to release you.' Something flickered behind his eyes, and Sophie saw it.

'Take care!' she cried. 'He has a gun!'

Her warning came too late. Harward had moved with cat-like speed. His pistol was already in his hand as he reached her side. Then the cold metal of the barrel was pressed against her temple.

'Drop your gun, my lord!' he advised. 'If you have any doubts that I will shoot, the lady will confirm it, won't you, my dear?' He wound his free hand into her hair, dragging back her head. 'Tell him!' he ordered savagely.

'He killed Nancy,' she whispered. 'I saw him do it.'

'I don't doubt it!' Hatton's tone was cool. 'Don't compound your crime, sir. You can't escape. Your men are already taken.'

Harward did not trouble to hide his amusement. 'Do you tell me that your little band has overcome a hundred men?'

'Not at all! We had the help of a company of Militia, the Dragoons and a number of the Bow Street Runners.'

'You lie, damn you!' Harward snarled.

'If you don't believe me, why not call for help?'

Sophie saw the uncertainty on her captor's face. 'Stand up!' he ordered. With the pistol still pressed firmly to her head, Harward dragged her to the doorway. Then he called down the stairs. No one answered him.

Then there was a movement around the table.

'This criminal is unknown to us, my lord,' one of the men observed. 'He broke in here and tried to hold us up.'

Hatton smiled at the speaker. 'He disturbed your business meeting?'

There was a quick chorus of agreement. 'We have no connection with him,' another speaker said. 'Whatever he may tell you, he has not the slightest shred of proof.'

Hatton shook his head. 'You disappoint me, gentlemen. I fear you are a band of innocents. When we search this room, as we intend to do, the evidence will be found. You have underestimated your accomplice. If I am not much mistaken, his records will be sure to implicate you. He is not the man to miss an opportunity.'

Sophie heard an ugly laugh. 'You have the matter to rights, sir. Allow me to direct your attention to the desk in the far corner of this room. There you will find the evidence you need.'

He dragged Sophie away from the door. Then, as all eyes turned in the direction of his pointing finger, he opened a massive cupboard just behind him. He pulled her inside and turned the key in the lock.

Chapter Fourteen

Sophie screamed aloud, but he struck her sharply across the mouth.

'Be quiet, or it will be the worse for you!' He reached above his head for a tinder box and lit a lantern, ignoring the pounding on the other side of the door.

Well aware that Hatton would not fire for fear of hitting Sophie, her captor showed no sign of undue haste. He lifted the lantern high to illuminate a steep flight of steps.

'Down here!' he ordered.

'I can't! I'll fall! Please let me go! Won't you leave me here? I can only delay you—'

'You could also save my life. Hold out your hands!' He seized the end of the rope which bound her and untied it. 'Down you go, and be quick about it. Hold on to the rail! If you fall you are likely to break your neck.'

He pushed her ahead of him down the wooden staircase.

Terrified though she was, Sophie was trying to think of some way of escape. If he'd gone first she might have pushed him down herself. She might even have managed to unlock the door for her rescuers before he recovered enough to fire, but he'd been aware of that. He'd thrown the key far into the darkness.

Fearfully, she continued to descend the stairs, unsure of her footing. They must be very near the river. She could smell the stench and she recalled that the Thames had been described to her as an open sewer running through the heart of London.

It was very quiet. She paused and listened, but the pounding from above her had stopped. Nicholas must be trying to find some other way of reaching her, but he would be too late. She and her captor had reached a long passageway with a door at the far end.

Harward unlocked it and pushed her through. They seemed to be standing on some kind of jetty.

Sophie was seized with a feeling of despair. Who could find her here? The fog which billowed all around her was thicker than ever. It hung like some evil miasma over the swirling waters of the river.

She had no cloak and she was shivering uncontrollably in that all-enveloping vapour. The acrid mist was choking her and her eyes were streaming.

Her companion looked about him with every sign of satisfaction. 'My luck holds!' he announced. 'I couldn't have wished for better than this. We shall not be followed.'

He raised the lantern above his head and whistled low. Then she understood.

This man was a survivor. He left nothing to chance. He would escape by water—a plan which must have been always in his mind if anything should go wrong. And he would leave no witness to his villainy.

She looked about her wildly, but there was no chance of escape. If she ran he would fire before she could disappear into the fog. She looked down at the swirling waters. Could she jump?

Harward read her mind with ease. 'I don't advise it,' he said almost kindly. 'In the unlikely event that you were rescued, you would not survive. That water is a flowing stream of poison. Look!' He gestured towards the bank and a floating mass of jetsam caught beneath the jetty.

Sophie's hand flew to her mouth. The bloated carcasses of animals bobbed about below her. Worse, a human hand was pointing skywards from a shapeless bundle of clothing. The sight of the corpse destroyed the last remnants of her self-control.

'Let me go!' she pleaded pitifully. 'You can have no further need of me—'

'Patience, my dear! Let us not be too hasty. Must you rush upon your death?'

'So you do intend to kill me?'

'Naturally! What else can I do? I take it that you have no wish to share my future life? Your passion for the estimable Viscount would rule that out, I think.' He was peering into the mist, and for the first time she detected a slight note of impatience. He whistled again, and this time it was piercing.

Sophie knew that she must keep him talking. 'When did you first suspect him?' she asked quietly.

'I never trusted the gentleman, my dear, even before I knew his true identity. He seemed to me to have the habit of command. Even allowing for your undoubted charms, I felt it unlikely that such a man would spend his time at an isolated country inn unless he had some other purpose.'

'You said that you trusted me.'

'Ah, yes, but I could not be sure, even of you. I did not know of your feelings then, my dear. I doubt if you knew of them yourself.'

Sophie did not answer him.

'It is all so unfortunate.' He sighed. 'I offered you great wealth. It didn't take me long to realise that it was not enough. So typical of a woman!'

'You don't think highly of our sex?' she challenged.

'No, Mistress Firle, I don't. Women are a mystery to me. They are capricious, governed by emotion, and often oblivious to danger where their loved ones are concerned.'

'I take that as a compliment,' she snapped.

'It is not intended as such. Great heavens, woman, did you think me blind? Your face gave you away when I was forced to shoot your unfortunate friend. I knew then that you would not forgive me.'

'Do you blame me?'

'No! I had expected as much...' He paused and peered into the mist. 'Ah!' he exclaimed. 'Here comes our salvation!' He waved the lantern as a skiff appeared beside the jetty.

Sophie closed her eyes. Would he shoot her on the spot, or was she to be knocked on the head and consigned to the murky waters of the river?

Harward appeared to hesitate. Then, evidently fearing that a shot might be heard, he motioned her forward.

Sophie could do no other than obey him. There were only two oarsmen in the skiff, and one of them, she saw to her surprise, was Wat. So he had betrayed her at the last, in an effort to save his skin.

'Well done, Wat!' her companion called. 'You shall have the pleasure of seeing to the lady.'

Sophie's eyes were upon the other figure in the boat. Could she be mistaken? The man was hooded, muffled to the ears, perhaps against the fog, but beneath his coat she saw the glint of metal.

Slowly, she began to climb down the rungs of the ladder which rested above the little craft. Firm hands caught her and sat her in the bow.

Harward had dropped his guard. Sure of his companions, he turned his back on them as he came down the ladder.

'Stay where you are!' Wat's companion threw back his hood and Sophie gave a cry.

With his pistol aimed steadily at Harward's heart, Nicholas drew her to him. 'It's over!' he told her quietly. 'They are taken to a man!'

'No! Don't give me over to the law!' Harward was pleading for his life. 'I meant no harm to Mistress Firle. I would have released her.'

'That isn't true!' Sophie told him coldly. 'You told me not an hour ago that you would kill me.'

'I didn't mean it! I was trying to frighten you! I will testify, my lord. You shall have your men.'

'I have them already. You, above anyone, will not escape your fate. You will hang for murder, sir.'

'No!' With lightning speed, Harward slipped a small pistol from his sleeve, but he was given no time to aim the weapon. Nicholas fired, and the shot took him in the shoulder. With a despairing cry, he lost his footing, and tumbled overboard. The water closed above his head, and he was gone.

Sophie gasped in horror. Then, sobbing with relief, she threw herself into Hatton's arms.

'I thought you'd never come!' she cried. 'Is it really over?'

'It is, my darling.' Too overcome with emotion to say more, Hatton enveloped her in the warm folds of his cloak. Then, holding her against his heart, he signalled to Wat, and the skiff drew away from the jetty.

Within minutes they were ashore, to be welcomed by

a cheering crowd, and there was Wentworth, smiling as he came towards them.

'Ma'am, you must give up my cousin,' he advised. 'He is much too fond of drama. He has a positive passion for a last-minute rescue! My nerves will not stand it!'

'Nor will mine!' Hatton told him grimly. Picking up Sophie in his arms as if she weighed no more than a leaf, he shouldered his way through the crowd to the waiting carriage.

'My father is here?' he asked.

'At the town house, together with my parents, and my uncle Perry. You have quite a reception awaiting you.' Wentworth swung himself up beside the driver and gave the man the office.

Sophie threw both her arms around her lover's neck. 'I thought I'd never see you again,' she whispered. 'Oh, my love, I've had such bitter thoughts. I sent you away without a word of love, and you might never have known how much I regretted it.'

He kissed her then, with such tenderness that all her doubts were banished.

'I don't deserve you,' he said very quietly. 'You speak of regrets, my dear one. I can't begin to tell you how I felt when we found Nancy's body. I was so sure that you...that you...' He could not go on.

'You didn't hear the shot?'

'No, but remember that you were well inside the tunnel. The walls must have deadened the sound. Had we heard it we should not have waited.'

'They were too many for you at the time. You did well to wait until we reached this place.'

'Did we? I went through the tortures of the damned wondering what had happened to you.'

'You did not find my brooch?'

'We did. That was when we suspected that they might have taken you hostage. It was the first small glimmer of hope, but I'll never forgive myself for exposing you to so much danger.'

'Don't blame yourself, my love.' Sophie pressed her lips into the hollow of his neck. 'Your plan would have worked except for Nancy. We could not have known that she would reappear at just that moment.'

'She too weighs heavily upon my conscience, Sophie. I should have listened to you. You sensed from the first that something was amiss.'

'But, Nicholas, we had no idea that her mind had given way completely. Poor Nancy! I shall always wonder if she might have been restored to health.'

'I doubt it, my love. Matthew almost caught her. She'd been hiding within the panelling of the walls. Unfortunately, he turned his back on her and she felled him with the butt end of his pistol.'

Sophie nestled in the shelter of his arms. 'What will happen now?' she asked. 'Those men around the table? Were they the ones you wanted?'

'Some of them. We have the names of others, many of them in high places. Harward kept the most detailed records of all his transactions. I suspect that he was planning blackmail as an easier way to riches than the smuggling trade.'

'I'm glad you've caught them. They have much to answer for, especially Harward...'

'The others are just as guilty. This was a dirty business and they knew it. They may have turned a blind eye to his methods, but in the search for profits they condoned them, if only by doing so.' Hatton took her hands in his and kissed each of them in turn. 'It is thanks to your bravery that we caught them.'

'I didn't feel very brave,' she told him with a shaky laugh. 'I was terrified. Oh, my love, I could think only of you and Kit. When it seemed as if…as if it was the end for me, I prayed that you would care for him.'

'How could you doubt it! Even when we have children of our own, Kit will always have his own special place in our hearts.'

Sophie looked up at him. 'May we go back to the inn today?' she pleaded. 'I long to see him. We have not been separated for so long before.'

'You will see him sooner than you think. I left orders for Reuben to bring him up to London. My family wishes to meet both of you.'

Sophie did not answer him.

'What is it, my love?' he asked. 'They are sure to love you as I do.'

'I hope so, but…well…'

'Well, what?'

'Oh, Nicholas, just look at me!'

'That is no hardship. I can't take my eyes off you.'

'No, be sensible! What will they think of me? My gown is torn and crumpled and I am…well…unwashed…'

Hatton shook his head. 'Women never cease to astonish me,' he answered solemnly. 'Not an hour ago you were in the most appalling danger. Now your *toilette* is uppermost in your mind. Must we shop in Bond Street? I know of an excellent mantua-maker…'

She heard the laughter in his voice. 'Now you are making may-game of me,' she reproached. 'I cannot think that your relatives will welcome someone as grubby and unkempt as I feel at this moment.'

'You are beautiful, my darling!' Hatton lifted her face to his and kissed her tenderly. 'A lifetime won't be long enough for me to convince you of it.'

Sophie sighed with content. 'I can't believe that we have our lives ahead of us, especially as we came so close to losing them. Now I feel that every day will have a special meaning for us. I'd given up hope, you know, when I was standing on the jetty...'

Hatton shuddered. 'I should have spared you so much suffering. If only we had realised...if we'd seen them putting you into the wagon...but there was so much confusion as they loaded the cargo, with men and ponies milling about. They took good care to hide you.'

'I knew nothing of it at the time,' she confessed. 'I must have been unconscious for some time after Wat was told to hit me.'

'Wat hit you?' Hatton stiffened. 'I'll make it my business to settle accounts with him.'

'Oh, no, please don't! He tried to help me. It was he who left the brooch for you to find, and he loosened my bonds as best he could. He planned to help me get away. It was only when I saw him in the skiff that I thought he had betrayed me.'

'I don't understand the man.' Hatton frowned. 'We feared to lose the wagons in the fog, and we didn't know which of them to follow. Some were decoys, as I'm sure you guessed. Then we saw a length of lace trailing from one of them. I thought you might have tried to signal to us.'

'I intended to, but Harward watched so carefully that I dared not risk it. Wat must have seized his opportunity, but he took a dreadful chance.'

'Why did he try to help you? There can be no doubt that he was one of Harward's band.'

'Wat is a fisherman, my dear. He was forced into smuggling as the only way to feed his children, but he didn't hold with murder.'

'He could have slipped away and left you to your fate.'

'He felt he owed me his life. Didn't you see the scar upon his face? At the very least, Harward might have blinded him. I couldn't bear to watch that beating. I made Harward stop.'

'I see.' Hatton grew thoughtful. 'Then that explains his actions when we entered the warehouse. He called a warning to us, and told me where you were. When we entered that room I thought that you were safe. I should have been prepared for trickery.'

'Harward was clever,' Sophie mused. 'Who could have guessed that such an innocent-looking cupboard was his escape route? He must have prepared it months ago. I was so frightened, Nicholas, I thought that you would never find me by the river.'

Hatton held her close. 'We might never have done so had it not been for Wat. Harward trusted him, believing that he, above any of the others, had good reason to hate you. He told us of the skiff. It was the simplest of matters to take the place of the second man.'

Sophie cupped his face in her hands and kissed him again and again. 'Let us not speak of it again,' she whispered. 'But, my darling, what will happen to Wat? We owe him so much. He risked his life for me, you know. I could not bear to think of him transported…or worse…'

'Nor could I, my love. It will not happen. Wat's bravery will be recognised.' Hatton looked at his betrothed and smiled. 'His future is in your hands. Shall you care to employ him in some way? There are cottages enough on my estate, quite large enough for Wat and his family.'

Sophie kissed him again. 'Then I may offer him a living? Nothing would please me more…'

'I'm hoping that a great many things will please you

more!' Hatton kissed her ear as the carriage drew to a halt.

She was still blushing as he led her up the steps of the family townhouse in Brook Street. Any anxieties she might have had were quite forgotten as a small figure rushed towards her and threw himself into her arms.

'Mama! Mama! Reuben has been teaching me how to tool along, and take corners to an inch!'

'Has he, my darling?' Sophie clutched her son. 'How are you, Kit? Were you well wrapped up?' It was an inadequate greeting, but she was very close to tears, remembering how she had feared never to see her son again.

'Of course!' Kit dismissed the enquiry with some impatience. 'Mama, you are squashing me again!'

Sophie relinquished her hold on the child and rose to her feet as a slender woman walked towards her.

'Mistress Firle, I am Prudence Wentworth. You must be very tired. Won't you allow me to show you to your room? You may care to rest before you meet the family.'

Sophie gave her a grateful look. 'I thank you, ma'am. I am more in need of hot water than a rest, I believe. You must excuse my appearance...'

Prudence laughed. 'My dear, you may believe that the men of this family care much more for spirit than for the niceties of an elegant *toilette*. Even so, a change of clothing will not present a problem. You and I are much of a height, I think.'

She led Sophie up the curving staircase and into a well-appointed chamber. A maid was already in attendance, presiding over a steaming bath which stood before the fire.

A number of gowns were laid across the bed, and Prudence eyed them critically.

'I hope you will find something to your liking, Sophie.

I may call you Sophie, may I not? My sons have spoken of you so warmly that I feel I know you already.'

'Mr Wentworth is your son, ma'am?'

'Thomas is the eldest of my boys. All three of them have the highest admiration for you.'

'You are very kind.'

'No! It is no more than the truth. But your bath is getting cold. Is Bess to help you, or do you prefer your privacy?'

'I shall manage without help, ma'am, I thank you.'

Prudence motioned to the girl to leave them. 'Good!' she said. 'I have long suspected that we ladies are not nearly as helpless as our maids would have us believe. Perhaps if I were to unfasten you at the back...?'

Sophie turned obediently, but Prudence was not done. 'Do please call me by my given name,' she pleaded. 'It may not describe me very well—in fact, it has amused my husband famously ever since we met. He feels that Prudence is hardly my outstanding trait of character. I threatened to change it, but he would not hear of it.'

Sophie saw the twinkle in the eyes which met her own, and she warmed to this warm-hearted woman who was still so lovely, although, with three grown sons, she must be in her middle years.

'Call me if you need me, Sophie. I shall be in the dressing-room next door, looking out some underthings for you.'

She was as good as her word, leaving Sophie to revel in the luxury of slipping into the scented water. The warmth was soothing, but she had no desire to rest. She bathed quickly and was drying herself by the fire when Prudence returned at her call.

'I'll leave you now...' her companion laid a pile of snowy underclothes upon the bed '...choose whatever you wish, my dear. Claudine assures me that any of these gowns will fit you.'

'Madame Arouet is here?' Sophie was beginning to feel nervous. As young Wentworth had predicted, there must be quite a crowd awaiting her below.

'She is, but you must not let that trouble you. I shan't allow the family to descend upon you in a horde. First you must meet your prospective father-in-law, but even that may be delayed if you should wish it. Are you quite sure that you don't prefer to rest?'

'I couldn't!' Sophie told her frankly. 'I feel that this is all a dream. I want to convince myself that it is happening and that there is no longer any danger.'

Prudence laid a comforting hand upon her arm. 'I know the feeling, Sophie. My own adventures as a girl almost matched your own. I'll tell you about them sometime. Now, let me fasten this gown for you. The blue is a good choice. It will suit you to perfection.' She waited by the window as Sophie slipped into a petticoat and drawers of the finest cambric, then her deft fingers dealt with the rows of tiny buttons as Sophie arranged the matching fichu of the garment over her bosom.

Prudence spun her around. 'You'll do!' she said drily. 'If Nicholas doesn't long to eat you alive, my nephew is not the man I think him!'

Sophie cast a nervous look at her reflection in the mirror and could scarcely recognise herself. Suddenly she felt more confident. In her borrowed plumage she would not disgrace her love. The blue gown fitted her to perfection.

'Prudence, I have you to thank for this,' she said shyly. 'I feel like a new woman.'

'But not *too* changed, I hope,' Prudence cried in mock dismay. 'Nicholas won't forgive me if he cannot recognise his love…though there is little danger of that, I think. My dear, won't you take a little refreshment? You must be very hungry. Let me send Bess to you with a tray.'

Sophie shook her head. 'If you don't mind, I'd prefer to go down now.'

Prudence didn't argue. She guessed rightly that Sophie was feeling nervous at the prospect of meeting the old Earl, and wished to get the ordeal over with as soon as possible.

'Very well!' she said. 'His lordship won't eat you, Sophie. You've taken a great worry from his mind. He'd begun to wonder if his heir would ever wed.'

'I hope he will approve of me...'

'How could he not do so? Besides, your little Kit has been an excellent ambassador. I haven't seen the Earl so entertained for years.'

'I hope Kit has behaved himself. He is no respecter of persons, as I'm sure you have discovered.'

'It is that happy, open quality which has endeared him to all of us, my dear. Kit and the Earl have been closeted together for a full hour this morning. The Lord alone knows what plans they've hatched.' Prudence began to chuckle. 'Come on, let us go down to them.'

She took Sophie's hand and they moved to the head of the great staircase. Then, even as they began to descend, Nicholas strode across the hall below.

'Your love is impatient for you, I see.' Prudence prepared to slip away. 'Go to him, my dear. You have all my wishes for your future happiness.' She turned and whisked away along the landing.

Sophie did not see her go. Her gaze was fixed on Hatton. She had a curious sensation of floating towards him in some kind of dream.

He stopped her before she reached the hall. 'Stay there

for just a moment!' he begged. 'I shall remember you all my life just as you look now.'

Sophie blushed, but she did as he asked, though she felt disposed to tease. 'I am in borrowed plumage,' she smiled. 'Your aunt has been very kind.'

'In borrowed plumage or your own, you are the most beautiful woman I have ever seen.' His look was so ardent that she blushed again. Then he took her in his arms and kissed her with an overwhelming passion which took her breath away.

At last she was forced to protest. 'Nicholas, the servants!' she whispered. 'They will think this most unseemly.'

He held her away from him and gazed into her eyes. 'Look about you!' he suggested.

Sophie glanced about the hall. She could see no footmen, and even the porter's chair was deserted.

'Don't you sense the air of celebration?' he chuckled. 'If I am not mistaken, they are gathered below to drink a health to us.'

She looked at his laughing face. The air of strain had gone, and happiness had smoothed the worried lines upon his face. She reached up to caress his cheek. 'You look like an eager boy,' she told him fondly. 'They must have guessed our secret just from your expression.'

'Certainly my father did so. Come and meet him, Sophie. He cannot rise to greet you, but you will understand...' He took her hand and led her into the study.

Any doubts which Sophie might have felt were dispelled as she looked at the scene which greeted her. Kit was seated on the Earl's knee, with an arm about the old man's neck.

'His lordship can't get up,' he told his mother instantly. 'He was injured when he fought the smugglers.'

'That is my claim to fame,' a deep voice remarked. 'It seems to find favour with your son. How are you, my dear? I hear we have much to thank you for.'

Sophie curtsied low, reassured by the kindly tone. 'I was somewhat overtaken by events, my lord.'

'Even so, you showed great courage, and Kit is proud of his mama, are you not, my boy?'

'Yes, sir. Hatton says that she is…she is a pearl of great price.'

'Well, we must all abide by what Hatton says,' the Earl agreed solemnly. 'Bless me, I had no idea that I had produced such a marvel of perfection.'

'He can skate backwards, too,' Kit offered.

'Astonishing! I am overcome! Such godlike perfection!'

'It pales beside the qualities of my coachman, Reuben, I assure you, Father. Now, Kit, the girls are waiting for you. They've challenged you to a game of spillikins. Let me take you to them.' He stretched out his hand and Kit went with him willingly.

The Earl of Brandon looked at Sophie. 'I had not thought to see my son so happy, my dear. I am most deeply in your debt.'

'I love him,' Sophie said simply. 'Kit does not think more highly of him than I do myself. My worry was that you might find this match unsuitable.'

'Why so?'

'I am a widow and I have a son. When Nicholas met me I was running an inn. It was not the most auspicious of backgrounds, my lord.'

'I think you have forgot to mention certain other matters. My son loves you, Sophie, and not only for your beauty, though you are indeed a lovely woman. I had begun to think that he would never wed. In fact, I have been guilty of trying to pressure him into marriage. I didn't understand that he was looking for something which he has found only in you, and that, my dear, is a strength of character which he can admire.'

Sophie looked up at him with brimming eyes. She could not have wished for a nobler tribute. On an impulse she stretched out both her hands to him.

'That's right!' The old man took her hands in his. 'Now give me a kiss, my dear. Let me welcome you to our family.'

Hatton returned to find them deep in conversation. When his father held out his hand, he shook it heartily.

'Congratulations!' Brandon said. 'You are the luckiest man alive, I think!'

'I think so too!' Hatton's eyes devoured his love. 'Sophie, when shall we be wed? It could be tomorrow if you wish it. I can get a special licence.'

The Earl of Brandon shook his head as he looked at the two lovers. 'See what you have undertaken, Sophie! My son has not the least idea that ladies need time to buy a trousseau and to invite their friends to share their happiness in an elaborate ceremony!'

Sophie clutched Hatton's hand. 'I don't care about such things,' she whispered. 'If you wish it, Nicholas, it shall be tomorrow.'

His look was reward enough for her, but now the old Earl chuckled. 'My boy, you are likely to be far too much indulged,' he teased. 'Sophie, take care that you don't always let him have his own way.'

Hatton slipped an arm about his love. 'My darling won't do that. Father, you have no idea! She can be the most difficult woman in the world.'

Sophie's laughing protests died upon her lips as

Prudence entered the room accompanied by Claudine Arouet.

The little Frenchwoman's eyes were twinkling as she looked at Nicholas. 'So you have won your lady, my dear? I guessed that this would be the outcome from the first.'

Sophie blushed and shook her head, but Madame came to kiss her. 'It is good!' she said quietly. 'You are well matched, I think. Allow me to wish you every happiness.'

Prudence added her own congratulations. 'Shall you wish to dine with the family this evening?' she asked with her usual frankness. 'If you wish it, Sophie, I will send a tray up to your room. You must be exhausted.'

'I should be,' Sophie admitted. 'But I'm not. I'll be happy to dine with you tonight.' It was true. She had never felt more alive. Now she wanted to savour every moment. It had taken a brush with death to convince her that nothing was more precious than life itself. And that future life would be filled with happiness, she knew. Nothing mattered now except the love which would encompass Kit and herself.

That evening they dined at an unfashionably early hour, but the gaiety could not have been surpassed at the table of the Prince Regent himself. Any doubts which Sophie might have had about her welcome were soon dispelled as one toast followed another to her future happiness.

She smiled as she looked about her, unfolding like a flower in the sun as the warmth of the family's affection flowed towards her. How alike they were—these Wentworth men with their dark colouring and their massive build! The Earl, his brother Sebastian, her own Nicholas and Sebastian's sons resembled each other so strongly. Beside them, their women-folk looked fragile, but Sophie was undeceived. Both Claudine Arouet and

Prudence had overcome hardship in the past. That much she had learned from Nicholas.

Then the Earl of Brandon raised a hand for silence. 'My son has set us a good example,' he announced with a twinkle. 'Claudine, have I your permission to let the family into our secret?'

For answer, the little Frenchwoman took his hand in hers.

Sebastian laughed. 'Brother, let us guess,' he teased. 'Claudine has agreed to become your wife?'

Prudence looked at her husband in mock indignation. 'You have spoiled the surprise!' she said.

A murmur of amusement rippled around the table. The Earl looked at the circle of laughing faces and threw up his hands in a gesture of resignation. 'What a family!' he said. 'Never try to keep a secret in this household, Sophie! You won't succeed, I can assure you.'

His news was the signal for another round of toasts and congratulations. Then Prudence rose and led the ladies from the room, leaving the men to their port.

Sophie hesitated in the hall. 'Prudence, will you excuse me for a moment?' she asked. 'I must look in on Kit. He is a restless sleeper. By now, his coverings will be thrown aside.'

She hurried up the staircase. Kit was settled in the dressing-room which adjoined her own bedchamber, and, to her relief, he appeared to be sound asleep. For once, his blankets were undisturbed.

As she bent to kiss him, a pair of chubby arms slipped about her neck. 'I was pretending!' he announced. 'I like it here, Mama, don't you?'

'I do, my pet!'

'I'm glad to hear it!' A large hand rested lightly on her shoulder and Sophie turned to find Hatton by her side.

'I was playing possum,' Kit informed his friend.

'What on earth is a possum?' Sophie asked.

'It is a small animal which lives in the colonies. Possums hide from danger, but they also sleep for hours and hours and hours, don't they, Kit?'

'I expect so.' Obediently, Kit closed his eyes, but as Sophie and her lover left the room they heard a happy sigh. 'I love Hatton,' the small voice whispered. 'Do you love him too?'

'I do, my darling!' Sophie lifted her face to look deep into the eyes of her betrothed. What she saw there convinced her of a love beyond her wildest dreams. With a little cry of happiness she melted into his arms.

* * * * *